Whose Death in the Tunnel?

The Tale of a Princess

by

Aaron McCallum Becker

Robert D. Reed Publishers
San Francisco

ISBN 1-885003-20-X

Library of Congress Cataloging-in-Publication Data

Becker, Aaron McCallum, 1946-
      Whose Death in the Tunnel? : The Tale of a Princess / Aaron McCallum Becker
            p.   cm.
      ISBN 1-885003-20-X (cloth)
      1. Diana, Princess of Wales, 1961-   --Fiction   I. Title
PS3552.E2524W48   1999
813' .54--dc21

                                                            99-12659
                                                            CIP

Robert D. Reed Publishers

For Maxine, Ada, Jennifer and Di

Author's Note

Although this novel is based upon known historical events and circumstances, it is above all a work of complete fiction. We remind the reader to separate the many facts from the fiction.

PREFACE

I am doing the unthinkable. I will tell you the true story about a woman's life. Her story is embroiled in trauma and distrust and make-believe love. She is known to the world as a magical woman, the beautiful ingenue chosen by the world's most eligible bachelor. She is thought to be the luckiest woman in the world. Overnight she becomes a fairy-tale Princess, the most talked about and admired of all the beautiful people. Her daily life is constantly reported and evaluated by the press. Her every movement is anticipated. The nervy paparazzi never cease to linger hoping to capture today's front-page telephoto shot. Her fairy tale becomes a nightmare, and this is the story of how she awakens from her terror.

I know this woman. I have known her for years, not publicly but privately. She talks to me. She confides in me. She shares with me her destiny. I promise you that she does not feel like a Princess.

To herself she is a ghastly catastrophe. Her unhappiness is so deep that suicide was not only contemplated but also attempted. Her life is one of entrapment. Even divorce does not provide freedom. She looks for an escape, any escape. One small idea unfolds. At first, the idea seems so absurd that it is almost unthinkable, a joke. But with more time and thought, perhaps...

This idea may provide her only hope. Maybe it is not so far-fetched after all. But wait, I am getting ahead of myself. First, I must go back and provide to you the whole story. It is intricate and filled with deceit and many a false turn.

Can you imagine the feelings of a young woman who realizes on her wedding day that her soon to be 'beloved' husband truly loves another? Before this day she overlooks the recurring feeling that burns deep within her soul. It is a message that echoes within her, time and time again. Somehow she knows it's true, but she so wants her feeling to be unfounded that she wishes it away. Like the solid beat of her heart, the message relentlessly recurs. Its reality is as blazing within the innermost depths of her existence as are the sun's rays at noon. She now understands the reality of her commitment, and the fear is overwhelming.

"For better or worse until death do us part." What is the unlimited power that these nine small words command? They resound in her mind, day after day, hour after hour, and finally minute after minute, until on the threshold of a breakdown she bursts.

Hours before the wedding she contemplates walking away. She turns to her family. They offer no solace. She is instantly faulted for her feelings. Her heart and emotions are unimportant. She is told to march forward with her head held high. The opportunity this union provides to her family is first. This is the commanding force. Her well-being is a lowly second. She is told to speak no more of such a despicable act of cowardliness. I ask you to imagine yourself in this situation. How would your family react? What type of a family would turn deaf ears to the intimate cry of a young woman embroiled in such internal turmoil? I do not know your family, but I intimately know this woman's family. I can promise you that the family's concern was in no way centered on this woman's happiness. It is a selfish family. Each member looks after his or her own needs first to the exclusion of the others.

Almost over the breaking point, she turns to me. She requests that I come to her immediately. Asking for a moment of complete privacy, she reveals her heart. This is not the first time we have spoken candidly. This is not the first time she has expressed her innermost heartache to me. We have talked before of the torture she endures as it bores itself deeper and deeper into her being. This is not the first time we have spoken with absolute frankness about her 'beloved,' about his relationship with another, and about her role in this saga.

She tells me that she cannot go forward. She asks me what I would do. She reiterates that her decision is solid and well-founded. She begs me to assist her in a quiet, sudden death. Her mind is stable. Her limits are well-defined. She can endure the termination of her life. She cannot endure a make-believe life. She cannot playact her life as the essence of harmony to the outside world while experiencing a private life of agony. Death is preferable. What would you do? What would you ask of me?

The ceremony is only hours away. Somehow through our talking she agrees that suicide is not the choice, at least for today. Too much is at stake. The entire world is looking on with elated anticipation. Maybe there is a way for her to win his love. Maybe in her own simple and sincere way, with time, she will be able to bring him to love her for what she is, for who she is. Maybe after living together day by day, he will come to realize that she is so much more than merely the woman who fits the formula.

Could you marry someone only because the person fits the correct formula? Could you marry someone knowing that your 'spouse to be' had chosen you because you matched an ordained blueprint? I know this woman. I understand her sincerity. She is so much more than a mere formula wife. She is real, unaffected by the standards of what is accepted as correct. She has so much to offer. The bottom line is her love. How could this be so very unimportant?

What type of a man could or would marry a woman only because she is the perfect formula? What type of a man could feign true love when he truly loves another? Is it possible for such a person to truly love anyone? What price must be paid? Is there any hope?

This same man has been engaged in a supposedly passionate, loving relationship with another for years. His 'true love' is not suitable. She is a mere commoner and is married to another. What type of a woman is she? Can you imagine a woman agreeing to a continued relationship knowing that her 'beloved' is betrothed to another? Can you imagine a woman agreeing to a relationship knowing that her 'beloved' would lead a very public life with another woman by his side?

The triangle evolves. The heroine quickly realizes that her worst nightmare is reality. She is not the beloved wife. Nearly overnight she is delegated to the role of the third person out in a three-way relationship. Through the common thread of this triangular patchwork, the plot unwinds. The thoughts of ending it all recur, but they are overcome by her passionate desire to live. This desire provides her with strength. She does not succumb. She clutches to her hope that, with time and energy, things will be different. Deep inside she understands. She has been relegated to a living death that is her reality. She pines for it to be different, knowing her hope will never be more than a dream.

At first, she contemplates the idea merely as a whim. The idea serves as a momentary reprise from the unbearable trauma of her daily existence. With the passage of days that turn into years, she is pushed more and more aside. The triangle endures. Its complexities are so enmeshed within her soul that the turbulence of mere existence is overwhelming. Life almost becomes unlivable.

I feel her pain. I understand all of the intricacies of the situation. I am special, for I alone have attained her trust. I am her only confidant. I know her story, and I will share it with you in the following pages. I share it with you because it is a story that must be told. It is a story of hope and passion for life. She will not suffer by my revealing her tale. The foundation of her protection is solid and unbreakable. You will be rewarded by the knowledge. If you knew what I know, would you, could you do any differently?

Oh yes, there are bright moments. In all of this, there are the children, two wonderful boys. They provide to her hope, and yet, they create for her the greatest dilemma. Could she act out her plan, knowing that she might never feel their embraces again? Could they ever be allowed to know?

There are thoughts about selfishness. So many worthy causes use her as a figurehead. How will they continue if she is no longer their spokesperson? What type of a woman could, would turn away from all of this? I know this woman. I can tell you that somehow her threshold of selflessness was violated. She was given no alternative. Her only hope was to replace her body and soul. Is it selfishness? Or perhaps only survival? Only you will be able to answer these questions, after hearing her story.

Not all of you will agree with her decision. Some will fault her. Others will praise her. It is a very personal story about life, and there are no absolutes.

Maybe for the best, maybe for the worst, the plot takes a turn that was never contemplated. Something goes terribly wrong. No one was ever to be seriously injured. Moreover, no one was to be killed. I understand death and its enduring effect upon all of those it touches. In this case the effects are overwhelming. The world is still responding. A day does not pass when her legacy is not eulogized through the charitable acts of others. Her crusades are now the crusades of the world. But what was the price?

Possibly the answer to this question is the reason I decided to come forward with her story. Never during the endless hours of planning her escape could she have imagined the outcries that would resound from around the world. Time seemed to stop when the news report was broadcast. Not for a moment. Not for a day. Not for a week. Still, the staccato moments remain enduring, almost eternal.

The images of the twisted wreck are frozen in all of our minds like the photos of the Kennedy assassination. Maybe they provide a small insight into the true purpose of man's existence. Possibly she exemplifies to the world the quality of humanity that each of us hopes to achieve in our individual walk through life.

The sincerity of the love expressed is overwhelming. It renews in me a trust in the goodness of mankind. It empowers me to tell this story. It allows me to ask the question time and time again. What type of a woman could have, would have chosen this path?

1

London, Early Summer 1996

The deep ache in her stomach crept to the base of her throat. The pain was constant. It had been with her now for days. Actually, it had been with her longer than she could remember. This infinite cavity of internal numbness surrounded her every action. The reality of the agony was more powerful than the horror of continuing.

Di forced herself to take charge of the day. It was getting late. She still had four telephone calls to make before her luncheon appointment. The most important and lengthy would be the one to her attorney. How could she possibly be in this situation? How could her entire life be exploding into unshaped bits and pieces? She had endured so much from the start. Now, her whole world was crumbling in upon her. The result, total devastation.

The marriage of the fairytale Princess was ending in divorce, not just divorce but a flagrant, publicly scrutinized divorce. Her turbulent relationship with her husband, her powerlessness under the law to maintain custody of the boys, her personal financial affairs, her supposed psychotic tendencies, her personal relationships, were all subjects of a worldwide media blitz. Her life was repeatedly, authoritatively rehashed by every talk show host from Larry King to that little redneck twerp, Elmo, who broadcasts every night, all night from some little nowhere in the middle of Kansas. There were hundreds of chat rooms on the Internet active twenty-four hours a day. They were filled with people scrutinizing her life. Every day a new 'insider' came onto the scene; each was privy to the real scoop. Everyone had a compelling opinion to express. Never could she have imagined such a ghastly fate.

Standing at the entry to her enormous walk-in wardrobe, a room larger than most women's entire bedroom suites, she was overwhelmed. Thoughts of her own extravagance came to her mind. Had she truly spent over two million dollars on her wardrobe? Was Charles right? What difference did it make, anyway? Her appearance was important. A new image for the Royals had been long overdue. Certainly, she had provided a very positive image for them. She was the most photographed woman in the world.

Why should her wardrobe, of all things, be a subject of the divorce? Did she pamper herself too much? Did she really own over 3000 suits? It was true that many of her most elegant ensembles still hung unworn in their plastic bags, looking like packages wrapped to be placed under the holiday tree. She always gravitated to the same small group of suitable choices. Somehow, she felt right when wearing them.

Today was no different. She chose the clean-lined, soft pink Chanel silk suit that had served her well on so many occasions. It was appropriate for the working luncheon and planning session that was her only appointment of the day.

Trying to focus on the demands of the day, she felt as though she was at the end. How could she, the soon to be ex-wife of the future King, go on? What future could she ever find in England? The sound of the Queen's voice rang piercingly in her ears. The thoughts so calculated. The demand for the divorce so lacking in compassion. Divorce had simply been decreed. Astonished? No. Demoralized? Yes. Was there any possible reality in...? Her thoughts were jarred by the telephone's ring.

"Good morning, darling. Do you have the time for lunch?"

"Unfortunately, I am already engaged," she responded.

"I have some news for you. I spoke with Adam. Arrangements are falling into place," Katherine said excitedly.

"Do you really mean it?" she asked with welcome anticipation.

"Please, we must meet, very soon."

"Could you join me for dinner this evening, at my apartment?" Di asked.

"What time?"

"Seven."

"Lovely. Until then, my darling."

The line went dead.

Shocked by the stillness, her thoughts returned to the reality of her destiny. Her inner pain once again mounted. Somehow, she forced herself to dress. She would do her own hair and face today. It was easier when she busied herself. She could not bear the hurt that swelled within when she sat idle allowing others to do her hair and make-up.

As she readied herself, her mind wandered into the future. She did not think of herself as a feminist. She did not really even consider herself strong. But one thing was for certain. She could not, would not, accept the humiliation of lingering in the shadows. No doubt, the public sympathy would remain with her, but pity offered her no solace.

She would maintain her title of Princess, but she would be an annoyance in the background. Camilla would be center stage. What would be Camilla's relationship to the boys? Would she one day, rather than Di, become the Queen Mother? How demoralizing. Di could not live as the underdog. She could not accept this fate. The Queen could dictate the divorce, but the Queen could not dictate her future. The plan provided her with an escape from the life sentence imposed upon her by the divorce. Could Adam actually develop a foolproof, perfect plan, turning a magical dream into a real-life probability? Was it possible?

Her racing mind jilted back to the moment at hand. Thoughts of her tight schedule jarred her into action. She picked up the telephone and pushed the speed-dial button for her attorney.

Experience had taught her to employ every caution when using the telephone. Important conversations were placed on hold until complete privacy was assured. It was never possible to control what an overly-ambitious maid, secretary or receptionist might leak to a reporter. The tabloids lingered like famished piranhas. By maintaining personal, direct communication with Anthony, there was much less chance for external intervention. Telephone lines could always be tapped. The highest standard of security had been built into her communication system through a labyrinth of call-forwarding cutouts patterned after the one employed by MI-5. It was regularly checked for bugs. Even so, her policy was to say very little over the telephone.

Part of her hoped that Anthony would not respond. It was vital for her to remain calm. Anthony saw her as the victim. This image was important for her to maintain. Never could the plan work, if ever she gave the slightest hint.

"Your highness, sorry to keep you waiting," he answered. "I have drawn the papers with our counter-proposal for the financial settlement. Do you wish to come by the office or should I drop by with them?"

"Could I come to your office at three o'clock sharp? I have a luncheon. Alfred is driving me today, so it is terribly easy for me to come by."

"Three o'clock is perfect. Until then, your highness," he said.

"Until then. Good day, Anthony."

She replaced the receiver, her mind again racing with the thoughts of the plan that would change her internal suffering into a future of hope.

Later, engaged in conversation at her luncheon meeting, she listened with only half an ear. How could she honestly be totally committed to participating in a program to increase the average life-span of African tribal babies when she was helpless to control her own destiny? Thank God the others were caught up in their own importance, doing most of the talking. They were asking few questions that required specific answers. She smiled and responded only when necessary. Soon it was over. She committed her support, and the others left content, that because of her, their goals would be realized.

Leaving the restaurant Alfred and Sean flanked her as they craftily dodged the hungry paparazzi. She lunged into the back seat of the car. Gasping for breath, she was content that Alfred was driving today. He was the best and was always so compassionate. She hated being escorted. How often she had wanted to renounce her protection, but she knew it was not the right thing for her to do. Not yet, anyway. She knew she especially needed the protection today. She had no strength to face the possible encounter with the media.

Whenever she went out, the press was there with insatiable appetites hoping for a taste of anything. With the support of Alfred and Sean, she did not have to worry. They were the most respected members of The Royal Protection Squad. Former SAS and trained marksmen, they were the ultimate of the ultimate. They shielded her from it all.

As the crowd of onlookers disappeared into the background, her internal struggle again kindled itself into a roaring blaze. The unbearable thoughts of her programmed destiny frothed within her soul. She knew she could not bear to live in the prison of this destiny. Only she could change the plotted course. She had the power to do it. She could do it. She would do it.

><del></del>—O—<del></del>—<

Code-named the Puppet Master in an 'off the books' intelligence operation, he was known to his friends and associates as Adam. The American intelligence genius served two tours in Vietnam and turned

CIA in 1974. His photographic memory catalogues for immediate recall in perfect order every detail he reads or observes. He misses nothing, ever. He speaks several languages, impeccably, with native accents and complete fluency. His parents had been wealthy. They spared no expense to assure the best education for both Adam and his sister. The two had been educated in Switzerland, in the finest of schools.

On special assignment with the CIA, he learned from the ground floor upward in an intelligence operation similar to the witness protection program. The operation called 'Wayward' was developed to hide high-profile defectors. Adam rose to the top immediately. His skill level and creative genius were unmatched. His solutions were repeatedly workable, doable, and believable. After less than two years of service, he was promoted into a career advancement track designed for only the most promising of agents.

His new assignment was Iran. He delved into the challenge with an unrelenting presence. Threatened by Adam's astuteness, a conflict soon developed with his immediate supervisor. The conflict relentlessly escalated during Adam's two years in Teheran. Adam was convinced that the Iranian regime was unstable and ready for a revolution. His supervisor vehemently disagreed. Strongly challenging Adam's theory, his supervisor saw to it that Adam's reports were mockingly shredded.

While serving in Iran, Adam was given the opportunity to assist the Shah. The two developed a mutual respect that grew into a personal friendship. Adam quickly gained the Shah's trust and maintained confidential contact with him. It was because the Shah took him into his confidence that Adam did not relent in his efforts to warn the U.S. government about Iran's internal volatility. Unable to gain his superior's ear, Adam went over his head. Adam's actions only strengthened his estrangement with his superior who continued to write off Adam's pleas as insubordinate. Finally, Adam stepped over the fine line of authority one too many times and was abruptly transferred back to the states under censure.

One week after his arrival in the U.S., Adam's parents died in a midair collision over San Diego. The date was September 25, 1978. They were victims of a crash between a private plane and a Pacific Southwest 727. The distraught Adam took an emergency leave of absence from the company.

His nightmare had only begun. Upon his arrival in San Diego to deal with his parents' death, Adam learned that his sister's husband and child had been murdered in their home in Mexico. His sister had disappeared, and the police were looking for her. The evidence pointed strongly to a drug deal gone terribly wrong.

Adam was devastated. He could do nothing but proceed. He coordinated the necessary arrangements for the proper burial of his parents. Simultaneously, he arranged for a proper interment for his sister's husband and daughter. He worked in concert with the Mexican police investigating his sister's disappearance. The burden of the unsolved disappearance hung heavily upon his heart. Through it all, his adrenaline flowed. An inner voice told him that his sister was alive, heartbroken and angry. His vitality returned, knowing she was a survivor. He trusted that she was angry enough to endure. She was keenly astute. These qualities would allow her to out-think even the most sophisticated of hit men.

Adam listened to the inner message he had received. He and his younger sister had been able to communicate with one another from afar since the time they had been small children. More like twins than mere siblings, only thirteen months apart in age, they had always known when one or the other was in trouble. Direct communication was never necessary for them to reach out to one another. When there was a need, one was always there for the other.

No one, including their parents, ever understood their relationship, their true closeness, their near oneness. Their friends all thought them to be estranged, because they seemed so different and rarely spoke of one another. It was never the case. They quipped to each other that together they made one great person. Their true relationship was their secret. They shared it with no one for fear that someone might intrude into their special and intimate cradle of life. They promoted their facade of being vastly different to the outside world. Politically she was the liberal and he the conservative. However, neither of them had developed a philosophy centered on political bedrock. They were both children of the times. In another time, in another place, they both could have been as apolitical as Adam was today.

It did not take long. Contact was made using their prearranged childhood code. Adam's assessment was correct. His sister was in grave danger, even worse than he had imagined, but she was alive. Adam saw no alternative. The only solution was to arrange her permanent disappearance. It took several weeks to craft the perfect plot. Every detail was enacted with precision. Finding the replacement body was the easy part. Changing her identity and assuring her safe passage out of Mexico were more difficult. During the preparation period, Adam could insure her safety only as long as she remained in complete seclusion. Her enemies were following every lead. Adam even manufactured and used false leads to buy time.

Adam knew he could do it. Adam's work with The Company had provided him with contacts worldwide. This, his first real challenge, had been placed in front of him before he was ready. He always knew what he wanted to do, but he never imagined that the challenge of proving his capabilities would be on such a personal level. He always imagined being removed from his clients. Now his client was his sister.

Adam got down to work. He extended his leave of absence from The Company for six months. He devoted all of his energy to assuring that every detail was in perfect order. Finally, all props were in place. It was time to take action.

A distraught Adam confirmed the police report that his sister died trying to leave Mexico by boat making her way to Cuba. She had been a target, the one person who knew what had really happened to her husband and daughter. Her only hope was to escape the wrath of her family's killers. In desperation she had attempted the impossible and paid the price.

Adam, her only living relative, traveled to the small fishing village near Cozumel where he identified the decomposed body. A small, Catholic funeral and suitable burial followed in Mexico City. Adam arranged for a tombstone fit for a Princess to mark her grave. Adam's grief was visible to all. He attended to all of the necessary formalities, publicly expressing his disbelief to the local authorities and returning to the states with all appearances of a broken man.

Surrounded by the security of his old friend, his English green leather library chair, he sipped a gin and tonic with his feet resting on the magazine-stacked coffee table. Adam reflected upon the last weeks. So much had happened. The deaths of his parents and extended family had destroyed his idealism. His naiveté had been pillaged by the tragedies. He had proven to himself his self-worth by the success of his sister's transformation. He had always known he could do it, but he had never before had the opportunity. It had dropped into his lap. Not out of choice but out of necessity. As he allowed his muscles to relax, he stretched his tired limbs to the four corners. His thoughts turned to her. *Will I ever get used to calling you Elizabeth? The name is so unfamiliar. I have so damn much to say to you. So many questions to ask. Damn it all to hell. We have done so much and said so little.* The time would come when they could again communicate, maybe even work together, but not yet. Contact at this point would not be smart intelligence work.

Adam no longer felt compulsion to re-enter the bureaucratic monster, but he knew it was the correct thing to do. Through the years, it had served him well. Now, professionally, he no longer needed it, but, strategically, returning to his job was wise. Initiating his very own special service business was nearing reality. This was his passion. His goal. All his dealings pointed in this direction. He dared not make a mistake. The time was not yet prime.

With the expiration of his six-month leave of absence, Adam followed normal procedure and accepted his new assignment. He did not want to draw attention to himself. He set himself to accomplishing his new challenge with his normal level of persistence. Just days into the project, criticism from his immediate supervisor, again, welled up. This one was a career man, only a year from retirement. It was the same problem that evolved during Adam's previous assignment. His supervisor was threatened by Adam's insight and, consequently, misinterpreted Adam's intent. The situation rapidly escalated. Adam was repeatedly and relentlessly stereotyped as a rogue. Less than three months later, Adam left The Company for the last time. Again, he was under censure.

After his dismissal, Adam became ostensibly an insurance investigator, but this position was merely his first cover. Then, he accepted a temporary, freelance assignment with a high-profile private investigative firm. The conclusion of this project provided a natural transition to initiating a private agency. Contact had been reestablished with Elizabeth, and she had agreed to work in unison with him. His vision was to assist only those in the highest profile positions: heads of state, corporate magnates, dons, the like. Success was born very rapidly. It took only one very high profile achievement to assure a solid client base. Word travels quickly in the very elite circles of power.

What an achievement it was. In 1979, the religious opposition led by Ayatollah Ruhollah Khomeini drove the Shah of Iran into exile. Khomeini relentlessly sought the capture of the Shah. When it was learned that the Shah had been admitted into the United States for medical treatment, Iran's response was the initiation of the hostage crisis at the U.S. Embassy in Teheran. The Ayatollah placed the Shah under a sentence of death. The spiritual leader of Iran promised immediate entrance into heaven in the presence of Allah to the man who succeeded in killing the Shah.

Adam was permitted to see the Shah of Iran while hospitalized in America. The Shah was devastated. He saw no hope, but Adam offered a plan. Adam unfolded his scheme, and, after much contemplation, the Shah agreed. The Shah was convinced that religious fanatics would hunt him to his death. Adam's solution provided his only truly safe way out.

After dismissal from the hospital, the Shah fled to Panama where he again met with Adam to work out the last of the details.

Adam received his enormous fee, all in advance. It was part of the prearranged agreement. For Adam, advance payment is essential. In this type of work, it is the only way to be assured of being paid at all.

The Shah then departed for Egypt, where he allegedly died on July 27, 1980, at the age of 60. But this was far from the truth. The Shah gained a new identity through Adam's work and lived to the comfortable age of seventy-six. His official grave contains the body of an assassin who was sent to murder the Shah. Adam was with the Shah during his real death in the south of France, where he had lived out the remainder his life in peace and anonymity. They had remained friends to the end.

This achievement was all that it took. Now, the demand for Adam's services is always in excess of his ability to produce. His clients find him by word of mouth. He does not maintain a private agency or office, preferring to live almost as a recluse. He works directly and personally, and only with the actual client. No middlemen. He is able to take only one, on occasion, two cases at a time. He relies upon the services of others to assist with the practical, but no one other than Adam and Elizabeth ever knows the full equation. There are no paper trails. His brain is his storage bank. The Internet provides him with a means of communication, but all sensitive information is transmitted vis-à-vis.

Adam knows that he is not only the master of his trade but the only source who can truly provide the ultimate in protection. None of his clients has ever been discovered. He names his fee; his clients are always desperate. His fee varies depending upon his feelings about the client and upon the specific needs versus risk ratio. He has no formula, no hourly rate. Sometimes the more prestigious and complex the problem, the lesser his desire for financial gain. The caper itself always provides the stimulus to Adam. He regards the whole process as creative drama. He has arranged for the disappearance of several mob bosses, big boys on the Street, and even some Third World Tribal Gurus. Now, a multimillionaire, he is very selective about whom he agrees to protect. His wealth allows him to pick his projects out of desire rather than need.

During his tenure with the CIA, Adam drained the brains dry of the in-house computer wizards. He hand-picked a team of geniuses and hijacked them to develop the most sophisticated system in the world for changing a person's identity. The system has never been penetrated. All paper trails, permanent records, physical characteristics, replacement corpses are referenced and cross-referenced. Adam's computer technicians and subcontractors do it all; yet, each only knows a small part of the equation. No one has the knowledge of enough parts to ever piece together what he has done. His score is 100%. No leaks. No speculations. Now, even the U.S. government is rumored to have engaged his services for its highest security cases.

>⊢◆>─O─<◆⊣<

Katherine first met Adam in 1975. Recently divorced, it took only a few minutes of conversation for her to understand why. The event was one of those boring, Harvard alumni fund-raising dinners. Seating was prearranged by placecards with husbands and wives at separate tables. This form of seating provides a convenient means for blending midst the pairs the singles who often prove the most generous contributors.

Adam, an eligible single and hearty contributor, was strategically placed at the center table to allow contact with the evening's head table and its special guests. Brooks Brothers all the way, he was young and vibrant. His manner was refined and quiet. So quiet that his presence somehow generated a feeling of absolute power. He silently conveyed the persona that he alone could capture the pulse of the whole world.

His conversation with Katherine was stilted. His reality was not at all like the man who had been described to her several nights before. Adam, well actually his divorce and settlement with his ex-wife, had been the subject of conversation during this month's regular gathering of Katherine's group of college friends at the Plaza's Oak Bar. The seven of them had been meeting without fail every fourth Tuesday of every month at seven-thirty for over five years. Only Christmas Eve or Christmas could change the date. The gathering was a ritual. Imminent death or out-of-town were the only valid excuses for absence.

So unlike what she had been told, Katherine quickly sized him up as a loner, a very independent type. He had been described as an expert in a variety of martial arts, but when quizzed, he underplayed his abilities. It was obvious that this man was special; yet, he was so aloof. His parents were wealthy and traveled extensively. His sister lived in Mexico with her husband and three-year-old daughter.

Katherine took to the challenge. She compassionately mentioned her divorce. Adam's expression immediately changed. The tone of his voice softened.

"I thought everyone other than myself carried nothing but contempt for his ex."

"Why would you think that? Sometimes people love one another but simply cannot make it together," Katherine replied.

"I've never thought about it that way. I guess you're right," Adam said.

Katherine noted a glowing harmony emitting from within Adam as he reflected about his ex-wife. The conversation flowed. He spoke of her with great understanding and emitted a deep sadness that he had failed to make it different.

"Ours was a special situation. We fought with a vengeance that was unequaled. Today, we remain the best of friends, true friends. Without a second thought and in a moment's decision, either one of us would give our life for the other. How many people who are happily married could say that?" Adam queried.

Katherine could only smile and nod her head in acceptance.

Ignoring everyone else at the table, Adam went on to tell Katherine that he and Natalie had never been lovers, not really anyway. The thought of intimately touching one another was something that had never occurred to either as a need in their relationship. But they needed to talk, to share, to enjoy one another's experiences. Even with the divorce, nothing had changed. Their friendship remains as pure and consecrated as the day they were married. They still seek solace in one another. Adam could not explain why, but they just could not stay married. They had no children. They had no reason to continue. Ending the marriage was a positive step. It provided a future to each of them. It provided to them both the life pulses of friendship and independence.

The speeches were endless and the food uninspiring, as is always the event at those functions. Unable to endure another minute, Katherine remembers well Adam whispering to her with a sheepish smile, "Let's get the hell out of here for a nightcap. Are you game?"

Katherine giggled and flickered her eyes with approval.

They left the banquet hall separately. Katherine excused herself for a quick trip to the powder room during the applause between the presentation about the University's Five-Year Building Projection Plan and the plea from Erma Bradson to fund a special scholarship for minority National Merit Scholars. Adam met her in the rooftop bar about fifteen minutes later.

They talked until the bartender asked them to leave sometime after two in the morning. Katherine had never before met anyone like him. Never had she been as fascinated with any one person. He told her little and only hinted about his work, but she could feel it. She knew that this man could, no, would, change the lives of many.

2

London, later the same day

Di's thoughts were with Katherine. Her mind danced imagining what Katherine wanted to tell her. The urgency in Katherine's voice on the telephone said more than her words. Di worried, thinking, *This evening, privacy is essential. What will I do with the staff?* She could ask Paul to serve drinks and then tell him to take off the remainder of the evening. She would use the excuse that she and Katherine wanted to do silly girl things. The others were easy to dismiss. Of course, they would protest, but in reality they would be glad to leave. They would jump at the opportunity to have some additional hours of paid time off. She and Katherine would cook for themselves. *No, maybe it's better I ask the cook to prepare a big salad and fruit platter. Food will be the last thing on our minds.*

Her mind turned to her concern about the privacy of her quarters. *Anthony always tells me that I cannot be too careful. He says, 'You never know who is listening. Be on guard, always, everywhere.'* She thought her home was secure, but it was not impossible that a bug had been planted. She would not put it past the establishment to do such a thing. She had taken every precaution to have her premises inspected. She had arranged for regular spot checks, almost weekly. No problems had been found, but no one was kidding her. The reports were only as honest as the people making them. In her circle there were more hidden agendas than could ever be imagined.

She and Katherine would just have to be especially careful tonight when they spoke. She knew the only way the plan could possibly work was to assure absolute confidentiality. Katherine would know what to do. She was close to Adam, and he would have prompted her. He would not want exposure either. Di was confident of that.

As the car pulled in front of Anthony's office, Di could not hold back the tears. She felt so lonely. Not just lonely because the boys were with Charles but lonely because she could not confide in those she trusted. She had so much bottled up within her. She tried to get hold of herself, but the loneliness and pain swept over her in giant waves.

How she would love to tell Anthony about the plan. She yearned for his advice. She trusted him completely. She coveted his reaction. Was she out of her mind to consider such an absurd proposition? He had always fought for her, putting himself out on a limb in the face of his partners to protect her privacy. She wanted to. She ached to. But she knew Adam was correct. If she broke the line of confidence and allowed even one person to enter, even Anthony, her most trusted, the result would be the plan's demise. She tried to get herself together. During their meeting she dared not give any indication she was feeling anything beyond her normal pain. Anthony could see through her. He seemed to always sense what she was able to hide from everyone else. She forced herself to regain her composure and tried to calm her heart.

In the process she thought back to her last session with her therapist. She had not been able to stop crying. She had blown it when it came to composure. She could not allow such a ghastly replay today when meeting with Anthony. She had told Susie that she was overwhelmed with all of the decisions she had to make. She felt so helpless with the boys. She had no rights when it came to their long-term upbringing. How could she fight the power of the establishment? William was firstly the Heir to the Throne and only secondly her son. The Queen had never allowed her to forget this reality. It was decreed the moment the Queen learned of William as a twinkle in her eyes. If Susie knew the possibility, what would she advise? Di thought she knew the answer. Susie would tell her to go for it. If only she could know for sure. Her therapist has repeatedly told her to build her own life within her own framework. Now, the framework was changing far beyond any boundaries that anyone had imagined.

Katherine's voice rang in her ears. "The only way to achieve what you want..." She began to smile and held back a giggle. Her vision of

Katherine lecturing to her remained vivid in her mind's eye. Older, yet still elegant, looking at her over those stupid reading glasses and telling her that delightful American expression. "Get a life." Her emotions were a yo-yo. She would cry one moment and laugh the next. She needed somehow to regain control.

She thought how naive she had been when she married Charles. She was so immature. She had been in love, in a dream world. Living a fairy tale. Divorce had never been contemplated. Surely, it would not be possible for the future King to do such a thing. No one in her family or anyone else for that matter had ever warned her of the possibility. It simply did not happen with an heir to the throne. Not even her brother, the skeptic, had uttered a word. His vision was that she was the luckiest woman in the world and, in fact, still is.

The consequences of divorce were even farther from anyone's thoughts. Now the reality sunk cold within her veins. She would become a nonentity in the House of Windsor, a dust speck in the establishment's eye to be blinked away. Her rights with the children would become nothing. Had anyone ever suggested this possibility when she married Charles? She could not remember, but she thought not. The warning signs were there. She had been so 'in love' at the time. She never would have listened. Now the reality was blatantly clear. *These are such inhumane standards in modern society, but they are the standards. I am powerless to change them.*

She had already spoken to Anthony about it all. He had confirmed that there was nothing she could do. She had no recourse. It would be a slow death, hard on the boys and, even harder on her. She thought of it in terms of death. How much better for everyone, a fast heart attack than a lingering illness. Not that death is ever easy, but it is better to get on with life than live in death.

Startling her back into reality, Alfred opened the door and extended his hand to help her out of the car. She had been so engrossed in her own thoughts that she had been oblivious. All of a sudden, they were everywhere. *Those damn paparazzi are here. My God, have they no decency?*

Hurriedly escorting her into Anthony's building, Alfred and Sean formed a human barrier to shield her from the paparazzi. Aware that she looked a bit tousled, Di attempted to dry her eyes and straighten her hair as they entered. It was wonderful that she did not have to put on a good face for Anthony. He understood her pain. She could allow him to see it, at least a part of it.

Whisked immediately into Anthony's office, she turned and asked the guards to wait. She declared. "This will only take a moment."

She wished the meeting to be over. She trusted Anthony and would support his recommendations. She did not want to review the details. If there was something that required her signature, she would sign and leave. It was too painful for her to dwell on the particulars.

Reading her expression, Anthony sensed her mood. He made light conversation but only for a minute or so. Then, he told her that all was prepared. "The proposal is tough, but I don't think they will reject it. We are in a good position. The Queen wants the divorce finished and final, effective yesterday. After some thought, Charles' attorneys will recommend agreeing rather than taking the chance of dragging out the negotiations. Time is on our side."

She thought back to what Adam had told her. *"Time is not your friend. The longer we take beyond what is necessary, the greater the risk of exposure."* Adam was right. The sooner they could execute the plan, the better for all concerned.

"You are right, Anthony. Time is on our side." His explanation had satisfied Di. Without reading the text, she signed and initialed in all places as requested. It was not a day for conversation, and Anthony respected that. *How fantastic he is. He can almost read my mind.*

Safely back in the car, her thoughts again turned to the news that Katherine would bring this evening. Was all of this just a dream? Was it possible for Adam, the man who she had heard about only as a legend, to orchestrate a fail-safe escape for her? Taking twenty deep breaths, she forced herself to relax, but her heart would not stop racing.

>─<•>─○─<•>─<

Katherine asked for Di to turn up the music a little louder. She motioned for Di to sit next to her, and they started to whisper.

Katherine said. "Adam has completed all of the first level planning and is confident that he will be able to complete the project without a problem. He wants to do it within a year, if possible. The time line is still flexible, but he estimates it will be close to a year from today. You must agree to follow Adam's directions exactly." Katherine repeated "exactly" again, telling Di that it was at Adam's request that she mention exactly a second time.

Di nodded to acknowledge the directive.

Then, Katherine began to explain the rest. "Adam feels that you can move another eight to ten million without creating too much suspicion. From this amount Adam's fee must be paid. If much more is moved, someone might question what happened. This will provide liquidity, and although the estate will not be as large as you had hoped, the risk of someone becoming curious and trying to trace the money flow will be eliminated. Properly invested, you will have a sizable monthly income, far more than you could ever spend in your new lower profile life style."

Di, again, nodded her assent but appeared a little strained.

Katherine looked at her and then put her arms around her.

Di immediately broke down and began to sob softly.

Katherine cradled her for a good twenty minutes and let Di cry herself out.

As she pulled back Di whispered, "Oh, look at what I have done to your top."

Katherine looked at her with eyes filled with love. "My love, it's nothing. But we need to get on with the plan. If I stay too late, someone might notice."

Di sat up straight and looked directly at Katherine. "You are right. Please continue."

"He wants for you to move the money using the same methods as last time, but in addition, he wants for you to use these two target accounts." Katherine provided a slip of paper. Then, she passed a second piece of paper with a name and an address in Texas. "Adam suggested that you send a letter to her as a memento. It could be important to you someday."

Di looked at her quizzically.

"It's your new name and address."

Di mouthed the name a few times and then looked to Katherine with a smile, the first real one all evening. She then whispered, "I like it."

For the first time since the dream began, it all seemed so real. Katherine could sense the resolve beginning to form in her friend. Di was going to make it. Seeing her new name in black and white offered hope, the first ray of light on the pathway that would lead to her new life.

"Adam said that it will be difficult when you begin to live your new life. It is important to write and give yourself a message to fall back upon to draw strength in the future. Also, he said for you to memorize or encrypt the information on the slips of paper and destroy them immediately."

She nodded. "I have already memorized the name and address."

"The other house will be in your new name by next week."

"Good."

Next, Katherine handed a thick paperback to Di. The title of the book was <u>Biographical Sketches of Twentieth Century Women</u>. "It looks thoroughly boring. Adam's intent. Read pages 150–237. You will learn the history of your new life. Adam thought that even if someone saw the book lying about, it would not attract much attention. He would like for you to read the biography several times. It will allow you to begin to truly know your new self and history. When you have finished, give it back to me. I will see that it's returned to Adam. Nothing should be left here that has your new name. Your new name is a real person's name and identity. No one will ever be able to challenge it. The schools in the biography are either no longer in existence or have records of your attendance. Even the most complete of background checks will prove you are who you say you are. You just need to memorize what is in the book and then fill in the gaps as you desire. Make the rest your dreams. They might come true."

Di caressed the book and pressed it close to her breasts. She began to sob softly. The tears ran down her cheeks, and she dabbed at them with a tissue. Taking a deep breath and forcing back the tears she said, "Now, we must get on. I will have a whole new life to cry, if I need it."

"Adam has made arrangements for your convalescence at a wonderful chalet in Gstaad, Switzerland. The speech therapist will work with you there and teach you to talk Texan."

Di snickered and said, "Howdy, y'all."

Katherine's normal reserve broke down. She giggled. "I think you had better wait for the speech therapist. I would never have believed that anyone could destroy that expression."

Di began to giggle too, and they hugged each other, long and tight, each drawing energy from the other. Katherine withdrew with the comment, "You are going to love it there. I just know it."

"I love America, but it will be so different to live there. I had never thought of living in the South, but after your explanation, it sounds perfect. It will be so nice to be away from pushy people and old memories. Texas seems so wonderful, I think it will be perfect."

"I know. That is why Adam suggested we find homes that are not weighted with centuries of memories. You will have a fresh outlook. Your life will be yours and yours alone. Both homes are new, well actually one is a complete remodel but like new. They will only have the memories you create. Adam said I can see them if I want, but I would rather wait for you to show them to me, so that I only relate to them as a part of the new you."

"Will you come right away, as soon as I am there?"

"No. Adam thinks I should wait for a few months. If anyone is slightly suspicious, the person might follow anyone who could have known. It's better if I act like everyone else and suffer with a stiff upper lip and all that rubbish. Besides you need some new memories, and I will just bring back the old."

Di pondered for a moment and said, "I feel so selfish. I worry about the boys. I worry about you, but it also feels so right."

"You have lived for the throne, and they have thrown you away. Now is your time. Don't let this nonsense get in your way. Get a life."

"Get a life." Di looked at her, and they both began to giggle again.

Thinking about the potential problems, Di asked, "How is Adam ever going to find a body that can pass for mine?"

"I don't know, but he has done it before. Maybe he finds one and freezes it until the time is right. I just don't know. He is the expert. He doesn't offer to give away his secrets."

"I guess, it's his business," Di replied, "but I don't want anyone to get hurt. You are sure he can do it?"

"If there's anyone in the world who can do it, it's Adam, affirmed Katherine. "Remember what he did for the Shah of Iran. No one has ever caught on. Even the Shah's family confirmed Adam's success to you. The first rumors did not even start to circulate until after his real death. That surely was the coup of the century, at least, until you. My God, can you imagine the books that would be written a hundred years from now, if any of this was ever discovered?"

"At least I will not have assassins looking for me," Di giggled. "Well, maybe if the Queen finds out."

"That was rather tacky, especially coming from you."

"You don't know her like I do. It must be the German blood. She is a very hard woman."

Katherine sensed she was on thin ice and changed the subject. They talked, now using normal voices, about girl things for a while. Then, Katherine got up to leave. Whispering again she said, "Love, please remember to be careful of what you say to both Paul and Rosa. The slightest hint of anything could prove disastrous. Just be yourself but don't be so much yourself that you give a hint of anything."

"Don't worry. I won't make a mistake," Di quietly replied.

Continuing in a whisper, Katherine said, "I really have been here too long. I must go or the wags will be talking about this old woman. I can only help if no one pays any attention to me. The paparazzi all think that I just work here. One even asked if I could let him know when and where you are going, so he could beat you there. I told him that I am not apprised of your agenda. I never see you other than in passing."

"Katherine, you're my angel," Di whispered, "and I hope I can look as wonderful as you when I'm your age."

"My dear, I'm not my age. I'm ageless."

They both smiled a deep assertion of hope, as Di showed Katherine to the door. Closing the door behind her and turning to rest on its solid framework, Di gazed to the high-cast ceiling imagining it as the universe opening its horizon to her.

3

New York, July 1996

Elizabeth was tired and a little demoralized. She had turned up nothing, not even a possibility at the three agencies she had contacted during the morning. London had produced only two weak leads the week before. Added to her lack of success, her quick lunch at Dawat was less than anticipated.

Curry is her favorite, the spicier the better. Today's fare was flat and boring. In the end it did not matter as she stuffed herself with the kulcha appetizer. It had been marvelous, as always. She took a little more time than she had intended, and her keeper was displeased because parking in the city is such a problem. She really did not care about that either. She had thoroughly enjoyed her short conversation with Madhur Jaffrey. He always loves to be complimented, and today was no exception. He expressed his concern that she had not eaten more than a bite or two of her curry. Worried that he would be insulted if she told him that to her taste the dish lacked pizzazz, she apologized by rationalizing, "You know me Madhur. I cannot control myself when it comes to your onion kulcha. By the time my entrée was served, I could hardly eat another bite." He smiled and seemed satisfied with her explanation.

Now, she was almost late for her two o'clock, her fourth appointment of the day. She was not worried. She knew that the agent would be so delighted to have a client who was real and who could pay her bills that it would not matter. He greeted her almost immediately upon her arrival. She liked that. No chit chat. He came to the point.

"How may I help you, Mizz?"

"I am looking for a female actress approximately thirty years of age. It's a long term contract, an understudy for another actress," Elizabeth replied.

The agent began to pull out dossiers. He went through stacks and stacks of papers. Elizabeth could not begin to keep up with him. Exasperated, she asked if she might be left alone for a few minutes to look through everything. Elizabeth searched through the photos, descriptions and resumes. She piled a stack of folders of possible candidates, only for disinformation. Elizabeth would show no interest in her real choice. She was always frightfully cautious, a family trait. She would reveal only what was imperative. She would leave a false trail in the process that lead in the opposite direction.

Bingo, she thought as she identified an actress who looked perfect. She casually but thoroughly absorbed the information necessary and then placed the file on the stack of rejected dossiers. Like her brother, Elizabeth had a near photographic memory. She had committed all the important facts to immediate recall.

Completing her selections, Elizabeth went into the outer office telling the secretary that she had some questions. Momentarily, the agent returned, hopeful that Elizabeth's search had been successful. She acted only partially optimistic but still requested prompt interviews with her chosen candidates. Arrangements were made, and upon completion of all of the normal pleasantries, she left.

On her ride down the elevator, Elizabeth reflected about the importance of details. She would earnestly interview the darker skinned women and then decide against them. If anyone ever remembered her even stopping by the agency, there would never be any connection to her search for the ideal fair-skinned female.

Asking her keeper to wait outside while she stopped at a small bistro on East 54th Street to unwind over a café noir, Elizabeth pulled her small communicator from her handbag. With near perfect photographic memory, she encrypted the stats about the woman named Jennifer, and posted them to the secure Internet FTP site that was being used for this project. The background check would commence immediately upon the retrieval of the information.

With a positive result, Jennifer would be contacted and, subsequently, interviewed by an ex-Scotland Yard detective named Tony. Tony would pose as a publicist seeking an actress to appear publicly with him. He would tell her that he needed a performing artist to accompany him as a cover for his homosexual proclivities. He was negotiating a contract with an extremely conservative company, and they would not hire him if they knew he was gay.

The interview would take Tony less than ten minutes. His skill level of painlessly determining a candidate's potential is unmatched. If she could pass Tony's interrogation, Jennifer would then be contacted by Elizabeth and told only a part of the story. No one could ever be allowed to know the complete tale. These compartments were necessary to the security of the whole operation. Adam's operating dictum runs absolute. No one individual is to know any detail more than is necessary to do the designated task. Concurrently, each person entwined in the plot is told more than enough to believe an entirely different story.

Leaving the comfort of the cozy and quaint Bistro, Elizabeth handed her keeper the address of her next appointment. Disgusted that he was such a bore, she said, "My appointment is at four. Please, hurry. I do not want to be late." The truth was that she was tired and wanted to cancel, especially since she had found Jennifer. She knew better. Years of experience had taught her well. Maintaining a back-up plan B was essential to the success of every operation. Plan A was never a given. Anyone who believed that was doomed to failure.

During the ride in Manhattan's typical bumper to bumper, horn honking, siren-laden traffic, Elizabeth reflected that New York is such an impersonal city. In Paris she would have chosen a totally different setting, a bistro with an exterior terrace and an ambiance of interaction. There she would have taken a strategically placed table that allowed for her to 'people watch' and, in turn, be 'watched' by others. In New York the vibrations are so different. Here, everyone escapes to a cocoon. People try to insulate themselves within a shell immune from the outside world around them. She thought, *This is the very reason I hate New York.* To her it was such a dichotomy. It is New York's non-human environment that makes this city such an ideal hunting ground for Adam's puppets.

Puppets, she thought, *is such a strange title for employees. But Adam's employees are puppets. Nothing more. Nothing less. Adam never hires managers. He does not hire assistants or secretaries. Never would he dream of calling an employee a vice-president or special consultant. Adam only employs puppets to man his projects. Ignorant of his total business plan, that he thinks of as his play, his puppets merely move to the motions of their parts. After their roles are complete, they pass out of his caper. Depending upon his need, he throws them away or places them on inactive status for his next performance. For Adam, the end always justifies the means.*

Placing her thoughts on hold, Elizabeth entered the ninetieth floor agency five minutes early for her four o'clock appointment. Head held high, she presented her embossed business card to the dour and matronly agent. The woman was clearly a lesbian on the make but without the finesse to make it work. The woman looked at Elizabeth and then at the card. She ran her fingers over the embossing and looked back up at Elizabeth in a new light. Quality was important to image. Elizabeth's card showed the Beverly Hills address of the firm of Goldstein, Hoch & Guttmann. Elizabeth introduced herself as Ruth Goldstein and slipped into her role. Elizabeth could change identities faster than most women could change their shoes. In two weeks the answering service would be disconnected and Goldstein, Hoch & Guttmann would vanish as a phantom in the night. The service had been paid for in cash; no trails were left behind.

With this agent Elizabeth skillfully singled out another possible actress named Susan. She posted Susan's stats in the labyrinth of her calculating mind poised for instant recall. Elizabeth's intuition remained firm that Jennifer was the perfect puppet. Nevertheless, as always, following her years of Junior League training, she registered her Plan B.

Leaving the giant steel and glass structure that served as just another of New York City's countless, faceless skyscrapers, Elizabeth stopped by the post box in the building's lobby. Slipping on a pair of light cotton gloves, she removed the yellow manila envelope from its protective cover and dropped the anonymous package into the box. Filled with a number of previously unknown facts that could later be verified, the half-truths would be accepted with little question. The big lie was so well coated with deceit that the government investigators would swallow it in smirking ignorance. *Stupidity has its own reward,* she reflected as she left the building. This information provided the missing link to draw to a conclusion the project that the Puppet Master had been orchestrating over the last year. Now, all attention could be directed to his present venture, the challenge of his life.

>-+-+>-O-<+-+-<

Back at her hotel, a sensitive staff who knew her as Ms. Wilson greeted Elizabeth. She felt comfortable and welcome at the Lowell, located on the Upper East Side. Small hotels were always more secure, a quality Adam demanded. The suites reminded her more of Europe than of the USA. A tribute to art deco, the hotel is somehow able to successfully mingle a touch of the elegant past with thoroughly modern opulence. Her favorite suite reminded her of her pied-à-terre in Milan. Taking a leisurely bubble bath while sipping a champagne flute of Perrier, she admired her reflection in the marble surround. *Not too bad for an old girl,* she thought.

It was soon time to begin her ritual of preparation for dinner. Elizabeth always dressed for dinner, even when she ate at home. Deciding on a black St John's knit dress, she accessorized it with sapphires and diamonds. She loved the contrast of the huge puffy sleeves with the high-neckline and deep scoop in the back. She thought, *Thank God it's fall.* She needed only a light wrap.

The last time she wore her sable coat in New York, some politically correct idiot had accosted her as she left the restaurant. Elizabeth could still hear the bigot telling her that she was insensitive to the suffering of the animals that were murdered for their skins. Elizabeth giggled out loud remembering her response to the earth chick. She could remember her words verbatim. She mouthed them once again. "Like hell. I personally drowned every one of the aggressive little bastards." The fat woman had gasped at Elizabeth in horror, as she continued with her keeper to the waiting car. "The politically correct are such insufferable boors," she had told her smirking keeper.

Dinner this evening was at The Post House and was excellent, as always. She adhered to the same philosophy as her brother. She preferred an exceptional dinner for two, herself and a damn fine waiter. There were no disappointments on either account this evening. Always petite, Elizabeth could eat anything and not gain weight. She maintained an excellent physique through exercise, not diet, and looked much younger than her years.

A handsome younger man repeatedly tried to get her eye, but she did not have the time for such nonsense. She ignored him, thinking that she should really take a break when this all is over and have an affair. Nothing too serious, perhaps a married man. Such affairs created less long-term entanglements. If he started to become too serious, she could disappear and leave him to his wife. His guilt would keep him from searching to find her.

She completed the meal in comforting solitude and enjoyed a small brandy before asking her keeper to take her back to the hotel. Elizabeth still had several hours of work to accomplish before she could find the comfort of her pillow.

Back in her suite knowing the information would be awaiting her return, she downloaded the initial report on Jennifer. She entered the decryption key and began to get a feel for the potential puppet.

Jennifer, a British subject, was raised in an upper middle class, untitled family. Her father and mother had been separated since Jennifer was eight years of age but never divorced. The mother was constantly medicated on antidepressants. The father raked up one sexual affair after another. There were rumors that Jennifer had been sexually promiscuous, but none was yet confirmed. Jennifer had been arrested on a shoplifting charge, but the charge was dropped after her father paid off the storeowner. Jennifer was arrested a second time, this time for possession of marijuana. Jennifer apparently had been clean since the second arrest. She had lied about her prior arrests when applying for a work visa. Currently, she was in the U.S. without a work visa. She had apparently entered through Canada, as there was no entry record in the immigration computer. No roommate. No steady boy friend. *Great.* She had signed a contract with two agencies, promising each an exclusive representation. *A deceitful little bitch. Perfect. Perfect. Perfect.* Her parents had reported her as missing to the local police in England three years ago, and clearly Jennifer and her parents had had no contact since that time. She was still listed as missing. Since she had been missing for three years and was in the U.S. illegally, no one would miss her here. *Fantastic. You, my dear, are perfect for the role. We will audition you and cast you in the role. We will make you an offer you cannot refuse. You will sing the puppet's song and dance the puppet's dance. My God, I am getting melodramatic in my old age. I had better get a grip.*

Elizabeth encrypted the dossier and uploaded it to the secure FTP site reserved for this project. She then wrote an encrypted message instructing Tony to contact Jennifer and posted it via e-mail. Hopefully, Tony would be able to arrange a meeting during the next few days. Elizabeth could not get out of stifling New York one day too soon. She longed to be back in Europe. First, they would go to Paris. Then to London and, finally, to Geneva. Elizabeth was ready. The adrenaline started to surge at the thought of placing their plan into action.

>-I-◆>-O-◆-I-◄

New York, three days later

Everything was falling into place with Jennifer. It was time for Elizabeth to do her follow-up for the rejected candidates. Like Adam, Elizabeth had a penchant to leave no unturned stones. It was her style to contact each of the various agents on a personal basis, returning all the information that had been provided to her. She would not contact the agency representing Susan. That door would be left open, just in case. She dropped by each agency, not calling in advance for an appointment. This personal contact, a simple courtesy, conveyed her seriousness. Her story was constant. "I am very sorry, but I have not found exactly the actress I am seeking. I will hire a candidate that I located in LA several weeks ago. I thank you so much for your assistance." The chapter was closed.

Back at the Lowell, she posted a message to Adam that all had gone as expected and checked to see if Tony had transmitted his report. *No such luck.*

Glancing at her watch, she realized that it was time to dress for dinner. Le Cirque was the evening's choice, and Adam was meeting her there. As always, they were meeting vis-à-vis, the only possibility for assuring absolute privacy.

He had arrived on the Concorde earlier in the day. He was staying at Morgans on Madison Avenue. Elizabeth hated the place, but Adam always stayed there when using this identity. His personal preference was The Pierre. Elizabeth liked it as well. For her, where Adam stayed was not important. She did not have to encounter the place that proved so distasteful to her. She really did not know why she disliked Morgans so much. There was just a feeling about it.

Elizabeth and Adam shared a bond that went far deeper than blood. They thought of themselves as twins in different costumes. They had been in boarding school together as children in Switzerland. Both could speak English, French and German like their mother tongue. Adam had never been able to rid himself of the slight Swiss accent that tainted both his French and German. But Elizabeth could pass for a Parisian or a Berliner. Elizabeth could also speak Italian like it was her mother tongue, but Adam had only managed to master it as a foreign language. They had that uncanny ability to communicate with each other by unspoken nuances. They could often complete each other's sentences. They were the Yin and Yang. Together they were whole, so much alike, and, yet, at times, they were so frightfully different. Both had been previously married, although the ending of each marriage was in sharp contrast.

Adam maintained a strong platonic relationship with his ex-wife, Natalie. She, to this day, served as a confidant when he needed a less cynical view. Elizabeth liked her, and their relationship was better now than ever. It had been strained in the early years; the two strong women had both been jealous of the relationship that each had with Adam.

Elizabeth's husband and six-year-old daughter had been murdered. Elizabeth was the other intended victim. Her daughter had merely been in the wrong place at the wrong time. Were it not for an impulsive trip to pick up some ice cream, Elizabeth would have shared the fates of her husband and daughter. She came home to a nightmare, realized the danger and escaped out the back door before she was found. Sometimes she was grateful she escaped; other times she was bitter.

Adam had rescued her from certain death. His ex-wife had helped to create the new legend of Elizabeth. The three of them were the only people alive who knew that Adam and Elizabeth were brother and sister. Although it was possible that Katherine had guessed. She was a sly old fox.

While excitedly dressing for her most welcome evening with her brother, Elizabeth allowed her mind to reflect back to that day several years ago when Adam had driven her to the abandoned factory. There, three of the men responsible for the deaths of her husband and daughter were being held.

Adam had already questioned the three and had extracted every detail. The two hit men knew nothing. They were merely stupid animals. Intimidated by Adam, their boss had identified the government contact who had hired him for the hit. The U.S. government official and the other accomplices would have to wait for another moment of justice. Their time of demise was for another day. Elizabeth and Adam were committed to making a clean sweep of anyone and everyone who had anything to do with the botched assassination. This day, their efforts were focused only on the three men sequestered at the factory.

Elizabeth remembered how the three looked like drowned rats in the bottom of the empty concrete tank. Ten feet by ten feet and eight feet deep, it had been designed to hold factory waste material. She remembered the sight perfectly. They were completely naked. Their faces were swollen, their bodies bruised and bloody. As she looked down upon them to photograph forever their brutal images in the hallow of her unforgiving mind, they covered their genitals. It seemed so strange to her to care about a thing like that as they prepared to die.

Adam and Elizabeth lowered the concrete top with the chain hoist and sealed the men in darkness, forever. They could hear the screams faintly through the ventilation cover. Adam had provided the men with enough water to be able to helplessly call for help for a week or so. Both Elizabeth and Adam wanted these men to have plenty of time to understand why they were dying. In three weeks Adam would return and flood the tank with the acid that would remove the traces. He had already extracted their teeth during his questioning. There would be nothing left to ever be identified. The other conspirators would have to wait. But they would never be forgotten.

Elizabeth's thoughts then jumped to when she had traveled to Switzerland through Mexico for the surgery that totally changed her appearance. At this same time, Adam and his wife created the 'Legend' that was to become Elizabeth. It was the longest and most sorrowful year of her life. She was so alone as Adam could not risk seeing her or calling her. She received post cards as he traveled, and they were always cryptic. Adam and Natalie left a trail of evidence that made it appear that she had drowned at sea trying to leave Mexico surreptitiously.

Startled back to reality, she remembered that her old self had now been legally dead for nearly twenty years. Sometimes it was very difficult for her to remember her old life. The images were fading. Then, like a shooting star, they would all come back too abruptly, wrapped in unbearable pain.

>–!–‹›–•–O–•–‹›–‹

Adam was already seated when she arrived. He rose, gallant as ever, while the Maître d' helped her into her chair. They looked into each other's eyes. A casual observer would have thought them to be old lovers. But the thought would have been instantly abandoned had the observer been able to look deeply into their eyes. Their eyes looked much too assured with one another and conveyed the message that they had seen far too much.

Their gentle conversation was in Jauner-Tüütsch, a Swiss German dialect that was even difficult for most Swiss Germans to understand. They exchanged banalities that provided all the information that each needed but would have revealed nothing, even if someone would have been able to understand the conversation.

Adam was flying to Houston the next day to work on another part of the financial package. It was necessary to have all finances in place and active before the Princess assumed her new identity. He would then travel on to Dallas to make other necessary arrangements there. He told Elizabeth that he would be at the 'Gun Club' in Houston and the 'Little House in Dallas.'

The 'Gun Club' was their code for The Remington Hotel. He would stay in his favorite suite that had been designed by Louis Cataffo with Adam in mind. Adam enjoyed the suite but studiously avoided the hotel's bar that was a Houston 'in spot.'

In Dallas he would stay at the Mansion on Turtle Creek. He and Elizabeth both laughingly referred to it as the 'Little House in Dallas.'

Adam updated Elizabeth on his meeting in London with Di's contact, Katherine, and provided the name of the dentist who Di used. Adam hated using a contact in the middle. In fact, it was against his policy, but Di was far too closely watched for Adam to meet with her more than once or twice. Adam and Elizabeth both trusted Katherine, but they had still agonized over the decision. It was the only workable solution. Katherine had known Di long before she married, and Katherine's relationship with Di had always gone unnoticed. Unlike Rosa who was a regular companion and confidant, Katherine was the invisible woman when it came to the press. She remained unknown because, in contrast to Di's other friends, Katherine never spoke of her relationship with Di or gave any tips to the press.

Elizabeth then told Adam about Jennifer. Adam was content that things had gone so well, so quickly. Adam looked deep into Elizabeth's eyes and told her, still speaking in the strange Swiss dialect, "Absolutely and thoroughly check out the girl. The wrong choice will spell certain disaster."

The returned expression told him that he was preaching to the converted.

He glanced down at the table, the closest that Adam ever came to apologizing.

After sipping a brandy and quietly looking into one another's eyes subtly communicating the complete understanding of the next steps demanded of each, Adam paid the bill in cash. He left a generous tip and escorted Elizabeth to the door where her keeper was waiting.

Snuggled back in her suite at the Lowell, Elizabeth was delighted to find Tony's report awaiting her. Thorough as always, it ran to several pages after it was decrypted. His reports always flowed like essays. Reading between the lines revealed almost more than was told by his outright statements.

Jennifer was desperate for work. Tony wondered how she had been able to pay her rent and buy food. Something was not quite on the up and up. He was doing a follow-up investigation and would report back as soon as his suspicions were confirmed.

However, the main concern in the interview had been laid to rest. Jennifer's accent could be easily modified to match. Jennifer had already demonstrated that she could mimic Tony's accent. Probably the most difficult problem with the entire caper was the accent. Tradition states that half of the population of England can determine, simply by listening to a person's accent, the location within twenty miles of where the person was raised. The other half can do it within ten miles. Only someone who grew up there can decode the subtleties of English speech patterns. It requires someone who understands the social order from the inside out. It would be possible to train an outsider, even an American, but it would take time that they did not have.

For a moment, Elizabeth allowed herself the luxury of feeling a warm fondness for Tony. Quickly, she placed her feelings to rest. He was a wonderful man, but he would never be able to understand what she and Adam did for a living. To become emotionally attached to him would be worse than suicide. It would be a living death for both of them. She had already once experienced a living death. Never again.

Tony believed that she and Adam worked for a corporate security firm that did some very quirky investigations. The cover was without flaw. It was best to leave it at that. It was prudent that she did not meet him face to face while he was in New York. It was much better to leave their relationship to the Cyberspace of the Internet. It was hard for her to believe that it had even been possible for them to work before the Internet. She remembered when they had depended on the fax and telex. Today, it seemed almost impossible that they had ever been able to accomplish anything. It had been like working in the stone age. Tony would fly back to London after he finished the follow-up and return to his private insurance investigation business. It was best that way.

Pampering herself with the pleasure of remembering, Elizabeth opened the secret compartment in her attaché case. She removed the photos of her daughter and husband. She knew that Adam would be furious if he knew she had kept them, but she had promised herself that she would carry out this ritual until the whole, ugly business was finally settled to her satisfaction. Three more men had yet to pay the price for her pain. And pay they would, when the time was right. She lovingly kissed each photo and softly whispered with a smile of contented satisfaction, "I will never forget. I will never forgive."

4

New York, one week later

The week passed quickly for Elizabeth. There was far more to accomplish than time provided. Tony's initial contact and investigation of Jennifer proved positive, but Elizabeth was still awaiting the final report. Tony had promised it by late in the afternoon. As always, he was exactly on schedule but not a minute before, posting it to the FTP site from JFK just before he caught his flight.

Merde. Tony had uncovered that the girl has turned an occasional trick to pay the rent. *Now a complete physical will be necessary. We cannot take a chance that she has contacted AIDS, hepatitis or some other sexually transmitted disease. We don't have the time for such nonsense. I really do not need this. Shit. Shit. Shit.*

Re-reading Tony's report, Elizabeth absorbed every word and catalogued every detail in perfect order in her amazingly organized brain. Reflecting upon what she had read, Elizabeth decided that Jennifer's positives far outweighed the one possible negative. Elizabeth smiled and contemplated, *This girl has a tremendous upside. She'll do anything for money. Fantastic.* If they were lucky, everything would be okay. Elizabeth forced herself to calm down and swooped into her innermost self. She felt satisfied. Jennifer was their girl. They would overcome the hurdles. The time had come to get on with it.

Pausing for no more than ten seconds, Elizabeth telephoned the doctor to arrange for an appointment. Next, she dialed Jennifer's number. The girl answered on the first ring. Elizabeth introduced herself as Tony's secretary and discussed the particulars of the job. "Tony wants to place you on a retainer, but there is one tiny problem. You must have a physical to qualify for our group health insurance. It's not our requirement. The insurance company demands it, and we cannot hire you without insurance. Do you have any objection?" Hearing the excitement in Jennifer's voice, Elizabeth continued, "We are rushed for time. I have already called the doctor. He can see you the day after tomorrow at two o'clock. Does that time work out for you?"

Jennifer responded with an immediate, "Perfect." Jennifer continued, asking only two questions. The telling one said it all. "When will I receive my first check?"

We have a ringer, thank God. Not wanting to sound anxious, Elizabeth continued the conversation on her terms. She was concise and professional. A bit abrupt. She gave the girl the doctor's address. Cautioned her not to be late for the appointment. She verified Jennifer's address and told her that a cashier's check would be posted the next day for the first month's retainer. Elizabeth provided the girl with an answering service number in France and told her to call if she had any questions whatsoever. The number would be disconnected in two weeks regardless. Jennifer would either be on board or set adrift by then. Almost sighing out loud with relief, Elizabeth quickly ended the conversation by thanking Jennifer for her understanding and saying, "I will be back in touch with you after the results of the physical are delivered to the insurance company. Good day." Elizabeth placed the receiver back on the hook. *The girl has possibilities, but she needs work. A hell of a lot of work. She is excessively obvious about showing her emotions.*

Satisfied that she had completed step one, Elizabeth called the Lowell's concierge and told him that she would be checking out the next morning. She logged on to the Internet, typed in the address for the TISS web site and booked her flight for Paris. *What will I do if she isn't clean? Shit, I don't even want to think about it.* Elizabeth hated the thought of returning to New York to pick up with Susan or, even worse, to search for other candidates. If Jennifer were infected, there would be no other choice. Time was of the essence, and Elizabeth resented that Jennifer's history had caused a possible delay. Knowing there was nothing she could do but wait, Elizabeth placed the whole project on hold somewhere in the memory banks of her mainframe brain.

It was time to get down to some serious shopping. Yesterday, she had seen a set of pearls that she felt she might need. No, on second thought, she was confident that she needed them. She called her keeper's room and asked that he be ready in fifteen minutes. Changing into her favorite, serious walking shoes, she could not get the pearls out of her mind.

As expected, her keeper was impatiently awaiting her arrival in the Lowell's lobby. This man was not her first choice. To be honest, he was not even her second choice. She never questioned his efficiency. It had nothing to do with that. There was no doubt he executed his assignment with robot-perfect skill. Her every need was impeccably fulfilled. But he was so incredibly boring and always seemed irritated. He could almost be Swiss. At least, she did not have to feign making conversation with him. He never said a word. Elizabeth thought how glad she would be to leave this one behind. *Why me with Mr. Efficient? This guy never misses a trick, but he is about as charming as a door post. This is the story of my life.*

Adam always rotated her keepers when Elizabeth was in the U.S. All of them thought she was an heiress who was a potential kidnap victim. She was probably as deadly as any of the keepers in hand to hand combat, but with a big man around, no one ever paid her any attention. She hated dragging someone around with her. It was like being in shackles, but she knew Adam was right. Alone, a small woman looked like a victim waiting to happen. *It's just as well to have a keeper.*

She would never forget the last time she was accosted. Adam had never again allowed her be alone in the big cities after that event. It happened in London about five years ago. She had been alone on a deserted street; she had taken a wrong turn while out for a late evening stroll. She broke a nail when she drove her fingers straight into the unsuspecting mugger's throat. It seemed to take him forever to quit thrashing around, lose consciousness and die. Not only was it messy as hell making sure she did not leave any evidence on his body, but she, also, immediately needed a manicure. She normally enjoyed a manicure. However, she kept a busy schedule, and it is so inconvenient when a nail breaks at ten o'clock at night and a meeting is scheduled for eight the next morning. She repaired the damn thing herself. Not a great memory. Doing a nail repair and a French manicure left handed was not at the top of her list of strong points. Shit, she hoped the inconsiderate bastard really suffered before he died.

>─┼─◄▷─O─◄▷─┼─◄

Houston, the same day

Adam had completed his work in Houston and was preparing for his departure to Dallas.

Step one was accomplished. Earlier that day, Adam had registered the new Mercedes in the name of Di's 'Legend.' It was sapphire blue and would seem like an old friend, closely matching the color of her BMW in England. He had finally settled on the Mercedes, although he first considered a 7 series BMW. The Mercedes was less noticeable, and service was free on the big car. Eventually, he wanted her to drive a Suburban or the new Ford Expedition but that would be too much of a culture shock for her this early in the game. The time had come for the 'Legend' to start leaving a paper trail in the U.S. Adam had deliberately over-parked at Houston International to receive a parking ticket.

Adam had ordered note cards and stationery from John Ludlam Fine Stationers. The Crane papers they offer are of the quality necessary to complete the image. Adam had been using this stationer's discreet services for years, although John had no idea of Adam's real name and business.

Step two was pending completion. The home in the exclusive village had been purchased, and a security firm had been hired to keep an eye on the place while the owner traveled. The 'Legend' split her time between Dallas, Houston and abroad. She would not be in Houston for several months, maybe even a year.

Step three was tomorrow's venue in Dallas. All paperwork was in place. The first tranche of funds had already been deposited as instructed. *How wonderful it is to work with someone who follows instructions perfectly. This woman is not only beautiful, she has a real head on her shoulders.* Now, it was merely a question of providing the 'Legend' with enough substance that no one would ever question her identity. It was not at all that difficult to do. It just took time and research to compile and create the verifiable facts.

The 'Legend' was the divorced daughter of a petroleum engineer who traveled widely. Adam's research south of the Rio Grande had unearthed the death of an American family in a private plane crash. The deaths of the parents were eventually recorded in their home state because of relatives who were interested in the inheritance. The infant's body had not been recovered, and there was no death certificate ever filed in the United States. The child had been a girl. Had she lived, she would be two years younger than Di. *Good news for her,* Adam thought with a smile. *Women always yearn to be a few years younger as time sets in.*

Adam had built a wonderful history for the girl that would withstand the closest of scrutiny. Her marriage and divorce were registered in Mexico. The 'Legend' would keep her married name. Even the remote chance of happening upon someone who might remember the child's death had been eliminated through the change of family name. The married name was common enough so that it would never attract attention. Social Security numbers had been obtained and bank accounts opened. Adam had hired a woman to acquire a driver's license in the new name. The picture would not match exactly, but with women they never did. Di could apply for a new one if she wanted. The 'Legend' had lived abroad for most of her life. A homemaker with no income. Her legendary husband was not an American citizen, so there was no tax history that might later cause problems, questions or suspicions. *A perfect solution.*

The banks and accountants had been informed that the 'Legend' was receiving an inheritance from a doting uncle who lived abroad. Precautions were made to minimize tax liabilities. No one would ever guess that this portfolio was developed as a cover for a change of identity. A tax form had already been filed with IRS for the current year to place the 'Legend' on the tax rolls. The more documentation of this type that could be accomplished prior to her appearance the better.

The 'Legend's' history in the United States pre-dated her disappearance from the world scene. No one would ever think to look in the past. It did not matter that no one had ever met her. She had paper trails everywhere. Credit cards had been issued and were already being used. A credit history had been furnished to TRW. She existed everywhere but in real life.

Adam left Houston using a credit card in the 'Legend's' name to fuel the big Mercedes. He then drove to Austin where he stopped for a delightful, light lunch at a small restaurant that was purported to be Italian. Adam had spent much time in Italy. This cuisine was not like any cuisine from any part of Italy that Adam had ever frequented. The fare was more of a cross between high Mexican, Italian and nouvelle cuisine. It was hard to define but fantastic none the less. Everything, that is, except the wine. Adam, upon the recommendation of the headwaiter, sampled a bottle of thoroughly boring Texan wine. A gorgeous deep red hue, it tasted more like a full bodied, sweet vinegar than the Merlot to which it had been associated. Adam was polite to the waiter but placed the wine aside and resorted to drinking his mineral water.

Mentally exhausted, yet superhumanly spirited, his mind wandered. *I have never felt so exhilarated. The exceptional nature of this project is a once-in-a-lifetime opportunity. I covet this challenge. I would do it for free if I had to, just for the excitement of it.* His thoughts continued to wander turning the three plus hour drive to Dallas into merely a moment in time. He could hardly believe it when he saw the freeway sign announcing a familiar Dallas exit. *How did I arrive so quickly?*

Adam drove directly to his hotel. He avoided pulling into the hotel's entrance and searched for a 'No Parking' zone. He drove around the surrounding blocks three or four times before securing a spot by a fire hydrant. Assured he would return to a parking ticket that carried a steep fine, he entered the tasteful lobby of the exquisite Mediterranean style Mansion on Turtle Creek. He checked-in using the 'Legend's' American Express Platinum Card. He was carrying identity to prove he was her brother with power of attorney should anyone ever question the card. As usual, no one did.

Adam was immediately escorted to his spacious quarters by one of the hotel's wonderfully trained bellmen. His every need was addressed with a perfect mixture of courtesy and formality. Adam kicked off his shoes and put up his feet. He relaxed over a Campari and mineral water perfectly prepared by the bellman from the suite's private bar. Adam loved it here. Dallas was like home for him with The Mansion his private residence. The Dallas panorama was so strong, so established and yet so young at the same time. It commanded a feeling of security. So much of Adam's past was here. Dallas was a part of him.

Allowing himself to let down as he sipped his drink, Adam felt exhausted. He was unsure if he could move. He knew he had to. He could not leave the car indefinitely. He forced himself to get up to move the damn thing before it was towed away. He really didn't care, but it was simpler just to pay a ticket than to deal with impoundment. When he reached the car, he found nothing. There was no ticket. His illegal act had gone unnoticed. *Shit. Where the hell is a cop when you need one?*

Accepting his defeat, Adam moved the Mercedes and deposited the car with the hotel's doorman. As he waited for the elevator to return to his suite, he realized how hungry he felt. His mouth started to water for the hotel's marvelous crab-cakes, a specialty of the house. Back in his quarters, exhaustion once again set in, but somehow he found the strength to pick up the telephone and touch the button for Room Service.

><+<>-O-<>+<

Dallas, the next day

Adam awoke promptly at 6:00 am. Stretching his arms and legs simultaneously, he reviewed the checklist of his body parts for aches and pains. He gave himself a clean bill of health. He felt rested and refreshed. Not wasting another minute, he threw off the covers and lunged out of bed. Searching for his glasses, he was happy that the speed dial button on the telephone was in big letters. Calling Room Service, he ordered coffee and a croissant, requesting delivery in ten minutes. He would shower quickly and then check his e-mail. While eating his breakfast, he would answer only the postings that were urgent. Everything else could wait until later. He wanted to be out the door before seven. Traffic would be heavy, and he had so much to do.

His first stop was Love Field, the Dallas regional airport. He again looked for a 'No Parking' spot. This time he chose a loading zone in the passenger departure area. He left the car for less than ten minutes feeling assured he would receive the desired ticket. He returned to success but success at a price, nearly a hundred-dollar fine. *Great.*

His appointment with the Realtor had been set for nine. If traffic was on his side, he would still be on time. He was posing as the Legend's brother. He had already communicated several times by telephone and e-mail with the woman who was the firm's number one sales agent.

Sensing he was an important man with little time to spare, she warmly greeted him immediately upon his arrival at her office and presented him with the agenda of the day. To his delight she had been responsive to his requests. She had organized several viewings of homes that generally met the criteria he had outlined. It appeared from his cursory examination of the information that one or more of the homes they would visit might suit his needs. He hoped that he could find the perfect home today, so he could move on to the other more pressing parts of the project. The day would be full, but it would not be wasted.

Adam adhered to the policy of contracting the best in any field to assist him with his needs. He had learned through his years of experience that the additional amount he paid for the services of the highly respected always saved him dearly in time and energy. He had learned the hard way that time and mistakes are very costly. It was a strange dichotomy, needing to spend more to save more. But he had proved this dictum accurate time and time again. Avoiding problems at all costs was cardinal in his line of work. There simply was no factor for error. The Puppet Master's plays had to be perfect, or they could turn deadly, very deadly.

Adam was very specific about his requirements. The correct area was everything. A presence of tasteful opulence would provide the perfect blend. Nothing so large that a single woman would feel insecure; yet, nothing so small that it would not lend itself to formal entertaining.

The home would be a refuge, an escape from the whirlwind of everyday life. Both privacy and accessibility were keys. Essential was the capability to install the most sophisticated of communication and security surveillance equipment. Access to high-speed digital trunk lines was necessary. The installation would be invisible to all who came and went from the home. Even the caretakers would not discover its existence. They would only know about the burglar alarm. That was nothing special. All houses in this price range had them. However, the real equipment and its capabilities would be known only to the 'Legend.' It would be her security blanket and her direct contact with Adam should she ever need help.

Adam and the real estate agent viewed more than ten houses, taking a thirty-minute break at one o'clock for a deli sandwich. Typical of American delis, the sandwich was huge, and Adam was unable to finish his. The sales agent, though, made a heroic effort and completed her meal in its entirety.

The day proved informative but unsuccessful. The agent was smart and very responsive. The choices she had made were close. Now that she and Adam had spent the day together, she had a much better understanding of his requirements. She had seen his reactions and learned from his descriptions exactly what he wanted. Their second meeting would be more productive.

Back at his Mansion suite, Adam downloaded the financial file that he had assigned to Thomas, a Swiss private banker. Thomas is an expert in covering tracks and moving money. This man created a miracle with the money President Marcos skimmed from the Philippines. The banker's schemes were brilliant. He placed major money in numbered accounts at the big Swiss banks, knowing that if placed under pressure, the Swiss would admit the existence of these accounts and block the funds. Concurrently, he moved and removed even larger amounts of money to secure locations. Some very high dollar art was purchased and sent to other countries for resale. It was a great way to cut the paper trail. Then, the funds were transferred again. Once, twice, sometimes three more times. None of these special funds that were hoarded by the Marcos family was ever found. The world has no idea of the truth. The world still believes that the Marcos' skimmed fortune is blocked in Switzerland. *Amazing.* Adam thought. *This guy really has his shit together.*

In the e-mail Thomas provided his recommendations for moving the 'Legend's' money. He suggested the purchase of some Old Master paintings. Such pictures are much less publicized than the big name

Impressionists. They can be purchased quietly and privately without creating a ripple in the art market. Thomas outlined to Adam how he often uses this procedure to move funds with absolute discretion. He engages the services of an extremely reliable Swiss team. He has worked with several dealers through the years, but when he uses this team, confidentiality is guaranteed. They organize the purchases and resell the paintings for the client after a period of time. Voilà. A large amount of money results with a legal reason to deposit it. Banks never think twice about the sale, and when the sale is claimed for tax purposes, the client's government is happy as well.

Adam thought for a few moments. *It worked for the Marcos Family. It is clean and simple.* He e-mailed an encrypted approval to convert another fifteen million into art. *Thank God for people like Thomas. I need to delegate more often.*

Then, Adam analyzed the rest of the plan Thomas had presented and approved it as well. Several annuities would be purchased from several Swiss insurance companies to provide a quarterly income. None was so large that it would create much notice, but together they assured an adequate cash flow for life. The other choices were also solid and involved some serious financial magic. Every investment had some form of a cutout so that none of the funds could be traced once they started moving. *Tricky, tricky, tricky.*

Adam and Thomas went back a long way. Adam had first met this genius when he was handling the Shah's project. Thomas was young then but imaginative. He had created some wonderful financial packages for the Shah. Both Adam and Thomas had aged well together.

Adam's newest asset was Jurg. Jurg worked at the same bank heading a special department for institutional investors. Although most of the bank people knew that Thomas and Jurg worked together, no one had any idea of the depth of their 'projects.' The bank's holding company would have suffered complete apoplexy with knowledge of the true nature of the business these two conducted. Yet, they were both men of high principle. They never handled dirty or drug money but undeclared funds or tricks like Adam needed were another matter entirely. They had assisted Adam so many times in so many ways. They had allowed him to save the financial lives of several political figures. Thomas and Jurg had creatively organized sweetheart funds that were carefully stored out of sight and out of mind. Many in the American government used Adam's services to create a nest egg.

Adam did not tell Thomas and Jurg often enough how fortunate he felt to have them on his team. He used them for his own personal financial matters, but he never seemed to find the time to deal with his own financial problems. Thomas and Jurg presented him with so many good recommendations, but Adam regularly procrastinated, putting off examining their suggestions for another day. For months Thomas had advocated that Adam purchase some Old Masters. Finally, today, he had agreed. Adam provided the go ahead at the same time he had given his approval for the purchase on behalf of the 'Legend.' He had not told Thomas how much he would invest. He needed to make a decision. *Maybe I should invest all...* The ring of the telephone broke his thoughts.

It was Elizabeth. She needed to talk. She could not get Jennifer's physical out of her mind. Adam, too, was inwardly worried about the physical. Outwardly, he reassured Elizabeth that her decision to continue with Jennifer was not faulty. Adam commented, "Elizabeth, you know as well as I do that Jennifer can surely be replaced. It would take us time, precious time. But we can do it if we have to. Hopefully, it won't come to that."

Both Adam and Elizabeth were keenly aware that time was their greatest enemy. Their timeline was strict. If it was violated, much of the work they had accomplished would be wasted. Adam, again, reassured Elizabeth that everything would work out. He signed off by saying, "Go to bed, darling, and please try not to worry. I'll be there in a few days."

Placing the receiver back on the hook, Adam compartmentalized the problem. He knew it was better to let his sister solve it. This area was not his strong point. The test results would be available shortly. There was nothing to do but wait and then make their decision. Elizabeth was more than competent and thorough beyond belief. It was her thoroughness that nearly got her killed with her husband and daughter. Adam remembered it all so well.

She had been working at the time with her husband doing research on World War II. Her husband was studying the case histories of the SS officers who had been declared war criminals. She was tracking them down and trying to find the trails of the ones who had disappeared. They were planning to write an exposé. In the process Elizabeth had unearthed a deadly secret. She discovered that the U.S. Government had given two of the 'animals' new identities and jobs. As unbelievable as it sounded, these two butchers had served as Federal Government employees for many years. Loaded with the facts, Elizabeth and her husband were about to go public with their story when the wrong people found out what they knew. She and her husband were placed on a hit list; the directive was to handle the case with extreme prejudice.

Pure luck and an impulse decision spared Elizabeth. She had stepped out to pick up some ice cream and happened into a conversation with a neighbor. She had taken a shortcut going out the back door, and the killers had not seen her leave. She should have been home. Her husband and daughter were brutally murdered. Elizabeth escaped the massacre, only because she was not where her assassins expected her to be. She returned via the back door and discovered the carnage. It took her only an instant to realize what had happened, and she fled before her stalkers could find her.

Adam had not believed that anything like this was possible. He had always been a loyalist, a true believer in the government. He was the conservative; Elizabeth was the doubting liberal. At the time, although cultured, Elizabeth was a bit of a hippie. She was cynical as hell about the government. She touted one conspiracy theory after another. Adam had thought it laughable until they awakened one day in the middle of this nightmare.

Both had been deceived but in different ways. Adam had secretly believed that the murders had to do with drugs or some other such underworld dealings. Such was the story the press reported at the time, and it matched the information that The Company provided to Adam. Elizabeth had sworn otherwise. She did not believe the press reports for one minute. After Adam tracked down the killers, he was sickened to find that his sister had been correct. The murderers were free agents working for the U.S. Government.

The tragedy changed both of their lives forever. It brought them together again. They had been so close during their youth; as adults, they had drifted apart. They had not taken time for one another. They led separate lives surrounded by their individual families and friends. To the outside world at the time of the tragedy, Adam and Elizabeth seemed more or less estranged. They were brother and sister in name only. Yin and Yang, fighting like cats and dogs in public. No one understood them. In reality they had always been of one mind and spirit. They had never lost their childhood bond. Had anyone realized the depth of their commitments to one another, Adam would have been targeted as well. The murders brought them together again. Now, they were a team with a mission forged in hell.

There was nothing Adam did not know about Elizabeth nor she about him. He knew of her nightly ritual of kissing the photos of her husband and little daughter. He ached feeling her pain. One day they would finally roll up the last of the team that had condemned Elizabeth to this living hell. This was Adam's pledge to her, a surety that he never questioned. So many years of living the memory had already passed for her. One day, final justice would be served. All who had been involved in the murders would be dead. Even with this, it would not be over. There would never be total closure. The bitterness was woven within both of their souls. It would endure in both of them forever. *No one ever said that life would be fair.*

Only three of the original people involved in the cover-up murder remained alive. Nine had already met their fates, including the contract killers. Two of the three who were still living no longer worked for the government, although all three still retained friends in power. Correct timing was essential. There could never be a hint of the plot to eliminate the team member by member. To do so would tip off the remaining members, who, in turn, might revert to any tactic to track down the avenging angels. Adam knew that he and Elizabeth had already used up a number of their nine lives. They could not afford to take undue risks with these people.

Adam was jarred from his memories as his laptop beeped to signal the arrival of e-mail. It was from Elizabeth. Good news. A thumbs up from the doctor. Jennifer was clean. He felt the tension drain from his body and realized that he had been as nervous as his sister about the results.

Overwhelmed with relief, Adam logged on to the Internet, booking a flight to London for the next day. He would fly a 747. The connections to use the Concorde were awful; from Dallas it actually took longer than flying direct by a slower plane. Dallas would be put on hold. He would call from the airport tomorrow morning to cancel his appointments. The star puppet had been cast. There was much work to accomplish in London. It was time to choreograph Act I. His blood was flowing, and he felt on top of the world.

5

Paris, the next day

Elizabeth finalized the arrangements for Jennifer's round trip flight to Paris. The return trip would never be used. For the moment it was better for Jennifer to think she was returning in a few days or, at least, could return at any time. Elizabeth needed to call her later in the day. With the time zones, it was three in the morning in New York. Elizabeth booked First Class TGV tickets to Lausanne for both herself and Jennifer in six days' time. The fast-train was the best way to enter Switzerland, and it actually took less overall time than flying, considering delays and the travel to and from the airports.

It was time to contact the girls. She sent an e-mail. They were a pair of former East German security service personnel. Eva and Brigit. One blond. One brunette. One stout and one gorgeously shapely. Both highly trained and loyal, absolutely loyal to the point of giving their lives in a moment. However loyalty extended to only one, the current paymaster.

They would be Jennifer's constant companions during the first phase of the project. They would act as her personal assistants, providing for her every need. Helpful to the extreme, they would serve her breakfast in bed, massage her shoulders after a hard day's work, carry her bags while she shopped, drive with her to appointments and open doors for her. They would also tap her phones, bug her room, and efficiently kill her if she deviated in the least bit from her instructions. Once the plan was in operation, it was imperative to protect Di, even if it meant the death of someone. It was unfortunate, but there was no other way to insure Di's safety. Jennifer would, of course, have no idea of this part of the plan.

They would arrive tomorrow, a day in advance of Jennifer and Elizabeth. They would bug the apartment and phones, place a GPS locator on the car that would drive Jennifer about. They would take care of all essentials before the arrival of the stand-in, leading lady.

Martin would also arrive tomorrow from Holland. He had served as a mercenary in the nastiest of business in various African countries. He was a bull of a man and cold as ice to those who did not know him. He would be Jennifer's chauffeur and bodyguard. He intimidated most men. From his acne scarred face to his dead eyes, he appeared as nothing less than a pure menace. He telegraphed a dangerous quality to anyone around him. Although he was always polite and correct, he conveyed a feeling that there was pure evil simmering just below the surface.

He was chosen for the assignment because his personality assured no danger of Jennifer getting too close or manipulating him in any way. He did not particularly like women. As far as Adam and Elizabeth had been able to uncover in their investigations, he had never had an affair with anyone of either sex. He appeared to be asexual. His persona would naturally draw Jennifer closer to the girls. It would become all of the girls against him. The arrangement, a perfectly calculated element of the plan, would keep Jennifer under complete surveillance and control at all times. All Jennifer would ever know was her individual role. Even so, there was no room for error. They could never be too cautious. It was imperative to protect Di at all costs, even if those costs involved the ultimate price.

When she awoke that morning, Elizabeth had found Adam's message. After receiving the news that Jennifer was a go, he had decided to change his plans. He was returning to London immediately. Elizabeth was not surprised. She would have bet on it. He would be staying at his pied-à-terre. *My brother. His plan is in motion, and nothing will stop him now. We will reshape history by the time it's over.* This project would be the crowning achievement of their career. It was a challenge in every way. The planning. The execution. *Even Di will never know the half of it. If she did, she would never go through with it. When it's over, it will be too late to have regrets. There will be no looking back. All that will be left is a fresh and new future.*

Catching herself while her mind was wandering, Elizabeth began to prepare the final instructions for Martin and the girls. She left no detail to chance. Suddenly, feeling a pang of hunger, she realized that she had nearly missed lunch in the midst of her planning. It was remarkably easy for her to become so completely immersed in her work that she forgot everything else. She looked at her watch and decided to just order from Room Service. She placed the call and got back to work.

She calculated that it was now seven in the morning in New York. Time for the happy wake-up call.

The sleepy voice answered the phone. Realizing who was on the other end of the line, Jennifer instantly tried to act wide-awake and failed miserably.

Elizabeth went right to the point. Everything was fine with the physical, and there would be no problem with the insurance coverage. The job was Jennifer's if she still wanted it. Time was of the essence, and it was necessary for Jennifer to travel to Paris immediately. "You haven't lost your passport, have you?" Elizabeth asked, a little worried.

Relieved by the instant response, all business, continued. She told Jennifer where to pick up her airline tickets. She instructed the girl to pack for a one-week journey and to travel light. Elizabeth told Jennifer that she would be waiting for her at the airport just as she walked out of the customs clearance area.

Jennifer could not hide the excitement in her voice. She had nailed her first real acting job and was bubbling over. It did not matter that it was not on stage. It would pay well and allow her to travel.

Damn. This girl must learn not to show her emotions. Elizabeth signed off wishing the girl a safe trip and moved on to the next order of business.

She placed a telephone call to Pierre, the caretaker. She asked him to ready the country house for six guests. She was sure that Adam would decide he had the time to sneak away from London for a few days. He would want to be there to see Jennifer for himself. Adam would, of course, show up unexpectedly. But he never fooled her. She would feign surprise, and he would act pleased, although he would not be fooled either. They were just too much alike for comfort.

Pierre would take care of everything. He would stock the refrigerator, prepare the rooms, and disappear until he was asked to return for the clean up. He was a spry old man who knew how to mind his own business.

Pierre had avoided many a problem in life by being able to mind his own business. Even the Nazis left him alone when they were strutting around thinking they owned the world. His cousin had been in the resistance. The Germans found him out and shot him. Pierre had always thought it served his cousin right. His cousin did not have enough sense to mind his own business.

Pierre had no curiosity about the Swiss man and French woman who were his employers. He believed that they were husband and wife, or, at the very least, husband and his mistress. After all, she was French, from Paris even. The Swiss were such boring people. What could she ever possibly see in this 'Mr. Nothing'? Pierre figured that the only possible answer was that he is rich. Everyone knew that all the Swiss are rich and bland. Pierre would have been shocked to find out that his bosses were neither Swiss nor French and, certainly, not lovers. They sometimes entertained foreign guests, and the villagers often asked what went on there. Pierre's response was constant. "They always pay the day they promise. What else is important?"

The auto had been purchased and would be delivered tomorrow. It was a black Mercedes with dark tinted windows. Sbarro, the Swiss custom auto builder from Neuchâtel, had heavily modified it. The car was much more than met the eye. It looked like a normal factory edition. It had not been armored. There was no need, and the extra weight would have proven detrimental to its handling. The car would be used throughout the entire project and then exported to South America. Arrangements had already been made. It had duplicate and forged registrations with plates to match in France, Switzerland, Luxembourg and Spain. It was very fast and handled like a sports car. The paparazzi would present no problem if they happened upon them.

>-+-◆>-O-◆+-<

Paris, the next morning

Ahead of the flight's scheduled arrival, Elizabeth took her station, as promised, outside the customs area at Charles de Gaulle International Airport. She preferred being early. Dressed in an unpretentious, light wool, taupe-colored business suit, she held a small placard. Jennifer's name was handwritten on its face. Until Jennifer was brought into the plan, it was important for Elizabeth to play the part of Tony's loyal secretary.

The wait seemed endless. Finally, Jennifer emerged. Elizabeth recognized her immediately. It was the first time that Elizabeth had seen her in real life. Jennifer was a near match in size and shape. She carried herself well. Her skin coloring was similar. Elizabeth thought, *This might actually work. I was worried, but she looks better than I imagined.*

Jennifer looked past Elizabeth twice before noticing the placard. Then, it finally caught her eye. Embarrassed, she quickly made her way to Elizabeth. She politely pushed herself through the masses and exited the roped-in space that separated the customs area from the waiting crowd. Jennifer was considerably taller than the diminutive Elizabeth, but she had the good manners to not hover too closely.

They quickly passed through the airport, as Elizabeth called Martin on her cell phone. By the time they had made their way to the exit, Martin was waiting with the trunk open. Jennifer was only carrying her purse, although Martin thought it was an overnight bag. It was huge. He only realized that it was her purse when he offered to place it in the trunk. Elizabeth was porting Jennifer's enormous overnight bag. It definitely stretched the limits of being considered an overnight bag. Noticing that Elizabeth handled it lightly, Martin was surprised as he lifted it into the trunk. He wondered if the girl was smuggling cannon balls.

The drive to the Paris flat was as uneventful as driving in Paris can ever be. Pure chaos. When they finally arrived, they found their reserved parking place filled with a Citroen 2CV. This little car was the French answer to the original VW Beetle. The 2CV was the height of camp, a car so very ugly it was cute.

Martin swore imaginatively under his breath and double-parked in the street. He took out the overnight bag and started to carry it to the door. Elizabeth stopped him and said that she would get it. "We don't want to get the Mercedes towed. We don't have the time." Martin took the cue, excusing himself immediately to return to the Mercedes.

Martin waited until the two women had entered the building. Then, he opened the driver's door of the 2CV. Checking that no one was watching, he released the brake and pushed the tiny car into the street. Pushing it further down the street, he gave it one final boost sending it into an intersection where another of its kind promptly sideswiped it. In typical Paris fashion, the driver did not even stop but careened on his way. The impact rolled the driverless 2CV into a parked car. Martin wanted to stay and see the eventual fireworks but thought it better to slip the Mercedes into its reserved slot before some other idiot took the space. He locked the big car and set the alarm. As he walked away he looked up just in time to see the owner of the 2CV walk up searching for his car. When he spotted it damaged down the street, the man ran to it, looked furtively about, jumped inside and simply drove off. The French could be so very casual about this sort of thing.

Martin entered the building. Like so many buildings in Paris, this one was registered as an historical site. It was an endangered species down on its luck. Changes had been minimal, but its general condition was not that bad. Actually, for a privately owned French building, it was rather well preserved. Martin could not help but feel the weight of decades pressing down upon him as he mounted the stairs. In most other European countries, the old buildings have a different feel. They might be run-down to the degree of almost falling down or perfectly restored with no traces of the past. It was different in Paris. Here, the weight of time was never ripped away.

He entered the flat to find Jennifer chatting excitedly with Elizabeth. The girl acted as though she was high on something. Hopefully, it was only caffeine. Jennifer looked over at Martin. She tried to hide her distaste but was amateurish in her attempt. Delighted, Elizabeth smiled from within. Martin was completely neutral; he was merely a fixture as far as Elizabeth was concerned. Martin appeared not to even notice Jennifer's reaction, although he was extremely observant and rarely missed anything. He was hard to read.

Elizabeth asked, "Martin, would you mind terribly popping out for some fresh croissants? And a little chocolate, too. You know how I am about croissants and chocolate. Jennifer is starved, and her mouth is watering for a real, French croissant. She is sick of the plastic copies they have in New York."

Martin turned on his heels and left without a word.

Jennifer asked, "Is Martin OK? You know, safe?"

Elizabeth told her that he was Matthew's favorite driver. Matthew was the name used by Tony when he had interviewed Jennifer. Elizabeth went on, "I personally have never had a problem with him. I must admit, he is a little severe for my taste."

Jennifer piped in, "And UGLY for mine."

Martin returned a few minutes later to find that Jennifer had gone to bed.

"She was suffering from jet lag," Elizabeth explained. "She has gone without sleep for nearly forty-eight hours because of the excitement. She could not take it any longer. She crashed five minutes after you left."

He merely shrugged and said, "The croissants are warm. We should not let them go to waste."

After enjoying the croissants, Elizabeth asked Martin to take a package to the girls. It contained some high tech surveillance gear they needed to complete their part of the project. She told him that she felt sure Jennifer would sleep through the night. "The girl is beat. Better she rest now while she can."

Showing him to the door, Elizabeth dismissed Martin. She told him that after making the delivery, he would not be needed until morning. Her only request was for him to check his e-mail and leave on his mobile phone in the unlikely case of an emergency.

Alone, at last, Elizabeth went to work on an update for Adam. He would be anxious to know her first impressions. So far, they were positive. She conveyed that the basic body type and carriage were very close. She went on to say that the rest they could alter. The only serious problem yet to be faced was how Jennifer might react to the proposal. She felt the girl was desperate enough to do it, even if she did not like the idea. However, this was the one major unknown that could send them back to the starting line.

Elizabeth logged on line. First, she checked her horoscope. She really did not believe in it, but it never hurt to check. According to her chart, tomorrow was to be a big day. The work she had invested would pay off. She hoped the stars were right. She decided to have one of their resident hackers ready to trash the galaxy web site if the horoscope proved wrong. She always believed in a good payback.

She returned to the report, encrypted it and posted it to the secure FTP site. She sent an e-mail to the surgeon in Switzerland and confirmed their arrival time. She could always cancel, if necessary. She returned to the secure FTP site before logging off-line and noticed that Adam had already collected the report.

With no loose ends remaining, she decided to kick back and watch television. Channel hopping, she found 'Les Visiteurs' only about five minutes into the start. It is a wonderfully stupid comedy that took her mind completely away from the project. She needed escapes like this now and then. Sort of a two-hour vacation from reality.

>─◆─O─◆─◄

London, the same day

Adam received a message from Thomas. More of the financial trickery was underway. Everything would be completed within the next month, except for the art purchases. They would take slightly longer, and no exact time line could be guaranteed. His Swiss dealers were thorough and moved at their own speed. Adam had instructed this team to purchase art works by Rembrandt van Rijn, Peter Paul Rubens and Sir Anthony van Dyck. Authenticity would be insured by digital verification through a Zürich firm, the industry leader in this breakthrough technology. The funds invested in art would not be liquidated for several years, so the delays presented no problems. It was actually better for this phase to move slowly so that it could never be tied to anything else that was happening.

Adam made an appointment for Jennifer at the dentist. She would be seen under a different name and identity. Di had confirmed that no emergency dental work had ever been carried out elsewhere. Everything was going according to plan and that made Adam nervous. So far, there had been no glitches. *There will be later. It's always the way. The story of my life.*

The plan would take months to reach fruition. It was by far the most convoluted and delicate plan of Adam's career. It was a little like the time he entered the golf tournament at Myrtle Beach. His handicap was 14. It was his first time on the course. He had not expected to do exceptionally well. The first hole was a par 4. He birdied it. From there things generally improved. He finished the 18 holes at 12 under, winning the tournament handily. The other competitors thought he was a pro who had lied about his name and handicap. He did not play golf again for a year. He just wanted to relish the memories of the best game of his life.

Adam felt much the same about this project. If he succeeded in making the most known woman in the world disappear without suspicion, he would take a year maybe more just to relish the memories. Elizabeth would think he was off the deep end, but she would need a break as well. With the clean-up work they had been doing for the current political powers and this project, they had not had a real break, not to mention a vacation, for almost five years. It was amazing how much dirty laundry needed to be sorted out in Washington.

Adam left for the airport to catch the flight to Paris. He had timed everything to arrive at the country house just before Elizabeth and Jennifer. *It will be a nice surprise.* He knew he was kidding himself. *The truth is, the only person who will be surprised is Jennifer.* It was impossible to pull one off on Elizabeth. Sometimes he thought she was a mind reader. At least, she always had the good form to act surprised.

><>-o-<><

Paris, the next day

Dressed before six the next morning, Elizabeth's mind was racing. Jennifer was still sleeping soundly. *The poor girl,* Elizabeth thought, *must be exhausted both mentally and physically.*

Soon, the doorbell sounded. Knowing it was Martin, always prompt, always correct, Elizabeth rushed to the door. He greeted her with fresh croissants that were still warm from the oven; she made the coffee. Enjoying the typical Parisian breakfast, they discussed the details of Martin's responsibilities. It was fortunate the girl was still sleeping. It gave Martin and Elizabeth much needed time to talk in privacy. Their discussion was guarded even though it was in German. Jennifer spoke some French, and they still did not have a feel for how everything would shake out with her.

Martin had worked for them on many projects during the years, and he required little explanation to understand his complete role. He was actually amazingly bright, although he hid it very well under his gruff exterior. He was loyal to the paymaster and clever enough to sense danger before it happened. He could be absolutely ruthless when necessary. He was paid a retainer and was kept on twenty-four hour a day notice. He had done no freelance work since Adam employed him more than ten years before. He was the closest thing Adam had to a full-time employee.

Jennifer was still off schedule. The jet lag had taken its toll. Elizabeth gently awakened her and asked if she would get ready so that they could go to meet the boss. Jennifer looked disoriented for a moment; then everything clicked into place. She was cheerful and headed for the bathroom to ready herself.

Elizabeth returned to Martin. They small talked about the new exhibit at the d'Orsay. Martin had a strong love for the arts and maintained a marvelous collection of drawings by Toulouse-Lautrec. Elizabeth was always humored by his art collection. If she were to imagine that Martin collected anything, it would more likely be human ears. She wondered what had made him the way he was? What were the early tragedies he had experienced? Certainly, they had molded him into the man he was today. So cold blooded and, yet, so sensitive. Evil and good, all in the same formidable package. She liked him because he was so complex. She had a natural distrust for people who seemed a little too simple on the surface. Often, it was a camouflage for deceit.

She well understood how this split personality could develop in someone. She thought back to when she and Adam had lost their moral virginity. The government raped them both, and the changes the experience had wrought were permanent. Like so many victims of sexual rape, the two of them carried on as though nothing had happened. They lived alone with their nightmare. Together they had found small solace in revenge. Together they had made a new life where no one else would ever have the chance to see the inside or ever know the truth.

Adam's ex-wife was the only one who had any idea. She did not know everything, but she had a good inkling. She was cut from the same cloth and could do whatever was necessary to finish a project. Her only fault was that she was not inured to violence. She would only resort to violence if there were absolutely no other possibilities. Elizabeth and Adam would use violence without a second thought if it provided the most expedient solution; although, both were careful about what they considered senseless loss of life. They looked at their alternatives like 'Chain Saw Al' looks at corporate problems. If a solution makes sense for the bottom line, the only alternative is to eliminate the liability. To be sure, Adam and Elizabeth made more permanent eliminations than 'Chain Saw Al', but the principal was still the same. Adam and Elizabeth concurred that it was better to keep his ex-wife informed after the fact when it came to parts of their projects that were settled with violence. If possible, they kept these matters from her completely.

Singing softly to herself, Jennifer entered the small kitchen. She looked fresh and ready to travel. "Will I meet Matthew today? How long of a drive is it?" As always, Jennifer did not mask her excitement. She had decided that she was on the gravy train working for this man. It sounded so easy. All she had to do was make a few public appearances and pretend that she and Matthew had a secret thing going. She was on top of the world.

"We should be there by five if Martin can keep the car out of a ditch," Elizabeth replied.

Quickly gathering their things, Martin loaded the car. Within less than five minutes, they were on the road. Martin cut through the center of Paris, rather than taking a more roundabout and faster route. It was his special, unspoken kindness for Elizabeth. In spite of the many years she had spent there, Paris was still magic to Elizabeth. Oh, how she appreciated Martin taking the extra, precious time to allow her that exquisite sensation of feeling Paris all around her. It was so bittersweet; she had shared Paris with her husband on their honeymoon.

Before they had traveled for an hour, Jennifer was again asleep and snoring loudly. Martin softly growled in German, "You better not allow that half-monkey to ever sleep where anyone can hear her."

The ghost of a smile flitted across Elizabeth's face. The old-fashioned use of the term half-monkey brought back memories of Switzerland and her youth. She remembered the day so well. She and Adam had gone into town after school to see a movie at a local theatre. They both were used to taking the trolley and knew the connection numbers. However, it had never occurred to either that the trolleys would only run until a certain time at night. They finished the movie, had a snack and then went to the trolley stop only to find out that the last trolley of the evening had departed five minutes before. Adam had told her, "We will just have to walk." The only problem was that neither had ever paid much attention to the route that the trolley followed. Elizabeth suggested that they just follow the power lines. It was a great idea until the line split a kilometer or so later. They walked a short ways in each direction until they located a small newsstand that looked familiar. By the time they finally found the school, it was three in the morning.

The headmaster was waiting at the concierge's desk just inside the entrance. Elizabeth remembered him as a brooding old man who terrified them both. He had enormous eyebrows that jutted out from his forehead like two platoons of advance guard. His eyes smoldered as he lectured them on proper human behavior, referring to them as 'half-monkeys.' He was actually a very tender man at heart. He had even flown to the U.S. to attend the memorial service for Elizabeth's husband and daughter and had stayed with Adam.

"Merde," muttered Martin as he swerved to avoid a car passing in the opposite direction.

The maneuver jarred Jennifer awake. She looked around with bleary eyes as she tried to put together what was happening.

Elizabeth smiled kindly, deciding she really did not like the girl. Not that it mattered. It likely even made the project easier. "We are only a few minutes away now. You might want to freshen up for the arrival," Elizabeth told the girl.

Jennifer opened her purse. It was so huge. It looked more like a midsize suitcase. *Poor taste*, thought Elizabeth. *It must go*. Elizabeth watched as Jennifer touched up her face and straightened her blouse. The girl smiled brightly at Elizabeth and asked if Matthew would be waiting for them.

Elizabeth just shrugged her shoulders and said, "You never know with him."

As they drove down the long curved lane and pulled up in front of the country house, Elizabeth noted the rental car parked next to the Fiat Uno the girls were using. The Fiat was, also, a special car. It had been especially prepared in Italy by a company that specializes in customizing rally cars. There was little original left of the car. The body had been preserved, complete with some scratches and small scrapes. It was white and looked dead stock except for the tires. They looked too large for the small car. This little sleeper could hit 150 faster than most Porsches, but it was invisible in the cities. People tended to just overlook and dismiss these little throwaway cars. It was a perfect undercover vehicle. Elizabeth was surprised that Adam had not parked his rental car in back to make the surprise more complete. Perhaps they were outgrowing the charades of trying to surprise one another.

Martin pulled around behind the house to park. He opened the doors and escorted the two women into the back door of the house. The girls were waiting. Immediately, they started fussing over Jennifer, distracting her and showing her about the house and grounds. Soon, they took Jennifer to meet Adam in the morning room; excusing themselves they left the two alone to talk.

Martin returned with the luggage and brought it into the kitchen. Elizabeth's look communicated that there was no need to put it away yet. It might be going to the landfill.

Elizabeth passed by the morning room where Jennifer and Adam were seated at the round oak table. They were talking about the weather. *Small talk for the moment. Good. The girl will relax somewhat before we get down to business.*

Quickly, Elizabeth went out to the car to find Martin. She wanted to confirm that everything was prepared. He assured her all was in order. He had lined the trunk of the Mercedes with heavy plastic. Several lengths of chain lined the trunk. A chilling smile ghosted across his features as he showed Elizabeth the garrote he had in his jacket pocket. For this kind of work, he preferred the garrote. It was silent. The clean-up was easier. She nodded to Martin and returned to the house. All was ready. If Jennifer did not agree to the proposal, she would join the fishes. Her clothes would be donated to the Red Cross. Her identification would be used by one of the girls to leave a false trail elsewhere, and, later, it would be destroyed. The rest would go to the landfill. All was ready.

It was an unfortunate possibility. They hated the thought. They had no desire to resort to such a thing, but protecting Di would be achieved at all costs. Soon Jennifer would know too much. If she did not accept the role, there would be no practical way to keep her silent for the year or two it would take to accomplish the project. They would have no alternative. She would just become an unfortunate casualty of a project she could never understand. It was merely a bottom line decision, cold and impersonal.

Elizabeth joined Adam and Jennifer at the table. Adam asked for the girls to go into town to pick up some fresh grocery items and cheese. They knew that they were to disappear for at least two hours. They could return if the Mercedes was parked in front of the house; otherwise, they were to come back late at night to collect their things. They would be called when they were needed again. They bid a sweet farewell to Jennifer and drove into town.

Adam turned to Jennifer and said, "Let us begin."

She looked mildly confused and asked if Matthew was coming.

Adam told her, "No." He went on to explain. "Things are not always what they seem. I will describe your acting role, and you can decide if you want the part. Please do not interrupt. I ask you to save your questions for later. Let us begin at the beginning. First of all your part has nothing to do with Matthew. He was on a special assignment from the Queen and has returned to his post in London. He was just playing his part to interview you for the position. The Queen herself wanted to be sure that you were qualified for the role. You will never see Matthew again. He is now working on another project."

The lies slipped easily from Adam's tongue, and Jennifer took them in with wide eyes. She especially homed in on the mention of the Queen.

"I will describe your acting role from the beginning. If you decide not to accept the part, we ask that you promise to never speak of the proposal until after the play is completed." He did not tell her that she would either be on board or dead in an hour. It was important for her to take the role because she wanted it or believed in it, not to accept it out of fear.

Her entire countenance was quivering with excitement.

"You will be acting as a double for Princess Di. She is hounded unmercifully by the paparazzi, and your part will be to distract them from what Di is really doing. You will receive no acting credits. No one can realize that there has ever been a double until after the project is completed. You will not be permitted to discuss what it is that you are doing with anyone, including the girls who will act as your assistants. This is an absolute. There will be no exceptions. Period. You will be free to write a book after the project is finished. The story will be worth a fortune. Your pay will be ten thousand U.S. dollars per month; all of your expenses will be covered, and you will be generously provided with spending money."

Her eyes brightened at the mention of the pay.

"The assignment is for two years at the minimum. Is everything satisfactory so far?"

She nodded and said, "Yes," a little too quickly.

This girl will demand close scrutiny, Adam thought. *We will have to watch her every action. She might try to sell the story to a tabloid or some other such nonsense during the project.* Adam knew the risk of a problem would diminish as the project moved forward. Jennifer would become addicted and realize that she had too much to lose. The real danger was in the first few months. He continued, "Now to you. Any questions?"

They spilled from her mouth like a cascade.

"Slow down," admonished Adam, "or I won't be able to answer anything. First, the question of appearance. You were chosen because your physique is nearly identical. You are convincingly the same size. You, at present, are only about one centimeter shorter. Your weight is about two kilos more. The height difference is insignificant, but you will need to lose a little weight."

Jennifer responded that she had been meaning to lose the weight anyway.

"Your complexion and eye color are the same. Your hair texture is a close match, and the color is easy to change. Now comes the hard part. We will require you to undergo some cosmetic surgery. We will pay for it fully and restore you to your normal appearance when the project is over or, perhaps, to a different appearance if you desire. The surgery will take place in Switzerland in a private clinic. The doctor is one of the best in the world."

"May I keep Di's appearance if I want?" The comment just exploded from her mouth like a shot.

Adam glanced at Elizabeth. She was smiling that knowing smile. They had the girl. She was all go.

"Of course you can," Adam replied.

"Now," Adam continued, "there is the problem of your speech. A speech therapist has been hired. He will work with you to match the accent, intonations, timbre and speech patterns of Di. We have a vast number of recordings to use as models. There is, also, the problem of mannerisms. There is an extensive library of video segments. They show Di doing almost everything that she has ever done in public. We have videos of her in private when she is relaxed. It should not be difficult for you to match the mannerisms. This is a standard skill for an actress. Our goal is to provide a convincing double to anyone who does not know Di intimately. It is possible that you will be able to convince someone who does know Di well, if the circumstances are rigidly controlled. Only time will tell, but this would be very difficult. We prefer to avoid this situation unless absolutely necessary."

The girl was still too obvious with her excitement. She responded instantly, "I can do it. I know I can."

Adam thought, *It's now a wait and see proposition to determine how good a product we can build. The girl has possibilities, but extensive refinement is an absolute.*

Adam went on to discuss background information. Di had furnished most of the information herself. There was supplementary information they had gathered from the various biographers. Di had read it all and annotated the texts, noting the rubbish, and there was plenty. She had, additionally, filled in the gaps and provided the missing details. This was critical in the event someone asked Jennifer something that had actually happened. Jennifer needed to know the real history and the correct answers.

Jennifer was ecstatic. It was time to calm her down a little and jolt her back into reality. This assignment was serious. It would demand total commitment.

Adam admonished, "This is not a game. This project is very serious. It will demand a great deal of work. If you accept the job, we will expect you to work eighteen hours a day to perfect your role. For our plan to work, you must be better than a perfect double. You must become Di. You must assume her personality."

Jennifer's eyes were staring away. They were filled with dreams of grandeur. Elizabeth excused herself and went out to find Martin. Telling him that the girl was a go, Martin was his usual impassive self. Elizabeth could never decide when she interacted with Martin in this manner if he was relieved or disappointed.

As Elizabeth returned, she heard the end of a conversation. "I'll be really famous if I succeed, won't I? People will remember me for long after this is over. Maybe even long after I'm gone. It will be some story, won't it?"

"I'm sure you're correct," Adam replied. "I can even imagine people making a pilgrimage to pass by your grave."

Jennifer lit up at the thought, and Elizabeth reflected that if Di's brother has anything to do with it, there would probably be tickets sold to pass by the grave. As quickly as it came, she buried the thought before she got the giggles. She nodded seriously at Jennifer and received a withering look from Adam. *Damn it.* He had read her thoughts. She stuck out her tongue at him. It was his turn to squirm. Jennifer was lost in her dreams and missed the whole exchange.

They heard the gravel crunch as the Mercedes was moved to the front of the house. Adam, in his most serious voice said, "Do not ever forget. You are never to say anything about what you have been told to anyone other than Elizabeth and myself. To do so would risk the whole project. It would place Di in a most awkward and, perhaps, a very dangerous position. She already is under too much pressure. It would result in the immediate termination of your position." Termination was a well-chosen word under the circumstances, although it was lost on Jennifer.

Jennifer immediately responded that she would never do such a thing. This was the most important opportunity she would likely have in her life. She was not about to take a chance on screwing it up.

Elizabeth went to the kitchen and noticed that Martin was seated at the bar. That man could move like a cat. She was sure that neither Jennifer nor Adam had heard him enter. She poured some wine and brought out some snacks as the conversation had moved on to scheduling. She overheard Adam telling Jennifer, "We will be using this place as a base, but we'll be in Paris and Switzerland, as well. Tomorrow, we have some photos to take for various documents."

"Documents?" Jennifer queried.

"Yes. We need a new passport for you. What with you being declared a missing person and all that, it would not do to be traveling to London on your passport."

The blush spread up through Jennifer's cheeks. Her embarrassment was not just obvious, it was a lighted billboard.

Elizabeth tenderly told her, "Its okay. We actually know everything about you, absolutely everything. Everything is fine. There is only one thing that is important. It is that you can perform the task ahead of you. Your history, your past failures mean nothing. All that is important is what you are able to do from here on." Elizabeth felt like a cheerleader. But it was necessary to instill confidence and drive. There would be only one chance. Once they had actually started, there would never be a second opportunity to start again. Jennifer had to perform flawlessly. Somehow, they needed to do whatever was necessary to make this one chance work.

6

The French country house, the next day

Brigit awakened Jennifer at eight in the morning. Alert and anxious, she was ready to go to work. Elizabeth was beginning to feel better about the girl. Her awkwardness and spaced out look must have been the products of jet lag and the uncertainty of her future. Today, she seemed determined. *A good sign,* thought Elizabeth.

The girls served breakfast with a flair, a touch, yet, not too familiar to Jennifer. Learning finesse was essential to the project's success. This quality would be integrated into every aspect of Jennifer's training. Elizabeth asked for an expresso, and Jennifer took tea. Elizabeth ate only a chocolate Madeleine. If Elizabeth ate anything at all for breakfast, it was always something chocolate. A croissant with a piece of Swiss chocolate was her other favorite.

Jean-Christophe had corrupted both Elizabeth and Adam when they had grown up in Switzerland. Jean-Christophe was a special old friend who was a chocoholic. They had indulged with him many a time, receiving the sensual and decadent pleasures of an early morning chocolate. Helene, the housemother, was always angry when she caught them. "You will be lucky to have a tooth left in your heads by the time you are twenty," she would rant. Helene was known for voicing her opinions in a dictatorial manner; everyone who had ever known her could quote them word-for-word.

Adam had already returned to London, sneaking away sometime during the night. His pre-scheduled meeting with Katherine was urgent. He and Katherine were organizing the logistics and working on security for the operation. Adam had only met Di once face to face. It was at a charity event where nothing could be discussed. Too much was at stake. Di's every move was watched by someone. Using Katherine as the intermediary was a far better risk. Adam hated using middlemen and made it a point to avoid using them under any circumstances. This project was the exception. There was simply no other solution. Katherine would end up knowing almost everything, but that was as it was. It was the only alternative. The time would come when Adam and Di could meet, but not yet and, certainly, not with the regularity that would be necessary.

Di was most anxious to meet Adam in private. She had many questions. She yearned to discuss every detail of the plan. She had heard so much about the projects that Adam had masterminded. She wanted to find out for herself if he was truly as capable as she had been told. She was disappointed that Adam would not allow such a meeting at the moment. She understood his reasoning but was, nonetheless, saddened. She agreed that if a suspecting or unsuspecting member of the press saw them together or learned of their meeting, the doors would open to all sorts of questions. Adam could be rumored as her new lover. The press would surround him like a pack of hungry dogs. Publicity spelled disaster. It was imperative for Adam to remain invisible.

Of great importance was for Adam to be advised of Di's day-to-day schedule. Adam incorporated Di's schedule into the planning of specific aspects of his scheme. Gerard, Adam's hacker genius, had written an automatic e-mail program for this specific purpose. It worked like a virus. The program copied Di's schedule file, encrypted it and then e-mailed it without leaving a record. The e-mail went to a special account that was instantly downloaded and then forwarded to Adam's special account on a secure server. There were always e-mail messages in the account that were never downloaded. They included messages that asked a husband to bring home milk, potatoes or some other such nonsense. These were purposely left on the server in the event that by pure chance someone hacked into the account. Any information found would be boring, causing the hacker to quickly become disinterested and move on to invading someone else's affairs. If by the unlikely chance someone hacked in during the three seconds or so that Di's schedule was on the server, the e-mail would appear as pure garbage. The schedule was encrypted with military grade encryption. It would take a supercomputer months to break it down. The system was not foolproof, but neither is life, and this was more reliable.

Jennifer preferred a hardy breakfast. The food was piled on high. She was even eating kippers. *My God,* thought Elizabeth. *No wonder the English have never produced a gourmet chef of import. They have no taste.* When the meal was finished, Elizabeth suggested that she and Jennifer adjourn to the study. She dismissed the girls with the order, "Under no circumstances are we to be disturbed."

The study was equipped with a sophisticated media center. The visual center consisted of a flat plasma screen that could be used as a television or a computer monitor. It was more than one meter in size, and with its supporting electronics, it cost as much as the Mercedes they were driving.

Elizabeth had decided to study along with Jennifer. She would watch the same films and read the same dossiers, as well as critique Jennifer's performance. It was Elizabeth's role from this point forward to be the coach. She would demand perfection in every aspect of the operation. Elizabeth had zero tolerance for error and held no delusions that Jennifer would ever want to be her friend.

Before they started, Elizabeth logged onto the Internet and checked her horoscope for the day. Jennifer was excited to check hers as well. During the past few days, Elizabeth's horoscope had been accurate with predictions proving to be realities. Elizabeth was satisfied and decided that there was no reason for her to call their young hacker to trash the galaxy web site after all. Maybe there was more truth in all this belief in the stars than she had ever imagined. Still, she accepted it with a grain of salt.

Jennifer knew nothing about computers. Never before had she experienced the Internet. She was fascinated. Elizabeth wondered how anyone in Jennifer's generation could survive in this world without being Internet literate. The Internet had become a part of Elizabeth's life. She could not imagine existing without it. She did her grocery shopping, purchased her airplane tickets, and even found some interesting acquaintances through the Internet. How could a young woman who, by her age could almost be Elizabeth's daughter, be so unaware? The time was long overdue for Jennifer to learn about the real world. Elizabeth would find a way to squeeze an interval within each day's busy schedule to teach Jennifer a little about cyberspace. It was the least she could do to help the girl. Today, they could spare ten minutes to play. Then, it was essential to get to work.

Elizabeth started the day's session all business. "First, I want you to work on Di's mannerisms for an hour and a half. You will observe the videos and copy what you see. Then, I wish for you to study the dossier for the same amount of time. I will work with you. I will coach you. We will role-play, and you will act the part. In the afternoon we will review everything we have rehearsed in the morning. We will practice and practice, repeatedly, over and over again until everything is correct. No, everything must be more than correct. Everything must be perfect. Perfection will require hours and hours of training. In the evening you can relax. This schedule will be our program for the next few weeks. Is this type of a schedule too much for you?"

Jennifer radiated her acceptance. She was excited and challenged. She said, "Really, it all sounds great. I think I can do it, and I don't mind hard work. I'm used to it."

The first day went well. Both Elizabeth and Jennifer settled comfortably into the routine. Elizabeth actually hated this part of every project, but she realized that it was the foundation. Without accomplishing this phase, the project would be doomed to failure. Normally, the photographic memory that she shared with Adam was a tremendous blessing, but during the preparation phase of a project, it was a curse. Elizabeth would become incredibly bored long before all of this 'training stuff' was over. The flip side was that she would miss nothing. She would be able to make careful and critical assessments of Jennifer's performance well before Jennifer was ready to perform.

▻┤◆┝━○━╾◆┝┤◅

Jennifer and Elizabeth followed this same schedule for several days with minor adjustments. The goal was to prime Jennifer for a dress rehearsal. The days progressed without problem. Each day Jennifer gained confidence and became more like Di, but there was still so much that needed to be accomplished before Elizabeth could begin to plan an actual real-life dress rehearsal. Progress was slower than Elizabeth had hoped. Still, Jennifer remained positive and perceptive of the subtleties that were demanded. Elizabeth's general opinion had not changed. She did not like the girl, but she was encouraged that Jennifer could and would do the job. That was all that mattered. The real question was how long it would take before Jennifer would be prepared for a real-life encounter.

Each evening, Elizabeth would disappear exhausted, and the girls would take over the responsibilities of keeping an eye on Jennifer. Elizabeth needed her space and time to send her e-mail reports to Adam.

The girls only knew that Jennifer was being prepared for a job. They had no idea of its nature. Their instructions were clear. It was all very black and white. They were to be overly friendly. They were to pamper her. They were to fulfill Jennifer's every demand with utmost precision and courtesy. They were to be extremely kind and considerate. They were to watch the girl's every move. If she ever tried to leave without permission, their instructions were simply to kill her.

Every phone conversation was monitored. If Jennifer called anyone, the line would disconnect after the number dialed was recorded. A French intercept would inform the person dialing that there were temporary line problems. "Veuillez appelez plus tard." In the meantime Elizabeth would be notified. Gerard would be called upon to hack into the phone service wherever it was that Jennifer had called and determine the registration of the phone number that was called. Elizabeth would know in minutes who Jennifer had tried to call and would take whatever action was necessary.

The days and nights passed without incident. Jennifer was content and committed to the project. Preparing her for the surgery was the next step. Elizabeth was a little worried. It was a delicate subject, to be approached with caution. One good thing, the surgery would be a break from the monotony. Jennifer could only go on for so long maintaining the repetitious and demanding rehearsal schedule. The negative was that the surgery would slow Jennifer's progress. There was no reason worrying about it. It was necessary. During the recovery period, Jennifer would have time to review and refine everything. She would be given whatever time was required to achieve perfection. *There is no Plan B on this one,* Elizabeth thought. *Everything is on hold until the girl is ready.*

Elizabeth decided to wait until the morning they were leaving for Lausanne to tell Jennifer about the surgery. There was no reason to give the girl time to think about it in advance.

>-+-◦>-○-<◦+-<

"Good morning, Jennifer," Brigit said brightly. "Time to slip into something comfortable."

Over breakfast Elizabeth told Jennifer that they would be leaving for Lausanne in two hours. Elizabeth asked Jennifer to pack quickly. They still had to drive back to Paris to catch the TGV, and Martin was already waiting. The girls would wait at the country house until their return.

Jennifer was eager about the trip. She readied herself far sooner than Elizabeth thought possible. Elizabeth and Jennifer sat in the back seat of the spacious Mercedes, and Elizabeth explained that they would be going to a clinic in Switzerland.

"This clinic is very private. It caters to only the very rich and influential. The surgeon is a fabulous artist, and Adam knows him well. You can't believe how many famous, as well as infamous and invisible, people wear his creations on their faces." *I am one of them,* she thought.

Jennifer was excited. She showed no sense of concern. It was funny how some women looked forward to surgery. *My mother loved it,* thought Elizabeth. *I hated it. I always worried that I might say something that should not be said while under the anesthesia. Thank God, it's all in my past.*

To avoid such a problem, Elizabeth and Adam never used a doctor who had not been thoroughly vetted. Even then, when Elizabeth went under the knife, Adam was always there. Adam insisted on being present to monitor what was said. Elizabeth would do the same for Adam should it ever be necessary. As of yet, he had not had the need.

Elizabeth and Jennifer entered their cabin on the train and began to scan a book about Di. Elizabeth pointed out several particular mannerisms as they paged through the photographs. The trip was pleasant. During times of reflection, it was a joy for Elizabeth to gaze out onto the French countryside as they passed by. The train started to slow, and Jennifer asked if they were arriving. Elizabeth told her that they still had some time to travel. The stop was only for the Swiss border control.

The Swiss frontier guard entered their cabin almost immediately. Elizabeth flipped open her American passport, and the guard gave it merely a glance. He turned to Jennifer as she was digging through her monster purse. The frontier guard's expression began to deteriorate from indifference to disgust as Jennifer dug though the maze to find her passport. She began to pile things on the seat next to her, trying to reduce the amount of debris through which she was sorting. If Elizabeth had not personally handed the passport to the girl earlier and observed her casually drop it into the yawning abyss of the bag, Elizabeth would have been worried. The guard was getting impatient. There was a huge stack of things filling the seat next to Jennifer. Soiled tissues, candy wrappers, a section of newspaper that looked as though it had been used to wrap a fish, an orange that had seen better days. Still, she dug deeper, and finally emerged victorious with the document. The guard was on edge and looked through the passport examining every entrance and exit stamp. The document was perfect. Less than forty-eight hours old, it looked as though it had been a part of the shifting sand of her purse for years. Satisfied the guard handed the passport back to Jennifer. Disgusted, he did not even feign a smile as she sheepishly expressed her appreciation for his patience.

Finally, the train arrived in Lausanne. A car from the clinic was awaiting their arrival. The drive from the train station to the clinic took about thirty minutes, and the traffic was heavy. Jennifer seemed enthralled gazing at the immense lake called Lac Leman. Most English speakers called it Lake Geneva, but Jennifer had the good form to call it by its given name. The shore-side town of Evian glittered like a jewel across the lake on the French side. The view was in little vignettes as they rounded corners to spectacular sweeps of scenery that were quickly swallowed by the area's imposing Baroque period architecture that stood as sentinels guarding the shore.

When the limousine turned onto a narrow lane and slowed to a stop, the chauffeur announced, "Here we are." There was no sign at the clinic's entrance. There was nothing material designating the purpose of the facility. Its appearance was that of a private villa. The entrance was gorgeous with a perfectly manicured landscape and strong gated presence. The chauffeur escorted Elizabeth and Jennifer into the marbled entrance. A nurse appeared immediately and showed them to a well-appointed waiting room. Barely seated, the nurse reappeared from a different door and motioned them to follow her.

The surgeon was waiting. He started without any of the usual pleasantries. Introductions were omitted. Not a minute was wasted. His agenda was obviously pre-planned to the moment.

With all of the charm of an IRS auditor, he abruptly asked Jennifer to sit in a chair that was surrounded by what seemed like a vast array of mysterious equipment. Jennifer was directed to pose one way, then another, then another. Cooperating perfectly, she was scanned with a laser-imaging device and then by ultrasound. Next, x-rays were taken. Then, some other scanning device measured every inch of her skull. The procedure went on and on for nearly two hours. Jennifer had no idea what was happening. She was uneasy and felt a little frightened but remained most cooperative. When finished, the surgeon thanked them without further comment. He instructed them to return at nine o'clock sharp the next morning.

Jennifer was taken aback by his abruptness and lack of explanation. She opened her mouth to say something when Elizabeth intervened, placing her hand softly on the girl's arm and nodding to her. Jennifer took the cue and forced a smile. Elizabeth thanked the doctor for his time. The chauffeur reappeared and promptly escorted them back into town to their hotel.

After they had checked in to their room, Elizabeth said, "Now we can talk about the good doctor. He is a brilliant man with all the social skills of a wart hog. He is easily bored with people. You will understand what I mean as you get to know him better. As you see what he intends to do, you will admire him in spite of yourself. Trust me. Now let's forget about him and not waste any more of the little shopping time we have."

While shopping, Elizabeth guided Jennifer into some new directions with her clothing. It was a subconscious decision, born from the many hours of watching Di and realizing the kind of clothes she prefers. "We might as well get started," she told Jennifer. "It's time for you to adopt the style."

Jennifer was like a child in a candy store. She took in everything that Elizabeth suggested and quickly grasped the idea. She made some selections of her own. *Not bad,* thought Elizabeth. *She's a quick study and has a natural feel for it.*

⊱─⊷─O─⊶─⊰

The next morning Elizabeth and Jennifer arrived at the clinic before nine. Jennifer had eaten nothing, complying with the instructions the surgeon had given, and she was starved. They were instantly shown to a gorgeous, executive office exquisitely appointed with wonderful French antiques. The only things that looked out of place were two large Silicon Graphics monitors and a wraparound keyboard that faced one of the monitors. All of this equipment was placed atop a beautiful Louis the Fourteenth writing desk. The wiring was completely hidden, and there was no computer in sight. There was a device that looked a little like a small cannon ball placed in a cradled rest; it appeared to be whatever it was that passed for a mouse. Classical music was playing softly in the background. Elizabeth thought it was a tape until it stopped abruptly. Then, it sounded as though someone was tuning a harp and a violin. After this interlude, the music commenced again.

The walls were covered with important Impressionist and Post-Impressionist art. Elizabeth and Jennifer stood admiring the paintings while awaiting the doctor's arrival. Jennifer had never before seen such art. The girl mentioned that she enjoyed looking through coffee table books about Impressionist art. *Good,* thought Elizabeth. *At least, she knows the Impressionists existed.* Elizabeth used the opportunity to talk a little about the different styles of these artists, pointing out an enormous Monet 'Nympheas.' She then compared Monet's brushstrokes to the smaller works by Manet and Cézanne across the room.

The surgeon entered. Disgusted that they were engrossed in his art, he asked them to be seated. He was all business. Again, he offered no pleasantries. He placed his right hand on the cannon ball and his left hand flew over the keyboard. A skull appeared on the screen and rotated in three-dimensional space. There was a small number 2 that looked as though it had been painted over the brow area. "This is you," he nodded to Jennifer. "With the packaging you look like this." Flesh appeared over the skull, and an uncanny likeness to Jennifer appeared. The flesh disappeared, and a skull appeared again. "These are the problems in what you desire to become," he said. He pointed out several areas on the skull.

Jennifer asked, "What difference does the skull make when it's covered anyway?"

He glared at her, thinking that only someone retarded could ask such a question. "This, my dear, is the problem," he responded. With a click, flesh covered the skull, and Jennifer reappeared. "It's more than duplicating the wrapper," he grumbled with distaste. "To bring it down to your level, it would be like trying to wrap a soccer ball so that it looks like a brick."

Jennifer blushed from the base of her throat to the crown of her head. The surgeon had absolutely no tact. Elizabeth thought this man would be a catastrophe in the U.S. where the politically correct are ruling the pack.

"Were I to do no work on the foundation," he went on, "the face would look like this." He played his fingers across the keyboard, and the face changed. The image looked a lot like Di at first glance. Then, another skull appeared alongside with a number 1 painted on the brow. The surgeon massaged the keyboard again; almost instantly, skull number one was clothed in flesh. It was Di. Comparing the two images side by side, the differences were subtle but obvious. Something was not quite right. The two faces were clearly different people who just looked a great deal alike.

The doctor returned to the images of Jennifer and Di's skulls. He said, "The problem is that the model you desire to resemble has some dimensions that are sufficiently different from yours. It is necessary to make some small changes to your foundation. Otherwise, you will look like a soccer ball masquerading as a brick. Fortunately, the things most difficult to change are close enough to be meaningless." He went on to explain that model number 2 has a longer run from the ridge of the brow to the tip of the top teeth than does model number 1. He said, "But the difference is only two millimeters. I cannot change this dimension; however, in my opinion, it is close enough to be irrelevant." Then, he pointed out that the distance from the top of the bottom teeth to the base of the jaw is three millimeters longer in model 2 than in model 1. He commented, "This, also, is not a factor to my eye, but it can be changed if desired. The surgery will be much more complicated if this change is added. The recovery time, too, will be longer. I personally do not believe that it is necessary."

He was losing Jennifer, but Elizabeth was tracking and cataloging every detail in her mind for instant recall. Adam would want an extensive explanation. He needed the facts before the decisions could be made. The doctor continued his complex evaluation for some time. He finished by clicking the changes he described onto the screen. He said curtly, "To make it simple enough for model 2 to understand, what you see is an overview of what we need to do."

Jennifer blushed again but was silent.

He continued, "You have what could be best described as a very petite nose. Model number 1 has a fuller nose. It is much broader at the base, especially at the area just below the eyes. You will also notice that model number 1's nose is not exactly symmetrical. This is perfectly normal. The tip of her nose is pulled ever so slightly to her left side. Most people do not have symmetrical faces. For example, yours and mine are not symmetrical, but the asymmetry is really only noticed with careful study. Elizabeth is one of the rare people who has a nearly perfect symmetrical face."

Why you old rogue, Elizabeth thought.

"The next issue is the lips. Model number 1 does not have full lips, but yours are visually thinner. The last important change is in the line of the chin. Model number 1 has a more pointed chin, rather than the more squared off chin that you sport. The width of both of your chins is almost exactly the same, so the changes here will be rather simple. All in all, I anticipate that it will not be difficult to obtain a convincing image of model number 1 from the bone structure of model number 2. The only thing that might create difficulties is the nose. From experience, the procedure will cause some rather long-term discoloration under the eyes. The bruising is a result of the surgery, and there is no way to avoid it. This discoloration may persist for as long as six to eight weeks."

The surgeon continued his lengthy explanation. He told Elizabeth and Jennifer that the changes he would make would be accomplished by using organics rather than inorganics, like silicone. The surgeon looked directly at Jennifer to emphasize his seriousness. He said, "The significance of this is that should you ever be submitted to an x-ray, the changes will only be apparent to a very well trained surgeon familiar with my procedures. The other details like the small natural colored mole just above the left corner of the lips and the similar mole to the right of the chin are easily duplicated. In fact, they must be duplicated, since model number 1 is likely the most photographed woman in the world. There is a tremendous amount of reference material for people to use if they want to make comparisons. This surgery is only interesting to me because I am convinced that it can be nearly perfect. Otherwise, there would be no real challenge in doing the project, and it would be better to not even consider it."

Both Elizabeth and Jennifer looked at the surgeon in reflective astonishment.

He returned to his computer and cloaked the skull of model number 1 with flesh. It was Di. He then clicked to the skull of Jennifer and cloaked it with flesh. It looked like Di as well. He continued to fuss with his keyboard, and the screen went black for a moment. Then, the two heads appeared side by side. "Now, tell me, who is model 1 and who is model 2?" He asked.

Elizabeth and Jennifer looked at the images. They turned to look at each other. They were silent for several minutes. Then, they started discussing their observations between themselves. At first, they chose differently; then both decided on the same choice and pointed to it.

"No," the surgeon answered with an egotistic smile, "wrong choice."

Elizabeth and Jennifer broke into smiles. *He could do it.*

"When shall we start?" he asked. "Remember that there will be as much as six to eight weeks of swelling and discoloration."

Jennifer drew her breath to speak, but Elizabeth softly kicked her. Smiling Elizabeth interjected, "Five or six months from now would be about right."

The appointment was scheduled, and the two women were promptly shuttled back to their hotel by the clinic's chauffeur. Once in the privacy of their room, Jennifer asked, "Why do I have to wait for six months? Why can't we do it now?"

Elizabeth explained the strategy. "After the surgery, either you or Di will have to remain in hiding until the end of the project. It would be too difficult for you to complete your preparation in seclusion. Before you can appear as Di, you must be convincing in your speech and mannerisms. You must assume Di's persona. This will take many more weeks of time and practice. If anyone ever becomes aware that a double for Di has been created, the project will fail. You must perfect your role before the costume is fitted."

Jennifer thought about Elizabeth's explanation and said, "You are right, of course. Well, let's go shopping."

As they freshened up, Jennifer asked why the surgeon never used her name or Di's but referred to them as model number 1 and 2.

"He does not know your name and does not want to know it," explained Elizabeth. "You will be admitted to the clinic under an assumed name. If five years from now you do something illegal, the surgeon does not want to be named as an accessory. It provides him with what is considered plausible deniability. Like when a painter paints a copy of a masterpiece painting, he does not want to be arrested if someone tries to pass it off as an original."

Elizabeth's explanation seemed to satisfy Jennifer. She did not bring up the subject again.

After several hours, not a single boutique in Lausanne had been spared. Elizabeth returned to the hotel feeling she had made a major coup. She had quietly helped to pick out a cute Hermes clutch for Jennifer. Her hopes were dashed, however, when Jennifer placed a few things in it and then dropped the elegant little purse into her monster bag, like it was a wallet. *One thing at a time,* Elizabeth kept reminding herself. *At least, she had enough sense to place her passport in the clutch. Now, it will be easier to locate in the landfill that passes for her purse. We're making some progress!*

Jennifer asked Elizabeth when she would be able to go home and collect some more things. After all, when she came she was told that her assignment would only last for a week or two. It now had been several weeks.

Elizabeth sat Jennifer down and explained, "Darling, since you accepted this position, it will be unlikely that you will be able to return to the U.S., other than as the Princess. Certainly you will not be able to return otherwise until after the project is completed. It is unfortunate, and I am sorry for this disappointment, but this is the way it has to be."

Jennifer looked a little panicked and said, "I need my things. You can't do this to me."

Elizabeth tried to calm her. "Your things have already been moved. When we return to the country house, everything that was in your apartment will be there. You may decorate your room in the country house however you would like."

Elizabeth's statement ricocheted off Jennifer. Offended she said, "You mean someone went through my things?"

"No one searched your apartment," Elizabeth continued. "Professional movers were used to pack your belongings. Adam assigned a couple to observe to insure that nothing would go missing. Your rent has been pre-paid in full for the next two years. If you want to go back to the same apartment, you may when the project is over."

Jennifer was obviously even more upset, although she was trying to cover her anger. Elizabeth knew that this was a critical event horizon. Perhaps she should have just surprised the girl with her belongings when they returned to the country house. *Oh well. What is done is done.*

Jennifer simmered for a few minutes longer and then said, "Well, I just wish that you would have asked me first. I don't like what you did to me and my privacy. When do we leave for the country house?"

Elizabeth took the opportunity to lay out the plan. "We will travel to Geneva tomorrow morning. There, we will open a bank account in your name. Your salary will be paid directly to this account."

Jennifer immediately brightened. With the thought of money, all was forgiven.

"Then, we will take the TGV back to Paris and return to the country house. So you know, and there will be no surprises, I will be a signer on your bank account. This precaution is necessary in the event any banking business needs to be done in person. You cannot go to the bank looking like Di. All paperwork will be sent to the country house, so that you can keep track of your personal finances. The account will be a numbered account. That way your tax liabilities will be minimized. There is no reason for anyone to ever know you have the account."

Like a sprite in the wind, Jennifer changed directions completely. "Is that horrible man going to pick us up at the train station in Paris?"

"Horrible man? If you mean Martin, yes. He will be our driver." Elizabeth responded.

"He gives me the creeps," Jennifer complained.

Elizabeth smiled, feeling reassured that the girl was still a go, "He is not my favorite, either."

7

Lausanne, the next morning

They took a taxi to the main train station in Lausanne and purchased first class tickets for the train to Geneva. Elizabeth watched with horror as Jennifer dropped the ticket into the abyss of her monster bag. Elizabeth suggested, "Perhaps you should place the ticket where you can find it easily. The train conductors will check it during the trip."

Jennifer shot Elizabeth a glance that could kill and said, "I can find it easily. I know exactly where everything is in my purse."

It was all Elizabeth could do not to grind her teeth or shoot back an acid comment. At times, she wanted to strangle the girl, slowly and painfully.

Elizabeth used the time on the train to absorb more of the information Di had provided to them about her particular likes and dislikes.

Jennifer watched the views of the lake drift by as the train sped toward Geneva. When they left the lakeside and started traveling through the tranquil countryside filled with orchards, Jennifer asked, "After this is all over, could I move here? Switzerland is such a peaceful country. It would be a good place for me to live while I write my book about being a double for you know who."

Elizabeth shrugged and said, "Possibly, although it's very difficult to obtain a permit to live here."

"Could you help me?"

"Let us wait and see how you feel after all of this is over."

The countryside soon broke and buildings and highways filled the skyline demarcating the outskirts of Geneva. Elizabeth placed her materials away and organized herself so she could leave the train quickly upon arrival. Jennifer remained captivated by the sites of the ancient buildings intertwined amidst the modern. The announcement that the train was arriving brought her quickly to attention. Hustling to organize her possessions, she caught up with Elizabeth who was already waiting at the exit doors as the train began to slow.

Elizabeth was grateful that the conductor had not asked to see their tickets during the journey. In spite of Jennifer's protestations that she knew the exact location of every item in her purse, her ticket might not have surfaced until the next ice age had she been asked to produce it.

Once inside the train station, Elizabeth directed Jennifer to the lockers where they deposited their luggage. Elizabeth said, "We do not need to be carrying all of this stuff around while we are in the city. I feel like a hotel porter. It's much too heavy."

Leaving the station, Elizabeth found the taxi stand and gave directions to the bank. It was a small, private bank where Elizabeth was obviously well known. Everything was typically Swiss. The employees. The décor. The feeling. Once settled in the windowless, tiny conference room, Elizabeth introduced Jennifer to the banker. "We have known one another for almost twenty years. This is Mr. Reliable." The banker grinned from ear to ear and did everything in his power to make Jennifer feel especially welcome. He was so courteous and polite, so unlike the surgeon at the clinic.

All necessary papers had already been prepared and were merely awaiting signatures. Elizabeth smiled and said, "He is Mr. Organized, too."

Jennifer responded with a warm smile and an agreeing nod of the head.

The banker asked for both Jennifer and Elizabeth to sign in the designated spaces. There was a plethora of forms. The Swiss had a paper for everything. He asked for their passports so that he could make a photocopy for the bank's files. Fortunately, Jennifer had placed her passport in the Hermes clutch, and it did not take her long to locate it. When the signing ceremony was complete, Elizabeth handed an envelope to the banker that contained ten thousand U.S. dollars in crisp hundreds. He counted the bills and verified the amount. Then, he rang for his assistant. Almost before he had placed down the receiver, a brisk knock was heard and a matronly looking woman opened the door of the tiny room. As she entered, the banker handed the paperwork, passports and money to her; he asked her to deposit the funds in the designated account and make copies of the passports. Expressionless, the woman slipped out of the room closing the door silently without saying a word.

Elizabeth smiled and said to Jennifer, "Your first paycheck. How do you feel?"

Jennifer all bubbly, asked, "Is this really happening?"

The banker interrupted, asking Elizabeth if they were going to be in Geneva over the weekend. He told the two ladies about a pageant that they might enjoy seeing. Before either could answer, there was another brisk knock at the door. The assistant returned with the receipt for the deposit and the passports. Elizabeth told the banker that, unfortunately, they were leaving Geneva that afternoon and could not enjoy the weekend there.

The banker escorted the two women to the bank's main entrance, thanking them repeatedly for their business. Emerging from the bank the two found themselves entrapped in a large crowd that had gathered to watch a sidewalk musical group. Elizabeth and Jennifer moved into the mass and positioned themselves as far forward as possible, so that they could see what was going on. The sounds that emerged were hauntingly beautiful. Baroque chamber music, full and robust. There were only three instruments: a violin; a cello; and a flute. After allowing themselves to float in fantasy for quite some time, something shocked Elizabeth back to the business of the day. Without a word she dropped a five-franc coin in the open violin case. She took Jennifer by the arm, filtered through the crowd, and pulled the girl away down the street.

"I want you to see my favorite store in all of Geneva," Elizabeth told Jennifer as they headed for Patek Philippe. The store was, at a normal pace, no more than a ten minute walk, but they window shopped along the way, making the walk a little longer. When they arrived, Elizabeth pressed the doorbell saying, "Their doors are always locked."

Immediately, the buzzer sounded and a tastefully dressed woman of about fifty opened the door and pleasantly motioned them to enter. The manager, sitting at his Louis the Fourteenth writing desk, watched with reserve over his half-lens reading glasses as the two women entered. Recognizing Elizabeth instantly, he sprang from around his desk and greeted Elizabeth warmly with a hand shake and the 'bise,' the typical three kiss Swiss greeting that is commonly exchanged by good friends. Then, he pleasantly introduced himself to Jennifer, shaking her hand robustly. He welcomed her to the store showing every courtesy. He seated both ladies at a handsome, carved table in the formal showroom.

Elizabeth asked to see the styles for women that had been introduced this year, and the man went to the store's ancient vault drawers to produce several trays of watches of different sizes and shapes. There was one sport, eighteen carat, yellow gold beauty with a royal blue crocodile wristband that was especially admired by both of the ladies. After examining the watch for less than five minutes, Elizabeth told the manager to send her the statement. She would take it with her.

Trying to mask his excitement, the manager said, "With pleasure, Madame. Is there anything else I can do for you?"

Elizabeth told him that she had left a watch for cleaning a few weeks ago. "Perhaps it's ready? If it is, I'll take it with me today."

He left to check on the watch, and Jennifer asked if they normally send out statements at Patek Phillipe. Jennifer had never before been in a store where it was not necessary to pay by cash or with a credit card. Elizabeth told the girl that she bought at least one watch a year and that she had a long-standing relationship with the store. "I'm sort of a special case."

The manager returned with the repaired watch and presented it to Elizabeth. After examining the fine quality of the workmanship, she placed both watches in her purse. The manager escorted the two ladies to the door, inviting them both to return at anytime.

As they stepped out the door, Elizabeth glanced at her watch and understood why she was starved. It was almost noon, and they had gone without breakfast. Elizabeth had spent enough time with Jennifer to know that the girl would be hungry, too. Jennifer was always starved. Elizabeth suggested, "Let's go to Café de Paris. It is only a short walk. I love it there." Elizabeth explained the restaurant's fare to Jennifer, knowing that the girl was an on and off vegetarian. Elizabeth knew it would only take a little coaxing for Jennifer to accept.

"A steak sounds great today," Jennifer replied.

Café de Paris is typical Parisian. The waitresses dress in the traditional black and white costume of a Paris bistro. It is a long, narrow restaurant with an entrance on each end. Elizabeth and Jennifer arrived just a few minutes after noon when the restaurant opens. Fortunately, they were early enough to get a table. Like in Paris, tables for two are placed only inches apart side by side, lining the two long walls. A long bench stretches along each wall. The tables are covered with cloths of different colors and then topped with paper coverlets. Space is limited, and seating is highly choreographed. As guests arrive, the waitresses pull out each table allowing the person taking the bench-side of the table to slide into the backside seating. The process is reversed when the person leaves. After the seating ritual, Elizabeth and Jennifer organized their possessions with some difficulty. Finding a resting place for Jennifer's gigantic purse in the tiny space that had been designated to them required near architectural skill. Barely settled, the waitress arrived and asked how they would like their entrecôte prepared. Jennifer looked puzzled, and Elizabeth took the cue ordering for both of them. The waitress wrote their order on the paper table covering and left to get the wine and mineral water.

"Where is the menu?" Jennifer asked.

"There isn't one. All they have is entrecôte. The only choice is how it is cooked. I ordered yours burnt, just like you like it."

Soon, the waitress returned with their drinks and fresh bread. Waiting behind her was a second waitress who served their salads.

After her first bite Jennifer said, "I have never tasted such wonderful salad dressing. Is it mustard? It's delicious but strong. It sends streaks of pain up the back of my neck."

Elizabeth smiling, replied, "Yes, it's wonderful, hot mustard. It's so full and, yet, so light. This is the only place I've ever been served anything like it. It's quite different from the American honey-mustard dressing, isn't it?"

The entrecôte was served with sauce spooned onto the meat by the waitress. The waitress then added pommes frites to the plate to complete the presentation. The fare was mouth-wateringly wonderful, as always.

Elizabeth explained that she loved to eat here. "This is one of my fun restaurants. Be careful though, when the waitress offers you a second portion. Don't take too much. The desserts are fabulous."

When the plates were cleared, the two women took several minutes to contemplate the dessert menu. It was the only menu in the restaurant and was filled with delicacies. "My two favorites are the crème brûlée and the profiteroles, I can never decide between the two," remarked Elizabeth.

"They both sound great to me."

"Such a dilemma. Why don't we order one of each and share?"

Jennifer immediately responded with a resounding, "Yes. Let's do it."

While waiting for their desserts to be served, Elizabeth presented the new watch to Jennifer and told her that it was a gift. "There is only one condition," chided Elizabeth. "When you die, you must will it to me. I love it, too."

Tears came to Jennifer's eyes. She was so touched by Elizabeth's outward expression of kindness. She placed the watch on her wrist, dumping her Timex unceremoniously into her enormous bag. Digging deeper into the abyss, she removed a well-used tissue and blotted her eyes. She tried to say something but was unable to get the words out.

They were interrupted as the desserts were presented. The waitress looked at Jennifer with compassion, as the girl's expression suggested she had just experienced a death in the family. Trying to assure the waitress that everything was fine, the two women smiled and directed their total concentration to the sensual tastes of sheer heaven. Their conversation became nonexistent. Scraping the plates to taste every last morsel of decadence, Elizabeth glanced at her watch and realized that the time had slipped away. She said, "We must hurry, or we will miss the train."

Fortunately, there was a taxi unloading a fare as they left the restaurant. They popped in before the door could be closed. It was a very short trip to the main train station; actually, it would have been a nice walk after such a large luncheon, but their hope of catching the train was iffy even with the taxi to speed the way.

At the station they hurriedly collected their bags from the locker and headed for the area that handled the trains traveling to France. A French immigration officer was standing at the entrance and asked to see their passports. Elizabeth handed her passport to the officer, but as Jennifer opened her bag, Elizabeth's heart sank. Miraculously, Jennifer pulled out the Hermes clutch and then her passport. She presented the passport to the officer and flashed a smug look at Elizabeth. They were waved through the clearance area and were soon comfortably seated in a first class car.

The train left on schedule to the minute. Elizabeth quickly went to work, losing everything that was around her. Distracted by the sound of soft snoring, she glanced briefly at Jennifer who was crumpled in her seat. The conductor came by to check the tickets, and Jennifer awakened just long enough to locate her ticket. She was back asleep before the conductor had finished checking the next section of seats. Elizabeth could not imagine that the girl was still suffering from jet lag. It had now been almost three weeks. Perhaps she was not sleeping well. It would be good to watch her carefully for the next few days.

The train arrived in Paris on time, and Martin was waiting, looking as a sentry when they disembarked. He had a porter in tow who took their bags. As they walked to the car, Martin informed Elizabeth that everything was ready at the country house. "Are we going there immediately?" he queried.

Jennifer started to interject but Elizabeth cut her off and said, "Yes, we will go there directly."

Elizabeth was beginning to become annoyed with Jennifer always wanting to assert her opinion. In her puppet role, it would prove necessary later, but her assertiveness was a pain when they were trying to organize their plans.

>+++-0-++-<

French country house, several hours later

The boxes had been thoroughly searched before they were sealed and shipped. Jennifer would never know. No big surprises had been found in her belongings, and everything of hers had been sent. She was renting a furnished apartment in New York, so there had been nothing bulky to transport.

Jennifer was excited to find the sealed boxes of her possessions awaiting. She was like a child at Christmas as she tore open the cartons and started unpacking her things. She decorated her room with her mementos, things that had some special meaning to her but probably meant nothing to anyone else in the world. A cocktail napkin with a heart drawn on it in smudged ink and a few faded photos of people who had faded from her life were displayed with pride. Elizabeth thought, *How sad. There is so little of her life. No wonder the girl is so quirky.*

When everything was in order, Jennifer reappeared in tattered jeans and a Phantom of the Opera sweatshirt. Elizabeth told her that the next few days would be spent studying her role. Then, early next week they would be going to London to see a dentist who would examine Jennifer's teeth. It was necessary to insure that she would have no dental problems during the next two or three years. This was very important. Once the surgery was completed, it would be difficult to do this sort of normal life business without attracting a large amount of attention. Looking like Di, it would be impossible for her to just breeze into a dental office to have some work done.

Jennifer asked, "Why are we going to London? The dental care there is not that great. We could go to Germany or Switzerland where it's the best in Europe."

Elizabeth replied, "We have an appointment with Di's dentist. Using the same dentist will provide consistency to the project. Not only that, he is probably the best dentist in England. I don't think you will have any complaints."

8

London, the next week

Elizabeth and Jennifer arose early to make the flight to London. It was a long drive through heavy traffic, and Martin did not want to be pressured to drive over the limit. Their goal was to be at the airport early. The flight was overbooked, as seemed to be the case with all flights this season. They were flying on a commercial commuter flight, arriving at London Central, where access to the city is much easier than from the area's other larger airports.

The three separated to clear immigration. Jennifer went through the line for EC entries with Martin who held a Dutch passport, although she was treating Martin as if he was a leper. Earlier Elizabeth had warded off an insurrection when Jennifer was informed that Martin was coming with them. Jennifer had been in an absolute twit over Martin. Elizabeth had tactfully smoothed everything over telling Jennifer that they needed Martin to provide security to them while in the city. Elizabeth was using her American passport and had to go through the queue for non-EC. She was behind a group of Arabs from the Emirates and a family who appeared to be Pakistanis. She resigned herself to a long wait and was not disappointed. It was becoming a real pain to travel in Europe without an EC passport. There were special queues for those with EC passports and one crowded queue for non-EC passports. It seemed every time she had been in an airport of late, she had been behind some third world refugee who spoke no language known to the civilized world. The waits in line were becoming interminable.

The trio regrouped in the baggage claim area and was pleased that the wait there was short. No sooner had Elizabeth arrived than their last bag appeared on the luggage carousel. With luggage in tow, they entered the arrival greeting area to find Adam impatiently waiting. Greetings were left to a minimum, as Adam directed them to the hired car double-parked just outside the entrance.

The car took them directly to Blakes, a small 'in' hotel, reserved for the beautiful people set. Elizabeth and Jennifer were sharing a small but well-appointed suite, and Martin was in a black and white 'decorator-look' room that resembled an elegant converted closet. The room was so small it seemed that placing a window in it must have been a real challenge. Adam was staying at his flat in Knightsbridge.

The four lunched in Blake's restaurant located underground. The chef made a gallant but futile effort to overcome the traditional dreary cuisine of England. Jennifer was the only diner who was complimentary. She seemed to think that the luncheon was one of the best she had ever eaten. The rest of the party kept their opinions private and smiled politely at the thoroughly boring meal.

The plan was laid out. Martin would accompany Jennifer to the dentist the next day. He was to stay with her during the appointment. Adam insisted that Jennifer was never to be out of Martin's line of sight. Adam underlined to Jennifer her need to cooperate with Martin. After the dentist, Martin would take Jennifer to Harrods for a shopping spree. Jennifer was still chafing a little at the thought of being accompanied by Martin. Thinking over what Adam had said, she acquiesced realizing that Martin was her ticket to Harrods.

Adam and Elizabeth would meet to make their plans during the time Jennifer was away with Martin. They had much to do and seldom the opportunity to be together at this stage in the project. They, additionally, had an important appointment, but this was not mentioned during the conversation.

Elizabeth was looking forward to the break from Jennifer. It had been so long since she had felt any peace. Her every moment was directed to sculpting Jennifer into the perfect princess. Elizabeth desperately needed some space. *I'm enduring the girl, but I don't have to like her.*

With plans in order, Adam suggested that they all relax for the rest of the day. They had earned the luxury. Jennifer was excited to be in the city and wanted some action. Staying at the hotel and resting in their suite was not her idea of the perfect adventure. She had suggested that they go bar hopping that evening. Adam blanched at the idea thinking of what a catastrophe it would be if Jennifer was on the loose and met someone she knew. Elizabeth caught Adam's concern; grasping for something to do, she suggested they go to the theatre that evening. Blake's concierge arranged orchestra seats for them, some of the best in the house. The performance was Miss Saigon. Elizabeth was mildly surprised that Jennifer had not seen it before. Elizabeth had seen it twice, including the premier German performance in Stuttgart. She actually thought the script a little sappy, a thinly disguised re-make of Madame Butterfly. But it seemed to appeal to the younger set.

Jennifer was wide-eyed and fascinated throughout the performance. The theatre in London was a new adventure for her. Elizabeth realized how limited Jennifer's experiences really were. It was surprising that with her family history, she had been so sheltered. Elizabeth took note and placed a 'yellow sticky' in the 'To Do' section of her mainframe brain. *Add the ballet, the opera, the symphony, and more legitimate theatre to Jennifer's training program.* Like mastering her speech and mannerisms, conducting herself properly at these events was a must.

During intermission, Jennifer was out of her mind with excitement over the glass of champagne that awaited them at their own private table in the theatre's lobby. Elizabeth had arranged this surprise before the performance. Jennifer commented, "I already feel like a Princess. This is such fun. Not at all like the off-Broadway shows I've seen in New York."

After the performance they found a trendy little Chinese restaurant in the theatre district to enjoy a late supper. Elizabeth's belief about London restaurants was reaffirmed, pedestrian food at equestrian prices. They finished eating well after midnight, but Jennifer was in no mood to go back to the hotel. The performance had been magical to her. She was talking on and on like a child who had been to Disneyland for the first time.

Elizabeth reminded her, "We have a busy day tomorrow, and it really is inappropriate for two ladies to be out unescorted at this time of night. It's time I call the driver."

Disappointed, Jennifer shrugged her acceptance. She had learned through several bad experiences that Elizabeth's word was law. But she thought, *With a little time, all of this will change. I am becoming too valuable to you. Soon, you won't be able to push me around anymore. Just wait and see. I'll get even with you, you pushy arrogant bitch. I can bide my time.*

Ten minutes later, the driver met them at the restaurant to escort them to the car. The restaurant was in a 'pedestrian only' area. He had parked as close as possible, about a five-minute walk away. Entering the street, Elizabeth was relieved she had called the driver. It had been the right thing to do. The streets were still packed. *London can be tough,* Elizabeth thought. *Especially, late at night. The project is too important to take any chances. Two well-dressed women alone at this time of night would have been an invitation for trouble.*

On the drive back to Blakes, the beauty of the tiny lights that outlined Harrods attracted the two women as they passed by.

"It really is one of my favorite stores, anywhere," Elizabeth commented.

Reminded that she would be shopping there the next day, Jennifer asked, "Could I borrow some money from you to make some purchases tomorrow? I'll pay you back, I promise. The minute I'm in Geneva, I'll go to the bank and draw out the money."

Elizabeth responded, "It's no problem at all, but maybe you should wait and see what happens. Adam and Martin have prepared a small surprise for you. You might want to change your mind after you know what it is."

Jennifer was overcome with excitement. She quivered like a puppy. Elizabeth again sensed that the girl had really been through some hard times. *She does not know how to handle it now that her ship has come in. Poor thing.*

They returned to their suite to find a box beautifully wrapped in gold foil and silver ribbons on Jennifer's bed. Placed atop was a card with "Jennifer" written in Adam's smooth flowing script.

Glancing at the handwriting, Elizabeth reflected back on their school years. Adam had experienced such difficulties perfecting the level of penmanship required in the Swiss schools. Unlike in the U.S. where mere legibility is the goal of the schools, perfection and beauty were the ideals at their boarding school. It had been so much easier for her. She never had a problem forming the letters, as the teachers demanded. Maybe it was because she was a girl. Elizabeth truly believed that boys and girls are innately different. Adam had constantly been marked down in his grades because of his handwriting. He finally managed to develop the required skill, and as in everything else he mastered, the result was perfection. Now, he used his computer for all communication. So what did it all matter, after all? All that work and agony for nothing. Elizabeth thought, *It has been years since I have seen his handwriting.* Elizabeth felt such warmth for her brother. She choked up feeling a lump emerge in her throat. *My brother. My life. Wholeness all in one gorgeous human being. What would I ever do without you?*

Jennifer tore open the card to find a message and another envelope inside. The message asked her to open the second envelope after the gift. Jennifer dutifully set the envelope aside and attacked the paper. She looked nothing like a princess in the process. She appeared more like a hungry dog digging through the trash for food.

The box emerged. It was a beautiful wooden box with gleaming brass fittings. It looked as though it was made of cherry wood and was finished with a patina that gave a glowing effect. It must have been hand polished; it would be nearly impossible to attain such beauty with a machine. Adam believed that attention to details was of prime importance, and it was so like him to take this level of care over the selection of a box. Its size was perfect for holding a necklace or some other piece of jewelry.

Jennifer was shaking. She held back, afraid to open the box. She waited several moments, and as her eyes started to tear, she closed them and flipped the latch. Squinting, with her eyes only partially opened, she peeked into the box. It was a fitted box, lined with a luxurious, deep purple-blue velvet. Lying within were two credit cards in Jennifer's new name that matched her fresh passport. One was an American Express Platinum Card, and the other was a Harrods Card.

Jennifer looked slightly puzzled and turned to Elizabeth for guidance. Elizabeth nodded to the unopened envelope. Jennifer ripped open the envelope to find an enclosure with Adam's handwritten message. "The cards are new. I have deposited ten thousand pounds on the Harrods card and five thousand on the American Express. It's just expense money for you to help you develop a wardrobe and make certain you have all those little necessities of life. I know how they add up for a woman. Martin suggested I arrange the cards for you. It was his idea. He really has a good heart under his rough exterior. You should go a little easier on him. Have fun shopping tomorrow!"

Adam had included the comment about Martin hoping it might defray the undeclared war that was ready to break out between Jennifer and Martin. Their perfect plan was already beginning to develop some problems. Martin was creating hostility rather than bringing Jennifer closer to Elizabeth and the girls.

Jennifer sat quietly for a moment staring at the credit cards and Adam's note. Then, the tears began to run down her cheeks. She sobbed and sobbed for several minutes. Looking up at Elizabeth, she said, "No one has ever done anything like this for me before. Never, ever before."

Elizabeth came over and put her arms around the girl, holding her tight. The sobbing only became more intense. After several minutes, Jennifer pulled herself away from Elizabeth and without saying a word scurried to the bathroom where she locked the door. Nearly half an hour later, she emerged with her make-up freshened. Looking bright, she said, "I must go to see Martin so I can thank him. I want to thank Adam, too."

Elizabeth suggested that it might be better for Jennifer to wait until morning and thank Martin at the same time she thanked Adam. "Remember darling, it is already tomorrow. Martin likely would prefer his thank you at a civilized hour."

Jennifer looked at her shiny, new Patek Philippe. Astonished, she saw that it was well after two in the morning. Then, she looked at the watch again and began to weep once more.

Elizabeth said, "Why don't we go to bed. It has been a big day. We have an even bigger one ahead of us tomorrow."

As they undressed, Elizabeth realized that the most difficult part of the project was not going to be teaching Jennifer to act like Di, nor was it going to be the necessary surgery. The challenge was stabilizing this emotional wreck called Jennifer so that she could do her job. *This girl is turning out to be more unpredictable than I ever would have believed.*

▸—◈—◂

London, the next day

Before eight, Elizabeth and Jennifer went down for breakfast. Martin was already finished, working on a second or third cup of coffee. Seeing Martin, Jennifer brightened and ran to him. She threw her arms about his solid musculature and hugged him hard. It was the first time in her life Elizabeth could ever remember Martin being surprised. He looked a little dazed as Jennifer said, "Your idea was so sweet. Thank you!" She then planted a big kiss on his cheek.

He tried to ignore the whole thing and merely grumbled that he had discovered the real reason that the English drank tea. Jennifer bit his challenge and asked him why. His response was the obvious. "Have you ever tasted their coffee?"

She giggled shamelessly at the tired old joke and started assembling her breakfast with a vengeance. Elizabeth took one look at the croissants and decided to pass. She would try the coffee.

Martin said, "You only have it half right, Elizabeth. You should skip the coffee, too."

Elizabeth watched Jennifer in amazement wondering how any one person could eat so much at one sitting, especially after such a late dinner the evening before. After finishing everything on her plate and going back for seconds, Jennifer excused herself to find the powder room. The minute she was out of sight Martin said, "What the hell happened? I liked it much better when she hated me. Okay, I know the reason that Adam did it, but I just don't like that silly bitch."

Elizabeth chuckled and replied, "Martin, you don't like any females. Your statement doesn't mean very much."

Martin shot back, "I like you, but don't you get any ideas."

Looking at him with amusement, Elizabeth caught out of the corner of her eye Adam descending the stairs. At the very moment he reached the bottom, Jennifer reappeared. Seeing Adam, she ran to him and threw he arms around him. It was evident from afar that she was graciously expressing her appreciation 'ad nauseam.' Adam, finally able to disengage himself from both of her arms, encouraged Jennifer back to the table. He greeted Elizabeth and Martin with Jennifer still clinging to his arm. Glancing at his watch, he mentioned to Martin, "You and Jennifer better get going, or you will be late for the dentist. It would be better to be there on time or even a little early."

Not wanting to leave Adam's side, Jennifer reluctantly took Martin's arm, but only after Adam skillfully removed her arm from his and moved it to rest under Martin's left biceps. Turning to leave, Jennifer wished Adam and Elizabeth a nice day. As the two headed up the steps, Martin shot Adam an evil look back over his shoulder.

Alone with Elizabeth, Adam switched to Jauner-Tüütsch. They discussed the plan for the day. His flat and the office they had sublet were being swept for bugs at that very moment. By the time they arrived, the work would be finished. Martin and Jennifer had a car that had been hired for the day; they would be on their own. Martin understood his orders. Adam and Elizabeth did not need to worry about being interrupted.

"We are going to meet her this morning," Adam started. "Surprisingly, the only regret she seems to have is deceiving Paul, her butler. She said that he is the kindest man in the whole world. She finds it so difficult to mislead him. She feels that someday, at the right time, she will again be able to contact the boys. Possibly, she's right, but, personally, I doubt it. In a few years she will be so into her new life, the old will seem like a dream, someone else's dream. She rationalizes that her nonexistence will allow Charles to marry Camilla. He has broken her heart, but she still wants to do the best for him. Camilla is the only gift Di will ever give to Charles that he will truly appreciate. She is really a remarkable woman. She hopes that Charles can learn to care, truly care, about someone. I think we need to help in any way we can. Paul is our only potential problem, and we need to keep an extra eye on him. It would be terrible to have him leak the project. Elizabeth, you need to talk with her from a woman's perspective. You know what I mean. You must convince her of the necessity of leaving no loose ends. You can do a better job than I can explaining these things."

"Okay. Talking with her will be no problem. Sometimes you amaze me though, dear brother. As well as you are able to figure out everything else, you sure are at a complete loss when it comes to women. Why should it be so surprising she cares for Charles? You still love Natalie, and she loves you."

He looked at his watch. "That's different. I never betrayed her. We need to leave. We need to be in place before she arrives. I'll fill you in some more in the car."

The car, a black Daimler, blended in well with the traffic. The driver was a large black man who had a lilting Caribbean accent. Adam used this driver from time to time when he was in London. Adam liked his style. He was cautious and obedient and immediately forgot anything he heard that should go unremembered. The driver smiled broadly when he saw Elizabeth and asked, "Young lady, when are you going to get this man to marry you, anyway?"

Elizabeth replied, "I have better taste than to marry a rogue like Adam. I wouldn't wish him on anyone."

The black man laughed in his good-natured way and opened the car door for them.

Adam picked up the thread of conversation again in Jauner-Tüütsch. "She is meeting with an advisor today. We were able to sublet a small office in the same building. She will be going to confer with this advisor numerous times over the next year or so. It might give us several opportunities for meeting her face to face. We have locked in the office for the next two years. The building management thinks we are moving to the Docklands when our offices there are completed and that this space is just a small satellite operation to provide us with a London mailing address. Everything is paid. There is a secure phone line, and Gerard built one of his magic boxes to monitor it. I have installed voice mail. She can contact us; however, the number she will dial is call forwarded to this number." He pointed to a slip of paper. "Gerard will monitor the main British Telecom computer. If anyone ever tries to determine where this number is located, we will fold up shop. To be extra cautious, we will change the number that she is to call every few weeks. If anyone ever tries to track her phone calls, it will be a dead end." Then Adam handed the slip of paper to Elizabeth.

Elizabeth mentally subtracted the true year she was born from the last four digits to decode the number. She committed the number to memory and tore the slip into small pieces. She gave half the litter back to Adam. He would throw his part away in a different location than the one she chose.

Adam continued cryptically, "The office is being debugged by the same crew that did my flat. You never know with these old buildings; they can have real infestations. The crew will be finished and gone by the time we arrive. She has a meeting scheduled for an hour and a half. She will excuse herself a little early and come to see us. The time line is very tight. We need to be very directed so she can appear again when and where she is expected."

Elizabeth nodded tightly. She was always directed.

The car slipped to the curb, and the driver let them out. Adam asked the driver to return to pick them up in two hours at exactly eleven forty-five. The driver beamed broadly saying "I'll be here. See you at eleven forty-five."

Adam thought, *Like hell. He will be late. He always is.*

Adam and Elizabeth quickly entered the building taking the elevator directly to the eleventh floor office. "How long do we have?" Elizabeth asked.

"We won't know until she arrives. If we are lucky, ten or fifteen minutes." Adam replied.

After entering the office, Elizabeth asked for directions to the ladies room. She excused herself to freshen up and dispose of the shredded telephone number. She returned to find Adam examining a file.

Adam said, "The room is clean. We can talk strategy."

They discussed a number of issues and decided that Elizabeth would do most of the talking.

"She'll relate better to you."

"Adam, you just like me to handle women so they don't end up handling you."

Adam held up his hands in surrender.

Changing the subject, he briefed Elizabeth on the status of the remaining three men who were yet to receive their judgment for their acts against Elizabeth's husband and daughter.

"One has reservations for a ski holiday in Switzerland," he commented. "The vacation is planned in about three month's time. The man is bringing his mistress. The story he has told his wife is that he is attending a conference at the UN in Geneva. The reality is that he has contrived a vacation to do a little skiing and a lot of nookie. The man and his wife live somewhat separate lives. It has become a marriage of convenience. The marriage is what I would call a graphic illustration of the true meaning of 'Cold War.' The wife is delighted that she does not have to attend. She hates freezing weather and snow. She will be furious if she ever learns of the mistress, and even more angry when she realizes that the trip is nothing more than a sex and ski vacation."

Adam drew an even larger picture for Elizabeth. He had located the Swiss bank account where the man keeps the money he siphons off from his black project financing. Adam had gathered enough information to send the man to jail for much longer than his life span calculated by his insurance company. Certainly, much longer than his life span as calculated by Adam and Elizabeth.

Then, Adam outlined his general plan. Elizabeth liked his ideas for the most part but suggested some refinements. Adam smiled one of his rare genuine smiles. "I should have thought of that myself," he admitted.

A quiet knock at the door interrupted their conversation. She was here. Adam responded immediately and escorted Di to the conference table asking her to be seated. "Please excuse us for being so blunt," he said. "We need to make the most of our time. This project can only be attempted once. If anyone ever learns of what we are doing, we would have to abandon the plan. Discovery would make the whole project impossible. We must keep our meetings to a minimum. They cannot be discovered."

She nodded but said nothing.

Elizabeth asked, "When are you expected at the building's entrance?"

She replied, "In about ten minutes."

Elizabeth sensed Di's concern and dove into the minefield with the question. "Is something wrong? Are you having second thoughts?"

Di looked at her with eyes that held far too much pain for a woman of her age. "To answer your questions, yes, everything is wrong. The situation is ghastly, to say the least. That is why we're here. Yes, I have second thoughts, but I do not see another solution. It's the only way I'll ever have a life of my own or find any happiness. My children are becoming less mine by the day. If the establishment gets its way, I'll be little more than the biological curiosity who birthed them. I have been prohibited from ever marrying again. I'm a virtual prisoner. I'm being held captive by the press, the establishment, the population at large. I'm a prisoner of people I have never met. I will never be free for the rest of my life unless you are to accomplish what you have promised. This is my next great worry. I don't see how you can do it."

Elizabeth breathed an inner sigh of relief and responded. "We can deliver on our promise. You know we have done this before. But you will have to follow the plan exactly. That includes keeping everything that you are doing for the success of the plan from everyone, absolutely everyone. That includes Paul."

For the first time Di smiled and commented, "You aren't a mind reader are you?"

"No, but we do our work very thoroughly." Elizabeth replied.

"I can see that."

Adam provided Di with a business card. He told her to use the mailing address or the phone number if she needed to leave a message. The card was in the name of a food importer that did not exist.

Di looked puzzled for a moment until Elizabeth explained, "If anyone ever sees the card, no one would ever think a thing. It's the kind of a card that gets handed out everywhere and people find in the bottom of their briefcases wondering where in the world they got it. This is the reason we printed the card instead of writing the number and address on a piece of paper. It's close to invisible due to its commonness."

Di nodded her understanding and slipped the card into her clutch. "I understand that you have found a girl to be my double."

"Yes, we have, and it appears that she will be ideal. She still needs a lot of work, but we are confident that she will be able to deceive those who don't know you personally."

"When can I meet her?" Di asked.

"You will only meet her in passing. It's better that you not get to know one another," Elizabeth responded.

"And why, might I ask?"

"Because she is a security risk. The less she knows about you and what it is that we are doing, the better. We do not want her to ever comprehend the end goal of this operation. If she becomes too familiar she might..."

Di interrupted, "I'm just bloody curious, you know."

"Of course. Please understand, we are just trying to protect you from risks that we know from experience could become realities. You need to continue to use the Royal Protection less and less. These men present a high risk to the operation and could be a source of discovery. The guards know you well. They could quickly spot a switch. They would recognize the differences immediately, just like Paul. It's the same with Rosa. We could never use your double when she is present. It is only the people who do not know you intimately whom we can mislead with your double."

"I think I understand," Di responded. "You are sure that no one will be hurt? It is very important to me."

"Not even a scratch. The plan is completely foolproof if all instructions are followed exactly," Elizabeth replied.

"Okay. Let's continue. I need to leave very shortly."

Elizabeth went on, "If you need to contact us, telephone on the number we have provided. Otherwise, you may pass a message through Katherine. We will continue to place a small advert in the personals to inform you to contact us if we have an urgent need to meet with you, or we will reach you through Katherine. Your presence under your new identity has already been established in the U.S. You have bank accounts, investments, a credit history, and real estate. We are adding more to your legend every day. You even have some parking tickets. We will tell you more about all of this at our next meeting. Everything is going according to schedule. Do you have any questions? I know you must leave."

Di responded quietly, "Thank you. No. I understand. I won't make any mistakes. Don't worry. I truly am delighted to meet both of you." Looking directly at Adam and smiling, she continued, "I feel secure and relaxed about the project. The Puppet Master is much more than what I have been told. I did a little checking, you know."

Elizabeth walked out into the hall to secure the elevator. When it arrived, she waved a clear sign, and Di sneaked away descending to her waiting entourage, as though she had just left her scheduled appointment. Adam's portable phone was ringing softly. When he answered, silence filled the room like a thunderbolt. Then he whispered "Merde. Merde. Merde."

>-+-<>-O-<>-+-<

The nurse escorted Jennifer into the dentist's examination room. Martin tagged along, peeking about like he had never been in such an office before. He looked like a man who was bored, trying desperately to find any small thing to interest him. Jennifer thought he must hate being in a dentist's office and told Martin that she would be just fine. "I can handle the dentist with no problems. Don't worry."

Martin ignored her and sat in the extra chair. The dentist arrived and looked surprised at the big man sitting in the room but said nothing. He asked Jennifer a few questions and then told her that he would need to take a complete set of x-rays so that he could see if there were any problems. Martin was asked to step outside while they took the x-rays. He stood outside but just outside the entrance to the room, returning the moment the x-ray shots were completed. The dentist and his assistant excused themselves to process the film, and Jennifer and Martin were left alone. Martin rose and looked out the window. He walked gingerly to a closed door and appeared to listen for a moment. Then, he returned to his seat.

Jennifer asked, "What ever are you doing?"

Martin merely raised his finger to his lips to indicate silence. She shook her head and decided to ignore him.

After a few minutes time, the dentist returned and said that Jennifer's dental work seemed to be in good condition. He foresaw no immediate problems. He had been told that Jennifer would be abroad in Africa for two years. Since dental care was so spotty in the areas where she would be traveling, it was important to confirm there were no potential complications.

The dentist recommended that Jennifer have a good cleaning and told her no other work was necessary. The assistant asked if they wanted an appointment for the cleaning, and Jennifer looked at Martin for help. He made a subtle nod of his head, and Jennifer carried it off very well by saying, "No, not today. My fiancé or I will call back later for the appointment. Our schedule is so unsettled right now."

Martin rose and asked if he could use the toilet before they left. Jennifer followed suit and asked as well. They were directed down the hall. Martin knowingly made a wrong turn and wandered into a back office. He quickly covered, acting as though he realized his mistake and turned to go in the right direction. He finished quickly and waited outside the door marked 'Ladies' for Jennifer to emerge. Martin called the driver to tell him they were on the way. They left the office together and stood for less than a minute before their driver pulled to the curb and collected them.

Martin instructed the driver to take them to Harrods and return for them in six hours, unless he heard otherwise. Martin pulled out a small notebook and began to make copious notes as the car wound its way through the London traffic. As they neared Harrods, Martin returned the notebook to his pocket. The driver pulled to the entrance and told them that this was the best place to collect them, due to the traffic at the time he would return. Martin agreed and escorted Jennifer toward the main entrance of the store.

As they neared the entrance, Jennifer asked Martin if he was hungry and told him that she had heard of a fabulous restaurant, just around the corner. He shrugged, nonplused by the invitation. Ignoring his lack of interest, she directed him through the crowd. They rounded the corner onto the side street where they nearly ran into a gang of three punks who were headed the opposite direction. The leader had a shaved head, except for a Mohawk that was in red spikes. He was wearing a dog collar, silver rings in his right eyebrow and a thing that looked like a flag grommet in his earlobe. His followers looked equally rough and refused to move out of the pathway of Martin and Jennifer. Jennifer pulled back, but Martin refused to acquiesce. The leader glared at Martin and glanced quickly to see if there was a bobby about. Concluding that there was no threat of being caught, the punk reached into his pocket, pulled out a butterfly knife and began to flip it open. Realizing what was happening, Martin made a quick half turn. His foot shot out, and the kid collapsed with a sickening crunch to the pavement. Martin admonished the followers who were looking in disbelief, "Your friend fell down, and it looks like he broke his kneecap. Perhaps, you should take him to see a doctor. It would be a pity if someone else fell down. The pavement here seems to be a little slippery."

By this time the leader was thrashing around in pain, gasping for breath. Occasional pedestrian traffic continued to move by on the opposite side of the street, but no one seemed to pay any attention to the injured punk, except for his followers. Martin took Jennifer's arm. Stepping around the injured gang leader, they were off again. Before they rounded the corner, Jennifer glanced over her shoulder. A crowd had begun to form. One of the followers was trying to scoop up the leader's butterfly knife but was having a problem as the leader was battering about beginning to catch his breath and screaming, "Oh God! Oh God!"

Jennifer asked, "What happened?" Frightened, she had moved behind Martin and missed seeing the whole event.

Martin replied, "The clumsy oaf fell and hurt himself."

Jennifer rolled her eyes and giggled as they walked on.

The restaurant was a Nouvelle Cuisine, an 'in' sort of place. The two placed their orders, and after about a fifteen-minute wait, two waiters brought their plates with art deco dome shaped silver covers. With a great flourish, the waiters removed the covers in unison to reveal three lonely raviolis in a dribble of sea green pesto sauce. Over it all was scattered what looked like a few lawn clippings. Martin looked at the waiters and asked in all seriousness, "Is this some kind of a joke?"

Shocked, the remaining waiter responded with disdain asking, "Sir, would you prefer something a little less sophisticated?"

Martin shot the waiter a hot glance of pure menace and then thought better of it. He replied, "No, this will be fine."

Martin knew that Adam would be furious if a scene had resulted. In fact, Adam would be furious when he found out about the punk Martin had disabled. Martin had not wanted to do it, but he had been worried about not reacting. The possible consequences of inaction were unacceptable. He had seen no other solution other than turning tail and running. That had its own dangers, especially with Jennifer in tow who likely could not have run that fast. Martin did not want to push his luck. He would eat this ridiculous meal and not complain. Adam and Elizabeth were the best thing that had happened to him since he left Africa. He didn't want to take the risk of becoming a liability to their operation.

Martin finished the meal in complete silence as Jennifer tried to bring him into a conversation. She felt the waiter embarrassed Martin, and she wanted to make him feel better. She did not understand that Martin was not the kind of person who would ever be embarrassed. He was only worried that he might have placed the operation in jeopardy with his action on the street. He knew that calling notice to himself in the restaurant would have been the wrong thing to do. He was not pleased with himself. He was getting sloppy and needed to pay closer attention. If he were not very careful, Adam would terminate his employment. He could not afford to make any more mistakes.

Adam was a soft-spoken man, but Martin had no doubt that he could be deadly, if crossed. When Martin thought about it, he decided that perhaps Elizabeth was the more dangerous. He tended to underrate her because she was a woman, but he had seen her in action. He knew that she was coldblooded and ruthless. They were a strange pair. They seemed to love each other. He could not understand why they had never married. They were both straight.

Martin asked Jennifer if she would like a coffee. She smiled brightly, thinking she had finally made him feel at ease. They ordered coffee, and Martin began to work in his notebook again.

Jennifer asked, "What are you doing?"

"I'm going to write a book someday when I retire. I write down the thoughts as they come to my mind. Right now, I'm writing about clumsy oafs who fall down on sidewalks."

She tried to sneak a look at what he was writing, but he closed the book and put it away before she had a chance.

They left the restaurant and walked around the block in the opposite direction they had walked before, pacing in a large circle before coming back to Harrods. Jennifer said nothing thinking Martin was just enjoying the walk, but Martin was checking to see if there was anyone looking around for them. Satisfied that pedestrian traffic and everything else seemed normal. They crossed the street and entered the side door of Harrods.

Jennifer immediately headed for the designer ladies' wear. She looked at a number of things that might work, and Martin stood patiently in the background appearing absolutely useless, as only a man can look while waiting for a woman to decide on clothes. She took her choices to the fitting rooms. Fortunately, there was a chair near the entrance. Martin planted himself and settled in for the duration. He began again to write in his small notebook. Had Jennifer been able to see the notebook, she would have been puzzled. It was only drawings, numbers and a few cryptic notes written in Dutch.

Jennifer made her selections and decided to change into one of the new suits that she had purchased. After using her shiny new card to pay for the clothes, she returned to the changing rooms. When she emerged, she was dripping with class. Even Martin had to admit, she looked smashing, far more elegant than the woman he had met for the first time less than a month ago.

Next, Jennifer directed Martin to the jewelry section. She looked for the longest time trying on several necklaces and sets of earrings. Finally, she chose some subtle but rather attractive costume jewelry. Her selections were well chosen, looking as if they might be the real things. She was assuming the appearance of a different woman, and Martin could not help but notice how the clerks now fawned over her. If she would only get rid of the overnight bag that passed for her purse, the image would be complete. *Maybe I can arrange to have it stolen. I'll ask Elizabeth.*

Jennifer then asked Martin if she could go to a boutique. She had read about it. "Everyone is talking about it."

Martin replied, "It's okay with me. I'll call the driver and have him pick us up early."

Jennifer suggested that they just take a taxi. "The driver could be anywhere. It may take him forever to arrive. I hate to just stand and wait and do nothing."

"I'm sorry, Jennifer. We must use the driver. Adam's orders. He is a good but demanding boss."

Pulling out his small portable phone, Martin touched the speed dial and connected with the driver instantly. He told the driver they were on their way to the pick-up point and closed the connection. Martin decided to walk around the building in a different direction than the one they had entered. He could not be too careful. Someone could still be looking for them. As they rounded the last corner, they saw their driver waiting for them. They scurried to enter the car, and the driver abruptly pulled into traffic. Jennifer gave the driver the address of the boutique. He hummed his acknowledgment and seemed to know the place.

>—+—+>—O—<+—+—<

Adam disconnected the phone and told Elizabeth that Martin had an altercation with a thug near Harrods. He had shattered the man's knee but seemed to get away cleanly with Jennifer.

Elizabeth's face darkened. She said, "That man is too dangerous to use for this stage of the project. We must remove him from this phase. His testosterone-charged attitude could screw up everything. If that bastard mucked this up, I'll personally castrate him."

"Leave it for now. We will talk to him later and hear his side of the story. Don't rush to judgment. He has always been damn good at what he does for us. It appears that no one is looking for either him or Jennifer. All the same, I want him on a flight to France tonight. Bring one of the girls here to replace him to look after Jennifer. Brigit is best, I think."

Elizabeth agreed and said, "Okay. I'll take care of it. But think about it. We don't want to attract any attention right now, and he is memorable. People who meet him rarely forget him."

"I know. That is Martin's real disadvantage as far as I'm concerned. Certainly, we might do things differently than he, but when we analyze his actions, he always chooses good solutions for the problems he faces at the moment. I wish he could be invisible, but he never is. Still, he always pulls through for us."

Mollified, Elizabeth started the autopsy of their meeting with Di. "Di is ready. I hope she can hold up for the next year or so. I wish we could speed up the process. The time line is my only real worry. She is under tremendous pressure. I hope she is strong enough to take it. I am convinced that we can pull off the project, if we can control the stage set. Di is a bit of a wild card though, and I'm not sure we can always get her to do exactly what we want when we want it done. Jennifer is the other potential problem. She is turning out to be far more difficult to predict than we thought."

Adam agreed that the real threats to the project were Di and Jennifer.

These two were the only wild cards. Somehow, they needed to control what Di might say and do. Jennifer was a problem too, but at least they had her under their surveillance all of the time. It was much easier to control her. Di was by far the most difficult part of the project.

He asked, "Do you think that Paul needs to have a little accident? It would take some time for Di to become close to his replacement. Perhaps that might be the best solution to that risk. As far as I'm concerned, the possibility of Di filling him in on the project is our biggest risk from her side."

"I'm not sure. It would have to be very carefully orchestrated so it looked as though it was really an accident. Even then, unless he was unconscious or dead, she might feel sorry for him and tell him. And, a big problem I might add, is what if Di became suspicious? She might become distraught and say something to someone else or even back out entirely. I think the risks are too high to take that step in the operation."

They tossed around the variables some more and finally decided that Paul's loyalty was to Di. If he ever discovered something, it was unlikely that he would do anything to jeopardize the project. Probably, he would just talk to Di about it. If they kept an eye on him, they might be able to head off a problem before it started. They could deal with him later, if he became a risk. For now, he was not a problem. There was a possibility that they would need to eliminate him after the operation, but only if he looked ready to blow the whistle. They did not want him to become a casualty of war, but only time would tell.

Elizabeth looked at her watch and said, "We should go. It's after a quarter till. The driver will be waiting."

"I doubt it. I think he is still on Caribbean time."

"Why do you use him? He is always late. He isn't that reliable. You certainly have better things to do than wait on the king of reggae."

"Oh, he is very reliable. It's just that he is usually late. Besides that, I like reggae."

"Reliably late," Elizabeth snorted as she tapped out a reggae beat on the tabletop.

They exited the building at five till. The car was nowhere in sight.

"Touché," Elizabeth said.

At that very moment the driver rounded the corner and pulled to the curb. He popped out and ran around the car to open the door for both of them. A bobby, standing near the corner, nodded and touched his hand to his helmet as they drove off. Elizabeth was just about to make a bitchy comment about being on time when the driver said, "Sorry I was late.

That bobby made me leave. He told me I couldn't park there. So I drove around the block. When I came back, he wasn't there, so I parked again. Damn, if he didn't come around the corner and see me again. I had to drive around the block again. I wouldn't have dared stop a third time, but I saw you there and figured I'd take the chance."

Elizabeth bit her tongue and gave Adam a guilty look. A smile ghosted across his face. He had scored a small goal. The two had stopped keeping score long ago, but the victor still tried to make the point whenever possible.

Adam asked the driver to take them to the S & P, a quiet and wonderful Thai restaurant not too far from Blakes. The driver told them that he had tried the place a few months ago. He was curious after he had taken Adam there a couple of times, so decided to try it for himself. "Damn!" he said. "That food is too hot for me, and I like hot food. I took one bite and almost croaked. I don't know how you can eat it. I sweated for three damn days afterwards. I was grateful I couldn't eat it all. I'd still be holding my throat."

Elizabeth rolled her eyes, and Adam smiled. As they pulled to the curb in front of the restaurant, Adam told the driver that he would call when they were finished. The driver gave the two of them a big wink and said, "Be good."

They entered and were warmly welcomed. Adam had known the owners for many years, although they had no idea what Adam did for a living. They were very successful Thai entrepreneurs, first importing Haagen Dazs ice cream to Thailand and then moving on to other ventures. Adam was always treated like royalty here, and today was no exception.

The son of the owner brought the menus but suggested that it would be his pleasure to ask the chef to prepare something special. Simultaneously, Elizabeth and Adam nodded their acceptance knowing it would be a real treat.

They were early for lunch in the city. Only one other table was occupied. It was a party of three very prominent and mature looking executive types. The man was quite tall. He was accompanied by two petite women, one an Asian and the other a blond Caucasian. The Asian woman rose and went to the toilet area; when she returned, the son introduced her to Adam and Elizabeth. She was also an old friend of the restaurateurs. She used the name, Art, since her Thai name was so difficult for Westerners to pronounce.

Adam told Art in near perfect Thai that he hoped she would enjoy the meal and that S & P was his favorite restaurant in London. Art smiled and thanked him in Thai, returning to her table and her companions.

The son continued chatting with Adam and Elizabeth telling them that the couple at the table with Art was Swiss; he wanted to introduce Adam and Elizabeth to them, as they seemed like very important people.

Ready for some privacy, Adam glanced significantly at Elizabeth. The unspoken message was clear. "We better not discuss business in the event they speak Jauner-Tüütsch." Adam then politely told the son that he did not want to disturb these fine people. He quipped, "They look as though they are involved in a deep conversation. It might be better for us to meet another time or perhaps after the meal."

In addition to what the chef was preparing, Adam ordered starters of green curry with extra hot peppers and a chicken Satay. The food was excellent and so very satisfying. And as always, there was so much food. Of course, Adam had augmented the problem by adding to what the chef was preparing, but what did it matter? They ate and ate, enjoying the sensual pleasures of the wonderful delicacies. The nice sparkling water they ordered was a perfect compliment to the spiciness. They noticed that the other table was enjoying a second bottle of fine red wine with the meal. "They must not have to work this afternoon," Adam quipped to Elizabeth.

Elizabeth nodded in agreement and sitting tall placed her hand to her stomach. Taking a deep breath and sighing out loud, she said, "I feel much too full. Would it be all right if we walked back to the hotel?"

"Sure, I'll call the driver and tell him to take the rest of the day off."

The walk was just the right distance to settle the food properly. They stopped several times along the way for a closer look at things that caught their eyes as they passed by the numerous antique shops in the area. In the end they had enjoyed looking, but they found nothing very interesting, nothing anyway they could not live without. Both Adam and Elizabeth loved fine antiques but preferred the more Baroque continental styles to the heavy and more cumbersome British tastes that were on display in the area.

Elizabeth's flat in Milan resembled miniature rooms from Versailles. Gianni Versace was a friend and had helped her to decorate it. He, too, was fond of the elegant Baroque, a style that often inspired much of his fashion. Elizabeth had a number of his ensembles salted away in her wardrobe. She only wore them, though, when she was not working on a project. His taste was never understated, and his designs tended to make her a little too memorable.

Milan was Elizabeth's favorite place to stay when she was away from her home in the Georgetown area of Washington, D.C. She and Adam jointly owned a Hill Country estate in Texas where they often stayed together between projects. The also owned a wonderful estate in Virginia; it contained a lovely home that looked as if it had been lifted directly from France. Unfortunately, they had not been there together for nearly two years. They had been so busy with their projects, they simply had not had the opportunity. Adam's ex-wife split her time between the two homes, and Natalie really kept both places in wonderful condition. The three of them had one rule. Discussing business on the premises was absolutely forbidden. They were committed to preserving these retreats as a sanctuary.

Elizabeth looked directly at Adam and said, "Let's take some time off after this one. I need the break and so do you. I want to do silly things like go on a picnic or sit on the bank of a stream and drag my feet in the water. I might even let you beat me at a game of golf."

Adam looked into her eyes like an old lover and replied, "Maybe we should just quit. Anything else after this one would be a come down. It's best to retire when you have reached the top. It's like being the President. What is there to do next? We still have a lot of life ahead of us. As far as the golf is concerned, you are a dreamer. I could spot you three strokes and still beat you."

A flash of pain crossed her eyes. Understanding her turmoil, Adam assured her that they would finish all of their private business first before they retired.

"Adam, it's not that. It is just that I have no one left but you. I know exactly what Di is feeling. I have no past. I have no future. I merely exist. Without you, there is nothing." She reached up and tenderly touched his lips as she looked into his eyes.

He took her face in his hands and said, "I love you, my sister. It really is just the two of us. No one will ever be able to share our lives. That is why Natalie and I could not make it. She and I were unable to share everything. There is only you."

"Di will have a hard time when this is over. We will need to be there and be her friends until she can develop some on her own. Otherwise, she will not be able to cope. The others have all had some sort of support group. With her, there will be only the two of us. This is my greatest worry. That what we are doing is futile. She may be overcome with loneliness. She is very social. I was not, but even with my independent personality, the loneliness was consuming."

Adam thought about what Elizabeth had said for a minute and then asked, "What about a man for her? Some male companionship might help, and if we can..."

"Adam, stop. Please stop. It would never work. Let her meet her own man. You are not cut out to be the matchmaker. Hell, you're not even a good judge of character for your own relationships, let alone try-ing to be a matchmaker for someone else. She will look great, and she has a great personality. I predict that she will be married within two years of her birth in Texas. We just need to help until she can get her feet on the ground. It will only be the first year or so. Then, we can begin to wean her from our constant attention."

"I like her. She is far deeper than I would have thought."

"Don't even think about it. She needs a stable man. My God, if she is a wreck now, imagine what she would be if she had you for a beau. I wouldn't wish you on anyone, even Jennifer."

"Hey, I can't be that bad. Natalie and you both love me."

"Not in that way, darling. That's why you and Natalie are not still an item."

They walked in silence holding each other's hand. There was a spe-cial bond. Neither would have been able to explain it if asked. Their bond was far greater than something than could be physically described; it was founded on a simple and accepting love for one another.

As they rounded the corner and approached Blakes, they stepped back into their public personas and were once again the professionals. Distant from one another and yet bonded together. It was easy to see why people were confused by their relationship. It seemed so much more than partners, yet it was not sexual in any way.

Adam and Elizabeth went to the suite that Elizabeth was sharing with Jennifer and caught up on the reports that were being submitted. Each had several hours of work to complete.

Adam remarked, "No police report has been filed on the punk. It appears that the authorities are treating the incident as an unfortunate accident. Even so, I don't want to take any chances. I want Martin on a flight out of the country today."

Elizabeth contacted Brigit and arranged for her to fly in the next morning. It took little explanation for Brigit to understand the need for her to replace Martin.

Adam and Elizabeth continued to download files and exchange information. They worked silently for over two hours. Finally, Adam looked at his watch. It was five o'clock. Time for their Happy Hour. He suggested that they go down to the bar for an aperitif and wait there for Martin and Jennifer to return. Elizabeth welcomed the break.

Leaving the suite they chose to take the stairs, as Blakes' elevator is so tiny. It is something out of the last century, impossible to use with baggage. The porter loads it, pushes the button, and then runs up the stairs to unload it at the top. It's all very comical.

Entering to find themselves the only guests in the hotel's lounge, the bartender was anxious to accommodate them. In unison they ordered. "Campari with a twist of lemon and a little sparkling water, please." Campari was traditionally served with orange juice or soda water, but both thought the sweetness took away from the taste. They always ordered it with fizzy water. They had converted to fizzy water some years ago, quite by accident one evening when, in desperation, they had substituted it for soda water.

They had just finished their drinks and were considering a second round, when they heard Jennifer's laugh floating down the stairs from the hotel's reception. Within a few seconds, Martin and Jennifer descended the stairs engaged in an intense conversation. Surprised to see Adam and Elizabeth, Martin and Jennifer joined them immediately. Adam asked if they would like anything to drink, and both ordered a sparkling water. Martin rarely drank and never when working on a project. Jennifer excused herself to find the ladies room to freshen up before sitting down.

As soon as she was out of sight, Martin told them both he had a problem and needed to discuss it. Adam said, "We know."

Elizabeth shot Martin a glance that would have curdled milk.

Adam told Martin that they would talk about it later, although he wanted Martin to leave tonight for France. "I want you out of here on the first available flight. Don't fail me."

Martin hung his head in acceptance.

Jennifer returned and asked, "Has someone died? You all look so solemn."

Elizabeth laughed and told her that they were sad that Martin needed to leave tonight for France to take care of some things there. They were just disappointed that he could not stay to spend a little more time here.

Jennifer asked, "Why didn't you tell me you were leaving?"

Martin merely grunted and shrugged his shoulders.

Adam asked about the dentist, and Jennifer told them that she was fine and only needed a cleaning. Adam asked if the dentist shot a full set of x-rays and made a thorough check.

Jennifer responded, "Yes." Then, looking over at Martin, she brightened. A full smile came across her face. All of a sudden she blurted out,

"Since everything is okay at the dentist, why don't I head back to the country house with Martin and go to work on my part? There is nothing else I need to do here, is there?"

Elizabeth and Adam turned to one another. Their frozen expressions soon melted into affirmation as they contemplated Jennifer's suggestion. In harmony they responded, "Why not?"

Elizabeth instructed Jennifer to pack quickly. They would be leaving for the airport shortly. Elizabeth would call the airline to make the flight reservation. All Jennifer needed to do was ready herself. Jennifer smiled brightly and headed up the stairs.

"Why do I believe the girl likes you, Martin?" Elizabeth asked impishly.

Martin instantly shot her a violent glance, then thought better of it and dropped his eyes.

"Naughty, naughty Martin. I can read your mind."

Returning to their suite, Elizabeth secured Jennifer's reservation and e-mailed the change of plans to the girls. "Brigit is to stay put," her message said. "Jennifer is heading your way. Be ready."

Still alone in the bar, Martin and Adam spoke softly. Martin, sweating profusely, explained what had happened. Adam leaned forward to express his displeasure with Martin's stupidity. Martin sat up straight and handed Adam his notebook. Adam paged through the notes. Adam looked up and said, lowering his voice even more, "Obviously, you will not be able to see the architect tonight to brief him on the dentist's office to work out the plan. You had better meet him in Paris tomorrow morning. I'll have him on the first commercial flight. Was there much security there beyond what you noted?"

"No." replied Martin. "Just some motion detectors. I noted the company who did the installation and the model numbers of the units I found. With the floor plan, it should be possible to defeat them."

Adam responded, "Work out the plans tomorrow and make sure that the architect does not recognize the physical location of the building."

Martin excused himself to pack, and Adam returned to the suite. Elizabeth asked Adam how he felt about what had happened. Adam motioned Elizabeth to move to the other side of the room so no one would overhear them. He said, "Everything is okay, but I want to cut Martin out of the project as soon as Jennifer goes to Switzerland for the surgery. It's not really that I fear another incident, but I think we should use him to organize the virtual reality project. We haven't done one to this level before, and he is a problem solver. Since he will need to depend on the setup to complete the project, he should be there and have a feel for what is being done. We need to bring him back at the end. No one is better than Martin for what we have in mind."

She nodded reluctantly and responded almost whispering. "Yes, you are right. He is the best for that. Do you want to use Gerard for the VR project?"

"Yes, if it's okay with his mother. I hate using him in our projects because of his age, but I can't find anyone better who we can trust."

"I agree. He is one of a kind. I still remember when you investigated the company that was doing the computer Internet project and found out it wasn't a company, merely a fourteen year old boy behind the facade. He is a very clever young man."

"He's not fourteen anymore. Soon, he will need to go out and make his own life. We need to cut him loose. We need to encourage him to build a real life, not a shadow life like we live."

"I told his mother we would pay his tuition at any school he decides to attend. I think we should set up a trust fund for him that is administered out of Liechtenstein. He very likely will figure out what we have done in our projects after a while. It would be better if there were no ties that could ever be traced to us. I am confident that he'll keep it to himself, but who knows ten years from now?"

"Enough business. I think we should see the two 'lovers' off to the airport and then go out for a decadent dinner."

"In London?" she asked with a laugh. "Where might we go? You've got to be kidding."

"Well, if you feel that way, let's just go back to S & P. We love the food, and it is so hard to find a good place where we can relax. We can dress casual and let our hair down."

Elizabeth smiled an okay, and the two went back to work.

Later, Martin carried the bags to the awaiting car. They would have plenty of time to get to the airport. Adam asked Martin to call him when they were near the airport. Adam wanted to provide Martin with an update on the architect's travel plans. Jennifer and Martin settled into the back of the car, and the driver pulled away.

"Personally, I'm glad to get her out of here," Elizabeth said. "There's always the chance that someone from her past might recognize her and tell someone she is back."

"It's not over yet. Let's hope they get back to the country house without any more problems."

The two returned to Elizabeth's suite to freshen up for dinner.

"Adam, why don't you stay here tonight? There is plenty of room."

He smiled at her gently and said, "Sure. Why not?"

The suite was actually small, but Elizabeth was a little lonely. It happened to her every so often, and Adam knew that she would never be over her pain. Paying out justice to the killers was a charade. They had continued carrying out the project because it had seemed like the thing to do all those years ago. Neither now knew how to stop. The sad part was that although they kept crossing names off the list one by one to attain justice, the pain did not subside. There was no cure. There was no closure.

9

Paris, the next day

Jennifer came down to breakfast at Le Bristol in Paris and found Martin hovering over the morning paper, while sipping his coffee. Since the plane had arrived so late the evening before, Martin had decided it was better to stay in Paris for the night. Brigit was arriving to pick up Jennifer within the hour. Martin was counting the minutes.

Jennifer had fantasized that she and Martin would share a room, but he had insisted on separate accommodations. As she walked up to Martin, she thought, *I will capture him yet. I must be patient. I can break through his wall. I know I can.* She knew Adam was a better catch. It was just that she could not figure out his relationship with Elizabeth. Were they lovers? Were they just partners? It was impossible to tell. She was smart enough to know that putting the make on Adam would be like walking on thin ice. She would wait until she was better established before she tried for him. Martin was enough for now.

Actually, Martin had potential. He was generous. He was a little quirky, but she was confident she could learn to handle him. When she was honest with herself, she had to admit that he still scared her a little. The worst, though, was his appearance. He was so ugly. The upside was that no other woman would want him, that was for sure. She would just have to wait and see. Perhaps she would decide to set her sights higher.

After her surgery, she might have a good chance of landing a really wealthy man who wanted to parade his Princess look alike. *Not a bad idea,* she thought.

She knew her biological clock was ticking. She needed to settle down soon. Now, she was on her way. She had received her big break. She would use every ploy she could muster to make the most of the opportunity that was knocking at her door. She knew she could be ruthless, if necessary.

Over breakfast Jennifer and Martin made small talk. Actually, Jennifer did all of the talking. She tried to draw out Martin, but he merely answered her questions with minimum yes or no responses. She was not discouraged. *I just need to give him some time. I'll have him begging at my feet. Then, I can decide if I want him or if I should hold out for a better catch. Time is on my side.*

As Jennifer was finishing her fourth croissant, Brigit walked into the hotel's breakfast area. Seeing Jennifer and Martin seated at a corner table, she hurriedly walked up to them. Greeting Jennifer warmly but abruptly, she said "I'm parked just outside, and I can't stay there long. Are your bags in the lobby? I will load them."

Jennifer replied, "No. I'm not quite ready. I'll go up and finish. It won't take me but a moment."

Brigit smiled sweetly and offered to help, but Jennifer assured her there was no need. Jennifer disappeared to finish her packing, and Martin could not hold back his dismay any longer. "My patience has run its course with that callous bitch. She is so plastic. She tried to come on to me last night. Thank God you're taking her before I did something rash. She's all yours with my blessing."

"I'm overwhelmed by your kindness," Brigit replied.

Jennifer reappeared with her huge purse and a porter in tow. The theatrical entry was a bit much for Brigit who rolled her eyes and nodded at Martin to be quiet. Brigit's eyes twinkled and a huge smile covered her face as she turned to Martin and whispered, "I had better get the cow to the country house."

⊱┈⊰─○─⊱┈⊰

Several minutes later in the privacy of his room, Martin added to his notes. After calling Room Service to order a pot of coffee, he sat in what looked like a trance for some time. He resembled a Buddhist monk in deep meditation. Suddenly, he opened his eyes when he heard movement in the hall outside his room. Walking to the door, there was a soft knock and a woman called out, "Room Service." Always cautious, Martin stood to the side as he opened the door. The woman started to bring the tray into the room, but Martin silently took it from her and abruptly closed the door in her face. Shocked, she started to knock again to ask for his signature, but realizing that she was shaking all over, the woman thought better of it. He was so ugly and mean looking. She did not want to chance making him mad. She quickly scrawled a signature across the bottom of the bill and returned to her station.

Engrossed in his thoughts, Martin poured himself a cup of coffee, returned to his desk and continued to make copious notes for another thirty minutes or more. Finally, throwing his pen onto the floor and stretching his arms backwards, he relaxed. A soft smile emerged across his lips. *Adam will be pleased. I have discovered the solution. It will work.*

Feeling smug with himself, he opened his overnight bag and pulled out a pack of Gauloise cigarettes. It was an unopened pack. He maintained a policy of smoking only one cigarette from each pack and throwing the rest away. Smoking was a filthy habit, but it did provide him with a certain amount of masochistic pleasure. He never smoked in front of anyone. In fact, he rarely smoked at all. Often, he would go for a week or two without a cigarette. He was hard on himself, denying himself a cigarette anytime he craved one. He only smoked as a reward. Today, he had earned his reward. *I deserve this cigarette,* he thought as he inhaled deeply. He made a mental note to purchase another pack, as he wadded up this one, crushing the nineteen cigarettes that remained and tossing the mutilated pack into the trash. He allowed his well-earned cigarette to burn low and then pinched out the coal between his fingers. The pain almost made him wince, but he had learned to control pain. He enjoyed his mastery of it.

The phone rang as he was washing his hands to rid himself of the disgusting smell of the smoke and burned ash. He moved swiftly to answer it. The architect was waiting in the lobby. Martin gave the man his room number and returned to the sink to collect a towel. He first dried his hands and then went back to dry the phone. Martin reflected that it was an unwritten law. *As soon as your hands are wet, the damn doorbell or phone always rings.*

Martin answered the door in the middle of the knock, and the architect nearly jumped out of his skin. He was a small, nervous man. A Dutch Jew in his sixties. He had lived in England since the first years of World War II when his mother and he had escaped the Nazi holocaust. His father had not been as lucky. Beneath the man's right arm was an artist portfolio. In his left hand, he held an attaché case that contained the tools of his trade.

Martin cleared the table, and the architect laid out his paper to begin his drawings. The maid knocked on the door, asking if she could clean the room. Martin politely told her to go away. He said, "It's fine for today. You can clean tomorrow." The two men continued to work together for hours. Martin would answer questions about small details and then quietly sit and observe as the architect charted out his handiwork. By early afternoon, there was progress, but the task was far from complete. Starved, the architect asked if he could have something to eat, and Martin sent down for some snacks. By five o'clock, everything was assembled. Both men were satisfied with the result. They had a complete floor plan of the area that was critical. The rest didn't matter.

The architect handed Martin a slip of paper with a Luxembourg bank name and account number. "My fee should be paid to these coordinates," he informed Martin as he prepared to leave. Martin nodded his understanding and showed him out.

The architect was such a strange, little man. Martin had worked with him twice before. He appeared feeble and acted anxious. The casual observer would think him to be cowardly. Martin knew otherwise. Adam had helped locate the Dutch man who had turned in the architect's father to the Gestapo. The little man had extracted his own crude revenge.

Somehow, it seemed that nearly all of Adam's workers were bound together in a brotherhood of violence. It was a common thread, although few would suspect such activities of his helpers. The only exceptions were the electronics men. Martin chuckled to himself at that thought. They were electronics boys, not men. He doubted that any were over twenty. They were a strange bunch. Gerard for instance, was quite amazing. This kid could take anything electronic and massage it to do what he wanted. He could understand the most intricate of computer code or electronic pathways, but the kid was a miserable failure at understanding people. In spite of himself, Martin could not help but to feel protective toward these young kids who were involved in Adam's dark projects.

▶┼◆▶─O─◀◆┼◀

Upon her arrival back at the country house, Jennifer went back to work learning more about Di. She was dedicated to the project and to impressing Adam. Resigned that Martin was a nothing, Jennifer decided that the best way to attract Adam was to master her role to perfection.

She was sure she could land him, if she worked at it, and he was obviously rich. It would take time, but her pay was good, and she was already being treated like a Princess. It was a dream job.

She settled into this same routine over the next months. Her goal was to master her role. Then, she would write her own ticket. She began to eat, sleep and breathe Di. In her mind she knew that it was the only way. If she could convince herself she was Di, she could convince anyone.

During this period, Elizabeth came and went, offering countless suggestions and providing few complements. Her damn criticisms were almost more than Jennifer could take. What did the bitch think she was anyway, an acting coach? Brigit and Eva were constantly doting over Jennifer, and Martin was frequently there, too, even though it seemed he was no longer directly working on the project. He remained quiet and aloof, but Jennifer wondered if it wasn't just his way. Jennifer began to have doubts that he would ever show any real feelings for her. He ignored her regardless of what ploy she tried. She wanted him to make an advance. She wanted to snub him. She had set her sights much higher, and she would take pleasure in rubbing his nose in it. *Someday you will be sorry that you didn't come crawling to me. I want to make you squirm, you bastard.*

10

Virginia, December 1996

Elizabeth was jolted out of her daydream by the sound of the key opening the door to her suite. Adam entered and nodded. They were staying at a hotel in Virginia. The hunt was on.

Their target was preparing to leave for Switzerland the next day. He was at home packing. His wife was organizing dinner, and their son was home for the holidays. The man's mistress was flying out on a slightly later flight, and the two lovers were meeting in Atlanta to fly on together to Switzerland.

The house was being monitored acoustically, and so far, all the conversation was predictable. The wife was unhappy because her husband would be away for part of the holidays. She wanted to attend numerous parties, and he would not be there. Angrily she asked, "What will everyone think?"

The college-aged son was listening to his stereo, trying to ignore the sparring between his parents. Disgusted, he phoned a friend. He bragged that he was smoking a joint. He was spacing out to avoid the shit that was flying around at home. He suggested to the friend that they meet later to do some serious shit. The boy was stupid to talk of such things over the telephone line, but at this point it really didn't matter.

The target was trying to console his wife. He rationalized that he really didn't want to go, but he had no choice. His boss had ordered him to attend the conference. It was his job. There was nothing he could do. He apologized to his wife and told her he would try to shorten the trip. He promised that he would make it up to her somehow. Perhaps, they could go to Miami.

What a family. The only child was a druggie who was yet to be busted and have it stick. His father had pressured the police to let it go the last time and bought a good lawyer the first time. The first time the boy had been high on crack and drove over a black child playing near the street. The attorney succeeded in getting the homicide charge reduced to fleeing the scene of an accident in what must have been the plea bargain of all time. The father was a philanderer, a rapist, a thief and a murderer. The wife was an alcoholic who gave her son money to indulge his drug habit. She saw nothing wrong with a little fun at his age; after all, it had only been a black brat. Soon, the whole picture would change. None of their past sins mattered except the sins of the father. One in particular. He was the man who had masterminded the murder of Elizabeth's husband and only child.

Adam and Elizabeth reviewed the plan again. They brainstormed, trying to think of anything that could possibly go wrong. They had contingency plans for every possible scenario that they could imagine. They were as ready as they could ever be. In the backs of their minds was the knowledge that the unexpected had happened three years ago when they had tried to move against this same man. They had aborted the plan and disappeared into the night. They had now waited three long years for this opportunity. They had no schedule to meet. They could abort again, if necessary. There could be no mistakes. It was very important for them to extract their collective revenge over a period of time so no one would ever see the pattern. The only criterion was to extricate revenge perfectly, without any trail that could ever lead to them.

An eye for an eye, a tooth for a tooth. It was brutal but correct justice. The pattern was the same. Elizabeth's family had been killed in cold blood. Her reputation had been ruined by disinformation about her being involved in a drug deal gone wrong. She had been forced to hide from the police who questioned her involvement in the tragedy. She had been blamed as causing the whole disaster through false information leaked to the police by the real killers. She had escaped certain death, but her escape had cost Elizabeth her life as her natural self. To her friends, to her past, she was dead. She was living no longer as herself but as another. She had experienced death, her own; at the same time she was experiencing life anew. She was two people in one body, and the pain of the past was not dissolved by any joy of the present. She want-ed no less than what she was suffering for everyone who had been responsible for the agony that now seared her soul. She and her brother would extract it.

After this target, only two would remain. This target was the only one still working for the government. The other two left disenchanted years ago. It didn't matter. They would pay their prices in blood in due time.

At the moment, all attention was focused on the current target; it was important for him to pay dearly for his inhumane acts. There was even poetic justice for this target. He had been accused of sexual harassment several months before; when the plaintiff's case proved to be weak, the charges had been dropped. Earlier, two rape charges had been filed against him. One of the rape victims disappeared without a trace. After weeks of investigation that led to no concrete evidence, all charges were dismissed. The other rape victim had died in what was termed a drug overdose. Again, all evidence was circumstantial, and the allegations led nowhere. All of the earmarks of corrupted power were present.

Adam and Elizabeth went to bed before ten. They needed to be oper-ating at one hundred and ten percent for the events of the next day. It would be a long day. Tossing about, Elizabeth was unable to sleep; she was tortured by the memories of what had happened to her so many years ago. She wanted to put it all behind her, but she could not. She knew it would never be behind her. The memories were a part of her, still as vivid as the day the tragedy happened. They could not be destroyed. She could not even hide them.

Adam was sleeping soundly. That he could fall asleep on command was the family joke. He, also, would awake at the slightest sound and be completely alert. She rolled over and listened to her brother lightly snor-ing in the next bed and thought, *Oh God, how I love him.*

Even while sleeping, Adam could sense her agitation. He could read her mind. Almost asleep, Adam lifted his head and spoke softly, "I love you too." Then alert, he opened his eyes and smiled. "It won't be long now."

"You should be asleep," she replied.

"So should you. I guess we both are breaking the rules."

She closed her eyes forcing herself to breathe deeply, her remedy to create sleep. Within a few minutes, she dozed off feeling warm and pro-tected by her brother's love. Her dozing turned into a deep, restful sleep until she awakened startled, sensing movement in the room.

Adam was just getting up and smiled. "We beat the alarm."

They changed into the business clothes they had set out the night before. Adam was wearing a slightly ill fitting, dark gray suit that he had purchased off the rack; Brooks Brothers to be sure but with every appearance of a ready-made suit. She was wearing a black, tailored, polyester woman's power suit. Together they came across as low level government employees with aspirations. They checked their guns and holstered them out of sight.

Very inconspicuously, they left the room and the hotel. They drew no attention to themselves. They were driving a plain Chevrolet, black in color. Aside from the plates, it looked absolutely like a 'Government Issue' car. They drove for thirty minutes at the speed they had previously clocked to arrive near the house at the right time and parked around the corner.

This was the easy part. The house was on a cul-de-sac, and no houses faced the street where they had parked. There was no way the target could leave without their seeing him, and no one was likely to notice them parked on this thoroughfare. With it being very early on Sunday morning, there was no traffic at all.

They monitored the action in the house. They heard the shuffling of the suitcases and the catty parting remark made by the wife as the door closed. At about 5:30, the target drove by them, later than they had expected.

"He seems to be cutting it a little close for his flight. He certainly won't come back if he forgot anything. That's good news." Elizabeth commented.

Adam agreed. They decided it was safe to make their move immediately. The time of death was important. The only wild card was the maid, Maria. She was an illegal alien and would be anxious to keep out of trouble. Should she present any problem, they had a contingency plan that they would enact, although it was distasteful.

They drove into the driveway. It was circular, allowing them to stop directly in front of the door. Elizabeth and Adam put on their most concerned faces and knocked on the door. The wife, who was still in her bathrobe, answered the door somewhat startled. Elizabeth and Adam showed their government IDs, and the blood drained from the woman's face. Apologizing for stopping by so early, Elizabeth asked if they could come inside. They needed to speak with her about something. Adam assumed a passive role and said nothing.

The woman said, "Of course. Please come in." She brought them into the kitchen. She cautiously brightened up and said, "You just missed my husband."

Elizabeth responded, "We know."

The woman turned pale again.

Elizabeth began, "There have been some irregularities with your husband. We are here to try to keep them from hitting the press. An investigative reporter is accumulating a story about your husband and two other important men. Before I go on, I need to know if anyone else is home who might overhear us speaking."

The woman replied, "I am sure my son is asleep. The only other person here is the maid. She is sleeping, too. She has Sunday mornings off. She usually sleeps in and then goes to church. Would you like some coffee?" She suddenly interrupted.

"No, thank you. We are pressed for time," Elizabeth responded. Then, she continued, "I'm going to tell you some things that will be painful, but there is no other way. Did you know that your husband is having an affair?"

The woman stared at Elizabeth in disbelief. "Impossible. You must be mistaken. He would never... It must be someone else. He is loyal. He is a perfect husband."

Adam opened his attaché case and brought out a plain envelope of photos of her husband having sex with a young blond woman. She looked at each photo in disbelief; her expression turned from amazement to anger to disgust. She tossed the photos on the counter.

"He is flying with this same woman to Switzerland this morning. He is also embezzling funds from a discretionary account and banking them in Switzerland," Elizabeth continued.

Adam provided the woman with some papers that had been impeccably forged with her husband's handwriting. The papers listed offshore bank accounts and balances. She looked at them and holding back hysteria said, "I think I should contact my attorney right this moment. I don't want to say anything else."

Adam responded, "I understand."

It was of no importance now. She had handled everything, and her prints were on every document and photo. Adam then said, "There is one more thing." He again opened his attaché case and swiftly brought out a silenced Colt 45 automatic. It was a special 'Government Issue' gun, fabricated for use in covert operations. It had no serial number. It fired a special subsonic cartridge that made the shot sound like the mild pop of a champagne cork.

The woman had no chance to even register surprise when the bullet caught her under the chin and passed though the back of her skull spraying carnage across the counter behind her. Elizabeth caught her as her still twitching body collapsed to the floor. There were some small noises, but none that would awaken anyone. Elizabeth put on her cotton gloves and folded the financial papers, placing them in the pocket of the dead woman's robe. The photos she tossed on the clean counter. She folded the two envelopes that had contained the photos and papers and placed them in her bag.

Elizabeth decided to leave the kitchen the back way to collect the maid, as the pool of blood was getting so large. It would be difficult to leave the front way without a long jump, and she might awaken someone and attract attention too early. The time of death was within minutes of the target's departure. There would be no problem.

All of a sudden, Elizabeth had a second thought. She turned on her heels to pass around the kitchen and climb the stairs to collect Adam. He was just leaving the boy's room and nodded that it was done. Elizabeth quickly told Adam her plan, and he smiled.

She hurried down the stairs to find the maid. Entering the maid's quarters, she thought it incredible how these poor people must live to survive. The small room looked like it was out of a ghetto. The paint was drab and peeling, and the bedding would have been rejected by Goodwill as a donation.

The heavyset maid awakened startled and panicky when Elizabeth entered her room unannounced. Elizabeth instructed the maid to be quiet and listen to her, that she was from the Government. She spoke to the woman in Spanish with a slight European accent that the maid found a little difficult to understand. Elizabeth explained that the man of the house had, only a few minutes before, murdered his wife and son and then ran away.

Astonished, the maid started crying out in disbelief.

Elizabeth continued in Spanish, "It is possible that the man will worry that you saw or heard something. He may think you could testify against him. He even may try to kill you. Or he may say you killed his wife and son. You know he is an important man in the Government. People believe him. You are an illegal alien, aren't you? If the police question you, you will be thrown out of the country or maybe blamed."

The maid withdrew into herself sobbing, trying to look invisible. It was a quality that Elizabeth had often noticed with illegal aliens in the U.S. When threatened, they tried to be invisible.

Elizabeth continued, "I want you to come with me. I will help you to be safe, but you must do as I say. Pack everything now that means anything at all to you. You can never come back here. Do it as fast as you can. We have very little time."

The maid still sobbing and shaking scurried around gathering a precious few things. *How sad,* Elizabeth thought. *It took her less than thirty seconds to place her whole life in a battered cardboard suitcase.*

While Elizabeth was organizing the maid, Adam found the man's slippers in the master bedroom. Slipping them on, he walked down the stairs and entered the kitchen. He thought it quite amazing how large a puddle of blood results from a head-shot. *The heart must keep pumping for a while after the brain is dead. I really never thought about it before. I must remember to tell Elizabeth.* Adam stepped carefully in the edge of the puddle of blood, just so a very small amount would smear onto the sole of one slipper. He then walked upstairs and entered the boy's room. Finally, he returned to the master bedroom leaving the slippers in the closet where he had found them. A very careful homicide investigator would track them through the house. Changing back into his own shoes and making sure everything was in order, Adam descended the stairs. Elizabeth and the maid were waiting by the telephone near the entryway.

He nodded to Elizabeth, and the maid was given her instructions. She dialed 911 and set the handset on the table next to the phone. Her prints would now confirm that she had made the call. Then, Elizabeth and the maid quickly left for the car.

Adam turned on the small, high fidelity minidisk player. Sobbing emerged from the speaker. The person on the other end asked what was wrong, but the sobbing continued uncontrollably for a few seconds longer. Then, in a mixture of Spanish and heavily accented English, a shaken woman's voice said, "He killed his wife and son. He would have killed me, but I hid, and he couldn't find me. There is blood everywhere." Adam pushed the phone onto the floor where it landed with a loud bang. He exited by the front door, leaving it slightly ajar. The neighborhood was still dark, and no lights were showing in any windows.

Elizabeth was behind the wheel, and the maid was in the passenger seat. Adam slid into the Chevrolet's rear seat, and Elizabeth pulled out of the driveway turning left out of the cul-de-sac onto the through street. They were several blocks away when a police cruiser sped past them without a siren but with lights flashing.

"Efficient police here," Adam commented in Jauner-Tüütsch. "I thought it would take much longer for them to trace the call and find the address.

"Good neighborhood," Elizabeth replied.

They drove to the freeway entrance and asked the woman how much money she had in her bank account. She looked worried and told them that she only had about five dollars and didn't have a bank account. She offered to give it all to them for saving her life. Elizabeth told her in Spanish, "We don't want anything from you. We just want you to be safe. The man may try to blame you. We need to get you away from here. We just didn't want you to leave your money behind. If you did leave money behind, you might want to come back."

They drove on in complete silence for about forty-five minutes and took a freeway exit at a different community. They stopped at the bus station, and Adam told the woman in halting Spanish that they had something for her. He provided her with an envelope that contained ten thousand U.S. dollars in hundreds and a second envelope that contained about five hundred dollars in small bills.

The woman began to cry and laugh at the same time. Never before had she seen so much money. "You aren't going to hurt me?" She asked in broken English.

Elizabeth spoke calmly and told the woman to listen to her carefully. Elizabeth instructed the woman to hide the big money, buy a bus ticket with the small money and leave town immediately. "By tomorrow, the police will be looking for you everywhere. You should go home and leave America for a few years."

The woman hugged Elizabeth with wet cheeks and looked like she wanted to do the same for Adam. Changing her mind, she quickly turned and ran inside the station.

"When does the next bus leave?" Adam asked Elizabeth.

"In about ten minutes."

They moved the car to a vantage point where they could watch the stocky woman board the bus. Momentarily, they saw her get on; less than five minutes later the bus pulled out. Content that everything was going as planned, they pulled back into the parking lot.

Entering the bus station, Adam and Elizabeth found the man behind the ticket counter absorbed in a well-worn girlie magazine. Clearing his throat to attract the man's attention, Adam pulled out a twenty-dollar bill and told the man behind the counter, "I bet this woman that you would remember where the little Mexican woman was traveling."

The ticket agent looked up and said, "San Antonio." He pocketed the twenty and returned to the magazine.

As they were leaving Elizabeth said, "Good. She's heading back home. There's a pipeline for aliens that ends there."

Adam nodded agreement and sighed, "Step one complete. Now, on to step two."

Back in the car, they reviewed the plan's next steps in graphic detail.

Arriving at the airport, they searched both the short and long-term parking lots to find the target's car. It took them over an hour of driving slowly up and down aisles before they found the car. Parking a short distance away and walking to the car, Adam slipped a flat metal piece against the window and down into the door. The lock snapped up instantly, and Adam opened the door. Elizabeth stood casually to the side but was watching everything. No one was paying any attention. The lot was almost deserted. Adam placed the silenced gun under the driver's seat. Certain there were no prints to be found, he locked the door, closed it and checked again to make sure that it was locked. Then, he methodically wiped down the outside of the door to eliminate any prints or marks he might have left.

Elizabeth and Adam returned to their car to collect their luggage. While unloading the suitcases, Adam changed the car's license plates by slight of hand with a skill that only years of experience could have perfected. The two headed for the terminal, dropping the plastic Macy's bag that contained the removed plates deep into the Dumpster they had located during their trial run.

Entering the terminal, they went to their predetermined restrooms to change. Wearing cotton gloves, each placed the clothes that they had been wearing into a generic, plastic trash bag. They separately deposited each bag into two pre-selected Dumpsters. Regrouping as planned at the check-in counter, they had nearly an hour before their flight was scheduled to board. Satisfied with their successful mission, they headed for the Business Class lounge to relax over a well-deserved cup of coffee.

Their flight arrived in Switzerland ahead of schedule, a little earlier than the flight of their target. They had traveled to Zürich; their target was flying to Geneva. They entered Switzerland using their Swiss passports and took the green lane with the 'Nothing to Declare' sign. Adam was called over for a spot search of his carry-on, but the inspector quickly lost interest when he saw a heavyset man of about forty with two bulging duty-free bags. The inspector waved Adam on and turned to the more promising suspect.

Adam joined Elizabeth outside the restricted doors, and they headed to the railway station located in the airport terminal. Connecting at the Zürich main station, they boarded a train to the lakeside town of Zug, a tax haven within a tax haven. Many a famous man has disappeared to Zug. Marc Rich and Pincus Green are among the notables.

Upon their arrival in Zug, they took a taxi to their flat and, before freshening up, checked their e-mail. Nothing was pressing. They could respond to their messages later. Jennifer was doing well according to the girls, although she had been asking about Adam and Elizabeth.

"Adam, when this is over, I need to get back there to spend some time. I must see for myself how well Jennifer is really progressing. I must help her with the final touches. I know she is doing well, but doing well is not good enough for this project."

"I agree. We can't have anything go wrong on this one. There is no room for error."

Adam turned on the fax machine and placed a telephone call leaving a very terse voice mail. Seconds later, the fax machine began to hum as it printed out the newspaper clippings. The headline on the first article brought relief. It shouted "Husband Sought in Brutal Murder." Adam read the details and smiled. The police had released only a limited amount of information. It was clear that there was only one suspect. The police had deducted that the suspect had likely fled the country. *Good. It's going according to plan.*

Adam handed the papers to Elizabeth. She read the clippings and said, "We should expedite our plan. The police are much further along in their investigation than we imagined possible. The last thing we want is for the Swiss to arrest him. The Swiss police will find him quickly once they know he is in the country. They are so anxious to please the U.S. at the moment. They will be checking every hotel as soon as the request is made."

Adam nodded his agreement.

Adam's car was a special limited edition Audi Sport Quatro station wagon that was a bit of a collector's item in Europe, especially Switzerland. It was to the max with highly modified suspension, brakes supplied by Porsche and a nearly race-tuned turbocharged five cylinder motor. Adam had turned the car over to a race tuner for even additional modifications shortly after he purchased it. The car was unbelievably fast and handled like it was on rails.

They headed straight for Crans Montana where the target had made a reservation at the Crans Ambassador. Adam drove well over the speed limit and was nailed by radar at least once.

Fortunately, Switzerland is a very civilized country when it comes to speeding tickets. A sophisticated stationary camera not only shoots a photo but also records the vehicle's speed. Later, the fine is calculated, and the ticket is merely mailed to the offender. Generally, there is no delay resulting from being pulled over and ticketed by the police. There is no trying to talk the officer out of the ticket or fine. It is the Swiss version of a fly now, pay later plan.

Arriving at the gorgeous mountain resort before the hour they had given themselves as a deadline, they checked into the Mirabeau. The town was full. The snow was wonderful. Thinking that this might be the case, they had booked their room several weeks in advance.

As soon as their luggage was brought to their room, Adam went to the Ambassador to gather information. The target had not yet checked in. Returning to the Mirabeau, he collected Elizabeth and the portfolio. The two returned to the Ambassador together. Adam verified that the target had still not arrived, and he and Elizabeth found a well-positioned seating area in the hotel's lobby to wait.

Within half an hour, the target entered displaying the young trophy blond on his arm. He was loud and obnoxious, attracting attention to both himself and his companion. He took no note of Elizabeth or Adam seated to the side. The target registered, and the desk clerk copied his passport number. The paper trail was now complete.

After the two lovebirds were escorted to their room, Adam waited about ten minutes. He wanted to give the lovers a chance to unwind and unpack. Using the house phone, Adam dialed their room number. The telephone rang several times before it was answered brusquely by the target who sounded out of breath. Adam identified himself as being from the agency. Adam told the target he urgently needed to speak with him in person. Adam continued that he would be waiting in the lobby. The target, seeming alarmed, told Adam that he would be down in a few minutes. The target added that he was in the middle of something.

Adam responded, "She will wait. Just put on your pants and get your ass down here."

The target sputtered and then was silent for what seemed like two or three minutes. Finally, he replied, "I'll be right down."

Adam looked a bit dismayed at Elizabeth. "We waited too long to call. The randy old man has been playing bedroom games already."

She shrugged, suggesting everything would work out.

Shortly, the target appeared in the lobby, red faced and flustered. Looking around as though he was waiting for someone he did not know, Adam walked up to him. Adam commanded softly, "Follow me. We must talk in private."

They sat down in a corner away from the traffic flow, and the target asked, "Who the hell are you? I've never seen you before in my life."

Adam replied that he was from damage control. "There is a very serious problem. I wish I did not have to break this news to you, and I wish there were an easy way. Unfortunately, I know of none. Your wife and son have been brutally murdered. It was apparently part of a plot to discredit you. All of the evidence recovered by the police links you to the murder. They have issued a warrant for your arrest, and they are searching for you."

The target looked dazed for a moment and replied, "What is this bullshit? I don't understand what you are saying. I'm going to call and find out just who the hell you are. I don't believe a word you are saying."

Adam held out a folder containing the newspaper article and said, "Read this first. Then, call your home number, or contact the police, if you have any questions. Do not call the government under any circumstances. They will have to turn you over to the local police, and we will not be able to help."

The target scanned the newspaper clippings and, instantaneously, his belligerence disappeared. Horrified he said, "I need to call home." He stood up and walked in circles to find a phone.

Adam intercepted him and said, "Not that way. Let's go to a public phone. You don't need the call traced to here. The Swiss Police would arrest you in minutes."

The target nodded, and Adam led him outside to the PTT booth nearby. Providing a telephone card to the man, Adam stood outside the booth while the target made the call. The target listened and said nothing. He quickly put down the receiver. He opened the door in astonishment and said, "What the fuck. A man answered my phone at home. He asked who I was. I just hung up. What should I do? What am I going to do?" The target was distraught.

All was going according to the plan, although the target had expressed no concern for his wife or son. The man was an even bigger bastard than he had thought.

"It must have been a cop," Adam told him. "Let's leave it for now. We need to get you out of here. It won't take long for the police to figure out where you went."

Returning to the hotel, the target was shaking. Adam could not tell whether it was from the cold or out of fear. It was freezing outside, and the target was only wearing a thin shirt.

Back in the warmth of the hotel, Adam told the target to return to his room and pack an overnight bag. "Tell the slut that you are sorry but there is an emergency at the office. Only you can take care of the problem. Tell her you must leave but will only be gone for a few days and that you will come back as quickly as possible. Wish her a good time and ask her to miss you a whole bunch or some shit like that. I don't think you'll have to worry about her having a good time. Just have her charge everything to the room. And for God's sake, stop shaking and act normal. Another team will come by later to pick her up and get her home. Don't worry. Everything is taken care of already."

Elizabeth added, "Be fast, the Swiss Police will be looking for you shortly. If they show up, we won't be able to help. You need to hurry."

The target nodded and tried to pull himself back together before he went upstairs. The man was in shambles. He exuded fear and anguish all wrapped in one. He had yet to express any concern for his family. He took some deep breaths and somehow returned to his lover. He was back in record time with the woman shouting after him, "You can't do this to me."

Adam was standing by the door and motioned for the target to follow him. The target abruptly broke away from the woman with no show of affection, without even saying good-bye. Chasing after him, the woman lost heart when she saw it was snowing outside. She turned away in disgust and stormed through the lobby of the hotel back to the elevator. The man behind the desk had that Swiss look that can only be described as being baffled by foreigners.

Elizabeth was waiting in the driver's seat of the Audi at the front of the hotel. Adam loaded the target in the front seat and plopped himself into the back seat directly behind the target. They drove away from the mountains and headed toward Martigny. There, they took a turnoff that led to the tunnel toward Italy. They drove without incidence to Milan, changing drivers once. The target was silent the entire way. No questions were asked. No information was offered. In Milan they drove to the airport and parked in the lot. There, they provided the target with a forged Canadian Passport, a driver's license and other supporting papers. The whole suite had been purchased in Israel and was first class. He could probably go anywhere in the world other than Canada and experience no problem with the document.

Adam explained, "You will fly from here to Africa. You can hide out there in a safe house. No one will ever think of looking for you in Africa. There is a man who will accompany you. He will help you. He is a subcontractor to the agency. He does not know what is happening. It is important that you tell him nothing. Don't worry. The whole thing will be cleared up in a few days, and then you can return to your girlfriend. We will send her back to the States, so she does not become impatient waiting alone in Switzerland. You will be able to call her in a few days."

The target looked so grateful. He thanked both Adam and Elizabeth profusely. They chimed in together, "It's just our job. No thanks are necessary."

The three got out of the car and walked to the Milan airport terminal where Martin was waiting. After being introduced to Martin and
saying his good-byes to Adam and Elizabeth, the target accompanied
by Martin headed for the plane. Martin told the target that everything
was prepared. He should just try to relax and enjoy the flight. They had
open tickets and would catch the flight to Rome and then go on to
Cairo.

With the target properly deposited, Elizabeth caught a flight from
Milan directly to Geneva. She would travel to Crans and check out of
the hotel room at the Mirabeau. Then, she would continue on to France.
She was anxious to get back to the country house where she would stay
until it was time to move Jennifer. Elizabeth was running on nervous
energy, and Adam knew it. He thought, *She will collapse and want nothing but sleep and some quiet time for the next few days.*

Adam, too, felt a little weary. On the drive back to Switzerland, he
decided to spend a night in Ascona before traveling to Zürich for his
flight to Dallas. He welcomed the thought of unwinding from the pressures of the last few days, even if it was only for a few hours. He loved
Ascona. He hoped someday to purchase a vacation, retirement home in
this lovely area. Perhaps it would be rustica, his favorite architecture in
this part of Switzerland. He was beginning to feel his age. He wished he
had more time. He would have liked to extend his reprieve but business
was pressing. There was still much to do for the 'Legend.'

><+>-O-<+<

Martin and the target arrived in Cairo without incident and transferred to their later flight to Kinshasa. From there they took a Land
Rover on a long drive to the border crossing, pulling off the road and
sleeping in the car during the night. Martin felt calm hearing the night-
time sounds of Africa, but the target was fitful and, probably, awake all
night. At the border the next day, Martin spoke to the guards and handed over an envelope. Martin and the target were waved through without
any passport check.

It was blazingly hot and uncomfortably humid. Martin seemed unaffected, but the target was sweating profusely. They arrived at their final
destination and parked the Land Rover near a hotel. Martin explained
that he did not want to drive to the safe house in the Rover, as it was
sometimes watched. They took a taxi that looked like it should be in a
wrecking yard rather than on the streets, even in a Third World country.

Martin handed the address of their destination to the driver. After about a ten minutes, the taxi pulled to a stop in front of a large, rambling building that appeared purposefully dreary and oppressive. The building was surrounded by razor wire. Guards armed with submachine guns were posted at the entrance.

Martin told the driver to wait. "I'll only be a few minutes. There will be several more of these for you," and tossed him an American five-dollar bill. The driver's black face beamed and his white teeth shone like a light out of darkness.

Martin identified himself to the guard at the building's entrance. He and the target were admitted with a nod. Another similarly armed guard took Martin and the target to a barren room and asked them to wait. The room was small and starkly furnished with only a steel table and four steel chairs. Everything was bolted to the floor, even the chairs. The brownish paint was chipped, and the concrete walls were damp. The room had a musty stench that was hard to define. A combination of sweat, fear, urine, and tropical odors, all blended to create a uniquely African smell.

The target looked at Martin wearily and asked, "What kind of a place is this?"

"A prison, you asshole," Martin replied.

The target stood up and said, "What kind of shit is this? You are supposed to take care of me. I don't have to put up with this. I'll have your ass if you don't take me out of here instantly."

Martin commanded, "Sit down, asshole." His look convinced the target to comply.

The door opened, and a large black man entered wearing old military camouflage clothing. Martin stood, and the man gave him a hug. The man's face beamed with a full, familiar smile. He then turned and looked at the sweating man seated at the table and smiled again, but this time his eyes showed no humor. The black man demanded to the target, "Stay here. I'll be right back." The black man turned, and Martin started to walk out with him.

The target panicked and jumped up to leave. The target took two steps before Martin turned and dropped him with a well-placed kick to the crotch. The target collapsed like a sack of potatoes, curled up in a ball and began to vomit.

"Don't damage the merchandise," the black man chided with an evil chuckle.

"He won't be needing that equipment where he is headed," Martin replied.

The black man laughed heartily.

Then, Martin handed a thick envelope to the black man and turned around, spitting on the target before he left the room. The target was laying in his vomit curled in a fetal position, groaning and gently rocking back and forth.

The large black man escorted Martin to the entrance and watched as he departed in the taxi. The black man then returned to the room where the target had been left to recover from Martin's devastating kick. Sitting at the table and counting out the money bill by bill while humming tunelessly, the black man glanced at the target who was now on his hands and knees attempting to get up. The black man looked up and said, "Whitey, that's a good position. You might as well get used to it. I've got five hundred black men in lockup who would kill for a little white ass like yours. Oh yes. I almost forgot. I have a greeting from someone for you." The black man then bent down and whispered a woman's name in the target's ear. From the target's reaction, the black man decided that the name carried some very special significance. A wail of despair escaped the lips of the target.

The black man laughed again and called a guard. The black man told the guard to inform the prisoners that he would personally carve up the man who shagged this Whitey to death. "After all, there are no women allowed. There is no doubt a man needs a little ass now and then. We all know white ass is the sweetest. We want him around here for a long, long time." The black man knew that with AIDS rampant among the prisoners, this Whitey did not have a chance of satisfying the boys for too long a term. But, they would do the best they could before he died of the slims.

>−⊷−O−⊶−◅

Adam was again in his usual suite at the Mansion in Dallas. He had become somewhat of a regular posing as the 'Legend's' brother. The e-mail message from Martin arrived more quickly than expected. It was short but to the point. "Project completed without incident. En route home. M."

Adam was pleased that one more name could be eliminated from the list. Progress had been made in fulfilling their commitment of revenge. Adam encrypted a quick e-mail to Elizabeth telling her that the patient had been properly admitted for his rehabilitation as prearranged.

Adam was relieved that he had finally been able to schedule the closing of the 'Legend's' Dallas home. Finding the home had proved far more difficult than he ever imagined, especially since Di had provided so many criteria that he had never anticipated. The more he thought about her, the brighter he decided she was. *This woman is truly intuitive,* he thought, *almost superhuman. I think I'm making her superhuman, if only in my own mind. Everyone else seems to feel the same way about her, so why not me as well?* He leaned back in his chair cradling his head in his hands and remembered their conversation of several weeks before.

She had told him that her feelings are complex. The life she had known for some fifteen years had always placed her in the spotlight. She had learned to be the smiling hostess, the desired cover girl for the charities of the world. As abruptly as she had gained stardom, it was being stripped from her. In her new life, she would be an ordinary human being to the outside world. No one special. No one to be sought after. This time it was her choice, her decision. In appearance, in speech patterns, in mannerisms, in background, in likes and dislikes, she would be a new person, nothing special. This new image would only pose as her real persona. All the while her true self would be hiding within. She would not lose her real soul, the essence of her being. She would ache for the closeness of her boys. Her constant dream would be just to have one short conversation with them. She would pine for the fanfare and the attention, even though she hated the press. She would even miss the anxiety of the untruths that were written about her and her loved ones.

Her new home needed to reflect her new image. It would assist her in becoming her new self. It could not be too grand. It would serve as a constant reminder of her new identity. She wanted it to be safe. Something simple and carefree. Nothing stuffy and formal. She had requested contemporary architecture that lent itself to casual, intimate entertaining.

Di thought of herself as strong and capable of mastering whatever challenge was placed before her. When she married Charles, her goal had been to become worthy of being royalty. She welcomed speech and diction lessons and mastered the required accent. At the time, she could not imagine a challenge more stimulating.

Now, she was faced with a new challenge, an undoing of sorts. Her new surroundings would be formative in her search for success. Adam was grateful that she had called to explain her wishes. Her desires were quite different than the ones Adam had outlined to the Realtor. His misjudgment had proved costly in time and money when he withdrew an offer, losing the earnest money he had deposited on a secluded and traditional Southern estate.

Startled back to reality, Adam looked at his watch realizing he had cut it too close for the drive to the closing. He would just take a cab. He prided himself on being prompt, feeling it insulting to those he was meeting to arrive late. Flying down the hall towards the elevator, he stopped dead in his tracks. It was such a hot day that he had walked out the door without his jacket. "Shit," he mumbled to himself. He turned away and jogged back to his suite; the door was wide open. The maid was straightening up after him. Taking quick note, he marveled at this hotel. Uncannily, the staff calculated his every move and was able to maintain everything in perfect order. At the same time, no one ever interfered with his privacy. Such service could not be taken for granted. *These people are fantastic.* Adam posted a note in his mainframe brain to tip each staff member heartily on his departure.

11

France, March 1997

Adam turned onto the long lane that led to the country house. He always took the road slowly to enjoy the idyllic pleasure of the huge trees that lined either side the roadway. It seemed as though the arms of rich green foliage were outstretched to provide protection and comfort to the weary traveler. Pulling up in front of the house, he parked his Audi. He had driven from Switzerland, stopping only for gas and a coffee. The plan was to return with Jennifer and Elizabeth by car.

He felt physically exhausted, but he was mentally alert. He approached the front door with Yusuf and Reem by his side. Yusuf was Martin's replacement for the next phase of the project, and Reem was Yusuf's wife. Reem was a talented make-up artist and hairdresser. She would assist Elizabeth and Jennifer in learning the ways of Islamic women.

Brigit greeted the three travelers at the door, obviously struck by Reem's appearance. Reem was wearing hijab that covered her head and face with only two peepholes for her eyes. Yusuf was dressed in western fashion. Not a word was spoken.

Before the three had time to walk over the threshold, Martin appeared from the kitchen. He nodded toward the study's closed double doors. The vibrant resounding voices of two women engaged in a heated argument filtered out from within. The voices became louder and more strained. The sense of urgency was imminent. Adam returned Martin's nod and knocked on the closed doors. Not waiting for a response, he entered to find Elizabeth and Jennifer embroiled in a shouting match. Adam noticed that Elizabeth's voice had dropped slightly in timbre. A prelude to violence. *Oh shit!*

Seeing Adam, Jennifer spun onto him and launched into a foul language tirade about Elizabeth. Adam stood calmly in the face of the storm that would have made a sailor blush. When Jennifer paused to catch her breath for the next onslaught, Adam softly said, "I can't believe the Princess ever speaks like this."

Jennifer's face turned several hues of red, and she spun and glared at Elizabeth.

Attempting to take charge of the moment, Adam directed the two women to accompany him to the living room. He said firmly, "We will have no more of this. We have work to do. There are some people I want you to meet."

In the living room Adam introduced Yusuf and Reem to the two women. Elizabeth rose to the occasion and greeted the couple warmly. Jennifer, still fuming, ignored Yusuf. She refused to engage in even courteous small talk with him. Reem's hijab startled her and provoked her even more. Starting to attack Adam once again, the atmosphere became tense. Responding to Adam's facial gestures, Martin quickly intervened to show the two newcomers to their room.

Realizing the situation was out of control, Elizabeth tried to curtail her mounting anger and force herself to be calm. Knowing her as his twin, Adam could feel her seething in spite of the placid exterior.

Jennifer spun around looking directly at Elizabeth and shot, "This is the craziest group of bastards I have ever met. The two krauts who never sleep. The asshole driver with less warmth than a marble statue, and now you bring in a rag-headed Arab and his ninja woman. This place is a regular bloody zoo. What's next, a fucking dancing bear?"

Elizabeth bit her tongue and pierced Adam with an evil look.

Adam put on his best smile, took a deep breath and said, "Things seem a little hot here. Maybe everyone has cabin fever. Why don't we try to start over and go out for a nice dinner at that marvelous little restaurant just down the way?" Like most men, Adam was at a complete loss when he found himself included in a female conflict. His modus operandi was to take the path of least resistance and gloss over the problem. A regular male-oriented denial syndrome.

Elizabeth rolled her eyes, and Jennifer looked at him like he was from a different planet.

Damn it, he thought. *What I said was worse than amateurish, but, maybe it will defuse the situation a little.*

Quickly, his hopes were quashed. Jennifer did not let up. She continued forcefully, "Adam, I must speak to you in private. Right now. This very minute."

With no choice but to agree, Adam led the girl back to the study and closed the door. Jennifer gave no slack in airing her complaints. "Elizabeth is too God damn, fucking demanding. She has no patience. She is a total bitch. No, she is more than a total bitch. She is a total fucking bitch. She does not understand me in the slightest way. She pushes me constantly. I never do anything that satisfies her. All she can ever say is 'no.' I am so fucking sick of hearing 'no' that I don't even listen to her anymore. All she ever says is 'no' to this and 'no' to that. Your accent is too hard. Your voice is too loud. On and on, that bitch can never be pleased."

They spoke for about forty minutes. Actually, Jennifer did all of the talking. Adam played the role of the perfect listener. Jennifer seemed to calm down the more she vented her emotions. Adam thought it better to allow her to continue to ramble on and on repeating the same complaints again and again in different colors and shapes.

When Adam finally felt that Jennifer had expelled all of her frustration and that nothing more was to be accomplished, he told her that he would work on the problem. He said, "I'm confident everything will work out. It's just a little misunderstanding. I'll speak with Elizabeth. Can't we forget about it all for tonight and go for a nice dinner? I'm absolutely starved."

Agreeing somewhat begrudgingly, Jennifer said, "I expect you to speak to Elizabeth tonight." She turned away and stomped out of the room slamming the door behind her.

Adam moved onto the next crisis, Elizabeth.

It started with Elizabeth's auspicious statement, "I love you dearly, my precious brother, but you are a complete idiot when it comes to dealing with women."

Adam replied simply, "I may be an idiot, but my approach works. No one is screaming at the moment, not that I could hear it after that scorching onslaught."

The two scowled at each other for a few moments until smiles that turned to laughter began to spread over both of their faces. Feeling that Adam was now ready to listen to what she had to say, Elizabeth started.

She explained that Jennifer was the most selfish, stubborn and conniving female she had ever met. After observing her all of these weeks,
Elizabeth was convinced that the girl was absolute trouble looking for a
place to happen. Elizabeth concluded, "If anyone ever lets her get the
upper hand, she'll hold it for life."

Then, Elizabeth went on to confess that the only reason she had not
strangled the girl and moved onto another choice for a double was that
Jennifer was not only good, she was inspired. Jennifer was everything
they had hoped for and much more. The more Elizabeth pounded on the
girl, the better she became. She was relentless in perfecting her role. She
could not only play the part, she could play it to perfection.

Elizabeth's only concern was whether Jennifer would be willing to
go along with them. Would she follow their orders? If they gave Jennifer
any slack, even the tiniest bit, she would be out of control. Elizabeth
said, "Adam, she has a mind of her own. We must keep her on a very
short leash, or she'll be holding press conferences. She is attracted to
any male, as long as he has a potentially active weenie. She tried everything to seduce Martin and was completely shameless. Once she is
ready, we need to keep her away from men, all men. She is as subtle as
a bitch in heat. My God, can you imagine the problem if she jumped into
bed with someone while playing her role, and the press got wind of it?"

Adam thought for a moment and said, "Maybe we can use her
defects, as well as her pluses, to our advantage. I think she has the hots
for me."

"Don't flatter yourself. She's conniving and deceitful. She'll wrap
your weenie around her little finger and lead you around by it. You are
a male and have money. You could be a leper, and it wouldn't make any
difference."

Around eight, the four of them, Adam, Elizabeth, Jennifer, and
Martin climbed into the Audi. They had made a dinner reservation at one
of Adam's favorite restaurants in the nearby village. Martin was at the
wheel, and Elizabeth sat in the front seat with him. She welcomed the
break from Jennifer's spiteful tongue. Jennifer joined Adam in the back
seat and was all charm and smiles with him.

As often is the case in France, the restaurant was one of those special finds, hidden away in a tiny village known only to the locals. They
sat with Jennifer and Adam on one side of the table and Elizabeth and
Martin on the other. As Adam pulled out Jennifer's chair to seat her, she
hooked her gigantic purse over the back corner of the chair. Everyone
watched in fascination as the chair fought a valiant but losing battle to
remain upright with the huge burden that had overbalanced it. Adam

tried to save the day with a quick but unsuccessful lunge to grasp the purse or chair and was almost pulled to the floor himself as he made his off-balance dive. His only reward for his attempted gallantry was a few stifled snickers from the local audience.

After a champagne aperitif, in concert they ordered the 'menu digus-tation' that had been enthusiastically suggested by the wife of the owner. The first course was saumon fumé avec sauce raifort chantilly. It was followed by the house specialty, canard à l'orange, prepared to absolute perfection and presented with the masterfully artistic hand of the owner-chef who still grew his own vegetables and raised his own game. Adam chose a marvelous, full-bodied 1989, Nuits-Saint-Georges, La Richemone. The vintner was one of the best, Alain Michelot.

Several glasses of wine later and only halfway through the meal, Jennifer's temperament had changed completely. Her anger had dissi-pated, and she was more her old self. She was all of a sudden enthusi-astic about Elizabeth's travels and was chatting softly and amicably with her. The events of earlier in the day had melted away and were forgot-ten. While looking directly at Elizabeth and excluding everyone else at the table from their private conversation, Jennifer placed her hand on Adam's inner thigh and gave it a squeeze. *Damn it, the last thing I need now is a horny woman,* he thought.

Adam was sensitive to the fact that part of the reason Jennifer was putting the make on him was because she was seated across from Elizabeth and Martin. Martin had lacked interest in her. The girl did not understand Adam's relationship with Elizabeth. If they were lovers, tonight would be Jennifer's coup to win Adam away from Elizabeth. Her hand again began to wander closer and closer, until Adam finally reached down, gave it a tender squeeze and moved it back to her lap.

After a selection of French cheeses and another bottle of Nuits-Saint-Georges, dessert was served with a flair, a mousse au chocolat gar-nished with fresh strawberries to die for. They finished with expresso and marvelous petits fours.

As they allowed the feast to settle and enjoyed a second round of expressos, Jennifer's hand, once again, crept back into Adam's lap. She began to make playful little movements. At first, Adam tried to ignore her advances. Jennifer focused her attention on Martin and Elizabeth involved in a discussion about the area's wines. Above the table it appeared that she was ignoring Adam, but under the table the scene was very different. Adam started to move her hand away again but thought better of it. The operation was imperative, and, after all, he was no virgin.

With conversation flowing, they all let down even more. What could have been a disaster had turned into a thoroughly enjoyable evening. Amidst the light conversation, Jennifer could not keep her mouth shut about her job. Silence was of vital importance to the success of the operation. Still, she seemed completely impassioned to talk about her proficiencies as Di's double. Jennifer offered much more information than what Adam and Elizabeth wanted Martin to know, at least, at this point in the project. Later, Martin would be told more, but not before it was necessary.

The project was rapidly approaching a decisive point. In a few days it would be too late to turn back. Adam and Elizabeth had so far failed in their plea to convince Jennifer to reveal nothing to anyone. The success of the operation now hinged upon their ability to control Jennifer. They needed to find a way to insure that she would keep her mouth shut. An inappropriate comment made at the wrong place could mean the end of the project and the end of the only hope for Di. This caper was by far the most risky and politically sensitive project Adam and Elizabeth had ever undertaken. Before they had risked their lives. Now, so much more was at stake.

Back at the country house, Yusuf had impatiently awaited the foursome's return. He had changed into Arabic attire. Jennifer was unable to camouflage the fact that she found his dress disgusting. Bright eyed, Yusuf was anxious to go to work. He was perturbed that Adam had left him stranded with nothing to do. At the very least, Adam could have outlined Yusuf's first assignment, allowing Yusuf to commit it to memory during Adam's absence.

Yusuf owed Adam his life and treated him like a father. He was so anxious to please. Adam assured Yusuf that everything was on schedule and suggested that the most important thing was for all of them to get some rest. It was already very late. Work would wait until morning. The day would be full. There was much to accomplish. A bit disappointed, Yusuf departed to his quarters with a flurry of swirling cloth.

While talking with Adam, Yusuf's eyes had penetrated through Elizabeth and Jennifer; he acted as though they were not even there. He acknowledged only Adam and then Martin. He treated Martin like an inferior, as though Martin was a servant or inconsequential nuisance.

When Yusuf was out of earshot, Jennifer asked, "Adam, do you only hire rude men or is it by accident that all of your male employees are rude?"

Adam returned a glare and said, "It is by intent, my dear. I require that each potential employee take a rudeness test. Only those with superior marks are hired."

Jennifer realized that she was approaching the point of stepping over the safe boundary. After all, Adam was her boss, the master. He could fire her as quickly as he had hired her. She decided it was best to drop the subject.

It was true Adam only hired the best; it was for a good reason. It made him look better. The situation was no different for Jennifer. She had to be the best, and part of being the best was acting her role of the Princess, even when she was not working. Now was a perfect opportunity to show her abilities. Her motive was twofold. She needed to set a hook into Adam so that she could be more secure. She was not going to let him escape like Martin. Assuming her best stage presence, she asked carefully, "Adam, I would like for you to see what I have learned. Could I perform my role for you?"

Feeling tired, Adam was about to suggest that they wait until morning when Elizabeth interjected, "What a wonderful idea, Jennifer. Why don't you perform the short skit based on the last film segment of Di. The one we have been rehearsing."

Jennifer responded, "Great. I'll get ready quickly. Should I wear the suit?"

"Of course. Make it perfect for Adam."

Jennifer disappeared to prepare herself, and Elizabeth explained to Adam that they had been refining this piece for several days. Di had sent it to them with several other video clips. "Why don't you watch the original first before Jennifer performs?" Elizabeth started the tape and continued, "I think you will be satisfied when you see Jennifer's interpretation."

Jennifer had lost the necessary pounds, much to Elizabeth's amazement. The girl still ate too much, but her weight was now perfect. Di had provided the suit, complete with accessories that she had worn for the event. Jennifer had been practicing in costume to help her truly feel the role of the Princess. Wearing the actual clothing made such a difference.

Jennifer entered the room and turned on the main lighting to better illustrate her role. She had donned a wig, and with her make-up, she looked enough like Di to pass at first glance. She acted the video segment with motions and dialogue perfectly memorized. When finished, she continued with an improvisation that lasted about ten minutes. It was uncanny. Jennifer had perfected her part far better than Adam had imagined possible. She could easily fool anyone who had never met Di in real life, perhaps she could fool even some who had. The facial differences were slight and well minimized by the make-up. Still, they were obvious to a keen eye on second glance. Jennifer's eyes looked the same. Her voice was ever so slightly huskier than Di's, but the intonation was accurate. The speech pattern was identical. The mannerisms perfect.

Adam rose in applause, and Elizabeth followed, giving Jennifer a standing ovation. "It was a magnificent performance," Adam affirmed. "Damn, you have done it. After the surgery, you will be able to pass with anyone who does not know Di intimately. We will only need to keep you away from those who know her very well. Maybe we can even fool them if we are able to control the circumstances."

Jennifer took a stage bow and then threw her arms around Adam asking, "You really are satisfied then? You mean it?"

Adam dropped to one knee and kissed her hand, saying, "You are magnificent, my princess. Now, it is time for a good night's sleep. Tomorrow we begin the next segment of our project."

Smiling a look of contentment that she had more than satisfied her master, Jennifer's eyes spoke for her. She thanked Adam for the lovely evening and courteously told both Elizabeth and Adam good night. Silently, she slipped out of the room.

Taking a nightcap of mineral water, Elizabeth and Adam spoke softly for more than an hour about the next segment of the plan. Everything was, for the most part, under control. Jennifer could play the role well enough, if not perfectly. If she would follow their instructions, there would be no problem. Could they keep her under control? This was the question.

Jennifer was turning into somewhat of a wild card, always so anxious to voice her opinions. Achieving the goal was possible. Adam could feel it and so could Elizabeth. They both now had complete confidence. Still, they could not be too cautious. They could not predict what Jennifer might do, and they could not risk even one mistake. They had no choice but to monitor her every move. Exactly how was not yet determined. Adam and Elizabeth agreed to sleep on the problem. Maybe one of them would glean the magic key to assure Jennifer's loyalty and commitment to the project.

>-I-◆>-O-<◆-I-◀

Entering his room, Adam immediately smelled Jennifer's perfume. *Shit, this is the last thing I need. Hell, maybe it's a good thing. She might be easier to control, if she thinks she has me lined up. If she wants me badly enough, she may be afraid to do anything to offend me. Maybe this is the key we talked about.*

She was lounging in his bed. Adam was about to make a comment about entering the wrong room when she sat up and reached her arms out to him. The sheet fell from her upper body and revealed her beautifully rounded, sensually shaped breasts. Her nipples were darkened and erect. Noticing the several small moles that appeared on her body, Adam catalogued another need. *We cannot forget to match the girl's moles to those on Di's visible body. Someone could catch the discrepancies in a photo. This must be the reason she is waiting for me. I needed to think of this, and I should have thought of it before. Just like Elizabeth always says, "things always work out." It's just that they sometimes need a little help.*

Not really knowing what to do or how to handle the situation, Adam undressed without saying a word. He entered the bed knowing he did not want what was happening. She quickly took the lead, thrusting herself over his body onto her hands and knees. Without foreplay or soothing of any kind, she mounted him robustly. Her naked, smooth body hung over him as he lay there helplessly accepting her intimacy. She was wild and passionate beyond any expectations, kissing and sucking him and, finally, draining him of his passion. Then, almost instantly, she started all over again demanding more and more until she pumped him dry. In the afterglow, she curled up in his arm and gently caressed his chest. She changed from a wild driven animal to a child sheltered in his arms. *This woman has really been around the block, but she makes it seem like it's so real. How in the hell does she do it?* Adam then realized, *This is the way she should be. After all, she is still an actress whether in or out of bed.*

Several minutes later, she broke the silence and asked if she was more satisfying than that cold blooded Elizabeth. He told her that he wouldn't know. He had never made love to Elizabeth. She grabbed him tighter demanding, "Promise me that you never will."

"That's an easy promise, my princess. I have no physical attraction to Elizabeth. She is no sexual threat."

Jennifer reached down and grabbed his organs squeezing them tightly saying, "Not good enough. Promise me, damn it. Like you mean it." The child had disappeared and was again replaced by savage instincts. She was almost like a cornered and wounded animal expelling the last burst of adrenaline. The last vision of hope before experiencing an untimely, torturous death.

"Shit, please let go of me. I promise. I promise," Adam cried out in pain.

As she loosened her grasp, he began to breathe again. She cuddled up to him snuggling tightly taking deep and restful breaths. *Damn, it felt like she was going to tear it off.* After several minutes of silence, he realized that she had gone to sleep. *I'm going to have to play this very carefully, or she'll end up running the show. I'm not sure I won round one. This will be like walking a tightrope.*

Awakened just before dawn in the middle of an amazingly erotic dream, Adam discovered that what was happening was no dream at all. Finding it difficult to rationalize between reality and his dream world, she continued to pound on him extracting more and more of his manhood. As alertness settled in, he found his manhood drooping. His heart was pounding. Her seduction had drained his juices dry. He was like putty in her hands. Finally, after several minutes of lying in the aftermath of ecstasy, his breathing returned to normal. Getting hold of himself, Adam brought himself back to reality. He forced himself to take charge of the situation. How could he control her if he melted under her feminine spell? He could not allow this to happen again. Softly, he suggested that she return to her room. "It will be very bad for the morale of the staff to know we have been sleeping together. We must be discreet."

After a long and passionate kiss, she climbed out of bed. She turned slowly in front of him in the dim light and told him, "Remember, I am yours. Today and always." Gazing at him in satisfaction, she stooped to pick up her robe and left quietly closing the door without a sound.

Jennifer had not been gone for more than five minutes when Elizabeth entered his room and sat on the bed. Adam groaned and asked, "When will I ever get some sleep?"

"Oh, you poor man," Elizabeth replied. "Want to talk?"

"We had better," he responded, and they lapsed into Jauner-Tüütsch. They played out the different scenarios until the sun rose. They decided that in the overall scheme of things, Jennifer's desire for Adam might be an advantage, if it could be controlled. The difficult part would be to control her demands. He could not allow himself the luxury of again falling under her spell. He would make himself available every so often to keep her hooked but, hopefully, not on a regular basis. He would travel more than planned to avoid having to deal with her. Elizabeth would be responsible for the babysitting. He would have a difficult balancing act. The girl would want him every night, but he would make it clear that such an arrangement was impossible. He would intrigue her by suggesting that after the job was complete, if she was still interested, they could be together all of the time. If she thought him a good enough catch, she might conform. As the sun started to rise, Elizabeth said, "I had better leave before the entire household thinks you are the local stud."

Smiling but agreeing, Adam said in all seriousness, "Personally, I'm worried about my manhood. I need to get the hell out of here before she decides to return and tear it off."

At breakfast, Jennifer appeared with a bounce in her step beaming in confidence. She took a seat between Adam and Elizabeth. Reem and Yusuf were present, and Reem was dressed in traditional western clothes. The group ate quietly, exchanging only necessary pleasantries. No one seemed to have much to say. The silence seemed pregnant.

As Brigit cleared the dishes, Adam asked if Reem, Elizabeth and Jennifer would join him in the study. It was time to start the next group of classes. Once settled in the study, he closed the door tightly. He quietly explained the logic. "Once the surgery is complete, it will be a major problem for you, Jennifer, to move about undetected. The face is too well known, and even with superficial disguises, there is the chance that someone might comment about how much you look like Di. This could lead to later suspicions. We simply cannot afford the risk. The best place to move around is here in Europe, especially in Continental Europe where many women follow the custom of hijab. Reem, you take it from here."

Reem fell into her well-prepared dialogue. "Hijab is not merely a covering dress, but more importantly, it is behavior, manners, speech and appearance in public. Dress is only one facet of the total being. Women must do everything to avoid attracting attention to their femininity. To merely wear the cloak and veil would not fool anyone for long. I will help you learn how to walk and relate to men. You must master many qualities before you will be able to pass as Islamic women in any environment. When you can assume the role of the Islamic woman, both of you will be able to move about invisibly, especially in France where there are so many people of the Islamic belief."

Adam slipped out as Reem began to demonstrate how to walk so that there was no jiggling of the breasts or bottom. Finding Yusuf, they conferred on the plan for the next segment of the project. Yusuf commented about the level of tension in the air and asked if it would affect the outcome of the project. Adam told Yusuf that he thought they had a handle on it now. Adam was optimistic that everything would work itself out.

There was much to organize. Martin had already left for Belgium to prepare for his next assignment; it was an aspect of this same project, although Martin would not be aware of this until later.

Eva and Brigit would secure the country house the next day after everyone was gone. They would insure there were no traces, including fingerprints from anyone who had been there. All the bedding would be washed; every surface that could possibly retain a fingerprint would be cleaned, and all paper would be destroyed. It was a formidable task; it would be simpler to burn the place down, but it was such a lovely retreat. There would be a good use for it again in a few months. Further, a fire might attract attention of the wrong kind. It was worth the clean-up effort.

Yusuf and Reem would leave the next morning. They would meet Adam, Elizabeth and Jennifer in Gstaad in two weeks. Adam had provided Yusuf with a shopping list of things that needed to be acquired and contacts that needed to be made. Everything was prearranged; all had been programmed to go perfectly as in a good novel. Unfortunately, nothing ever happens as it does in a good novel. Something always goes wrong. Murphy's law was not written with a story line in mind.

They all regrouped at lunch time, sitting together around the large table in the kitchen. Reem explained to Jennifer the method of eating. Not that she would ever need to apply the lesson, but the information would help her to better understand the psychology behind hijab. The group spent a few minutes chatting after the meal, but Adam's schedule for the day was precise. They had only three hours to rehearse before performing for him.

Adam was working away at his computer when the three announced they were ready. Three black ghosts drifted through the room. He watched with fascination as they glided along.

The idea was a good one, a perfect way to hide Jennifer. The only problem would be to teach Di, as well, so that the swap could be accomplished without incident. The problem was easily solvable, even if it required cutting an instruction video. Di could play the video and copy the mannerisms in private. She was a quick study and well schooled in accomplishing the task at hand without notice. Adam decided to e-mail a message to her to see what would be the best solution. Perhaps she could speak to an Islamic woman's group. There were many possibilities; it was merely choosing the best alternative.

Adam was also concerned about the height of Di and Jennifer, as both were abnormally tall for a woman from the Islamic part of the world. He thought the appearance could still be believable. It was only that it might be memorable as well. Therein was the danger. He entered a reminder on his list of things to do, along with the problem of the moles on Jennifer's body. Worried about the moles, Adam decided to take a break and watch a video of Di to catalogue any skin imperfections or moles she might have on her arms, back and shoulders. He had already registered those on Jennifer.

Dinner was served at home and was excellent. Eva had developed into an accomplished cook. She prepared a full oriental meal, using fresh ingredients she had obtained from a Vietnamese market located about twenty kilometers away. Hot and sour soup was just short of painful. The stir-fried vegetables were crisp in the center, absolutely mouthwatering. The crispy beef was so much in demand that it was finished early in the meal. Eva skillfully prepared a secondary substitute, a wonderful chicken dish. They ate like there was no tomorrow and finally stopped, not because they could eat no more but because there was no more food.

Elizabeth, feeling as though she had eaten more than too much, excused herself from the table and said, "I need to go for a walk. If gluttony were a crime, we would all be convicted after tonight. Not even OJ's Dream Team could get us an acquittal."

Laughing, they all agreed and decided to accompany her. In spite of the initial discomfort of overeating, the walk refreshed everyone. The fresh air of the cool evening revitalized their inner beings. Returning to the country house for the last evening of this part of the project, their spirits were elevated. They were moving forward in their plan. Everything was in order. They all knew that nothing would ever be the same again. They had reached a turning point, and there would be no going back.

>-+-<>-O-<+-+-<

Adam stepped out of the shower to the sound of the closing of his bedroom door. He toweled himself dry wondering if it was Elizabeth or Jennifer. Hoping otherwise, he decided it was Jennifer. In reality, he knew it was Jennifer. Elizabeth would stay away to avoid causing problems for him with the girl. As he entered his bedroom, he thought. *Bingo. She is recharged and ready to go at it again. Oh Lord, please spare me!*

Jennifer was standing in the middle of the room waiting for him to enter. She was wearing a light pink, silk bathrobe and holding two glasses of champagne. She glanced down at him and licked her lips.

"Mademoiselle, you have me at a disadvantage," he commented. "Do you want to share your wares?"

She offered him a flute of champagne, and he took them both.

"Take off your robe first," he asked, "I want to drink in your body first."

She untied the knot, and the robe fell to the floor.

"Turn very slowly and let me admire all of you. I want to consume every part," he requested.

She deliberately and sensually moved before him, cradling her breasts and slowly thrusting her hips. She danced a lyrical seduction before him in three-quarter time, while in the back of his mind he reaffirmed his photographic blueprint of the moles that dotted her body.

She noticed that she was having the desired effect on his manhood and dropped to her knees to strengthen him. She was starting to feel familiar with his body. She knew the special touch and circular movement that made him explode with fullness. He nearly cried out as she began to caress him, and he took her head in his hands. He sank to his knees to kiss her. They had their fill of love on the carpet to the rhythm of a creaking floor. United they rose, and she led him to bed where they fell into the soft feathers still entwined. She dribbled some champagne on his chest and licked it off. As she began to move lower on his body, he pleaded, "Please, stop. Please. I'm an old man. I need a few minutes to recover."

"Bullshit," she replied and proved him gloriously wrong.

He lay exhausted and decided that he could only take her in very short doses. *Thank God she'll be incapacitated for a while after surgery. I'll make my escape before she is sufficiently healed to desire any athletic bedroom endeavors.*

She spoke huskily, "Do I really have to spend time with the others? Can't we just do this ourselves? It would be so much more fun."

"No, we can't." Adam responded. "We need the support of the company. A woman alone in hijab attracts much more attention than do three women together."

"If they ever make a marquee for a movie describing the female actresses, it will have to read 'the Princess, Ninja Woman and a Bitch in a Bag.'"

Adam snorted, "If Reem heard you calling her a ninja woman or Elizabeth heard you calling her a bitch in a bag, they would happily hold you down and cut out your tongue."

"Wrong, my Lord. They would do nothing. I am becoming far too valuable to everyone. Neither would dare harm me. This team has invested too much time and energy in me to back out now. I will soon be able to do anything I wish."

Adam smiled, moving his index finger softly around her breasts and said, "You may be right, my princess." At the same time alarms were going off everywhere in his mind. *How in the hell are we going to control this Frankenstein once we let her loose? Shit, shit, shit. She means it. She plans to do whatever she wishes and get whatever she wants.*

>-+-<>-O-<>-+-<

France, three days later

Jennifer took the passenger seat next to Adam in the Audi as they left the country house. Elizabeth was relegated to the rear seat. Adam rocketed down the narrow lane, limbering up the Audi sport.

The turbo-charged five cylinder had been customized by a small firm in Switzerland. It was one of those Swiss ironies; it is illegal to make these modifications to a car, but only if the car were involved in an accident would it ever cause a legal problem. The whole business creates a Swiss sub-culture of near race cars on the street that are driven very aggressively but carefully to avoid accidents. As a precaution, Adam had mounted state of the art radar detectors remotely so they were not visible; they are also illegal, and the police are not friendly if they discover them.

Adam was more careful driving in France than in Switzerland. The French police will take a person's car away if he drives too fast; the Swiss merely charge a small fortune.

Cresting a small rise in the road at nearly 140 kilometers per hour, they surprised a tiny Fiat 500 that had just pulled out of a side lane. Adam deftly passed the tiny car on the right, throwing up a cloud of dust and small rocks from the road shoulder and creating the appearance of a small explosion. Jennifer made a sharp intake of air and Elizabeth said, "Kiddies, don't try this at home." Jennifer recovered and launched into a "you are going to get us killed," speech.

Adam cut her off abruptly. He explained that the Audi was equipped with full-time four-wheel drive, Porsche brakes and other enhancements he had added. Unfortunately, his soliloquy was lost on Jennifer who fumed in silence for the next fifteen minutes.

Joining the AutoRoute near Auxerre, Adam pushed the Audi's speed up to the 200 kilometer range. The AutoRoute is the European version of the super highway and is generally the best way to drive long distances.

He was soon joined by a Porsche, and they played a changing game of follow the leader until they neared the turn off for Dijon. Adam suddenly swerved into the right lane and stood on the brakes as the Porsche rocketed past. A red light flashed frantically on the dash, and a buzzer grated in their ears. The tires howled as the Audi scrubbed off speed, forcing the three forward against their seatbelts. Jennifer sounded like a vacuum cleaner in heat as she sucked air. Adam had reduced the speed to the legal limit by the time he had crested a small rise in the road and saw the French police car. In a few seconds the officer sped past in hot pursuit of the Porsche. Pleased at his astuteness, Adam drove for several kilometers at the legal rate and then bumped up the speed again. Elizabeth was unmoved by the event and had no problem catnapping. Jennifer remained in a complete twit over the driving.

Adam exited the AutoRoute at Beaune and headed to the restaurant of Jean Crotet. This man was to marvel at, a local success in a restaurant called La Côte d'Or, located in the tiny village of Nuits-Saint-Georges. As the three entered the restaurant, they were greeted warmly as though they were long-lost locals. They were promptly shown to a lovely corner table.

Before Adam was seated, Jean Crotet appeared and first kissed Adam warmly on both cheeks. He turned to Elizabeth and repeated the ritual. He kissed Jennifer's hand and turned back to focus his attention on Adam and Elizabeth. They spoke animatedly for several minutes in French, and Jennifer sat in the background looking like a neglected child. Although she spoke some French, she had a hard time tracking a fast-moving conversation and was a little at a loss.

The meal was more wonderful than Adam had pronounced it would be. He had gone to great lengths describing the restaurant during their drive. The starter was a delicate crème d'asperges soup, followed with a salad of mixed greens and a main course of pigeon au foie gras, the specialty of the house. They enjoyed a fabulous bottle of Nuits-Saint-Georges, Les Cailles, 1976, bottled by Alain Michelot. Although some experts might dispute the choice of this wine for this particular menu, Adam and Alain were old friends. Adam felt a certain loyalty to Alain and loved his wine. This bottle was the logical choice. In reality, Adam always selected a bottle from the cave of Alain Michelot if it was offered on a restaurant's wine list. It was more or less a tradition for Adam.

As the meal progressed, Jennifer relaxed and by the time dessert was served, she was back to her bubbly self. Never did she falter on her pursuit to seduce Adam. Throughout the meal, she attempted to play footsies with him. They finished the meal with a small glass of Marc, an after-dinner drink of the region, and a very French expresso. Remembering their schedule, Adam suggested they continue their conversation in the car. They still had more than three hours to drive before they would arrive in Lausanne.

Adam held back a little on the throttle, hoping that both of his passengers would fall asleep after the perfect luncheon and several glasses of wine. His scheme was successful. Both slept soundly until he slowed to filter into the line of traffic at the frontier crossing into Switzerland near Jougne. They were waved through customs without a passport check.

Jennifer asked, "Is it normal that they don't ask to see our passports?"

Adam replied very accurately, "Sometimes. It's a little like roulette. But it helps that we are driving a car with Swiss plates."

They arrived in Lausanne a little more than an hour later and checked into the Beau Rivage Palace. They took two suites, and Jennifer made it clear that she was not about to sleep in the same room with Elizabeth. Adam suggested that Jennifer share his suite, and all was settled.

Adam's muscles were tight and stiff after the stress of the long drive. He needed to release the pressure he was feeling from being prey to Jennifer's seductions. He wanted to loosen up with a game of tennis on the hotel's courts. Both women, disinterested in tennis, refused to play with him. They suggested, as an alternative, a sauna and swim. Knowing this was his only hope of persuading them to do anything, he acquiesced.

The hearty swim well served its purpose. Adam felt refreshed and spirited. He excused himself from his companions, leaving the two in the bar to engage in a little female warfare. He felt the need to make himself scarce for a while, and he knew Elizabeth was tough. She was willing to provide him with a short reprieve from the demands of Jennifer. He would receive his fair share as the evening progressed. *Only one more night,* he thought, *and then, we will be free for a few days. Thank God. The moment cannot come too quickly for me.*

⊱⊶⊷⊙⊶⊶⊰

Adam had to nearly fight his way out of bed the next morning. Jennifer kept pulling him back. Her desire was insatiable. Finally, Adam was firm. There was no more time. They had to get ready. They could not be late for their appointment at the clinic. The surgeon was a very exact man. He would not tolerate tardiness. Reluctantly, Jennifer agreed to let him out of bed. However, she had one and only one requirement. "Adam," she demanded, "You must promise that you will not sleep with Elizabeth while I'm in the hospital."

Adam, without hesitation and in complete honesty responded, "My princess, this is a promise I have made before, and I make it again today with no problem."

They were collected by a driver from the clinic, and upon arrival were escorted to Jennifer's private room. The surgeon arrived minutes later and reviewed the procedure, confirming the changes that would be made. He asked Jennifer, "Madame, are you certain you have no second thoughts?"

Still excited and a little bubbly, Jennifer responded, "Not even one."

Adam and Elizabeth left Jennifer alone in her room to enable them to confer in private with the surgeon. They spoke about their requirements for a few minutes, and he agreed to keep Jennifer in the clinic until the stitches were removed. Normally, the clinic allowed a patient to leave after five or six days, but Adam and Elizabeth wanted and needed a reprieve.

Returning to the Beau Rivage Palace, Adam and Elizabeth moved into the same suite. There was a great deal of planning that needed to be done for the next part of the project. They were beginning to discover that the overall procedure was not as simple as either had originally thought. This girl had serious problems and would be very hard to control.

Elizabeth prodded Adam. "Did you see the shameless woman try to put the make on the surgeon? She will be sleeping with him before her recovery is over. Mark my word."

Adam looked at her as if she had flipped.

"Trust me. She is out for another conquest. I can feel it."

"Are you sure? I think she's just interested in the procedures."

"You are so naive. That woman is a man eater."

"Picking up on it must be a girl thing."

"It is."

Adam gave a resigned sigh and suggested that they get down to work. Both had their portables, and the keyboard on each started to fly.

Some time later Elizabeth said, "Adam, do you really think that Yusuf can make the contact we need, or do we need to launch another plan?"

"Yusuf knows the family well. He can get the suggestion through. That's not the problem, but you are right. It's possible Mohammed won't bite. You never know how he'll react. His feelings may be hurt because she turned him down the last time. Maybe we should take a parallel approach."

"Well, Adam, you know how I am about having a back-up plan. There is no doubt Mohammed has many reasons for wanting to get one up on the Royal Family. This may be his opportunity. Let's lay out the groundwork that way."

"God, are you ever right on that one. He is an outsider, and he hates it. As hard as he tries, he just can't change his image. Half the establishment still calls him a wog in private."

"For heaven's sake, what do you expect? He is an outsider to them and always will be. The establishment will never accept him. It's not money or success that counts. It's blood. To their upturned noses, he is a wog, and they will never change their minds."

"Don't forget Katherine knows him," continued Adam. Although I don't think it would be smart to use her. She is almost invisible in her relationship with Di. I want to keep it that way. It would be far too easy for Rosa to become suspicious and maybe a little jealous if she realizes that Di and Katherine are close. Besides Katherine is too straight. If she puts two and two together, she might tell Di. It's better to keep Katherine completely out of it."

"You're right, Adam. My God, Katherine is almost too straight for her own good. She is definitely not our link on this one. We must use a different avenue."

"Why don't we use a gossip monger?" Adam suggested. "They believe anything you tell them and are easy to manipulate."

"Agreed," Elizabeth responded.

Adam collected his e-mail and received good news from Martin. His team was assembled. They were all Belgians with African experience. Martin was using a Northern Irishman named Michael as his front man. Michael had lived in London during his teenage years and could speak with or without an Irish accent. He would be a perfect puppet for his role. The Belgium team had been briefed that they would be working for the British, so the disinformation had already begun for this segment. Michael was convinced his employer was the Irish. Martin had made the right inferences to allow the men to draw their own conclusions. Adam had trained him well.

Martin had laid out equipment lists. He had already ordered the laser from a South African custom arms contractor who he knew personally. Martin was going to London the next day. He was leaving the team in Michael's control with a list of exercises to practice. While in London, Martin would complete the architect's work and prepare for the break-in. The forger had been contacted and would be on twelve-hour advance notice standby starting June first. Martin would personally meet with the forger and brief him on the project while in London.

Adam re-encrypted the message and forwarded it to Elizabeth for her information. Progress was being made, but there were still many loose ends. It was a precarious mix. The plan needed to be precise. There was no room for error. At the same time, it was necessary to maintain the fluidity to adapt to changes and variables as they arose. The challenge was becoming more complex as they approached the next phase.

Some time later, Adam and Elizabeth took a break from their individual tasks. They discussed the logistics of the next act. There were so many tiny details to manipulate. To make a mistake of any kind would create a catastrophe. They agreed that there would only be one border crossing. When they left Switzerland, they would not return with Jennifer. There was too much risk involved in moving their doppelganger around, even when hidden by hijab.

12

Switzerland, four days later

Adam and Elizabeth entered Jennifer's room as she was being prepped for surgery. She was mildly sedated and seemed a little spacey. They asked the nurse if they could speak with her in private for just a moment.

When they were alone Adam asked gently, "Jennifer, are you still okay about all of this?"

"Don't worry about me. But what about your promise?"

"Good as gold. I've already told you it's an easy promise."

Elizabeth asked what they were talking about, and Adam told her. She laughed and looked at Jennifer, "You couldn't pay me enough to sleep with this rogue. He conned you, you poor, dear girl. Don't feel badly; he cons all the girls."

Jennifer smiled but was having a hard time keeping her eyes open. Interrupting their conversation, the orderlies came to take her away. They moved her to a gurney. The surgery would take several hours, and Jennifer would be drowsy for even longer. Adam and Elizabeth assured her that they would be praying for her, but their comments went unheard. She was long gone.

Adam told Elizabeth, "We need to make sure that she will never be able to sell a scandal. I can imagine the headline. 'The Day Surgery

Made Me Look Like Di.' What a catastrophe that would be!"

The time passed quickly in the well-appointed waiting room. Both Elizabeth and Adam caught up on their work. The clinic provided every need for the patient's family and loved ones in an elegant yet tasteful fashion. There were both standard and ISDN telephone lines for modem hook-ups, as well as private telephone lines, fax and photocopier. The clinic even provided computers with Windows, Mac and Unix operating systems, allowing virtually anyone to work while waiting. Adam and Elizabeth preferred to use their own computers for security reasons, even though the clinic provided the in-house service. A large-screen monitor was connected to the operating theatre, and updates of the surgery's progress were provided every thirty minutes or more often, if required. A private butler was on duty for each family group. This individual remained on stand-by to assure the patient's loved ones a most enjoyable and stress-free atmosphere during the surgery. Adam had never before encountered such service, even in the finest hotels of the world that he regularly frequented. Somehow, a normally unbearable experience was turned into a holiday.

Adam and Elizabeth were served luncheon in a private dining room. The menu was traditional Swiss. Tartare du saumon followed by a very nice carre d'agneau with rösti, the special Swiss potatoes, and a garden of vegetables. A flowery Fendant, Switzerland's signature white wine, was served with the starter; a Pinot Noir de Sierre from a valley just East of Lausanne accompanied the main course. Dessert was meringues topped with fresh fruits and crème Gruyères, a marvelously rich natural cream from one of the slightly mountainous French areas of Switzerland not too far from the clinic.

Shortly after lunch, Elizabeth returned to their hotel suite to place some urgent telephone calls. Privacy was essential. After completing the calls, she went to work to assure the demise of Jennifer's gigantic purse. Taking a razor blade, she carefully loosened the seam that secured one of the shoulder straps. The goal was for the strap to pull off one of the first few times Jennifer again picked up the purse. Thinking about it, Elizabeth became concerned that she had not eased the seam enough. To guarantee the success of her mission, she added a few small cuts along one of the seams at the bottom of the huge bag. Now, victory was like a time bomb with an erratic detonator. The bag would blow, the only question was when. Satisfied with her accomplishment, Elizabeth tried to slip the disabled purse into a shopping bag but could not find one large enough to hold it. *Shit. I don't dare just carry the damn thing. It could self-destruct while I have it, and Jennifer would smell a rat.* The day was saved when she found a large bag furnished by the hotel for soiled laundry.

The surgeon had provided his services for Adam on several occasions, and the two had grown to know one another well. The surgeon acted with the utmost of discretion. The man asked no questions, and Adam told him no more than what was necessary. As long as he was paid, the surgeon was content.

Normally, Adam did not accompany the patient to the clinic, so he was unknown to the staff. His posing, in this instance, as Jennifer's fiancé presented no problem. Adam had decided that it was critical for him to remain at the clinic throughout the duration. It was vital for Jennifer to feel his concern and sincerity. She might become distraught, or even angry, if she woke up to find that he was not there by her side. Every possible precaution was taken to prohibit her from saying something inappropriate. As long as she felt she had hooked Adam, she would comply with his demands.

Three or four expressos and two toilet stops later, the butler invited Adam to return to Jennifer's room where they would be reunited shortly. Adam had already received confirmation from the surgeon via the video monitor that the surgery was complete with the procedure enacted to perfection.

Within fifteen minutes, Jennifer was rolled back into her room. She was still heavily sedated and only semiconscious. Her breathing was regular, although a large amount of equipment was connected to all parts of her body. Adam tried to speak to her by calling out her name first softly and then more loudly. Her response was nil.

Feeling the need to dissipate his nervous energy, Adam took out his portable computer and started to work. As he was encrypting an e-mail to Martin, he heard a soft groan. Jennifer was rejoining the world. He dropped a quick e-mail message to Elizabeth asking her to return to the clinic at once and then moved to the bedside.

Adam took Jennifer's hand and gently rubbed it. She looked like a mummy with her face completely swathed in bandages. There had not been any major changes but many little ones. The entire face had been party to several hours of cutting, pulling and shaping. She groaned again, and he pushed the buzzer for the nurse.

The nurse arrived as Jennifer mumbled some nonsense and apparently went back to sleep. The nurse took Jennifer's vital signs and told Adam that everything was fine. She continued in French, "Ne vous inquiétez pas, Monsieur," telling Adam not to worry.

Jennifer had been sedated heavily. The surgery was intricate.

Perfection took time and planning. The surgeon preferred total anesthesia for major jobs like this one. An unexpected move by the patient at an inopportune moment could cause a slip of the knife that might prove disastrous to the desired result.

The nurse continued to fuss over Jennifer, and Adam chatted with her in French. While they were talking, Jennifer drifted back into reality to mumble, "My mouth is so dry. Could I have some water?"

The nurse did not understand English, and Adam translated the request. The nurse glanced at her watch and cautiously provided Adam with a glass of water and a straw. She instructed him to use the straw like an eyedropper, dribbling only a tiny amount of water into the girl's mouth. The nurse stayed to observe Adam, making sure he understood her instructions. When she was satisfied that he had mastered her directive, she left him alone with Jennifer.

Jennifer was rapidly gaining her wits and squeezed Adam's hand. "My lips are asleep. It feels as though I have been to the dentist. My face tingles and feels so numb, like there is pressure on it. Did he do a good job? Is there any more to do?"

"It's all over now," Adam responded. "The surgeon is completely satisfied and thinks you will look perfect."

"He should feel what I'm feeling from the inside. It doesn't feel so perfect to me."

Within five minutes, Elizabeth entered the room, holding the laundry bag low and out of sight as she walked up to stand next to Adam. She patted Jennifer's hand and asked the girl how she was feeling. Elizabeth said, "I saw the surgeon in the hallway. He said nothing could have gone better. You are his star patient. The results should be perfect. I am so proud of you!"

Jennifer mumbled, "Déjà vu," and attempted a chuckle.

As Jennifer started to ask them something about her role as Di's double, the surgeon entered with the nurse. Adam chimed in, "Oh here is the doctor," to alert Jennifer that they were no longer alone.

The nurse started rearranging Jennifer's bed linens and checked her vital signs, once again. At the same time, the surgeon shined a light into Jennifer's eyes as he said, "The procedure went very well. You must now rest very quietly to enhance the healing process. I do not want you to leave the clinic until after I remove the stitches. It will be about ten days, depending upon how quickly your body heals."

There were very few stitches, but Jennifer did not have to know that. The surgeon had opted to use an innovative technique that minimizes scaring. The cost of applying this technique is prohibitive for many patients, but in this case where absolute perfection was demanded, its application was essential. The surgeon had explained the need to Adam weeks before the surgery, and Adam had agreed to use the state of the art technique without a second thought. Adam would bear any cost to guarantee the required results.

The surgeon continued explaining to Jennifer, "You likely will experience some discomfort, but it should subside within twenty-four to forty-eight hours. The nurses will change your dressings every day and do whatever they are able to keep you as comfortable as possible. You will be checked on, at least, every fifteen minutes during your entire stay at the clinic. You may ask for whatever you desire. Your meals will be served at your convenience, whenever you are hungry, twenty-four hours a day. You may ask the chef to prepare whatever sounds good to you, but alcohol is forbidden. And, oh yes, I almost forgot the most important thing. If you have pain, tell the nurse immediately. She will give you something to help you feel better. I do not want you to suffer, even for one minute. We want your stay with us to be enjoyable. I will check in on you again in an hour or so. Do you have any questions right now?"

Dozing in and out of awareness, Jennifer only half listened to the surgeon's remarks. She complained, "I can't breathe through my nose. It feels like it's stopped up."

"Your nostrils are packed due to the surgery," the surgeon explained. "It will be a couple of days before you can start to breathe normally. Even then, there will be swelling that will make breathing through your nose a little difficult for a while longer, but I don't think it will bother you too much."

For the moment more alert, Jennifer asked. "You are sure that it worked, and everything went okay? I will look like her?"

"Yes, I am sure that you will be satisfied. There is no doubt whatsoever."

"Good."

"I'll leave you with your loved ones. Just let the nurse know whatever your needs may be."

Jennifer nodded and said, "Okay."

As the surgeon left, Jennifer turned her every thought to Adam. She now seemed very alert. "Adam, please don't leave me here alone. Please!" She reached out her hand to his, and when he placed his hand into hers, she clutched it tightly. "Will you stay with me all of the time? Will you stay with me all night? The nurse doesn't speak English, and I might need something."

A little taken back and not knowing exactly how to respond, Adam said. "Sure, I'll be here every day. You know that, my princess. But I do need to do some other work. I must continue with the project, or we will not meet our schedule. You must understand that I will have to be away some of the time. If I'm not here, Elizabeth will stay with you. The clinic will not allow me to spend the night. It's against house rules. There's nothing I can do. Please try to understand. I'm so sorry, my princess." Adam made a mental note to tell the doctor that there was a house rule against him spending the night in the event that Jennifer asked.

"Don't forget your promise." She started to say something else, but her voice fell into nothingness. She closed her eyes and seemed to drift off into a deep and restful sleep. Adam shot into action. He took the laundry bag and gently extricated Jennifer's purse to return it to the wardrobe.

>-I-<⋄>-O-<⋄>-I-<

Switzerland, ten days later

Jennifer seemed her old bubbly self, although she moved her head with exaggerated slowness. Elizabeth had left several days earlier for Gstaad. Jennifer was restless in the clinic and childlike in her demand for Adam's attention. He had been overly accommodating to her during her convalescence. Her mood swings were exaggerated. She was an angel when he was present and ruthless and unruly with the staff during his absences.

She now felt she held something over him. She could talk, and he knew it. She had a story to tell. Her talking could destroy the project. Adam did not have a replacement for her. No understudy was training. To find another actress and start over would be impossible at this late date. Jennifer knew this and was feeling smug. The project's success pivoted around her, and she was using her position to her advantage.

Jennifer remained happy as long as Adam performed for her. In her mind she was in control. She did not realize that she was in control because Adam allowed her to be. She did not know the real Adam. She did not fathom what he would do to assure that his plot was successful. She had no inkling of why he had been crowned with the code name, Puppet Master. He had well masked his true reality to her. She was his puppet; he would abort the project and terminate her the moment he felt the situation was out of control. He could always place the project on hold and start again. He had done it many times before with other projects. It would be very difficult for Di, but waiting was certainly preferable to exposure.

The morning of the unveiling could not have been more welcomed by anyone than Adam. Jennifer was seated in a chair that looked as if it had been designed for a dentist's office. There were various tools laid out on the small tray that was cantilevered over the left side of the chair. The only thing missing was the running water and a place to spit out the grindings.

The surgeon entered. He nodded to Adam and began to work in silence. His lack of people skills had bothered Jennifer from the start. The only time he had been in any way conversational was right after her surgery. She was so out of it then that she could hardly remember what he had told her. All she could remember was that he had tried to act like he cared about how she felt. She imagined that what he had told her was likely a memorized speech that he presents after every procedure. *He probably modifies it to fit the needs of the patient and gives it mainly for the benefit of the patient's family. Actually, to satisfy the person paying the bill. Today, he is back to his old, cold self. Maybe I can charm him. Maybe I can break through his wall. I have been trying for the last two weeks with no success. Maybe I'll score today.*

Adam admired the man. He was extremely intelligent and knew that his business could only thrive if he maintained strict boundaries. Like most doctors, especially surgeons, he was an egotist. He was put off when he had to talk with people he did not believe to be his intellectual equals.

Continuing his silence, the surgeon carefully removed the dressings from Jennifer's face and head. Adam watched with cautious anticipation. *My God,* he thought. *She looks awful.* The swelling was minimal, but there was much discoloration in various hues of blue and yellow and stains everywhere that looked like betadine. If Adam had not known better, he would have concluded there was no hope and considered starting over with another person.

The surgeon broke his silence after taking several minutes to examine both sides of Jennifer's face and neck with magnified lenses. Without comment as to why she looked so horrible, he looked directly at Adam and said, "The healing is ahead of schedule. There is no infection, no complications. Everything looks very good." He then turned to Jennifer and looked her directly in the eyes, "I am going to remove the stitches from your mouth; it may be uncomfortable and a little painful. I will be as gentle as possible. You will feel much better without all of the threads in your mouth."

Jennifer jumped and then groaned. Finally, she sighed with relief when he said, "They're all out. I'm finished. You must follow these instructions exactly for caring for yourself." He handed her a slip of paper printed in six languages. The recovery and care process was explained in detail.

Jennifer asked, "Didn't you forget the packing in my nose?"

The surgeon fired a look at Jennifer that suggested he thought she was retarded and told her that there was no packing in her nose. "It was removed days ago. What you feel is merely swelling."

Shaking his head and looking dismayed, the surgeon continued. "You may leave the clinic today. You must promise that you will carefully follow the instructions that I have provided. It is critical that you do not bounce around whatsoever or push on your face at all. Do not scrub your face to remove the stains. They will come off with gentle washing over a few days. The healing process is not complete. Some of your tissue is still very weak and can be easily damaged."

"I understand," she replied.

Interrupting Jennifer before she could say more, the surgeon went on. "Adam told me that you are traveling to Gstaad where you will recuperate. I recommended to him that you travel by ambulance rather than car. There will be much less risk of tissue damage, if you are in a reclining position. I have arranged for the ambulance, and it is waiting for you. The discoloration on your face and neck will fade gradually. The bruising under your eyes will last the longest, maybe as long as four or five more weeks. In another two weeks with good make-up, you should be completely presentable. I have given Adam some pills for pain if it continues. Avoid using them if you can. They tend to be addictive and should not be used unless absolutely necessary. Do you have any questions?"

"Yes. May I see what I look like?"

The surgeon walked to a cabinet and returned with a mirror. He held it up to Jennifer, again without saying a word.

"Shit! Fucking shit! I look like the fucking aftermath of a serious car wreck. Damn. I look more like how she would look after a serious car wreck."

"Give it a little time. The discoloration hides many of the changes, and it will pass soon. Remember that you need to avoid bouncing around. I am going to wrap you up again. There is no need for the ambulance drivers to see your face. Dying her hair black before the surgery was a nice touch, Adam." The surgeon applied the dressing and called for a wheelchair to take Jennifer to the ambulance.

"Adam, are you going to ride with me?"

"No, my princess. I need to take my car. I'll follow the ambulance and arrive at the same time you do. I will not let the ambulance out of my sight. I'll take your things with me."

"Promise?"

"Of course, my princess." The nurse thought it lovely how kind this older gentleman was to his much younger bride-to-be. He was obviously more educated and experienced than she. The nurse had appreciated his sensitivity to the girl during the past several days. *This young thing is lucky to nab such an eligible man,* she thought.

The nurse stood and watched in admiration as Adam pushed Jennifer to the clinic's entrance. The ambulance was ready with the rear door open. The attendants dressed in spotless, white uniforms were waiting, almost standing at attention, to greet their patient and assure her a pleasant and safe journey. The attendants lifted Jennifer into the ambulance and assisted her in stretching out onto the secured gurney, offering her extra pillows and blankets.

Adam gave directions to the driver and told him to go ahead. Adam told the driver not to worry, he would catch up with them in just a few minutes. Near Gstaad he would pass the ambulance, allowing the driver to follow him to the chalet. The driver suggested that they take the longer route through Bulle. There was some road construction that could be bumpy and cause delays on the shorter route through Aigle. They agreed, and the ambulance pulled out.

Adam returned to the clinic and handed a thick envelope to the surgeon. The surgeon preferred to receive his money in cash. This way he did not have to declare his fees for special services such as this to the tax authorities.

The surgeon handed Jennifer's file to Adam. He told Adam that he had even erased the computer entries that referred to her appointments, even though the appointments had not been made in her name. He told Adam to be careful with Jennifer. The girl could not be trusted. "She is on the constant make. She tried more than once to seduce me, and my silence always threw her off. She did not know how to come on to me when I would ignore her and say nothing."

Smiling Adam commented, "Believe me, my man, I understand what you mean. Her highly developed sex drive poses a problem for more than just you. I can't keep her away from me. She's like a shameless bitch in heat."

They continued to speak together cordially for several minutes. Then, glancing at his watch, Adam said, "I must leave, or I'll have to drive like a maniac to catch up with the ambulance."

Laughing the surgeon asked, "Isn't that how you normally drive?"

Adam returned to Jennifer's room and collected her things. The clinic kindly provided someone to help, and Adam allowed the orderly to take her clothing and cosmetic bag while he gently cradled her purse in his arms.

Pounding the Audi up the grade, Adam passed the huge cross that marks the dividing line between the cantons of Vaud and Fribourg. A sixth sense told him to slow down. He checked his radar detector and mirrors but could see nothing. Everything appeared normal; still, he felt something was wrong. He backed off his speed to 140 and was about to bump it up again when he passed a dark blue Volkswagen Golf. Glancing inside, he noticed the driver was in uniform. It was an unmarked car. *Merde. I should listen more closely when those little messages come my way.*

Sure enough, the Golf jumped on his tail with lights flashing. Adam immediately slowed down and pulled to the side of the road. *At least the police in Switzerland are civilized. I'll be back on the road in a minute or so.*

The policeman asked no questions. He merely informed Adam of his speed and the amount of the fine. Adam paid on the spot. It was much easier than doing it later, and the police always seemed to appreciate a man with cash. It was less paperwork for them. Speaking French, the officer wished him a pleasant remainder of the day, and Adam was on the road again with a minimum loss of time.

Jennifer felt a little nauseous and dizzy as the ambulance wound back and forth on the mountain route to the chalet. She was not herself and was just as happy to be lying down. She would have looked ridiculous riding in a car wrapped like a mummy.

To pass the time she calculated her plan. She had Adam where she wanted him, and she knew it. She was invaluable to him. Maybe she should hit him up for more money. The ten thousand a month had sounded great at first, but it was nothing compared to what the big stars receive. What was she really worth to him? If she sold her story to one of the tabloids, she would make big bucks. Maybe a hundred thousand. Maybe two hundred. She could contact more than one tabloid and play them off against each other. Then, she could write her book. What would they pay for a book? She would lose Adam, but she would have so many other opportunities once she was famous, it really didn't matter. For now, she could do nothing. Not until the bruising was gone. She would hit Adam up for a raise. *Twenty thousand a month sounds good to me. It's not that extreme.*

Tonight she would seduce him. He was helpless when she sucked on him. She would bring him once, then again and maybe even one more time. Then, when he was lying there void of all energy, she would gently ask him if she was playing her role well enough. When he told her that she was doing a perfect job, she would hint about the raise. She would ask him if he had thought about giving her a little reward. Maybe a tiny, little raise. She would be kitten-like. She would caress his ear with her tongue and move it across his cheek to his mouth. Thrusting it deeply within, she would kiss him passionately. Then, she would whisper, "Don't you think I'm worth twenty thousand a month, plus expenses" She could do it. He would be a pushover. He could not refuse her. She could wrap him around her finger. He had no idea who he was dealing with when he hired her.

Adam was near Gruyères when he caught his first glimpse of the ambulance several hundred meters ahead. Dropping back to the legal speed limit, he paced himself to stay several car lengths behind. He was daydreaming as he passed Château d'Oex when he noticed an Alpine rapidly closing the distance behind him. The Alpine was probably a more common car in Switzerland than anywhere else in the world. It is more or less the French answer to the Porsche. The Swiss French seem to love these little lightning rods, although only the Swiss Germans are able to afford their upkeep.

Adam resisted a burning temptation to play as the Alpine shot around him. Adam had not been in an impromptu road race for a long time. Nothing gave him a stronger adrenaline rush. Curtailing his urge, he sighed rationalizing, *I know the road well, but I must keep to the task at hand.*

As he entered Gstaad, Adam called Elizabeth and told her they were nearly there.

"Everything is ready," she responded. "How does she look?"

"She's all wrapped up. To be honest, I was shocked. She looks awful. She is very bruised, but I think we have the result we want. We just have to give it some more time."

"Thank God," Elizabeth sighed. "Oh yes, dear brother, are you staying with us for a few days to service your little princess?"

"Damn it, Elizabeth. I've taken about as much of her shit as I can swallow. Lay off of me," and he slammed down the receiver.

Elizabeth was waiting outside the chalet as Adam and the ambulance arrived. It was cold but clear and sunny. A crusted blanket of snow covered everything, except for the streets and sidewalks that were clear and dry. After the attendants helped Jennifer out of the ambulance, Elizabeth and Adam each took an arm and almost lifted her up the steps. Jennifer was protesting the attention she was receiving but seemed glad to have it. She asked to go immediately to her room; she wanted to freshen up. They showed her to her room, and she asked if it was all right for her to be left alone for awhile.

Yusuf appeared from out of nowhere and exchanged a quick glance at Adam. Adam shook his head, and Yusuf disappeared. Elizabeth and Adam went to their favorite corner of the living room. The space had been designed specifically for the two of them. No one else dared to use it. There were two oversized chairs that faced one another with a glass table in between; soft halogen lighting provided a relaxing glow, and the fireplace threw off a gentle warmth from the other side of the room. This area was their special think tank. Many a solution had been formulated here.

They began to exchange information. Adam had just received an update of Di's tentative schedule. Even in the midst of all her troubles, finalizing the divorce, dealing with her loss of authority with the boys and arranging her own personal affairs, she kept very active with one charity event after another. It was good for the project that she was still so visible. It was important that the world saw her as a survivor. Only a woman of sound mind could cope in such grave circumstances.

After talking about the various possibilities, Adam and Elizabeth decided that it was time to give Jennifer a trial run. They looked for possible opportunities to integrate Jennifer into Di's schedule. Elizabeth had arranged for a yacht to be leased in the name of a shell corporation that indicated Saudi ownership. Yusuf had acted as the front man, and the yacht carried British registration. It would provide a way to transfer Jennifer in and out of England without being noticed.

About an hour after they started talking, Jennifer interrupted their conversation. She walked into the room unnoticed and approached them saying, "How do I look?"

Both Adam and Elizabeth were taken back. She was absolutely smashing. She had overlooked the surgeon's orders and removed the Betadine stains. She had applied some make-up and donned her Di wig. She was dressed in a Channel suit and looked better than either Adam or Elizabeth had ever imagined possible. The darkness under her eyes showed through the make-up. It was a subtle defect; she merely appeared as though she was short on sleep. Neither Elizabeth nor Adam said a word. They just stared. Captivated, they could not take their eyes off her. Adam was searching for an obvious clue that might give her away. He was unsuccessful. He found nothing. Masking his excitement, he thought, *Holy Shit! We've done it!*

Jennifer broke the silence, "Not bad, eh?"

Elizabeth was the first to answer. "The result is far better than what I had hoped. I am sure Adam agrees with me. You look fabulous!"

"I feel weird though. Sort of like my face is part numb, and my nose feels like it's packed with wadded up newspaper."

"You may feel weird, but you look absolutely spectacular," Adam interjected. Adam then started commenting on every part of the surgery. "You look slightly heavier than Di in the upper nose area, but I suppose that it could be the swelling or the make-up. Other than the discoloration under the eyes that is peeking through, the result is absolutely perfect."

"Just like a man to fuss over a minor detail," Elizabeth responded. "You have to be the expert, don't you, Adam? Get a life, for heaven's sake."

Jennifer began to giggle at Elizabeth's comment and stopped herself thinking. *I had better be good. It still hurts too much.*

Adam asked Jennifer if she wanted some pain medication, and she decided against it. "It's time I start weaning myself. We can't have a Princess druggie, now can we? I'm going to take a nap, unless you need me for something. I'm not quite myself, and I feel so tired. What time will we eat?"

"It's good for you to rest. It will help you to feel like your old self more quickly. When would you like to eat? Is there anything I can get for you?" Elizabeth replied.

"Maybe some ice cream now, if possible. Then, I'll just wait until supper. Is that okay?"

Elizabeth responded, "I'll bring it up in a couple of minutes to give you a chance to change."

"Maybe Adam could bring it up."

Almost choking Adam responded, "Sure, I'll be happy to."

Jennifer headed back up the stairs, and Elizabeth smirked. Adam glared at her, and she laughed at him, "That won't work on me; I know you too well. Better not bounce her face loose."

"Why, you dirty minded old woman. I'll..."

They both began to chuckle as Adam headed to the kitchen to prepare the ice cream.

13

Gstaad, early May 1997

Jennifer looked smashing. The discoloration had disappeared from her face except for a trace under both eyes. The swelling was completely gone. With make-up and her wig, she could have fooled all but Di's most intimate friends.

Jennifer was spending a great deal of time looking at herself in the mirror. Often, she would feel frightened; she no longer looked like herself. She marveled at the surgeon's skill. He was truly an artist. Maybe his artistic nature is what made his personality so distasteful. He had captured Di's ever so tiny, unique features and artfully transposed them onto Jennifer's face. The result was a replica of the original, a doppelganger.

The days passed in a regular routine of rehearsal and more rehearsal. Jennifer was assuming her role at all times. She ate like Di, moved like Di and spoke with Di's intonations and rhythms. Elizabeth remained Jennifer's constant companion, analyzing her every action and sound. Now, criticism was infrequent and unnecessary. Jennifer had captured the essence of Di's public persona.

Tensions, though, were rising between Jennifer and Elizabeth. Actually, they were rising between Jennifer and everyone. Jennifer had been sequestered in the chalet for nearly a month. She was suffering from cabin fever and was taking her frustration out on everyone. She felt as though she was a captive. Restless, she wanted to see something other than the repeat videos of Di and the four walls of the chalet. She needed some space and some action.

The weather was unusually cold for April. Earlier in the day, an unseasonable storm had dropped several inches of wet and heavy snow. The storm had been short lived, and, now only a few hours later, the warm sun was bringing welcome relief to the trees and bushes heavily laden with the icy mass. Jennifer pleaded to go for a walk. She promised to be discreet and remain in control. With her large sunglasses and her black hair, she would not be noticed. She promised not to do anything to draw attention to herself.

Adam agreed that they all needed a change of scene. Maybe they could risk a walk into the village, but first Adam insisted on running a test. He asked Jennifer to dress wearing her ski parka and her dark glasses and to meet him on the balcony. There he shot several photos with a Polaroid and headed into the village with Yusuf.

Adam and Yusuf stopped at a busy little bistro in the center of town and showed a photo of Jennifer to one of the waiters. Adam, speaking the Schwiitzer-Tüütsch dialect native to the area, asked the man if he had seen this woman in town. The waiter studied the photo for a few seconds and then asked in dialect, if it was Princess Di with a black wig. The waiter told Adam that he had not heard Di was in town but that it was not impossible. Adam told the waiter that the photo was not of Di; it was a French woman named Nicole. The waiter looked puzzled and asked Adam if he was trying to joke with him, but Adam's face was impassive. The waiter then looked at Yusuf. The waiter finally shrugged his shoulders and told Adam that he had not seen the woman. Adam thanked him and they left.

"Bad idea, boss. You can't let her out."

Finding it difficult to hold back his excitement, Adam responded. "I'm torn between depression and celebrating the success of the operation. Shit, I had no idea we would score like this. It's like making a goal in international competition while blindfolded and in a wheelchair."

"Di is the most photographed woman in the world. Don't forget that, boss. Everyone knows her face. I'm even worried that Jennifer might be recognized wearing hijab by her eyes. The eyes are so recognizable."

"It would be more of a problem if we did not have support. That is one of the reasons that Reem is so useful to us. With her make-up artistry, she can help to hide the eyes. Plus, with the three women together, it is much less likely that anyone will notice one of them individually. We will just have to orchestrate the appearances well. The only thing that might attract attention is the height. Jennifer and Di are both quite tall."

"It would be better if we could keep the appearances to a minimum, even in hijab. To me, the greatest risk will be the times that we are orchestrating the switch."

"I agree. I had intended to use Jennifer more, but it would be better to keep her out of circulation and use her only when necessary. Perfect plans never seem to remain perfect. You must remember that, Yusuf. Never be afraid to change a plan if circumstances change."

They returned in silence to the chalet. Each was deep within himself, contemplating the reality of their discovery. As they entered the door, Jennifer jumped up and headed for the coat-tree where her parka was hanging.

Adam said, "Hold off a minute, my princess. You aren't going to believe what I have to tell you. Do you remember the old good news, bad news jokes? Do you want the good news or the bad news first?"

"I've already figured out the bad news," Jennifer snipped. "What do you think I am, brain dead?"

"The good news is, my princess, that the surgery was so successful that the waiter we talked to in town thought the photo was Di in a black wig and sunglasses. I'll admit Gstaad is a tough town to pull off something like this. Celebrities come here all of the time. The people who work here are attuned to looking for the rich and famous and seeing through their disguises."

"So, I'm right with the bad news. We're bloody, fucking not going into town." She could tell by Adam's expression that she was correct. Never at a loss for words, Jennifer continued. "Shit, fuck, piss. I just can't take it here any longer. Can't you understand that? I want out of here. Maybe I should just forget everything. Maybe I'll split and sell my story to the press. I could tell all about the surgery. I could sell photos of me as Di to the tabloids. What do you expect me to do anyway? I can't live like this any longer. I'm not your prisoner. How do you expect me to live cooped up in a mountain chalet in some little village in Switzerland that I have never even seen? For God's sake, Adam, answer me," she demanded. Without even taking a breath to give Adam the chance to respond, her verbal diarrhea continued. "What do you expect of me? Am I ever really going to be Di's replacement? I can't practice forever. Shit. Can't you understand that? Sure, maybe there are a few things I need to do better. But I can pull it off. I know I can. If she needs a fucking break so damn badly, why can't I just give it to her, now? Not six or twelve months from now or whenever in the fuck you get ready. I want some action, and I want it now. How are you going to make all of this up to me, Adam? Talk to me, damn it!"

Adam allowed Jennifer's rage to slide by, although no one missed her state of mind. Yusuf had made a quick disappearance at the start of the onslaught, leaving Adam alone to face the dragon. Elizabeth was standing in the background with a dark face. Jennifer had no idea how close she was to disaster.

Adam carefully maneuvered the girl by responding gently. "I had planned for us to stay here for another month, at least, but I agree with you, my princess. It is too confining here. We should leave. The chalet is too small, and there is nothing we can do for a change of scene. You deserve something better. We need to concentrate on the task at hand. You need to be happy so that you can perfect your role."

Turning to Elizabeth, Adam said, "Call Brigit and Eva and have them go to the villa south of Florence. The weather there is comfortable this time of year, and the grounds are isolated. We will go there. It's a lovely retreat, not at all closed in like it is here."

Then, continuing his explanation, Adam turned back to Jennifer and said, "I know you feel like you are ready, my princess, but all of the discoloration must disappear before we can allow you to be seen in public, even the very small amount that remains under your eyes. You are doing a wonderful job of preparing to be Di's second, but you still have some aspects of your character to perfect. Your language, when angry, is one of them. It will be beautiful in Italy, and I will stay there with you most of the time. Would you like that? There are some small villages nearby, and we can find some secluded restaurants where we will go unnoticed."

"Well, Adam, I guess it sounds better than…"

"Jennifer," Elizabeth said, "Excuse me for interrupting, but I just spoke with Brigit. The girls will leave within the hour for Florence. They will start preparing the villa tomorrow. It's a large complex, and no one has been there for several months. It will take them some time to get it ready. I think we should leave here a week from today. How does that sound?"

Jennifer glared at both Adam and Elizabeth. Pointedly she said, "Adam, I'll be in my room." Turning abruptly, she headed for the stairs. Yusuf appeared out of nowhere, he must have been hiding around the corner.

Sighing with exasperation, Adam said to Elizabeth and Yusuf, "We have work to do. Please, let's adjourn to the kitchen where we can speak in private."

Elizabeth poured a cup of Red Zinger tea for each of them, and they gathered around the table to plan their strategies.

"Yusuf, do you think Mohammed will act, or do we need to plant a hint another way?" Adam asked.

"I'm sure he'll invite her again. I've already told him that I heard she'll accept, if he extends another invitation. He was encouraged. He trusts me. He wants to do it. He just does not want to be rejected again. If anyone ever believes that money can solve all of the social ills or buy happiness, the person should talk to him."

"Elizabeth, make sure that Katherine gets word to Di that we need to know immediately if she receives an invitation. Also, tell her to accept, but only under the condition that no one knows about her acceptance. This will be a good opportunity for us to test out Jennifer, but if the whole world is watching, it will be much harder. It would be nice to do the first one without the press clamoring."

"Yusuf, can you handle the border crossing or do you want for me to arrange it?"

"I can do it through Ticino, boss, but if you want to cross into France and drive around, you had better make the arrangements yourself."

"Ticino is fine." Then, without a transition to indicate a change of thought, Adam looked at Elizabeth. "Have the villa swept for bugs. I don't think that anyone has identified it with us, but we cannot be too careful. Be sure it is done just before we arrive and after the girls are in place."

Always one step ahead of Adam, Elizabeth responded, "I have planned on it. I would like to use the American team. No one knows them in Italy, and I can fly them into Rome. They can make sure they are not followed and take the train to Florence. The girls can collect them."

"Good idea, as long as they can get right on it. Yusuf, call…"

He was interrupted by a voice drifting down from above. "Adam, did you forget about me?"

"Shit," he responded under his breath, momentarily ignoring Jennifer's call. He continued. "Yusuf, with her present state of mind, I want twenty-four hour surveillance on Jennifer. I don't trust her for a moment. Is it possible for you and Reem to cover at night? When I am with her, you can sleep. Elizabeth and I will take the days, except when I am away; then, you will have to help Elizabeth, as necessary. You know the procedure if she tries to leave. It's just as we have discussed. Handle it with extreme prejudice. Any questions?"

"Affirmative. I understand perfectly, boss."

Changing the tone of his voice to that soft, understanding timbre he uses when he speaks to her, Adam called up to her. "Of course, I didn't forget you, my princess." *God, how I wish I could forget her and forget her forever.* "I'll be right up."

Giving him no slack, Elizabeth adopted her most catty expression. "Why Adam, I do think you are becoming a bit henpecked."

Adam, unable to hold back a grin, looked at his two compatriots seated across the table. Rolling his eyes, he wearily said, "Not for long. Not for long. Just wait and see. Believe me, there's not only one great actress but also one hell of an actor in this group." He got up, kissed Elizabeth on the cheek and slapped Yusuf on the shoulder. As he walked away he said, "Off to the battle front. See you tomorrow, hopefully sooner."

⊱━◦━⊰

She was dressed in an ecru silk bathrobe that draped to the floor. Wearing her Di wig and make-up, she slowly pulled open the robe, first outstretching her left arm and then her right. She stood as an angel, fully exposing her anatomy. He stood and watched. He ached to approach her to cup her breasts in his palms and, at the same time, run his tongue across her flat, velvety smooth tummy. Dropping both arms to her sides, the robe fell into a mound at her feet like a cloud passing through the horizon. "How would you like to be royally laid?"

Caught up in the sensuousness of her request, he approached her, placing his left arm around her naked back and his right arm under her knees. Like a feather, he picked her up and carried her to the bed. His manhood was aroused and took over his consciousness. He dropped his pants and did not take the time to remove his shirt and underwear before mounting her. When deep inside, the passion turned to disgust. *Why am I doing this? She is shit to me. I hate this conniving bitch.* Feeling his manhood start to deflate before climaxing, he clicked himself back on forcing the passion to return. *Don't blow it now. She'll never forgive you. Just remember, old boy, only a few more days. Not much longer, at all. Keep your cool. It's better to keep her in bed with you than risk her sharing pillow talk with some reporter.* He continued the magic until he brought her not once, but twice and then again. She dug her nails into his back and cried for him to stop, but he just kept pounding himself into her, venting his anger until it was released in an explosion of shudders.

⊱━◦━⊰

Gstaad, one week later

They rose at four in the morning. Yusuf and Adam had loaded the two cars the night before. All that remained to do was ready themselves and pack their overnight bags with their toiletries and night clothes. Adam wanted to be on the road before it was light.

Elizabeth had heard a disturbing rumor when shopping in the village. Word was spreading that Di was in town disguised in a black wig. Everyone was curious, and no one seemed to know where she was staying. Usually, when Di was in Switzerland the paparazzi followed her. They loved to capture a shot of her on the ski slopes with her boys. There were no paparazzi in town now, and the villagers thought that a little strange. There was no sign of her anywhere. Still, the rumors were raging. They could not be too careful. They had no alternative but to drive through the village to leave. All it would take was one suspecting person to create all sorts of problems for them.

As they were getting ready, an outburst of foul language filtered out of Jennifer's room. Elizabeth quickly rushed up the stairs to see what had happened. Jennifer's monster bag had finally bit the dust, and she was furious. "This fucking, cheap piece of shit. I spent a lot of money for this, and look at this shit. The fucking strap pulled loose. How the hell am I going to get it repaired?"

Elizabeth said, "I'll think of something. In the meantime, I'll find something for your things."

Elizabeth left the room before she lost it with laughter. She ran down the steps into the pantry area. Adam and Yusuf, at first, thought she was crying as her shoulders were shaking from behind.

"What happened? Are you okay?" Adam asked.

She turned with a large cardboard box in her hands and collapsed on the floor in giggles. Yusuf and Adam were dumbfounded. Elizabeth finally managed to get it out, "That fucking purse is history. Adam, you take the box to her for her things. I just can't take it." She could not stop giggling.

Adam gave a thumbs up and headed up the stairs with the box.

"Oh Adam, can you fix it?"

He picked up the bag and examined it carefully, saying, "It looks like the bottom seam is ready to go as well. I think it's time to retire it."

Afraid that he might say the wrong thing if he said another word, Adam dropped to his hands and knees to help Jennifer transfer the important things into the Hermes clutch. The remainder was placed in the box until she could sort through it. There was an amazing amount of debris for the trash. The most remarkable was a desiccated orange. At first, Adam thought it was one of those things that women use to freshen the smells in closets, but as Jennifer tossed it into the wastebasket a flicker of a smile crossed her face. "It's a little past its prime, I guess."

Porting only about half the bulk, Adam descended the steps with the box in hand. Jennifer followed carrying her more modest clutch. Elizabeth had regained her composure. She was reasonably under control but did not trust herself completely. She did not dare comment. She was afraid she might lose it all again.

Elizabeth, Jennifer and Reem were all traveling in hijab and would ride with Yusuf in the Mercedes. Adam was driving alone in the Audi. The Audi was fully packed with the suitcases. Adam had folded down the back seat to fit everything inside. Care had been taken to economize space, as they had reached the limit with volume. The rear of the Mercedes was also loaded to the hilt. It was incredible the amount of luggage they were transporting. Adam thought it quite astounding what three women could do.

Adam and Yusuf had both placed silenced SIG automatics beneath their seats. Although the border crossing was pre-paid, sometimes dealing with Italian officials can be problematic. The Italians are noted for leaking word to a friend; Adam and Yusuf could not chance being shaken down.

Just the week before Adam had read an article in the paper about a man who had been carrying a large amount of currency across the border. At the border the man had claimed the money, as required by Italian law. He was passed through without a problem, but less than ten kilometers after crossing, the man was stopped by the Italian Police who confiscated the currency as evidence. Then they gave him a receipt. The only problem was that the 'police' were actually a gang, disguised as police, and the money was now gone forever. The real police had no leads on the case, or if they did, they were not telling.

They had too much invested now to run the risk of exposure. Adam was totally loyal to his client and would kill to protect Di. Very few people understood how seriously he took his business. His willingness to do anything to insure success was why he was the master of his craft. He would accomplish his promise to Di no matter what the cost might be to him or to others.

Most of the mountain passes were closed, even several of the lower ones. Spring had arrived, but in Switzerland spring has to turn into summer before the passes are open for travel. They had decided their best choice was to use the Saint Gotthard tunnel to head south into Ticino.

They departed Gstaad without notice. It is a small town. The police work eight to six, and even acknowledging that the Swiss are early risers, they timed their departure perfectly to avoid being seen. The roads were deserted as they headed down the valley towards the AutoRoute. They made good time. Once on the AutoRoute, about twenty minutes after passing through Bern, they took an exit for a rest stop that looked a little like a collapsing parachute. They topped off both cars with fuel, and Adam popped inside the fast-food restaurant that appeared to be part of the Mövenpick chain for some teas and coffees. He also collected some croissants to bide them over. Reem had packed some sandwiches for later, as it would be much too dangerous to stop at a restaurant to eat.

The drive to the villa would take about nine hours, providing they had no delays. It normally took less time, but the border crossing they had chosen was out of the way. It added a little more than an hour to the driving time. Adam had made the trip in five hours once, but today it would not be good to be stopped for speeding.

They experienced a minimum delay at the Saint Gotthard tunnel; often there are long delays, but today the traffic was moderate. They waited only about five minutes to enter the seventeen kilometer bore that cuts through the mountain. As they descended into the Italian part of Switzerland, the weather instantly changed for the better. The sun shone brightly and the temperature mounted.

Ticino is a well-kept secret. Few foreign tourists know of this paradise. It is an area crowded against the Alps yet blessed with a Mediterranean climate. Visitors are usually shocked to see the palm trees that grow in this little heaven and ask, "Are you sure this is in Switzerland?"

They took the exit at Locarno to head for the arranged border crossing. When they were near the crossing, Yusuf pulled over and exited his car. He and Adam conferred for a few moments. Back in their vehicles, each placed an unopened pack of Camel cigarettes on the dash of his car near the left side of the windshield. Adam pulled out first and was tailed closely by Yusuf. As they approached the frontier and passed through the Swiss control, they were ignored. This was normal for a Swiss car leaving the country. The Swiss are usually glad to see their own leave, assuming there will be taxes to pay upon the car's return.

As they approached the Italian side, the frontier guard walked up to Adam's side window. Adam was sitting on the SIG. He dropped his hand to his lap so the weapon would be closer. The guard asked if he could have a cigarette, and Adam handed him the pack from the dash. The guard waved Adam through and repeated the same ritual with the

Mercedes. The Mercedes passed through the checkpoint, and Yusuf punched up the speed to catch up with Adam.

The plan was that Adam would drive about a half kilometer ahead of the Mercedes. By doing this Adam could provide warning if there was a problem. After all, the women were with Yusuf, and Yusuf had a more difficult task to maneuver, if there was a problem.

They were about ten kilometers from the crossing when Adam's portable phone rang. It was Elizabeth. "We have company. Blue Lancia Kappa. Milano plates. Driver and one passenger. They are trying to stay out of sight, but we slowed down and saw them again after the last corner. They dropped back again."

"Tell Yusuf to speed up to ten kilometers over the speed limit, and I'll take care of it." Adam cruised into the driveway of a small restaurant and pulled to the back of the parking lot. He turned around and waited.

A few moments later, the Mercedes cruised by with the Lancia lagging a small distance behind. Adam counted to ten and pulled out. He held back playing the same game as the Lancia, staying just out of sight on the twisting road. Adam called Elizabeth and put his phone on the hands-free model. "I need info."

Understanding her brother like he was not a different person but merely an extension of herself, Elizabeth tracked exactly what Adam was asking. She began to describe the road and traffic conditions as they sped along. She was giving distances, describing small landmarks and the upcoming turns.

He continued to listen for the next two kilometers and, suddenly, broke the silence. "Good, ready or not here I come."

The report had been what he wanted; the upcoming turn was perfect since it had a small run out. Instinctively, Adam dropped the Audi down a gear and mashed the accelerator to the floor. The car rocketed forward; almost instantly the Lancia was in sight. He was closing in fast.

Elizabeth's report continued. "No traffic approaching from the other direction. The road seems clear. I'll keep you posted."

Without a response, Adam went for it. The Lancia was just beginning the right hand curve when Adam launched the Audi like a wire guided missile. He hit the Lancia hard on the right rear corner, then cranked the wheel and the Audi dove to the right. The Lancia spun off the road on the left across the small run out and down an embankment in a cloud of dust. Adam rocketed the Audi around on the road with tires screeching back to the crash scene. He told Elizabeth to get the Mercedes off the road and out of sight, then he leapt from the Audi. The passenger was just getting out of the car when Adam stuck the SIG pistol in his ear. "What the fuck were you doing?" he asked in his best Italian.

The man flaying his arms said, "Don't shoot, please. Please, don't shoot, Signor. I have a wife and three children."

Adam was not impressed. The guy was obviously an amateur. Adam was even more convinced that these guys were not professionals when the driver crawled out of the passenger side of the car in a stupor. The driver was definitely not tracking. Adam commanded. "Stand still." The driver did nothing. His expression was blank, and Adam could smell the wine on both of them. The driver was clearly no threat. He was in a daze. Still holding the SIG in the passenger's ear, Adam motioned for him to move closer to his partner. Again, Adam asked, "What the fuck were you two up to?"

This time the passenger responded, "Everyone needs to make a living. Arabs have money, Signor. Everyone knows it. They always carry a lot of cash." He then went on to tell Adam their plan.

"Well, you assholes picked the wrong target. Open the fucking trunk." Adam motioned for the two men to climb inside. They started to argue, and Adam said, "Listen, this gun is silenced, and your car is not visible from the road. It's easier for me just to kill the two of you and leave your bodies here. This is the last offer. In the trunk before I count to ten or die here on the ground. It doesn't matter to me. One, two, three…"

A few minutes later, Adam called Elizabeth. "I'm back. Tell me where you are, and I'll be right there. Just wait for me, and I'll fill you in."

Elizabeth described their location, and Adam was easily able to locate it. It was a graveled drive that went up a hillside on the right side of the road. Adam dropped his speed to a crawl, not to turn up a cloud of dust. He mounted the meandering lane to the flat wide space where the Mercedes was parked. The place afforded a good view of the road below. Adam was pleased to note that Yusuf had already turned the big car around and left the motor running so that he could take off quickly, if necessary. Adam pulled up and stopped in front the Mercedes, leaving Yusuf room to maneuver. He slipped out of the Audi.

Elizabeth and Yusuf started to get out of the big car, but Adam motioned them to stay put. He walked to the driver's window and filled them in on the developments. "The idiots thought you were Arabs smuggling money into the country. They planned on holding you up when they had an opportunity about twenty kilometers further down the road. Their partners are dressed as Italian Police. They were going to stop you and shake you down for your money. Definitely unorganized crime. The driver was sloshed. They were real bozos."

"Do we need to call for a cleaning crew?" Elizabeth asked.

"No. I locked them in their car trunk and told them I was booby trapping the back seat with a grenade. They will be very good until their partners find them. We just need to stick it out here until the road is clear."

"Is your car okay? There's a pretty nasty prang in the left front."

"I think it's mostly cosmetic. It ran fine and didn't seem to want to overheat. Call the girls and have them contact the garage to make the repairs as soon as we arrive. I don't want anyone looking for this car. Unfortunately, it isn't very discreet with the bright blue color and the front damaged. You can roll up the window and keep the air on. I'll just stand here and watch."

They were high enough to see all the movement on the roadway below, but it was unlikely that they would ever be seen. The overgrown, lush terrain provided the protection they needed. About ten minutes later a blue and white police car shot by. Deciding it was the car that had been set up to stop them, Yusuf dropped the window and smiled at Adam.

"Good thinking, boss. Let's get back on the road." He raised the window and pulled out, leaving Adam to jockey his car so he could get out.

Once back on the road, Adam called Elizabeth and told her that he would stay back as a rear guard until they had entered the AutoRoute system. No one would be able to track them then.

Jennifer was wild for the rest of the trip. She did not handle tension well. The incident had frightened her, and she had seen a side of Adam that she did not know existed. She was sure that he could have killed the two men who followed them, even though Elizabeth denied that it was ever a consideration. She was starting to realize that Adam was a different person than she had thought. He had looked like he has ice water, not blood, in his veins when he described the incident. *Maybe he is a dangerous man.* She was not sure, but she was still confident that she could control him. *What if Adam was wrong? What if someone else had been following them? Maybe someone from the press. Maybe someone knew. Or...* She knew that the establishment of England had resorted to all sorts of nefarious plans to protect itself in the past. *Maybe Adam is working for the English establishment. He mentioned something about the Queen herself. What have I gotten myself mixed up in?*

Unable to calm down, Jennifer started in on the hijab. "It's so heavy and hot." She rambled on and on complaining. "Please, Elizabeth, can't

I just remove the head piece for a little while? Who is ever going to notice me in this bloody car? The windows are nearly black. No one could ever see in."

Elizabeth was firm. Yusuf chimed in reminding Jennifer of the importance of their mission. *My God,* thought Elizabeth, *the only way this girl can vent her emotions is to talk. She is so damn shallow. I can't take much more.*

Trying to neutralize the tension, Elizabeth looked at her watch. "Jennifer dear, please try to understand. We are almost at the villa. Only another hour or two. Yusuf will get us there as quickly as possible, but you must be quiet and cooperate. If those men had seen you, they would have kidnapped you. Their only thought was the ransom they could raise from having the 'Princess' in their hands. Needless to say, Charles would not pay for your release. They would probably have later become frustrated and killed you."

Jennifer swallowed hard. "Okay. I'll be quiet. You win. I understand. I guess you are right." Jennifer had a strong survival instinct and decided it was better for her to remain invisible until she saw another option. But this whole thing was taking some strange turns as far as she was concerned.

They arrived at the villa not a minute too early for any of them. Adam had called ahead, and Eva was waiting to open the gate.

Jennifer's anger and concerns fell away as they drove into the spacious and well-manicured, mature grounds. The villa looked palatial. Pulling off her head covering and forgetting all of her anxiety, she said, "This place is gorgeous. How many bedrooms are there? Is there a bridal suite? How about a pool where I can swim and take some sun?"

Elizabeth's rolling of her eyes went unnoticed. Elizabeth wasn't sure whether to attribute Jennifer's reaction to her hijab or to her naiveté.

Everyone helped unload the cars. The unpacking seemed endless. About thirty minutes later, just as they finished, there was the sound of a horn from the gate.

"Who's here?" asked Jennifer nervously.

"It's okay," Adam said as he headed to open the gate. "I'm expecting him."

Brigit had made arrangements with Adam's favorite master mechanic to pick up the Audi for repairs. Adam trusted no other person in the area with the care of his cars. Adam's cars were almost more important than his weapons. Actually, he considered them weapons. He never took them for granted and always paid attention that every detail was in perfect running order. The condition of his car could pose a life or death proposition for him. However, never did Adam imagine that the man would actually arrive as planned. He was so prompt today. It was so un-Italian. Adam outlined what he wanted done, in addition to the obvious damage repair, and sent the man off with the car.

To keep Jennifer from disturbing Adam, Brigit had taken her for a quick tour of the estate. Jennifer was wide-eyed and impressed. Her anger disappeared, and she quickly settled into the new location.

After taking a few minutes to unpack her things, Jennifer decided the time had come for her to prove herself to Adam and Elizabeth. She was still contemplating slipping away, striking out on her own. She knew she would attract attention anywhere in the world. She just had not figured out a plan to capitalize on the attention she would receive. Until her plot was in order, she thought it better to stick it out with Adam. After all, she was making twenty thousand a month, plus expenses. Adam had accepted her proposal without a lot of arguing. He was like putty in her hands. Maybe she could arrange another raise in pay. Now was not the right time. Not enough time had lapsed. She would have to wait for the proper moment. It might be better for her to learn some more at Adam and Elizabeth's expense before making her escape. From a business standpoint, it would be smarter to wait until she had actually made a stand-in, or two, for Di. With that experience under her belt, her story would be even more valuable. *I am going to be one of the most famous people of all time. Then, I can buy people like Elizabeth and Adam. Then, we'll see who's the boss.*

Jennifer was starting to feel like she really understood Di. When she felt sorry for herself, she felt sorry for Di in so many ways. They had shared many similar life experiences. Like Di, Jennifer had not felt closeness from her parents. Like Di, Jennifer did not trust the sincerity of her lovers. Not even Adam when it came down to it. But, then again, she really trusted no one. She had learned that it was always best to look out for number one, but she didn't think that Di had figured that out yet. Perhaps, she would have a chance to give Di the hint; that could help her story too. Jennifer had mastered Di's mannerisms. She could imitate Di's voice to perfection, although she had not been able to rid herself of its so slightly huskier quality. Most importantly, Jennifer was no longer acting. She had assumed Di's persona.

The only problem was that Jennifer had no firm plan as to how to step out on her own. She now had good seed money in the bank in Geneva, but she would have to go there to draw it out. How could she prove her identity, looking not as herself but like Di? If she left, Adam would never give her a second chance. She was certain of that. Feeling confused, she tried to reassure herself. *Maybe Adam will marry me when this is over. He acts as though he cares for me. I could do one bloody hell of a lot worse. I turn him on. I know that much. I could marry him then wait until someone better comes along. I could divorce him and take him for as much as possible.* And so she settled on her immediate plan.

About three hours later Jennifer walked into the room. Motionless, their faces showed visible shock with the rush of blood to their brains. They were startled. She had said good-bye to her black hair. Her roots had started to show, and since her black hair had fooled no one, she had changed the color. Her natural light brown hair was now much lighter, highlighted in blond.

Adam was the first to comment. "You frightened me when you walked around the corner without a word. For a minute I fantasized that Di was here. I thought I had forgotten an appointment. God, the resemblance is unsettling."

"I just wanted to show you. I'm ready to be famous. Famously yours."

⊱┈❀┈○┈❀┈⊰

Yusuf received the e-mail message. The invitation would be extended. Excited, he searched to find Adam. The good news bubbled out. His emotions were high.

"Now we must really get to work," Adam said. "Our time schedule is closing in upon us. The farther this progresses, the less room there is for error."

Adam was concerned if Di understood how critical it was to the project's success for her to accept the invitation. Taking the boys was a perfect way to keep the press from jumping to conclusions, but Di was limited in what she could do with the boys. It was problematic, but they would think of a solution. Once there, she could certainly drop hints so she could return for an extended visit. They would work out something. They had to; there was no other option.

In the middle of his contemplation, Adam's portable signaled him that he had new mail. The message was from Martin. It was brief.

"Arrangements are in order. Plan to strike within twenty-four hours. Notify to abort. M."

14

Paris, 19 May 1997

They had arrived at the Paris flat a few hours earlier. Everyone was fatigued after the long, uneventful drive from the Italian villa. Elizabeth was helping Jennifer pack for Pakistan. Jennifer did not know where they were going, only that she would be substituting for Di. Elizabeth was marking off each item on her checklist to assure nothing was forgotten. Precision was essential.

They had stopped in the south of France the night before at a safe house that had been arranged to make the long drive from Italy more endurable. Adam had not wanted them to take chances with a border crossing into Switzerland. There were no longer border checkpoints between Italy and France. They were insured an uneventful border crossing by driving up the coast of Italy and crossing there.

Hijab was not the most comfortable form of clothing for such a long trip. Overheated, the women had demanded the air conditioning at full force, and Yusuf had complained of being too cold the whole way.

Elizabeth made a mental note to tell Adam that he needed to work with Yusuf to be a little more sensitive. Especially to those he did not think his equal. Women in particular. It was a problem of his culture, and he might never overcome it.

Fortunately, Brigit and Eva had gone ahead to ready the safe house and prepare a delicious dinner to welcome their arrival. Everyone's nerves were on edge. The car was confining, and the personality battles were raging. The delicate fabric of control was fraying.

Jennifer was in one of her incessantly bitchy moods. Talking was her addiction, and she left no room for doubt in expressing her dismay. She snapped at everyone. Nothing satisfied her. Adam was in the States. He had been away now for nearly two weeks, and she was furious. She was feeling sorry for herself. Her needs were going unserviced. She felt neglected and insecure.

Her threats to leak her story to the press were more frequent than ever, but they remained idle. So far, she had never attempted the leak. Elizabeth had tightened security, and the situation was becoming a 'Catch 22.' The more Jennifer threatened and complained, the more closely she was watched and the more uncomfortable she became. As she felt more abused, she would conjure new threats. Frustrations were escalating and were almost out of control.

Elizabeth sent a priority e-mail to Adam begging him to change his plans and return. Elizabeth feared losing her grasp on Jennifer. In Adam's absence the girls had assumed the responsibility of standing watch over Jennifer between midnight and six in the morning. They took three hour shifts, but the schedule was exhausting. No one really took Jennifer seriously, but it was impossible to know. If she tried an escape, it would certainly be at night. Adam's orders had been absolute. Twenty-four hour surveillance. These orders were being carried out, but everyone was weary in the process.

Before leaving Adam had tried to prepare Jennifer for his absence. The evening before his departure, he arranged a private soirée for the two of them. On the terrace overlooking the idyllic landscape of the valley below, he and Jennifer shared a candlelight supper served to perfection by Eva. Soft love songs played in the background as Adam complimented Jennifer on her success. He told her that he was so satisfied with her mastering of her role that he was giving her another raise. This one was five thousand dollars a month. He promised her that when the project was complete, he would take her wherever she wanted to go, anywhere in the world. They would spend two weeks in paradise. She merely needed to be patient. It would not be much longer.

Jennifer was reluctant at first. She told Adam that she was tired of being confined. Her salary was meaningless because she never saw any of the money. She could not spend her money. She had no access to her funds. They were in some stupid bank in Geneva. She was like a prisoner. Adam would not allow her to go anywhere at any time, not even when she was dressed as a stupid ninja woman. She demanded for Adam to pay her in cash.

Adam handed her fifty thousand French francs, knowing she could go nowhere to spend it. He told her it was just a bonus. He caressed her and flattered her. Skillfully, he turned her queries into understanding, at least, for the moment. But with her it was difficult. Adam had already discovered that the woman had a hidden agenda for everything she did.

Later that night, as they clung together in his large bed, he whispered in her ear that they were now close to her premiere performance. He explained that he needed to travel to the States to make some final arrangements. The arrangements were extremely sensitive. He needed to handle them personally. It would not be long, only two weeks. Then, they would be reunited. Adam promised to contact Jennifer daily by e-mail. Elizabeth would help Jennifer collect Adam's messages and would assist her with responding the minute they arrived. Jennifer's reply was much less submissive than Adam had hoped. She did not want messages; she wanted Adam. Finally, after arousing her to climax six times in a row in fifteen-minute intervals, she dropped off into a deep, sound sleep. Adam lay awake afraid to move for fear she might awaken with demands of starting the lovemaking cycle all over again. He was fatigued and more than a little sore.

If he hadn't had access to the experimental drug made from a root found in Africa he never would have succeeded. Servicing this young slut was becoming almost repulsive to him. When he first succumbed to her, he never dreamed it could turn into something so ugly. He had always prided himself on being able to handle anything for the sake of a project. Jennifer was pushing him over the line. He had known numerous women through the years. Jennifer was from a different mold. There was nothing real about this woman. She never stopped playing her role. At least, she no longer faked her orgasms; at least, he thought she no longer did. She could play act easily, detaching herself from her true emotions. As a lover, her role was strictly physical. Her desires for stimulation were insatiable. She was the hunter, aroused only by brutal manipulation. He should have figured this out earlier when the crew that packed her things in New York had discovered a vibrator and a plethora of other sex toys.

Adam turned off the alarm and leapt from the bed. He told Jennifer he needed to hurry. He was catching an early flight. Protesting, Jennifer begged him to cancel. He took a deep breath to regain his composure. *Why in the hell can't I get through to this little piece of shit? Damn. I need her. Somehow, I have to gain her trust.*

Walking back over to the bed, he sat down by her side. He was firm with her now. "My princess, the success of this project is dependent upon you and me. No one else can do what we have to do. We are a team. I have confidence in you. Your debut is now only three weeks away. I have work to do to prepare the stage for you. I need your help. I need your support. Please understand. Be my partner."

The last days at the villa without Adam had been difficult for Elizabeth. All Jennifer wanted to do was e-mail complaints to Adam. She would ask Elizabeth to help her send an e-mail; thirty minutes later, she would want to send another.

Elizabeth had become a master at attaining the response she wanted from Jennifer. The months of togetherness had taught Elizabeth what buttons to punch. Jennifer responded to stimulus. Elizabeth would reward Jennifer with e-mailing privileges when their day's schedule was successfully completed. It was surprising that Jennifer had still not figured out how to e-mail on her own. Manipulation was Jennifer's best friend, but she seemed to lack interest in learning if someone else would assume the responsibility for her.

During Adam's absence, Jennifer had perfected her role. They had worked on small idiosyncrasies of Di's persona. They had spent much time reviewing the dossiers that Di had provided. Jennifer memorized Di's likes and dislikes in food, music, dance, décor and designers. Anything that might or could come up in everyday conversation was now covered. Di had also prepared several video messages for Jennifer, talking about her childhood, her strained relationship with her mother, her life with Charles. They were all stories that the press had covered, but Di provided the truth of the matter. They were all personal feelings that Di had shared at sometime with someone. Again, these were things that could come up in everyday conversations. Jennifer had listened intently, assimilating every detail. Jennifer was very good at this portion of the task. She realized that making this information her own would benefit her later.

Elizabeth had observed the girl falling out of herself. She was forgetting her own past. She was accepting Di's past as her own. *Too bad she couldn't assume Di's personality,* Elizabeth thought. As kind and considerate as Di was, Jennifer was selfish and egocentric. Reassured that Jennifer could do it, Elizabeth's solace was still overshadowed by the recurring challenge of keeping the girl on track. As long as they were working, all was well. The minute they took a break, Jennifer's mind would begin to wander. She would babble her discontent and reinvent her unfulfilled demands. Elizabeth thought it preposterous that it was taking five people to keep this one female in line. *Damn it! Adam, get your ass back here.*

➤┈◆┈○┈◆┈◄

Hours after his arrival in Dallas, Adam received a call from Martin. The connection on his cell phone was fuzzy, and Martin's voice was fading in and out. Disgusted that Martin was carping to him, Adam tried to calm him down. *My God, he is acting like an old woman. I have never seen him do this before.* "Martin, shit. Just do what he says. Do you understand me? I know he's a kid, but he's damn smart. Don't piss him off."

"I hear you. It's just that he spouts some damn computer term and then looks at me like I am from another planet when I don't understand. Why the hell can't he speak some normal language instead of computerese. I think the little prick is doing it on purpose."

"You are from a different planet, and don't forget it. Unless dinosaurs like you and me get with it, we will be extinct. The whole world is going to be run by these damn kids if we don't wake up. What is he doing anyway?"

"Damned if I know. He is synchronizing the video recorders on the van, and he wants us to make another film run. He said it has to do with vertical and horizontal image disparity, whatever the hell that means. He said he has software that can make the corrections within certain limits. The production will be seamless through the VR helmet, whatever in the hell that is. He said something like that, anyway. Does it mean anything to you?"

"Yes, I understand. It's Gerard speak for 'line the fuckers up so that you can see the whole picture when you look at it.'"

"Why the hell couldn't he have said that?"

"Quit acting like a cretin and get the job done. You sound like an old woman bitching about her husband."

"Okay, but I really don't like working with this little shit."

"Cool off and e-mail your progress reports to me."

"Ya, sure. Okay, I understand. Talk to you later." The line went dead.

Adam was relieved that the kid was making progress. It disgusted him that Martin could not separate his own emotions from the task at hand. All that mattered was getting the job done. Realizing that he was nearly late for his dinner invitation, Adam telephoned the concierge to confirm that the limo was ready. He would be down in five minutes.

➤┈◆┈○┈◆┈◄

Martin stopped at an all night bar for what turned out to be a bitter, over-roasted expresso and headed back to the garage. He found Gerard tinkering with the alignment of the cameras. Gerard was oblivious to Martin's presence. Martin coughed to announce his return, not wanting to startle the kid.

"Glad you're back. Hey, would you hand me that screwdriver? It is hard for me to move."

"No problem."

"Thanks. Okay. Just one last connection, and I think I've got it. There. Let's go for a drive and test it."

"Are you sure? You want to go now? For Christ's sake, it's four in the morning."

"Perfect time. Not much traffic."

"Are you going to ride in the back again and constantly bitch at me to drive steady? It's a real pain in the ass."

"I have to. It's the only way I can tell if we have visual disparity. I can monitor everything on the screen. Then, I'll make the fly input adjustments, slip in a little code or patches and hot swap the drives if necessary."

"In other words, you have to muck with the damn thing."

"Close enough."

"It was a hell of a lot simpler when we just drew it out on paper and went for it."

"It was also a time when a hell of a lot of mistakes were made. The unexpected and unplanned happened. With the new computer simulations, there is much less room for error."

"You keep telling me that, but all computers seem to do is allow us to make bigger screw ups with greater confidence."

"God, you sound like my mother."

"Shut up, or I'll squash you like the little bug you are."

"Listen, Martin, you don't intimidate me. Sure you are big and tough and could pound my ass if you could run fast enough to catch me. But you have to sleep sometime, and I am as vindictive as hell."

Martin was about to make a preemptive physical strike when he remembered what Adam had said. "Okay. Okay, you win. Let's go for the damn drive. I feel like I'm bickering with an old woman."

"Be sure to stop long enough at the Ritz for me to register the cameras. I'll let you know when I've got it, and you can go on."

"Just be fast about it. Security will be all over me if I stop there for long."

"Tell them to piss off; you have to take a leak."
"Stick to your computers. You don't understand people."

>—·—<>—o—<>—·—<

It was almost three in the morning when Adam opened the door to his suite at the Mansion. His evening with Thomas had been enlightening. Thomas had been correct. The meeting was urgent. Dallas was a neutral location, a better solution than Switzerland.

Switzerland is a small country, and although heralded for secrecy, fading into the masses is much easier in a large U.S. city. Too many people knew Adam and Thomas in Switzerland, and it was important if anything ever came out about Di that no ties could be remembered.

Adam opened his e-mail program as he loosened his tie and started to undress. His messages downloaded quickly. There were seven in total. Two from Martin, and the rest from Gerard.

Martin's first message provided his assessment of the project. It appeared to be on schedule. The other was bitching about Gerard. Adam had no time for this petty nonsense and deleted it before reading it completely.

Gerard's messages were written in techno-speak, except for one. Tit for tat. Gerard was bitching about Martin. *They sound like a couple of old women bickering,* Adam thought as he deleted the message. Understanding Gerard's messages was a little like piecing together meaning from a scholarly article in a foreign language after only a six-week conversational course. From what Adam could assimilate, the project was a go, and the major problems had been overcome. Gerard was a little ahead of schedule.

Satisfied that his plan was falling into predictable order, Adam called down to the front desk asking that any incoming calls be diverted to his voice mail. He would steal a few short hours of long awaited sleep.

>—·—<>—o—<>—·—<

The trip to Pakistan provided the needed reprieve. For her normal composure, Jennifer had remained calm during their two days at the flat in Paris, excited that she would soon be reunited with Adam. They had taken time to relax and unwind; in retrospect, it had proven to be a bad idea. Any time Jennifer was not busy, she reverted to talking. Elizabeth had encouraged the girl to read a good book to take her mind off of everything, but such a feat was about as likely as Jennifer making a new breakthrough in higher math. During the two days, Jennifer had been overly demanding of Elizabeth's attention asking the same questions over and over again. She wanted to know how she should go about publishing her book. Her interest in telling her story placed the entire crew on alert. No one thought that she would try to contact the press, not so close to her debut, but the girl fooled no one. With Jennifer anything was possible.

Jennifer's severe mood swings were unpredictable. They could not be too cautious. Elizabeth was not sure that her decision to outline the first part of the plan to Jennifer had been smart. She could not turn back now. What was done was done. Elizabeth had left the details unsaid. She had provided Jennifer with only enough information to whet her excitement and stimulate her imagination. Jennifer did not know where they were going or what she would be doing. All she knew was that she would shortly have her first opportunity to substitute for Di. It would be a low risk situation. For the project to continue, Jennifer's success was mandated.

They arose before four in the morning. They were packed and only needed to ready themselves. The plan had been structured to the minute. Everyone understood the need to comply exactly as arranged.

Yusuf was driving the Mercedes with the three women in hijab. The women were to remain silent. They were to say nothing to anyone. Regardless. Yusuf would handle all outside contact.

Yusuf drove at the legal limit directly to the airport. Security was tight, the norm at Charles de Gaulle. Terrorist threats had been numerous of late, and the European airports were often key targets. The airport officials were taking no chances. There was no possibility of clearing security unless all regulations had been properly followed.

Yusuf had pre-driven the route the day before. He had memorized the appropriate turns and exits. He had driven at the same time of day. He had clocked his time and noted where he could have traffic delays. All variables had been contemplated and calculated into the schedule. He was prepared. He would maneuver the Mercedes without hesitation.

Arriving at his destination on time, almost to the second, the automatic gate opened before Yusuf had a chance to slow the car to a full stop. It was a remote side entrance at the farthest end of the airport complex. They were expected. A guard approached the car. Yusuf handed him the appropriate papers. All designated information was accurately noted. After a casual check, the guard waved them through.

The Mercedes ghosted across the runway to the custom-designed

Boeing 747 decorated with Arabic markings. A passenger ramp was in place with an officious looking young man waiting at the bottom. Yusuf parked next to the ramp and exited the car. The young man shifted nervously, uncertain of what to expect. Without acknowledging the attendant, Yusuf opened the back-seat doors and helped the women exit the car. The young attendant stood silently motionless. He made no attempt to offer his assistance. He merely stood there like a permanent fixture. As the three women glided up the stairs and disappeared into the aircraft, Yusuf turned on his heels. He tossed the keys to the young man and said, "Unload the car; then park it. You should learn some manners while you are at it."

With quick reflexes, the young man caught the keys and jumped into action. Asking no questions, he ran to the car and began to haul out the bags and drag them up the rear ramp.

Yusuf waited at the bottom of the ramp for the young man to return with his keys. As he waited, it started to rain. Yusuf opened his large black and white umbrella with Ping written on one of the panels. Adam had told him that Ping was a golf company. Yusuf had thought that with a name like Ping, it was probably Chinese. He didn't know that the Chinese were interested in golf, but they must be. As the air chilled and the rain continued to fall, Yusuf's mind began to wander.

He thought of how often the weather in Paris is miserable. He had grown to take it in his stride by now. When it got right down to it, Yusuf didn't think much of Paris anyway. The buildings were beautiful, but most were in poor repair. The Parisians were an arrogant people, especially to anyone looking Arabic. Worst of all, the city was filthy. Still, he could not deny it. Paris and the Parisians had served him well. Even with their arrogance, the Parisians would put up with anyone who could speak French. After all, they had put up with him. He had to give them credit for something. He had been able to live in Paris without much discrimination. All cultures of the world are represented in this city and he, like so many foreigners, had been able to blend into everyday life.

Paris had been his second home for many years. He had used it as a base when he changed his identity after being singled out in a terrorist attack against Israel. Adam had helped him assume his new persona. Yusuf remembered it all so well. Every time he thought of it, he had to fight off a shiver that made him look and feel cold.

Yusuf had sought out Adam to help him escape the Israeli hit squad that was looking for him. Adam had the reputation for being the best in the world. Ironically, Yusuf had heard of him through an Israeli security leak. The Israelis are the keenest in the world when it comes to covert activities, and anyone they trust is reliable. How strange it was. Yusuf's tip, his ticket to safety, had come from his enemy.

Yusuf remembered like yesterday how selective Adam was in his dealings. Adam worked under his own terms. He agreed to help Yusuf on one condition. Yusuf had no choice but to agree to give up his political beliefs and start a new life. Yusuf's decision took some time. It did not come easy. Finally, Yusuf accepted; he knew that without Adam, he was a dead man. That was bad enough, but his beloved Reem was on the hit list also. With Adam Yusuf would have life but could not be himself. Yusuf was a man of convictions, and without the ability to work for his cause, there was little reason for him to continue. But Yusuf had Reem to consider, and he clung to the hope that after going underground in disguise, he could again act for the honor of his cause.

Following Adam's orders, Yusuf religiously hid in Paris for nearly a year. During this time, he had carefully and, as far as he was concerned, skillfully reaffirmed contact with the terrorist organization. It was a splinter group of the PLO.

One afternoon Yusuf was looking onto the street from a window of the apartment he shared with Reem. He observed Reem, in hijab, approaching about a block away. He noticed that she was being followed. He could not believe that anyone had recognized her, but he realized something was wrong. Frantic and unable to act, he watched in amazement. The man who was following her took up a post near the end of the block. Soon another man joined Reem's stalker at the other end of the block. This man was neatly dressed in blue jeans and a denim shirt with a large leather belt and silver buckle. He epitomized the French idea of the American country hero. Hardly the look of a terrorist. Yusuf concluded that the man was obviously an Israeli. The two did not close in on Reem. She was allowed to enter the apartment building undisturbed. They did nothing. The streets were crowded with pedestrians. The two stalkers went unnoticed, blending into the busy atmosphere of the city. The two just watched, inconspicuously, and waited.

Yusuf began to panic. The norm for the Israelis was to extract vengeance. They epitomized the philosophy of a tooth for a tooth and an eye for an eye. Yusuf felt trapped; the men would not wait long once they had identified him. They might come for him that very night. They were on his tail. Suddenly, Yusuf's courage began to fail. These men would do anything to execute their revenge. They would kill Reem, as well. For one of the first times in his life, he felt real fear.

Yusuf told Reem that they had no choice. They would be dead by morning if they did not escape. They had talked before about their plan, should the need ever arise. They leapt into action. They primed the apartment so lights could be seen from every window. They turned on the television and played a taped conversation of the two of them in a soft but heated discussion. They had prepared the tape weeks before as a security measure, in the event an urgent situation arose.

It was twilight. The perfect time. The men would never anticipate their attempting anything before complete darkness. Dressed in western clothing, they made their escape through an attic window. They had taken a trial run shortly after moving into the apartment. They knew the escape was doable. They cautiously crossed the rooftops until they found an alleyway that was unguarded. Yusuf secured a rope and lowered Reem to the pavement below. He then expertly shimmied himself down. Their maneuver went unnoticed. They emerged from the narrow street draped around one another like two lovers who had hidden for a few minutes to escape prying eyes. Clinging to one another, unaware of the world around them, they made their slow escape from the area.

During the time they were in hiding, Yusuf had started to feel that being a freedom fighter was much more interesting to talk about than it was to experience in real life. He wanted to get away from it but found it difficult to sever all ties. He wanted to keep his promise to Adam, but he could not quash his bleeding internal urge to fight for his cause. His father had always told Yusuf that he was foolish. He had told Yusuf it was not his cause, but like youth the world over, Yusuf was caught up in rebellion.

As the wind caught his umbrella, Yusuf's thoughts were interrupted. *What in the hell is taking that stupid little prick so long?* As he turned in a three hundred and sixty-degree circle to see if the kid was approaching, Yusuf's thoughts again turned back to his past.

It had never been a question of money. They were wealthy. Yusuf's father had been a part owner in a bank in Lebanon and was a shrewd investor. He had never approved of Yusuf's political beliefs. He had told Yusuf that he was acting like a child, allowing cowards to manipulate him. Yusuf's father considered the terrorist leaders cowards because they always enlisted young people to stand on the front lines, promising them glory. These so called leaders were experts at organizing protests while remaining safely protected behind the lines. Taking no personal risks, they never faced death, but they never questioned expecting their fresh cannon fodder to carry out their operations and die for them.

The Israelis had begun to understand this reality and were looking for these cowards. The Israelis were eliminating them, as they found them, methodically, one by one. Maybe somehow, Yusuf had been pegged as one of these leaders. He had only been on the periphery of the group. He had never personally engaged in any overt act of terrorism, although he had been involved in several terrorist acts, including the one that exposed his name. Yusuf knew deep down that the leaders of the terrorist groups were not being fair, but he had been naive and caught up in the whole thing. Reem had followed him out of devotion for him. She had never felt a fire for the ideology. But she had a fire for him.

Yusuf realized that he had been stupid when it came to Adam. Adam had helped him, and Yusuf defied Adam's trust by breaking his promise. Yusuf had tried to carry on his shadow activities, even though he had promised Adam he would sever all ties. Now, it had all caught up with him.

After their successful escape, Yusuf had nowhere to turn. The blatant reality struck Yusuf. Adam had been right all along. Yusuf hated himself for being so foolish, for doubting Adam's judgment. Yusuf, now, needed Adam more than ever. This time Adam might refuse to help. After all, Yusuf had already betrayed him once. Swallowing his pride, Yusuf contacted Adam. Adam was furious when he learned of Yusuf's stupidity. The two went back and forth arguing for a week or so. Finally, Adam acquiesced. He would help Yusuf and Reem, but, only on his terms. Adam was serious. If he caught one infraction of the rules, Adam would personally hand over Yusuf's dossier to the Israelis. Yusuf agreed with a level of commitment he had never before experienced. He would prove himself to Adam. He would regain Adam's confidence. This accomplishment was Yusuf's new crusade, his new cause.

Yusuf began his new life exactly as Adam dictated. In the beginning he worked from time to time for Adam. As time passed, his workload was increased. He was given more and more responsibility. His relationship with Adam grew. They developed a bond that could not be penetrated. Now, several years later, he was one of Adam's most trusted operatives.

Some years after all of this had happened, Yusuf's father, who was terminally ill at the time, called for Yusuf to come to him. He had been lingering for months and his time was now very near. His father told Yusuf that they had unfinished business. He could not die without telling Yusuf the truth.

Intently, Yusuf listened. Yusuf's father confided that in the years before, Adam had sought him out. He and Adam had been friends forever. They had met during the debacle that took place when the Shah of Iran escaped. They shared a common bond. The two men had privately discussed Yusuf's allegiance with the terrorists. Adam had expressed his concern for Yusuf. Adam felt that Yusuf, a man with a big heart, had not always been smart. Yusuf often picked the wrong people as friends. Adam was convinced that Yusuf needed to see life from a different viewpoint. The two men conspired. They arranged to have Reem followed in Paris to frighten Yusuf into permanently changing his ways. They wanted Yusuf to be scared enough to take Adam's advice seriously.

Yusuf was furious beyond words. His anger mounted into rage when he realized how Adam had manipulated him. His father, sensing that Yusuf was almost over the line of control, suggested, like only a father can do, that Yusuf should be eternally grateful to Adam. Adam had offered him a new life, a hope for the future. What had the cowardly leaders offered him but hollow rhetoric and sure death? Yusuf still to this day remembered his father's words almost verbatim. "He is the best friend a man could ever have. Don't ever doubt his sincerity. You were putty in the hands of dangerous men. They were manipulating your mind. Adam helped you become your own man. Without Adam's help, you would have been dead before me." With this comment, Yusuf's father had feebly stretched out his arms to embrace his son for the last time.

After his father's confession, Yusuf told Reem the whole story. She just laughed at him. She couldn't stop. Somehow her reaction took away all of Yusuf's anger. He began to laugh as well, and the weight was lifted. Now, several years later, there was nothing that Yusuf would not do for Adam. Reem felt the same way. He was like a father to both of them and had given them life.

Adam was a strange one. If he liked a person, he would do anything, literally anything, to help the person. Anyone not included on his list of favorites was treated quite differently. Adam used the person like a pawn. As long as Adam had a need, he would relate to the person. When the need was satisfied, Adam would simply throw the person away.

Yusuf was not sure into which category Jennifer fell. He had yet to figure out what was happening. Clearly, Adam had developed her into a doppelganger for Princess Di, but what was he going to do with her? This was the big question, and Adam was a hard one to outguess. Yusuf was not a betting man but if forced, he would put money on including Jennifer's name on the list of pawns.

Yusuf realized that Adam was committed to the project. He was sure that it involved Di directly. He could tell by Adam's intensity that it was a major project. Yusuf hoped that nothing too severe would happen. As usual, Adam was playing his cards close to his chest, and Yusuf still had not figured out Adam's scheme. Adam was a master at providing only enough information for his operatives to accomplish their individual tasks. At the same time, he would withhold as much information as possible making it impossible for anyone to calculate his ultimate plan. Yusuf was as much of an insider as anyone. He had grasped the nature of the plan, although Adam had told him little. When Adam decided to tell him, it would likely prove to be a confirmation of what Yusuf had theorized himself. Still, he had been dead wrong on several occasions, and it kept him on his toes.

Yusuf, now somewhat drenched from waiting so long, was distracted from his introspection by the young man running towards him. The youth was trying to get to cover before he was completely soaked. Unfortunately, he was not having much success. Yusuf thought the young man a fool. Like Adam, Yusuf had little patience with fools. The young man tossed the keys to Yusuf as he started to climb the stairs two by two to the aircraft's entrance. Yusuf yelled to him, "Wait a minute. What in the fuck do you think you are doing?"

Stopping in his tracks about halfway up the staircase and more than a little shocked, the young man turned to look down onto the voice that was calling from below.

Yusuf continued, "Step away from the aircraft. Your services are no longer required. We will return in about one week. Find a cheap hotel. Notify the number on this card of your whereabouts. When we return the aircraft, you will be contacted, and you can return to your self-importance."

Accepting the card from Yusuf's outstretched hand, the young man started to say something until he saw Yusuf's expression. On second analysis, he decided it was wiser to keep his comments to himself. Without a word, he walked dejectedly through the rain towards the hanger.

Idiot. He must be related to the Sheik. That is the only excuse for hiring him. Yusuf climbed the stairs. As he entered the aircraft, he shook out the umbrella and signaled the ground crew to remove the ramp. Yusuf announced to the captain that everyone was on board. They could depart at any time.

Jennifer and the others had already been shown by one of the flight attendants to their spacious three-bedroom cabin. Yusuf charmingly told the attendant who greeted him at the door, "I would like to join the ladies."

He was shown to the cabin where he knocked at the double door entrance and waited for a response. Elizabeth, in hijab, answered the door. Reem and Jennifer had already peeled off their cloaks and veils and had made themselves comfortable in the cabin's large sitting room.

Upon seeing Yusuf, Jennifer jumped to her feet and ran to him. "Just look at this place. Have you ever seen anything so gorgeous? It looks as though it's right out of Architectural Digest."

Elizabeth felt almost like throwing up at Jennifer's enthusiasm. For her, the decor was blatant opulence, nouveau riche, and absolute crippy crap all wrapped into one giant package. The overpowering intermingling of the gold and silver lamé on the heavy brocade fabrics was more than she could stomach. Sensing Elizabeth's exasperation with Jennifer, Yusuf suggested that she change out of hijab. "You will be much more comfortable," he mentioned. "Why don't you use the study. You can work there undisturbed."

Yusuf would act as their personal steward throughout the flight, serving refreshments and meals to the three women at their individual discretion. He would assure that the flight attendants did not enter the cabin. No one would see any of the three women out of hijab.

The captain's voice blared out over the loud speaker. His English was heavily accented but understandable. "I welcome you all to the flight today. Please fasten your seatbelts at this time. Please remain seated until I turn off the fasten seatbelt sign. I will do this when we reach our cruising altitude of about 12,000 meters. We expect a smooth, nonturbulent flight to Lahore. The flight crew is here to serve you in every way. The crew will do their best. I remind you to fasten your seatbelts now, and I wish you a most enjoyable flight. You will have plenty of time to sit back and relax."

With the captain's message Jennifer was even more exuberant. Like always when she was excited, she started talking incessantly. As she heard the engines start to spool up she said, "This plane is incredible. Is it Adam's?"

Elizabeth was about to excuse herself to the study as Yusuf had suggested, but first she had to satisfy Jennifer's curiosity. "No. It belongs to a friend."

"I would ask who, but I know you wouldn't tell me."

"Correct."

"Can you, at least, tell me how many hours it is to Pakistan?"

"About ten hours, I think, but only because we are making a stop on the way."

"Are we picking up Adam? That would be wonderful. He promised me he would be here. It seems like I haven't seen him forever."

"No, he is already in Pakistan. We will meet him there. You won't have to wait much longer to see him."

"Then why are we stopping?"

"To refuel the plane. We have no choice." The real reason was that they wanted the flight to originate from the Middle East, not from France. But Jennifer did not need to know this information. Elizabeth often led the girl astray more out of habit than necessity.

>─┼─◆>─○─<◆─┼─<

They were jarred by sudden turbulence as they began the descent to the airport at Lahore, Pakistan. This bumpiness was the first they had experienced. The flight had been smooth just as the captain had promised. The landing was gentle, almost too perfect. Yusuf wondered where the pilot had received his training. He was better than most of the commercial pilots Yusuf had observed.

Upon deplaning, two Mercedes were waiting for them. The women descended the access stairs like black ghosts and entered one car. Yusuf told the pilot to be ready to depart at 06h00 on May 25th. The pilot shrugged acceptance and merely said, "That one is an unusually tall Arab woman."

Yusuf, showing no emotion, responded, "Yes." He hoped that most people were less observant than the pilot. It was a problem. One that Adam, Reem and he had discussed often.

Jennifer was too tall to be convincingly of Arabic origins. She was nearly as tall as Yusuf. Perhaps, their original thought of having her walk a little stooped to hide her height was a good one. He would, again, mention it to Adam.

Yusuf descended the steps to the other car and with pleasant surprise found Adam seated in the far side of the back seat where he had not been visible from the plane. Yusuf began to speak, but Adam signaled him with a sharp glance. Taking the cue, Yusuf remained quiet until they arrived at the luxurious compound they would be using as their base during their stay in Pakistan.

The compound was much larger than Yusuf had anticipated. It was laid out like a small hotel with numerous freestanding bungalows. Each donned its own secluded outdoor spa. The bungalows were situated so they wrapped around a central building that housed the dining room, library, game room and the owner's private quarters. The grounds were exceptional with tennis courts, a lap pool, a diving pool, and a sandy beach area by an artificial pond.

After they had released their driver, Adam told Yusuf that the driver had not been checked out completely. Adam was playing it cautious until he knew for sure. Yusuf acted a little hurt that Adam thought he would have said anything important. Adam looked at him for a moment and said, "Yusuf, you know how it is. We cannot be too cautious. I don't even want the driver to be able to tell what languages we speak. It's unlikely, but someone might try to question him later."

Yusuf said, "You're right, boss. I'm sorry I questioned your reasoning."

"Please quit calling me boss."

"Yes, boss."

The women had been placed in a separate area of the compound. The owner, a devout Muslim, insisted on correct behavior if they were to use his property. Adam had been delighted with the arrangement. He thought to himself as he assured the owner the arrangement would present no problems whatsoever. *Damn, how lucky can I be? I can continue my sabbatical from Jennifer.*

The arrangement, however, was a shock to Jennifer. When the women were herded to their dormitory-like quarters, Jennifer flippantly asserted her status to the maid assigned to her care. "Don't you know who I am?" she started.

Elizabeth broke in, "Jennifer, not now, please. This poor woman cannot understand a word you are saying. It has nothing to do with her. It is the custom here. You must understand that women here are different. We must comply and respect their way."

"Well, I'm not about to comply. I'll find Adam. He will work it out. He can do anything. He wants me with him." And with that she swished out the door.

Dealing with Jennifer had not been on Adam's list of top priorities. She was becoming more and more of a problem to him. Relating to her was like walking on eggs, not knowing when one might break. He allowed her to dispel her anger, not because he cared but because he could not afford a mutiny in the ranks.

"We've been separated for three weeks now. I've missed you. I'm hungry for you. I thought we would have a romantic interlude here in Pakistan. I imagined being treated like a Princess. Instead, I have been regimented to an austere dormitory like a fucking barnyard animal."

It took Adam nearly an hour to calm her down. He promised to make everything up to her. He suggested extending to four the two weeks he had already promised her in paradise. He would take her anywhere in the world, wherever she wanted to go. He hated himself for making these promises, but he could think of nothing else that would satisfy her.

He felt trapped, concerned that she would become too comfortable with him and demand more and more.

Finally, in all seriousness he said to her, "Please understand. We have no choice but to be on our good behavior here. We are guests. Whether we like it or not, we must follow their rules. It would be disrespectful to do anything else. Above all, it might place the project in jeopardy."

"Well, all right. But I don't like it now, and I won't like it even for one minute. I'll hold you to your promise, and I mean it." With that she turned away carrying herself as an Arabic woman. Her height provided the only hint she was Western.

Di was scheduled to arrive in three days. They had a great deal of work to do to make sure that they were ready. Di had cooperated with Adam's instructions perfectly, relieving him of the pressure to develop an alternate plan. Di had agreed to make this trip without an official police escort. The switch would be much easier if Di was not flanked by state security. Adam was excited to place into action phase one of the project. He was convinced that Jennifer could pull it off.

Adam had already tested Jennifer's appearance with the media. It was more than a close match; it was perfect. Adam had taken a candid of Jennifer at the Florentine villa. He sold it through an agent to one of the mainline tabloids. The photograph showed Jennifer standing next to Yusuf, with Yusuf turned so that he was not recognizable.

Katherine had e-mailed a message the day after the photo hit the newsstands. Di had shown the photo to Katherine. Di could not remember the surroundings or the man. Di was at a loss for where the picture had been taken. It was not taken with a high-power telephoto, but at close range. Di was completely puzzled.

Adam had e-mailed a return message to Katherine telling her the truth. He gave Katherine permission to tell Di. Adam did not want Di to worry that she was suffering from memory loss. Later, Katherine had sent a message that Di had succumbed to a near terminal case of the giggles when she learned that it was a picture of her doppelganger that was published.

Adam felt high. The adrenaline was pumping. The dress rehearsal had been successful. The scene was ripe. It was time to get on with the show.

15

Lahore, 23 May 1997

The black Mercedes pulled into the meticulously manicured grounds of the compound and slowed to a stop under the portico that led to the mansion's massive entrance gate. Yusuf, standing at military attention, was waiting to open the door. He extended his hand to offer support. Accepting his gesture of assistance, Di stepped out. Her eyes twinkled as she nodded her appreciation for his help. With her head cocked, she donned her signature, often photographed, smile. She stood tall and appeared relaxed yet determined. Without a word, Yusuf escorted her into the residence where he showed her to the library.

He opened the huge oak double doors with a soft swoosh. The room, reminiscent of something that would be found in an English country estate, was tastefully appointed. The ceilings were high. The walls were lined from floor to ceiling with heavy, dark oak bookshelves stacked with leather-bound volumes. The sofas and winged-backed chairs were covered in deep English green Connolly leather that obviously was not new but was well appreciated. The custom tables were carved to match the handwork on the bookshelves. The room was tastefully accessorized with various items of handblown Waterford crystal. There was nothing Pakistani about this room. It was as though it had been transported directly out of England with its full character maintained in the process.

Jennifer was standing motionless across from the entry with a colossal case of stage fright. As Di entered the room and looked up, her eyes froze on Jennifer. She stopped dead in her tracks. Jennifer's body reacted and turned rigid. The two women stared at each other. Their expressions mimicked one another. First amazement and then fright seemed to cover their stone faces. Nothing was said. The silence lingered, almost interrupting the flow of time. It seemed as though the events of the moment were frozen in time.

Elizabeth, not knowing exactly what to do, intervened. She could not tell if Di was horrified or pleased. Trying to break the silence, Elizabeth frivolously started to fuss with Jennifer, rearranging her hair to match Di's. The wind had whisked through Di's, leaving some lingering strands, and there was a slight difference that needed to be corrected. Everything else about the two women was identical. Their clothing and jewelry. Their accessories, nails, color of lipstick, perfume. Absolutely everything was a perfect match. Neither woman seemed to notice Elizabeth as she fussed about with Jennifer's hair, trying to soften the shock.

Taking charge, Adam startled both women out of their trances. "Jennifer, excuse me, I mean, Di," he said looking at Jennifer. "You had better leave before the driver becomes nervous. The schedule is very precise."

The static moment was shattered. Jennifer responded immediately. She walked over to Adam and reached out to place her hand in his. "Remember your promise."

Squeezing her hand hard and winking at her to acknowledge his understanding, Adam looked directly into her eyes. He said, "You are a dead ringer. Now, go break a leg."

Smiling with her head a little cocked in that so familiar manner of Di, Jennifer exited the premises with all the confidence of a professional. Her stage fright had been substituted with confidence. She aptly assumed the persona of her character. No longer was she Jennifer. She was Di. She was ready to prove herself to the world.

As Jennifer exited the room, Di held out her hand to steady herself on the back of one of the huge wing-backed chairs. "My God. It's almost like seeing a ghost. Please excuse me, but it's all rather unsettling. I had no idea..."

Interrupting Di's train of thought, Reem, in hijab, glided into the room like an apparition. She was carrying a beautifully appointed Victorian silver tray and tea service. Steadying herself on the furniture, Di moved to the sofa and melted into the comfort of its subtle leather.

She was speechless. Yusuf assisted Reem as she arranged the tea service on the coffee table in front of where Di was seated. Elizabeth thanked them, telling Reem she would pour. Bowing, the two, acting as servants, exited in silence.

Adam, Elizabeth, and Di now had complete privacy. The library had been sanitized just prior to Di's arrival. Because of the level of security required, Adam, himself, had since remained in the room. They were free to speak openly. Adam's orders to Yusuf had been absolute. They were not to be disturbed. Period. Whatever the emergency, Yusuf was to handle it. Yusuf understood well. Yusuf would comply.

Di turned to Adam and said, "It's like seeing a shadow or looking at a trick mirror that has a mind of its own. I had no bloody idea it could be so eerie. It is very disconcerting."

"I think she will do a good job for us." Adam's voice was comforting.

"I'm sure she will, but I'm a little overwhelmed. Please excuse me. I feel lightheaded. May I have a glass of water?"

"Of course." Elizabeth poured tea and water for the three of them.

"It was quite frightful, almost ghastly. I see myself regularly on video, but this was so different. I thought I was actually seeing myself. I could see her breathe. I realized it was not me but someone else."

"Don't worry about it. I expected no less," Elizabeth consoled. "It must be shocking. I can only slightly imagine how I might feel if I walked into a room and saw my twin, knowing I am not a twin."

Adam interrupted the two women. "I hate to sound rude or insensitive. Maybe the two of you can continue this conversation at another time. Our time together is very limited. If you don't mind, there is so much to be accomplished. This meeting may be the last opportunity we have to speak face to face before you begin your new life. It is important that we clarify our plans."

"Yes, of course. You are correct. I understand, but may I ask one question before we go any farther?"

"Of course."

"Adam, are you absolutely sure that this will work? My life is nearly unbearable now. If anyone were to find out about this plan and leak it to the press, I don't think I could endure the backlash. I would be completely done in."

Adam thought for a few moments before responding. He chose his words carefully. "The plan is workable, and I believe in it. However, there is absolutely no room for error. If you follow my instructions exactly, no one will ever know. It will be necessary for you to make some sacrifices to set the wheels in motion. Once we have set the stage, it will be over shortly. I estimate that everything will be finished in less than six months from now, but we need to be flexible on the time line. Do you feel you can do it?"

Excitedly, she answered. "Yes. Where do we begin?"

"To start, you must accept Mohammed's invitation to visit his yacht this summer. It is important for you to spend time in France. We will execute the project there. It would not be impossible to do it in England, but the risk of being discovered in England is much higher. You are watched more closely in England than anywhere else in the world. You must answer to more people there. Too many people know you well enough to possibly spot our doppelganger. France is a much better setting. I have the infrastructure in place to make all the necessary arrangements. I can program the events to meet our needs. The French are much more inclined to look the other way. So, if you have no objection, I would like to proceed in France."

"Okay," she again responded quickly. "France sounds like a good place to me, but you're the expert. I'll follow whatever you say."

"Now I need a little background information from you. How well are you known by Mohammed's family?"

"We know each other. My father and Mohammed were friends. I have spoken with him a few times, but we are not what you would call close. I have assisted him by making an appearance at his store. He invited me to the yacht last summer. It was a thoughtful gesture but not for me. I was very troubled at the time. I know the rest of the family, too, well enough to recognize them anyway."

"Do you think your doppelganger could fool Mohammed?"

This time Di took a little longer before responding. "Probably. I think so. I have not really seen her in action. The problem would be if something from my childhood were discussed. He really does not know me that well, but he may remember stories of my childhood. We have not spent much time together. How does she sound anyway? Does she sound like me?"

"If you were surprised by her similarity in appearance, I think you would be aghast seeing her in action. Her mannerisms are yours. Her verbalism is precise. Her intonations are accurate. She carries herself as you. She can do the job for us. Don't take me wrong. I'm not worried about her proficiency. It is just that we must be careful. Prudence is essential. I would be afraid to place her one on one with Charles or your boys. That would be far too risky. She might actually fool them at first but unlikely for more than a few minutes. There are just too many tiny personal qualities that cannot be assumed. The person I'm most concerned about is Dodi. She will need to be face to face with him, likely several times. What do you think?"

Again, Di's response was without hesitation. "That should be no problem. We barely know each other. But why Dodi? What is it that you have in mind?"

"If you were to express some interest in Dodi, it would provide a good excuse for you to spend enough time in France for us to organize the event. He would make it possible for you to stay at their villa or on the yacht."

"Adam, for heaven's sake, Dodi is not my type. He is very self-centered. He is the quintessential playboy with a rich Papa. He cares little for what happens outside of his own small circle. Not only that, but the establishment would be furious. A proper British lady does not mingle with an Islamic man. That goes without saying. Anyway, don't you know he has a girlfriend? She is a model, a beautiful young woman. I have been told he is planning to marry her. I think he has given her a ring, but I cannot imagine him marrying anyone. He is a little flighty."

"You are a very beautiful and perceptive woman. Your analysis is correct on all counts. This is why it is important for you to accept Mohammed's invitation. Mohammed will be excited. He will have his own agenda. He always does. He is well aware that you are now the most sought-after and eligible woman in the world. Who could be a better match for his son? He would like nothing more than to be the step-grandfather of the future King of England. It will give him the opportunity to gloat over the people who have more than once refused him British citizenship. He will encourage Dodi. I am sure of it. You will have to be involved, but we should be able to allow your doppelganger to cover most of the time. If not, you will just have to do it. The important thing is for you to keep the summer free of public engagements. We then will be able to organize everything we need to do around our schedule instead of the schedule we are dealt by your pre-planned public appearances. We will have a secure retreat for you in France. While your doppelganger is working, you, Elizabeth and I will be able to meet, if necessary. It is nearly impossible in England without someone wondering who I am. Oh yes, one more thing. It would be good if you could take your children with you on the yacht when you first go."

"Why? I don't understand."

"As I told you we will substitute your doppelganger as often as we can. Once Dodi becomes interested, he will want to meet your boys. We don't want to be in a position where we can't extricate the doppelganger.

It would be sheer disaster if she had to meet your children. It is better to address this issue before it becomes a problem. One time will be enough. Everyone knows you cannot take the children out of England without permission."

"I see."

"Can you make the necessary arrangements?"

She made her decision without hesitation. "I'll think of something."

"Dodi may not be there at first. This is why it is good for you to bring the boys. He will surely show up. I just don't know when. He will receive a great deal of encouragement to become better acquainted with you. Be careful. You don't have to come on to him but, somehow, keep him interested. That's girl stuff. I'm sure you well know how. As soon as he comes into the picture, your doppelganger will take over. We will use her as much as possible before that time, too."

She giggled and looked a little shy. "I'm not going to let him in my knickers. I'm not ready for something like that. I can't handle it. I've gone through too much, too quickly. I'm up to you know where with wrath from the establishment."

"I trust you to do the right thing. We have complete confidence in you."

"Adam, I have a question. I have thought about everything so much. I feel like I have made the right decision. I am excited about the houses and the artwork. I know you said the art was an investment, like buying stock to be cashed in for profit. I just can't get the painting of the Italian General out of my mind. He reminds me of you. It's something in his confidence and bearing. He is my General, like you are my General. I know that as I follow your orders, I will win this battle. Who knows, since I have Italian ancestry in my new blood, maybe he is a relative. A rather dapper one at that, if I do say so. I feel such a closeness to him, a connection. Could I hang the painting in my home? It would give me a legacy and always remind me of what you have done."

"I had never thought of it. I'll talk with the bankers. We'll think of something. There should be no problem."

"Adam, there is one more thing. My children. I have sorted out everything else. I can handle it all. The thought of leaving them forever is more than I can fathom. Could I confide in William? I have started to tell him so many times. I know him. He is loyal to me. He is strong. He can keep a secret. Isn't there some way we could maintain contact. Maybe through the Internet or some other secret channel. At the right time, he could tell Harry. What do you think?"

Adam stood up and walked over to Di. Kneeling down on the floor before her, he clasped the palms of his hands around hers and smiled looking deep into her tear-spotted eyes. His heart sank to his stomach as he realized the possible demise of the project. His skill was being tested as never before. His future was on the line. His hallmark was his keen ability to bring his puppets around to accepting the decisions he dictated. He was the Puppet Master. He was mandated to enlist her loyalty. The project's success was dependent upon her precise enactment of his orders. His strategy was to appear sincere and sympathetic. It was imperative for him to listen to her needs and relate to her fears. He spoke softly with concern and understanding. "I know this is difficult, but it would be the seeds for destruction."

He sensed her strength as she pulled her back straight and held her head high. She was dissatisfied. She was ripe for change. Her spirit, almost rebellious, was primed for the prescribed adventure. The monarchy no longer controlled her. Her infuriation for her own plight was turning to pity for those who had tried to destroy her. Her body language said it all. She had already made the decision. Now she was seeking the permission to continue.

"I respect your idea. It is not a whim. You have wrestled with your emotions, and I do not doubt your evaluation of your son. I do not take your request lightly. I will tell you why my reaction is so firm. Remember he is only a boy. It is true that he has been taught to be strong. Someday, he will carry the entire weight of a nation's history on his shoulders. The burden you are suggesting though is quite something else. It may be a much heavier burden than being King. Can you imagine his struggle? Imagine him trying to comfort Harry when the news is received and he knows it is false. The backlash would be overwhelming if by some slip of security, your secret was discovered. You know how his every move is watched. Even, if we agreed he could handle it mentally, I am not sure if I could provide the technology necessary to pull it off for any length of time afterward. It is a very complex problem, and it places a tremendous burden on his shoulders. I'm afraid of it."

Her concordance was spontaneous. "I agree. It's a ghastly idea, but, for me, it would be perfect."

Her expression remained solid. She was committed. Trusting that he was reading her thoughts correctly, Adam took a deep breath and said, "If you cannot agree to proceed without telling William, I advise we abort the project. The personal risk to you and everyone else is just too great."

Her response was without doubt. "Oh, no! No! We cannot stop now. I have already given you my word. I have not changed my mind. I understand. I just want to make this as easy for everyone as possible."

"Good." By making the burden too great for William, Adam hoped that Di would put the idea to rest. *There is so much for her to do during the next weeks,* Adam thought. *Maybe she can just lose the boys in the middle of it all. Before she realizes what has happened, she will have her new identity. The changes will be so severe that there will be no chance to go back.*

"I'm sorry that I continue to be so abrupt, but our time is so limited. I have critical information for you. I need to change the subject and provide you with some equipment that is essential."

She looked puzzled.

"May I sit by you?" Adam asked.

She nodded acceptance with her theatrically coy smile.

"What I have in my hand looks like a cosmetic compact. It was made especially for you. It's not a compact at all but a minidisk recorder." Adam handed the compact to Di and took a minidisk out of his pocket. "It's a very sophisticated piece of equipment. It uses this tiny disk and is very sensitive to human sound waves. It records conversations clearly from inside your purse, without static interference. It is sound-activated and only records when there is something to record."

Di held the tiny gold embossed compact in her hand. Opening it, she found a soft burnt red-colored blush with mirror and mink applicator brush. "It does not look like a recorder at all. I love the color."

"I, too, was pleased with the end result. No one other than you will ever imagine the true function of this little jewel. Please, may I continue?"

Again, she nodded for him to go on.

Adam took the compact from her hand and closed it. He pushed a small, almost indistinguishable button on the underside. The disk slid out. Adam slipped it back in saying, "This is how you change the disk. You push this button to activate the recorder; the recorder will record what you are saying or what someone else nearby is saying to you. In France, any time you are with someone whom your doppelganger might meet in the future, turn on the recorder. That way she will learn what was said. She has a very good memory and an acute ability to memorize. Reviewing your conversations will prepare her if she talks with someone you know or, more importantly, with someone with whom you have recently spoken. Likewise, your doppelganger has an identical compact. She will record her conversations and provide her disks to you. This will be security for both of you. A check and balance system. Your doppelganger is using her compact today. You will know exactly what transpired while you were here with us."

"What a marvelously wonderful idea."

"Oh yes, I almost forgot to show you how to play it back to listen." He pushed another tiny button. "We have installed a special jack in yours so that you can use Walkman earphones and listen to the recorder in private. The jack is located under this little gold seal. Merely turn the seal like this. See how it pivots out of the way exposing the jack? If you use the earphones, you will never have to worry about someone over-hearing anything. It is probably best for you to always use the earphones and only when you are certain you are alone. The battery is long lasting, but here are several spares. You change it like this."

"I understand, Adam. I am so impressed. Everything Katherine said about you is correct. You are my savior, my General! I still can't get that painting out of my mind."

Adam without reaction ignored her comment. He remained con-trolled and disciplined to accomplish the task at hand. He continued. "Here is a supply of diskettes. You can mail them by just placing them inside a greeting card or some other such thing. They are thin enough that the postal service will not care. Anyone handling the card will not pay any attention. Mail them to this address." Adam handed Di a slip of paper with an address in France. "Memorize the address, or write it down in parts intermingling it with other addresses. Destroy this slip of paper. Either burn it or tear it into bits and deposit the pieces in several receptacles. Both Katherine and Elizabeth will spend some time in France and will be available to you when you are there. Remember that someone likely monitors your telephone conversations. Therefore, be very discreet in what you say. You can meet with either Katherine or Elizabeth in person; both know how to avoid eavesdroppers. Alternatively, you can record information or questions on the diskette and mail it to us. Katherine will deliver the reply."

The black Mercedes pulled into the compound. Seeing it out of the corner of her eyes, Di rose from the sofa. Almost paralyzed she walked to the window. Pressing her face onto the glass, she gazed as Jennifer was helped out of the limousine. Di was finding it difficult to assimilate what she was witnessing. In trance-like stillness she stood. Jennifer passed by the window and entered the giant double doors that marked the mansion's entrance.

A few moments later a soft knock at the door startled Di back into reality. She turned as Yusuf escorted Jennifer into the library. Time stopped all over again. The two women stared at each other for a second that turned into what seemed like eternity. Then, without warning Jennifer plunged into an impromptu mirror act, mimicking Di's expression and stance. Adam, trying to normalize the situation, broke into Jennifer's act and asked for the diskette of her time away. Jennifer walked past Adam and approached Di with that special stride in her step that was so memorably Di. Handing the diskette to Di, Jennifer assumed her Di impersonator voice and said, "The driver talked about soccer. I mentioned that William and Harry are both big fans."

Not knowing whether to acknowledge Jennifer or ignore her, Di took a deep breath. Gulping she turned to Elizabeth. "Does she sound as much like me as I sense she does? It's hard for me to know."

Walking over to Di, Elizabeth concurred, "Yes, her voice is as uncanny as her appearance."

Turning her attention back to Jennifer, Di was again captured by the likeness. She studied Jennifer's face, her hair, her hands. She outlined Jennifer from head to toe, examining her every feature with intimate awareness. Di's emotions were confused. She felt exhaustion and exhilaration co-mingled into one contorted passion. It was like something from a Robert Ludlum novel. Fantasy turned into reality.

Feeling she could endure no more, Di turned away from Jennifer. It was time for her to depart. Unable to collate her feelings into any organized formula, she held out her hand first to Elizabeth and then to Adam. "I thank you both for everything. I understand my assignment. I will not fail you." She then turned to Jennifer. Sighing loudly she said, "I don't know how you have done it, but I must say you have bloody well done it right. You even fooled me. I will always be indebted to you. How can I appropriately thank you? I don't even know your name."

Jennifer started to respond, but Adam interrupted signaling her to silence. "It is better that way. You two can talk about this sometime in the future, if you desire, when the project is finished. Now, we need to get you back to the car. One last word, we will continue to contact one another as we have been doing. The procedure is working well, and we all are familiar with it."

Di nodded her agreement, as Adam motioned to Yusuf to show her to the waiting limousine.

>–┤◆>–O–<◆├–<

Lahore, 26 May 1997

Yusuf sat with Adam and Elizabeth on the expansive terrace to enjoy a cup of strong tea in the peaceful tranquillity of the early morning freshness. They had scheduled a very early departure. As usual, Adam had taken all precautions possible. Boarding the aircraft before sunrise almost assured them of leaving unnoticed.

The flap over Di's lack of security in Pakistan was already a thing of the past. It was amazing how quickly something newsworthy became old news and forgotten. The press had moved on to other, more pressing matters of the day.

Earlier, several newspapers had quoted a top Pakistani intelligence officer as reporting that for several hours the security force had completely lost track of Di. They had had no idea where she was. They looked everywhere but were unable to find her. She simply had vanished. Pakistani intelligence had been paralyzed with fear. These specially trained agents had been assigned to protect Di from possible terrorist activities. She had slipped away from them unnoticed, without any fanfare. Remarkably, she disappeared in a private car. Pakistani intelligence is nothing compared to British security. That is a well-accepted fact, and she had made this trip without the support of the British intelligence service. Even so, the Pakistanis were obliged to provide her with their highest level of security. As embarrassing as it was, to the eyes of the world, they had failed.

The other crisis, even more pressing, had received far more extensive press coverage. Jennifer had been briefed on what she was to discuss with the parents of the London doctor during her visit acting as Di in Pakistan. Jennifer had been overly enthusiastic in her discussion with the parents, and now rumors were circulating that Di was in love with their son, the doctor. Marriage bells were ringing in the minds of some journalists. Di was furious. Adam was furious, too. He hated the press. The less attention the better for the operation's success. A retraction of some kind was essential. It was likely that an official announcement would be made to lay the rumor to rest.

Then, the press had covered another statement. This one was an announcement from a cousin of the doctor. The cousin, who lives in America, affirmed the rumor that a wedding was in the making. The whole thing was a mess. Adam was happy that the thrust had been passed from Di to the cousin. Knowing they could not get close to Di, the press had turned its attention to pumping the cousin, and things were quiet in Pakistan for their departure.

The positive result of the coverage was that no one had observed anything unusual from Jennifer. Her picture as Di had appeared in several newspapers and even on television. She had carried it off without a glitch. Adam was more convinced than ever that Jennifer could succeed at whatever challenge was placed in front of her. The project would be successful.

Adam gazed across the table in silence as he thought of his escalating problems with Jennifer. She had been so upset that they had been unable to be together in Pakistan that Adam had agreed to her demand of their spending several days alone in bed immediately after the Pakistan trip. He had made the promise, and she was reminding him of it almost by the hour. She had even mentioned it in Di's presence. She would collect.

He hated wasting his time, but he had no choice. She only performed when she was serviced. It was not his style to allow anyone to control him. For the moment, he was compelled to allow her to feel like she was controlling him. On top of this, she had held him up for an additional ten thousand a month in salary. She pleaded that she was worth it now that she had proven her ability to fill in for Di. He had agreed but was furious inside. She was nothing short of an extortionist, but Adam knew she had met her match and was giving her as much encouragement as she needed.

Yusuf looked with concern at Adam and spoke softly, "What are you thinking about so seriously? You looked troubled. You never take the easy way, do you, boss?"

"To answer your question, I try to always do the best thing. My goal is to make every project a success. Whether it is easy or hard has nothing to do with it. What's on your mind, Yusuf? Why do you ask?"

"It seems to me that you are planning to remove Di and give her a new identity, making some kind of a swap with Jennifer. I have only one question. Is the swap permanent or temporary? I have been thinking, if it's permanent, it would have been so easy to have done it here in Pakistan. You could have had Jennifer fly back to London on the plane instead of Di. You could have brought the plane down with a small bomb. There would be months and months of investigation, but in the end there would be no real answers. The world would mourn Di, and it would all have been finished so easily."

Adam looked at Yusuf for a few moments in amazement. "You are very clever, Yusuf. Really, more clever than I imagined. You have learned well. In principle, your idea is workable. It is one that could have been used if circumstances were different. In this case, it presents too many potential repercussions. Your personal history has made you a little too prone to terrorist-type violence. You have grasped a part of the plan, to be sure, but you have not effectively evaluated the variables. A plane crash would be a poor solution for several reasons. The most important is that there would be unnecessary loss of life. We both well understand that from time to time there are casualties in our line of work. Sometimes they are unavoidable. The important point to remember is that the loss of human life must be avoided whenever possible. To destroy an airplane and take the lives of everyone on board simply to achieve our goal is an unacceptable solution. Also, because of the importance of Di, after a plane crash, there would be too much speculation. Theories would certainly evolve that she had not been on the plane. There would be a massive search of the wreckage to locate her body or any part that could have been from her. There would be extensive DNA testing of every piece of organic human material found. The search would be endless to give Di a proper burial. The investigators would never find a part of anything that they would conclusively be able to claim was a part of Di. Then, they would search to try to find her. It would be theorized that it all was a conspiracy. Some idiot would say that aliens or some such thing had captured Di. People would claim to have seen her everywhere. Then, think about this. Pakistan would be blamed for the disaster. Pakistan would rightfully deny that they had anything to do with it. Pakistan would try to shift blame to India, and the whole thing could end up escalating into a war between two countries that go through regular saber rattling. Both countries have nuclear capabilities and the resulting holocaust could add another few million innocent lives to the innocent lives already lost in the plane crash. Overall, bombing the plane is more than a bad idea."

Yusuf looked sheepishly across the table at Adam pondering over everything that had been said. Sighing a little acknowledgment of relief, he said, "Adam, I should have thought of all this. Please accept my apologies. I understand why you are the boss. I hope someday I can be more like you, so you will be proud of me." He glanced at his watch. "I need to awaken Reem and Jennifer. It's getting late and Jennifer asked for forty-five minutes to ready herself." Adam nodded and Yusuf rose and left the room.

Elizabeth said, "I think Yusuf is going to make it. He just has a lot of history to get over."

"You are probably right, but he scares me at times when he thinks of terrorist solutions to simple logistic problems. He needs to look farther ahead. That is exactly the problem in the Middle East. People don't think about the long-term implications of their actions. Perhaps there will never be peace there. Certainly, there will never be peace, as long as people think like Yusuf."

"His father was not that way. Yusuf learned to hate and react from others; he is outgrowing it. You are right though. The mentality in the Middle East needs to change before there can ever be hope for peace."

They sipped their tea in silence as they heard renewed activity in the back of the house. Adam's portable signaled that he had e-mail. It was from Martin. As Adam read the message, Elizabeth noted the change in his expression. Concerned, she asked if everything was okay.

"I think so. Martin and Gerard are bitching about each other, but it doesn't seem serious. I just would hate to see it get out of hand."

"Men can be so stupid about relationships," she theorized. Martin likes Gerard. Martin would never admit it, but he is intimidated by Gerard's knowledge. Martin well understands that we are living in a technological world, and he has not been accepted as a citizen. Gerard has passed the rites of citizenship and may even become a leader. Martin sees Gerard as an alien in Martin's world. Gerard is a weirdo; he doesn't understand people at all. Martin's nature is to be unfriendly. Remember how he treated Jennifer. All Martin can do is grouse all the time and try to keep Gerard from getting into a human situation that would compromise the project. Then, there is Gerard. He thinks that Martin is mostly bluff. He pushes Martin by being condescending to him on matters that don't concern technology. Gerard doesn't have enough experience with people to understand that Martin is not bluff and very dangerous. Gerard looks at Martin as a big teddy bear who is trying to mother him. Give Gerard a few years, and he'll develop some people savvy. In a few years Martin will become more techno-literate, and the two will probably continue to gripe at each other like a pair of brothers because they are used to it and don't know any other way to relate."

"Yes, dear mother and great authority on human relations."

"Shall we talk about Jennifer, my sweet brother? And how you are going to handle your problem with her?"

"Hell no. She can't understand that I get my kicks above the waist. I am just trying to relate to her on her level, only for the sake of the project."

"That's an interesting concept."

"This is going nowhere. We have important things to talk about. Shall I fill you in on Martin and the Paris project?"

"Go for it, you big stallion."

Adam ignored the barb and commenced. "Gerard designed the virtual reality seat and movement mock-up. Martin is having two small machine shops make the necessary parts. This way neither shop has an understanding of what is being made. It will take about three weeks before everything is ready. Gerard said that we have to stick with the one driving route. To program another route would take another two hundred hours or so of programming. There would not be enough time to debug everything. Gerard is dropping out of school for the next two months to make sure that he can have everything up and running on time."

"What did his mother say about it?"

"She was okay, actually she is more open-minded than I would have expected. She asked for me to sign a paper that confirms Gerard is working on a special computer project for a commercial firm. He can use this work experience to receive college credit that will balance out the school he will actually miss."

"He's got a great mom, but I hate using him because he's so young. Quite frankly, I don't know anyone any better. That is the problem. We can use one of our shell companies to make up the paperwork for him. No one will ever think anything of it."

"I thought the same. We need to be careful to insulate him from what we are doing. He is damn smart and will likely figure it out if we give him too many clues."

"We need to keep him clean at all costs. He is someone who could very well end up working for the NSA. For his sake and ours in the long term, it is essential we keep him in the dark."

Their conversation was cut short as the cars pulled into the long circular drive. Elizabeth said, "We'll continue later. I'm late. It will take a few minutes for me to get ready; hijab is rather burdensome.

⊱━◆◦─O─◦◆━⊰

Di's return to London, although uneventful, was contemplative. Relaxing on the flight, she sipped a bubbly glass of Veuve Clicquot Ponsardin's Grande Dame. She was stupefied as she glanced through the newspaper coverage of her Pakistani trip. Captured and enthralled as she perused the photographs taken of her, she realized that some were actually photographs of the doppelganger posing as her. Di examined every minute detail, searching for anything that looked out of place or false. The likeness was indistinguishable. She was overcome with an undeniable sense of helplessness. It had become a recurring scenario in her adult life. Again, her future was being molded by the decree of others. It was that total lack of control of her own destiny that was so frightening.

She trusted Adam. His plan was solid and doable. Most importantly, she believed in it. It was a positive solution for a complex problem. She knew she could not go on with the life that was now proclaimed for her. The transformation would be dramatic. *Actually, it will be quite exciting,* she thought.

She could only attempt to imagine existence as a private citizen. It had been years since she had gone anywhere unnoticed. Like the flash of a snapshot, everything would change. She would fade into the masses. How much better it would be than the fate of rejection that she was experiencing now. The establishment's goal was to push the memory of her under the table, out of sight and mind. They cringed at the publicity she received. They scorned her for her humanitarian gestures. Trips like this one to Pakistan were criticized as senseless and inappropriate.

She laughed when she thought of their gall at suggesting her actions inappropriate. *How bloody duplicitous they are. So quick to fault me; never accepting responsibility for their own actions.* She was always the first to be blamed. Her infidelities had been prostituted. Those of her husband had been pushed aside as acceptable for a man married to an unstable torrent.

My God! Beyond that, they are so petty, so insincere. They called them gifts. Bracelets, necklaces, brooches, so many things from various members of the family. Then, when it came down to the divorce, they all became party to the settlement. Crazy. Her stomach felt sour. These so-called gifts had altered her faith in human nature. Pleasures had been twisted into an ugly acceptance of the inhumanity of humankind. What had been presented as gifts were, in the end, deemed part of a life estate and calculated as a portion of the monetary settlement. She had listened endlessly to explanations from the attorneys. She was chided as being unable to understand business. *True, I am not a business woman. For me, business and emotion do not mix. How do gifts become something other than gifts? It is beyond me. My guess is that it's beyond most women. I know. Maybe in my new life, I should write a book.* <u>Divorce Advice for Women</u>. *Not a bad idea.*

Her outpouring of thoughts continued. She had been fortunate. Her years as the Princess had been hollow in so many ways and yet so fulfilling in others. Her position had provided her the opportunity to reach out to others. There were times when she could have done more. She accepted that. She was satisfied though with her contribution to humanity. Her efforts, joined by those of so many others, had raised millions for charity. She had already done more than most. She could continue to help but, now, in different ways.

The attendant broke her train of thought as she prepared the service for her luncheon. Di took out the little compact. Adjusting the minute earphones, she pressed the start button. She wanted to listen to the conversation again. She was still overcome with Jennifer's proficiencies. *This performance deserves an Academy Award,* she thought, giggling to herself as she listened to what sounded like her own voice.

16

Paris, June 1997

By the day, Martin was finding it more difficult to relate to the demands of the prickly kid. Trying to be nice to him was like hugging a cactus. He e-mailed regularly to Adam, and Adam's response was always the same.

"Hang in there like a man. You can handle it. He's only a kid. Don't take it personally."

Martin did not completely understand what the kid was doing, but Adam kept reassuring him that Gerard was together. Martin's orders were clear. He was to provide whatever Gerard requested. Cost was no object, neither were Martin's feelings about the matter. All that mattered was the result.

Martin had been canvassing the industrial areas of Paris for several days searching for small machine shops with the capability to tool the parts. It was a challenge. Martin's French was pedestrian at best, due to his accent. He actually spoke the language fairly well, but his accent sounded very Dutch. The French are normally unsympathetic to those who do not speak their language without complete fluency. They would rather make fun than attempt to decode what is being said. Martin's temper was challenged more than once. Knowing that Adam would tolerate no mistakes, Martin controlled his flashes of anger. Making a scene, even a small one, would cause repercussions that were intolerable.

Finally, after four days, he scored. Martin located two, tiny enterprises. Each was manned by a handful of employees. Each company proudly showed Martin samples of their work. The quality reflected the precision Gerard demanded, and both shops agreed to meet the deadline Martin outlined. The time line was critical. After the parts were fabricated, Gerard needed lead time to make sure everything worked and was debugged; everything had to be out of beta in the next six weeks. *Damn. I'm starting to think like him.*

After augmenting his amusing French with a lot of arm waving, Martin amazingly was able to communicate the necessary. He was satisfied the two owners understood. He arranged for the work to be done and felt comfortable that the jobs would be accomplished as specified, on time. Martin paid each proprietor fifty percent up front in cash. He would tender the balance when he picked up the parts in two weeks. "Deux semaines, pas plus. C'est important!" He was sure that they had understood; he would take it out of their hides if not. Martin provided each man with his cell phone number. If there were any problems, he was to be notified immediately.

When he returned to the garage, the kid wouldn't stay off his back. "Martin, are you sure that they can have the modules ready in two weeks? I have to have them by then. I can't wait any longer. Can we get them sooner?"

"Gerard, you can be a pain in the ass. Yes, a thousand times yes. Two weeks. It's the best I can do."

"My God, you sound like my mother."

"Hell, I wish she was here to take care of you. You wouldn't eat if I didn't bring you food. I'm not cut out to be a nursemaid to a... Shit, you're right, I am sounding like your mother."

"Martin, I need to talk to you about something else. It's serious. I have a problem. I need help to de-bug the code for the program I'm building. I'm afraid it will take longer than I thought. I can't do it all by myself. I need to hire someone to help me."

"What is this shit? I thought you could do anything. I'll have to run it by Adam."

"He told me to ask you."

"Can you get help without the person knowing what you're doing?"

"Yes and no. If I say it's a video game, no one will suspect that it's a car-driving simulator."

"How do I find someone for you?"

"You can't. I'll do it. I can find someone on the Internet. It's not a problem. I just want to make sure that it's okay before I go shopping."

"Okay, but let me check out the person physically before we let him in on the video game."

"No problem, although it really won't be necessary. The person does not have to be in Paris. I can use someone in the U.S. or Canada or even India. They have some great code writers in India."

"Okay. That sounds good. Let's find someone far away from here. India would be perfect. Let me know, and I'll take care of it for you. Don't let the person know who you are. Don't let him know anything. I never want you to meet face to face."

"Martin, I'm not stupid. There is no reason to meet. I never use my name on the Internet anyway. I even change my handle every three or four months and I always change it every time after I do some 'little thing' for Adam. Is he CIA or something? I can't exactly figure it all out. When I erase phone records and things like that, I can't help but notice the phone exchanges. His last two 'little things' involved the White House phone exchange."

"Gerard, shit. Why are you asking me? Do you remember the old adage about curiosity killing the cat?"

"Gotcha, man. Mum's the word. Oh, I forgot. When we get the parts, I'm going to need your help to assemble the modules in the flat. Some of the pieces are just too awkward for one person to hold and attach at the same time."

"Why don't we assemble them in a warehouse, test them there and then move everything when we know it all works? That will keep the flat quiet. The less the neighbors know about what we are doing, the better."

"Can you find a warehouse? Why are you so worried about someone hearing something? I sure as hell hope that this little device is not going to get me into hot water. I can't imagine how, but I guess I should ask."

"Not at all. Don't worry, kid. It's purely a training device for a one-time stunt to fool some TV journalists."

Gerard pulled down at the corner of his eye in a uniquely French gesture and said, "I'm sure, and Clinton is as celibate as the Pope. Right?"

"Listen kid. You need to eat. You must be starved. I'll be back in a few minutes. What do you want on your pizza?"

"How did you know I wanted a pizza?"

"You never eat anything else. Shit, you even ate a cold slice for breakfast. Now, that was utterly disgusting."

"What's wrong with that? A good pizza contains all the basic food groups."

⊱━•➤•━०━•◄•━⊰

Adam and Elizabeth were wildly plotting and planning. They worked intently and then would steal additional moments to brainstorm. It was almost like choreographing a dance, every move was coordinated and calculated in perfect rhythm. Sleep came in short intervals. Their bodies would cry of exhaustion and revolt against any more activity. Defeated, they would succumb for a few hours, only to start the process all over again the instant their bodies would allow.

Jennifer was controllable but only for one reason. Adam was regularly servicing her insatiable physical demands. Some God from above had placed a spell over him and was providing him with the necessary endurance. Well, that, coupled with a little help from an experimental drug made from an African root. Although he was living testimony of the drug's effectiveness, Adam vowed he would not recommend it to anyone who did not want to grow calluses on his manhood.

Jennifer was caught up in the notoriety that she had received in Pakistan. She wanted more. Adam refused to give her any idea of the plan. He just kept saying, "It won't be much longer, my princess. We are still trying to organize everything around Di's schedule. Until it's firm, we cannot set a definite plan."

Elizabeth and Adam had arranged time blocks each day to meet and brief one another. They stole moments when Jennifer was having her massage or pedicure, or taking a bath, or doing her exercises or some other such nonsense. Brigit and Eva were becoming skilled at keeping the girl occupied and away from them. These two women were great. Adam was committed to using the pair again, if he ever had the need.

Today, over a Campari and mineral water, Adam and Elizabeth took advantage of the few minutes they had together alone before dinner.

"We really should give the girls a raise. We never thought when we started, it would come to this. What do you think?" Elizabeth asked.

Preoccupied Adam responded, "Perfect. Do it. Whatever you think is right is fine with me. A few minutes ago, I received an e-mail from Katherine. Di signaled her that she wants to meet with me. She is worried that her lines of communication have been tapped. The people who sweep her lines for her told her that everything is fine, but she is worried because some information got to the press that should have remained confidential. She thinks the leak came from a phone tap. She is worried that someone in the establishment wanted to embarrass her. It's possible. She wants to fill us in on her plans. She will be in New York in a few days. What do you think?"

"Risky. She's getting so much press now with the sale of her dresses. Where could you ever meet?"

"I could be there for the auction or something like that. Maybe we could meet in London at the office there."

"What about Katherine? Why can't she be the courier? If she is careful, she can meet privately with Di. Katherine is not only responsible but our best conduit. We can depend on her, although I hate to involve her any more than necessary. Maybe Gerard can check out Di's phone lines. He can determine if there has been any funny business."

"No. Gerard is a little behind on the virtual reality project. We can't afford to take him away. Send in the American team and tell them that it must be discreet. If the phones are bugged, we don't want to tip off the people who did it that we are on to them."

"Good thinking," Elizabeth agreed. "I'll get right on it. We should wait to make our plans until after we know what's going on. I, too, had e-mail from Martin. He said that they have the virtual reality mock-up working in the warehouse. He tried it and said it made him nauseous. He prefers the real thing. Gerard told him that it would be fixed soon, so that we can use it for Michael's team to train. This technology is really going to change the face of our business. Hell, it will change everyone's business for that matter. It will be possible to rehearse anything with no risk of exposure or accident. Think how great it will be for the Delta Force or the FBI Hostage Rescue Team. It's definitely the sign of the future. Instead of building mock-ups in warehouses to practice, everyone will use virtual reality set-ups."

"They already do, although it is not yet a Standard Operating Procedure. In any event, it's great news." Abruptly changing the subject, Adam continued, "I'm a little worried. It's not like Gerard to take longer than he says he will. This is the first time he has ever needed help to de-bug a program. What did Martin think of the virtual reality program? Was he impressed? Is he worried about Gerard getting it all together?"

"No. He's not worried about Gerard. And yes. He's as impressed as that lump ever gets about anything. He told me that he thinks we should start using computer simulation for all physical aspects of our projects. Gerard has made him a believer."

"That's a switch. Maybe he'll stop bitching to me about the kid."

"Do you have any news on the laser?"

"The last test was near perfect. The subject went into sensory overload and was temporally paralyzed. He never knew what happened. He recovered fully in about an hour and thought he had just blacked out. The hospital where he was admitted had no clue as to what happened. They released him with a clean bill of health, although he is still seeing some spots. Of course, he has no idea what caused his problem."

"It was awful what happened to the last subject. Will he ever recover his sight?"

"Probably not. He saw a specialist, and the doctor could not explain what happened to his vision. A laser did not cross the doctor's mind. I made sure that our man is well taken care of. He is by far the wealthiest man in his village, and he has two new wives. He thinks it was a gift from the gods. A loss and then a gain."

"Still, I hate to use unsuspecting people for experiments."

"Damn it. He wasn't unsuspecting. He had been hired. He had been told about the potential risk. He accepted it."

"He sure as hell didn't know it would make him blind. You just don't think about him the same way you would if he was a London taxi driver instead of an African tribal villager."

"True. But he has no idea that his blindness had to do with our project. He thinks his blindness happened naturally. He considers himself lucky. He thinks we are the ones who were stupid because we went ahead and paid him and paid him big, even though he couldn't help us any more. He sees it as getting even with the crazy foreigners and all that."

"Forget about it. You just don't understand. When will it be shipped to Belgium?"

"It will come from South Africa by air next week. Michael will pick it up in Paris and drive it to Belgium. By building the battery pack into the back of the Fiat, we were able to get the weight and handling so that it's completely manageable in a small area. The car is a real little cracker."

"Will it work through the window?"

"Yes, but the window must be perfectly clean, or there could be some back splash or halo effect. Michael will change the rear window a few days before the caper so that it is scratch free as well."

"Make sure that Gerard doesn't find out anything about this. I want that kid to always be in a case of plausible deniability if something goes wrong."

"No problem. Martin is keeping him away from everyone. Oh yes, by the way dear sister, you were right. Martin's carping about the kid is only because he's being protective."

"That didn't hurt so bad, did it?"

"What do you mean?"

"Admitting I was right."

"Women are impossible."

⊶•○•⊷

"Gerard, this is great. It almost feels like I'm driving the car. I feel the motion and everything. It's so damn realistic, the jostle and crunch when the Fiat hits us. You do good work for a kid."

"Yeah, and you only thought I was good as a pizza disposal."

"Let's get to work and move it to the flat. We can have it there and up and running by tomorrow."

"Possibly. It might need a bit of re-calibration after it's set up. It could take me a few hours."

"It's okay. Just do it."

"Damn, Martin, you sound like a Nike ad."

"What the hell are you talking about?"

"Forget it. You wouldn't understand. Generation gap."

"Wise ass."

⊶•○•⊷

Everything was finally set up in the back room of the flat when there was a rap at the door. Martin, a little disturbed, got up from his kneeling position to answer. It was the pizza man with a delivery. Martin paid and returned to the room.

"Gerard, I wish you wouldn't give out the security code for the building. We could have gone down to pick it up."

"It's too much hassle. Hell, it's just a pizza man. It wasn't like I gave it to organized crime or anything."

"You will never understand, will you? God, you need a keeper. I'll be so glad to give you back to your mother."

"Makes no difference to me. You're just like her, a little more bitchy maybe, but just like her."

Martin threw a wadded up rag at Gerard that he easily dodged. The two had a discussion about eating the pizza and reached no agreement. Disgusted, Martin went to the dining room and sat alone at a table leaving Gerard to eat on the floor next to his work.

Completing the meal, Martin hacked out an e-mail to Adam with a copy to Elizabeth; he was not sure the two were together. The text ran,

"Status Victor Roger project, now ahead of schedule. Will take the 'Boy Wonder' home in three days. Michael will bring his team next week to try out your new video game. They should be impressed. I was. 'Boy Wonder' will return if I can't manage to set up the interface. There should be no problems. If you ever offer to take me out for a pizza, I'll strangle you, slowly and personally." He signed off with "M" as always. His message was a little cryptic; he could never be too cautious. He did not trust encrypted e-mail, even though Adam did. Gerard had explained several times that it was secure, but just the same, old habits were hard to break.

Martin returned to the back room to find Gerard absorbed in the computer screen. The pizza was still in the box where Martin had left it for him. "Time out. Eat. Now."

"Just a second, Martin. I'm almost finished."

"No. Now, or I'll unplug that damn thing."

"Yes, mother."

Martin gathered up the leftovers and headed for the kitchen to add them to the mounting supply of pizza rejects. When he returned, Gerard had an offer.

"Betcha fifty francs I can wax your ass at Duke Nukem."

"Belgian?"

"Hell no, Swiss."

"French, and you're on."

"Martin, you're a real wuss. But don't think I'm going to give you a break because of it."

"Get out the two controls, and we'll see who's the wuss."

17

Milan, 22 July 1997

Elizabeth and Adam had arranged to be seated a few rows behind the pew that was reserved for Di and the other notables. They had wanted to be seated back just far enough to avoid being photographed, yet close enough to have access to Di. Had Elizabeth not been a close friend of Gianni, they never could have wrangled the positions they occupied. They sat separately. They had positioned themselves at opposite ends of the pew to allow either a quick exit to intercept Di on the way out. They had Di covered, regardless of which way she turned. Each carried an identical minidisk with updated instructions.

The American team had found Di's telephone lines clean. Her worries were evidently unfounded. The press regularly ran stories and gossip that was supposed to be the inside scoop. Usually, the information was completely unfounded. Apparently, someone had been lucky with a guess this time that had triggered Di's suspicions.

With everything that was happening, it was no wonder Di was a little jumpy. She had told Katherine that she preferred to make her deliveries and receive her messages through Katherine. She did not trust herself at the moment. She was afraid she might make a mistake if she used her voice or e-mail. She was under tremendous pressure and knew she wasn't acting like herself. Then, when she learned that Adam was reluctant to use the doppelganger to give her any break from the current events and scrutiny, her anxiety was intensified.

Adam had been afraid to substitute Jennifer ever since Pakistan. Not only were the logistics a problem due to the public scrutiny Di was receiving, but Jennifer was becoming dangerous. Adam feared that Jennifer might announce that she was a double during a public outing to gain publicity. The writing was on the wall as far as both Adam and Elizabeth were concerned. Jennifer planned to defect; the only question was when. They needed the doppelganger only once more to complete the project. Adam had concluded that although tough on Di, Jennifer's services needed to be reserved for the finale. His challenge was to manipulate the girl to stay on board until they could complete the project. If they lost her now, the project would be aborted.

There was so much press after Di's controversial vacation on the yacht in the Mediterranean that her every move was being carefully watched; the media was circling like vultures. Di's request was recurring. She repeatedly asked Katherine to convey her desire to meet with Adam. She had continued to beg for a meeting in New York, but Adam's response had remained firm.

"A meeting, vis-à-vis, is an unnecessary risk. You are being watched too closely. If I can find a way to do it discreetly, I will. Unfortunately, I see no way to arrange it at the present."

Now everything had changed. The impromptu meeting was possible. Adam and Elizabeth had agreed, it was maybe even necessary. The untimely murder of Gianni Versace provided the opportunity. They could have continued to filter necessary information through Katherine, but both Adam and Elizabeth concurred. It was important to take advantage of this unexpected moment to see Di face to face. Di would feel more secure. Elizabeth had assured Adam that even if they could not get close enough to exchange the disk, their physical presence, alone, would give Di strength. It was important for them to reaffirm their support of her and rebuild her confidence that the project would succeed.

It was a dismal time. They knew that the killing was particularly upsetting to Di. The funeral would be difficult for her. She would be introspective, knowing that it would not be long until she would be the one having a funeral. The reality might prove a terrible shock. Adam and Elizabeth were both concerned that seeing a church filled with grieving friends would give her second thoughts. The timing could not have been worse.

Di entered and quietly took the seat next to Elton John who looked devastated. Katherine had told her that both Adam and Elizabeth would attend the service, but she did not appear to notice either of them when she entered. Several times during the service, Elton John broke down and began to sob. Di comforted him; her own sorrow was, also, apparent. Elizabeth could see that she was having a difficult time dealing with the grief that had touched so many because of this tragedy. Another senseless death. What was gained by anyone through this murder? The death of Gianni Versace had cheated the world.

On the spot, Elizabeth made a decision. She had extracted enough revenge. When this was over, she was going to tell Adam that she was finished. Finished with everything. She was putting an end to playing chess with other people's lives. Somehow, she needed to convince Adam as well. They had both lost their humanity.

After the service, Adam maneuvered himself into a position next to Di. The crowd was jostling people first one way and then the other. Adam had found it difficult to be polite and still make his way to Di. He had been able to wiggle his way next to her, but she was occupied with someone else. While exchanging banal pleasantries with a former business associate who was standing behind him, Adam elbowed an important looking, obviously gay, gentleman. He then stepped on the foot of an immaculately dressed woman of about forty securing his position next to Di in the migrating mass.

Di did not make eye contact. She did not acknowledge his presence. Frustrated, Adam was about to make a comment to attract her attention when she turned to face him, while at the same time looking beyond him directly toward a young woman who Adam did not recognize. Maintaining eye contact with the woman, she whispered to Adam, "This is so unbelievably sad and dreary. I hope you can arrange something a bit better." She spoke momentarily around him with the young woman and then directed her attention to Adam. Showing only very impersonal recognition, she outstretched her right hand to his. As they shook hands, Adam passed the minidisk to her. Di looked him in the eyes and said, "Thank you for coming. I understand why you came, but I can assure you that it was not necessary. Life must go on as best we can plan. I'm okay but weary." Without another word, she turned away from Adam and threw her arms around two young men who had pushed their way through the crowd to where she was standing.

Adam was a little taken back. He had not expected this type of a reaction. *She is so much stronger than I ever dreamed possible. The press has sized her up completely wrong. She's not impulsive. She's a decision-maker. She knows what she wants and goes after it squarely.*

Again jostled by someone jockeying for a position next to Di, Adam backed away. Finding a gap in the wall-to-wall mass of people, he moved in a different direction. As the crowd thinned, he was pleasantly surprised to find himself next to Elizabeth. She appeared out of nowhere. "How did you know where I was?"

"You do not realize my might, oh fearless leader. My undercover work is really quite exceptional. You fail to give this poor woman proper credit."

"Mission accomplished. Let's get the hell out of Dodge before the press catches one of us in a photo and someone wonders who we are. We have avoided them so far. I take great comfort in remaining a nonentity."

They walked for several blocks before stopping at a tiny café on a small square. They were lucky to get a table outside where they could people watch without having to resort to contortionism. The city was crawling with the press and inquisitive tourists. They could not decide which group was worse.

Adam and Elizabeth were masters at blending in with the locals. Dropping into Italian, Adam ordered an expresso and Elizabeth a caffè macchiato. Both were served in heavy porcelain cups with a side plate of hard biscottos for dunking. They sat side-by-side looking out onto the square enjoying the sweet sounds of the children playing in the nearby schoolyard. They kept their voices low. Adam related the comment Di had made. He remarked about her strength.

Elizabeth was excited. "The comment says so much between the lines. She is ready. She is committed to see the project through to the finish. I just hope it won't take too much longer. It is getting too hard to hold it together. Did she say anything about her schedule?"

"Nothing," Adam said, shaking his head. As he reached down to brush some crumbs from his jacket, his fingers passed over something in his pocket. *What is this?* A little confused, he lifted the flap on the pocket and pulled out a minidisk. Presenting it to Elizabeth, he mused, "We haven't given this woman enough credit. I didn't even know she had slipped it to me. She must have tucked it in my pocket when I was by her side. I thought she was oblivious to my presence. My God! I'm embarrassed! She has one up on me."

"Adam, women always have one up on you." She started to laugh. "Haven't you figured that out by now? We just humor you to save your fragile ego."

As he shook his head in amazement, he too started to laugh. Using his best Italian, he muttered, "This little jewel may be filled with the keys to the kingdom. We must open it and see what treasures it contains."

They both laughed even harder, noticing an extremely fat woman tourist in very short white shorts giving them a scathing look. Apparently, she thought they were laughing at her, and she had turned to glare. The woman's look was too much for Elizabeth. Unable to restrain herself, she broke into uncontrollable giggles. Adam tried his hardest to maintain a straight face, but he lost it and began to snort. The tourist glared at them even more severely. After what seemed like an eternity, she waddled off still staring at them over her shoulder.

"Oh my," Elizabeth quipped. "We needed that. I have been so nervous. I have been so afraid that everything would turn sour. I feel like a thousand pounds has been lifted from my shoulders."

The relief of knowing Di was committed to the project had washed away their tension. The trip to Italy had proved more than worth the time and energy it had taken from their preparations. For Adam, the escape from Jennifer was worth almost anything. She was like a parasite taking over its host until it killed it before migrating to a new host. Neither of them had any questions as to why Jennifer had no friends. She had used them up and killed them off.

"Maybe we should hire her after this is all over," Elizabeth suggested.

"You mean Di? That might not be a bad idea. I wonder if she can take something out of a pocket as easily as she can add it?"

"We should go back to the hotel and see what she has passed on to us. Maybe she has given us a date."

Adam left enough money on the table to pay for their drinks and provide a nice gratuity. He got up and pulled Elizabeth's chair back for her. The waiter swept by to clear the table puzzled that they should leave so soon. A table in a place like this was usually homesteaded.

They walked away holding hands. They drew strength from each other, and holding hands was a relic of their childhood. It seemed in a way to recharge their batteries, to restore energy in each of them. Again, Elizabeth reflected. *We have to stop. Someone else can solve the problems of others. The cost to us is just too high. The cost to everyone is too high.*

>─◀▷─○─◁▶─◀

The minidisk contained about fifteen minutes of input from Di. The decryption of the dialogue was transparent. The transmission was so crisp that Adam and Elizabeth felt like they were in the room with her. But the message sounded odd, as though she was reading from notes or a prepared speech. It was delivered almost in a monotone, like someone reading stock market quotes. She provided an update on the Dodi affair and then her tentative plans for the remainder of the summer. Details of wardrobe choices and other matters that were pertinent to the operation were covered. Adam and Elizabeth were both impressed with her organizational skills. Di was succinct, going straight to the point. After listing the specific dates and times, Di slipped into a conversational tone to bear her heart to both of them. Unlike the first part, this portion was delivered with emotion. Elizabeth, in particular, felt an urgency that the woman was near a breaking point.

Di was under tremendous pressure from the establishment. They were not pleased that she had taken the boys to see Dodi and Mohammed. The establishment thought that it was inappropriate for her to consort with foreigners, considering her position. What, for her, was merely a social matter had been twisted into a political statement with potential long-term consequences. Di had responded that she no longer had a position and could do as she pleased. However, she had been reminded that she was still the mother of the future King. It was extraordinary how her position and her activities became important, maybe even threatening to the well-being of the nation, when they challenged the agenda of the establishment. Otherwise, the staunch conservatives could not be too quick to remind the world that she was nothing more than a common citizen whose activities were of no interest.

Her vacation had been upgraded to a fiasco, and her continued access to the children was now threatened. Di was finding it difficult to maintain her composure. She was afraid she might say something that would better remain unsaid. She asked Adam to take whatever measures necessary to expedite the project. She wanted the whole thing to be over, the sooner, the better. Ending with the plea, "Please, just do whatever it takes to finish this agony. I'm not sure that I can hold up much longer. And by the way, I misjudged Dodi. He is actually a wonderful man. Very kind and considerate."

Elizabeth looked introspective for a few moments. Then, with concern she said, "I understand what she is going through. She is committed to go forward and has mentally prepared herself for it. As much as is possible anyway. Her old life is over. She knows this and relates to this on a daily basis. The problem is that she is still here. She is no longer who she was, but she is not yet who she will be. It's like an old person who has decided to die. The person progressively becomes detached from the living and fades away, feeling a lack of belonging in this world and losing interest in remaining. Di does not have this luxury. A person, especially one with a very public existence, does not change overnight. The impossible is being expected of her. She needs to have it over officially. I remember that once I had made the decision to move on, I wanted nothing more than to have it over. All I wanted was to do it. We need to make our move and make it quickly for Di's sake."

"Believe me, we need to bring this whole affair to a conclusion soon for my sake. I'm starting to feel like a worn-out old man."

"Why, Adam, I do believe that Jennifer is becoming a bit much for you. That's the main problem with men; they follow their weenies until someone slips it in a meat grinder."

"Don't be catty. You know that I'm involved with her only because of the project. I am worried that she might get out of control. She has money on her brain. Think how many times she has held us up for a raise. She wasn't the least bit impressed when I gave her the last one to boost her ego. She wanted to ask for more. I could see it in her eyes. She's not stupid though, and she realized it was not the thing for her to do at that moment. So, she was quiet and acted as though she was very pleased. I could see right through her. She thinks of nothing but herself. This is why she is so unpredictable. She would sell out Di in an instant, if she thought she could make a large profit. All that is holding her back are the unknowns. I'm one of them. She thinks I have big bucks. Maybe not as much as she would like, but if nothing better comes along, I'll do. She's setting me up; she plans to cash in for as much as she can get. Then, there is the intrigue of the caper. She sees it as an opportunity. The more she can find out, the more she thinks her story will be worth. That's why she is pumping everyone on our team for information. She has no real idea, but her imagination tells her that the story is worth millions! We'll lose her if we don't move quickly, and the loss could be catastrophic."

"Oh come on, Adam. I thought she was sincere. I thought she was developing a real love for you. Becoming your significant other, or whatever it's now called."

Elizabeth's facetiousness was almost more than Adam could take.

"Like I already told you," Adam said a little angrily, "the only thing Jennifer loves about me is my money. It wouldn't surprise me if she went through my wallet and pocketed small change while I'm in the bathroom. She told me that she had originally thought that she would marry me, but now with her new appearance, she is thinking about holding out for a really rich man."

"My, my. Aren't we sounding insecure."

Adam glared at her, and they both broke into laughter once again.

He held his hands together in mock prayer, "Not much longer. Not much longer."

18

The French country house, 29 August 1997

Adam checked his e-mail. Immediately, his body tensed. He sat straight up in his chair. The time had come. Katherine had delivered the minidisk with the instructions. The reply had been received. Tomorrow was the day. Adam flew into action.

He sent an encrypted e-mail to Michael instructing him to set the stage. Michael's team had arrived in Paris two days earlier. They were on twenty-four hour call. They had run the computer simulated event with the Virtual Reality equipment and pre-tested the route. They had even been able to try several different scenarios to confirm they had chosen the best options. The site of the accident was masked from nearly everywhere. They were convinced that only the people actually involved would see it. The computer equipment had functioned flawlessly. Everything was in order. The plan seemed foolproof. That was what concerned Adam. Things were going too well.

With the message transmitted, Adam quietly knocked on the door of the study. He did not want anyone to hear. As he opened the door, Elizabeth looked up, buried behind the pile of papers on her desk. One look at Adam's face was all it took. She knew, "It's time. Isn't it?"

He nodded in confirmation, "Tomorrow night. We will leave here mid-afternoon."

Elizabeth looked at him stunned for a moment. She was overcome by that familiar surge of amazement that often controlled her thoughts when she pondered the remarkable and complex individual who was her brother. She was so like him in so many ways. In personality, in tastes, in morals, they were so similar. In other ways, she was so lacking. She was so unlike him. Oh yes, she was great support. Give her a task, and it could be considered accomplished. But the creativeness, the ingenious intermingling of all the variables into a perfect fitting whole, this genius belonged to Adam, and Adam alone. It was his realm. He was the mastermind. His projects were always complex like the workings of a fine watch. Their success rested on his expert abilities to build and polish the parts separately and then bring the whole together in one big dress rehearsal that was the real thing. He was doing it again. He was like a conductor who trained each section of the symphony separately in private and then brought all the instruments together for a magical orchestral performance.

For her the wait had been unsettling. Maybe it was because she felt so close to what was happening. The plan was so like her own personal life experience. The news brought with it a sensation of calm, a feeling of peace. The time was right. All was prepared. Adam was in command. He would oversee the project flawlessly. Together they would change history. It was enough to know that they had changed it; they wanted no credit.

Adam's mind continued to race. He started to e-mail to Martin but on second thought decided to telephone. Martin normally checked his e-mail only two or three times a day. It was imperative for Martin to receive the news immediately.

The cell phone rang only once with Martin's voice barking, "Ja."

Adam spoke only one word before hanging up. "Tonight." Nothing else was germane.

Adam continued his preparation. He remained focused, tranquil and devoid of emotion. His mind was rapidly calculating contingency plans to use in the event any small component did not work out exactly as designated. The plan appeared to be completely foolproof, but foolproof plans generally just make fools of those who trust in them.

Jennifer entered the room and interrupted Adam's racing thoughts. "I understand that I'm on tomorrow."

"Yes. You will have a short role in Paris."

"Well, then, I think I'll take the rest of the day off to make sure I am fresh. Do you have any objections? Do you have time for me? Oh Adam, please."

Impatient with her, Adam caught himself before he sounded curt.

"Jennifer, my princess, I'm so very sorry. I'm sure you understand that I have much work to do. This opportunity came to us suddenly, and we don't have the usual amount of time to prepare. Take a rest and relax for the rest of the day. Why don't you soak in a long bath and take a nap. We will leave after lunch tomorrow afternoon. I want you to be in the city early to mid evening. In case there are any traffic problems, we need to allot plenty of travel time. We cannot risk your arriving late."

"Do you know the wardrobe?"

"Yes. I'll print a list for you. You can go over it with Elizabeth this afternoon, to assure that nothing is forgotten. Everything should be in perfect order, but I want to be sure well in advance. Just in case. I'll print the list for you in a couple of minutes. I have to take care of something else first."

"I don't need Elizabeth's help. After all, it's my part. I'm the star. She's just trying to grab some of the glory."

He covered his emotion and said, "It's not that I don't trust you to do a perfect job, and I seriously doubt that Elizabeth wants any of your glory. It is just that the matter is so critical that it's advisable to have someone else check the work as well, merely as a precaution. It's important to have a crosscheck. Just like in Hollywood when they make films. There is always someone who checks to make sure that the dress is identical for sequential scenes."

"Do you really know people in Hollywood?"

"I've told you I do."

"When this is over, I expect you to make the proper introductions for me. I want something more than just a fucking thank you."

"Yes, my princess, of course." *My God, I sound like an old henpecked married man. This has got to be over soon.*

Yusuf entered the room without knocking, and Jennifer glared at him for taking Adam's attention from her. Adam told him that they had received the green light. Yusuf was to prepare everything according to the plan for tomorrow evening. Yusuf would take the Mercedes, and Adam would follow in his Audi. They had gone over every detail countless times before. Every curve and turn, each small component was ingrained in Yusuf's mind. The stage was set for a flawless performance.

>–◦–◦–◦–◦–◦–◦–◦–◦–◦–◦–◦–◦–◦<

London, the same evening

Martin had found an inconspicuous, corner booth to nurse his pint while waiting for Abraham. He wiped off the cloud of white froth that covered his mouth with the back of his shirtsleeve, as he watched the old man enter.

Abraham, ruthless and wizened from his years of experience, was pushing seventy. He looked as though he could be the poster image for a 'Feed the Homeless' charity. The bartender started to head off Abraham as the old man shuffled across the floor toward Martin's table. Martin, stone-faced, signaled to the bartender and shook his head while mouthing, "No." Abraham clutched a well-used paper bag to his chest as though it contained all of his worldly possessions.

"You're late."

Abraham shrugged and collapsed into the seat across from Martin. Unresponsive, he sat for a moment. Then he asked, "Could I have that glass of water?"

Martin pushed the glass across the table, leaving a trail of moisture on the Formica surface that outlined the path the glass had slid.

Drinking it all in one gulp, Abraham set the glass down with a clang and winked at Martin, "Later, you can buy me a pint."

Martin growled, "Shit. What in the hell do you think we are doing? Going to a tea party? I ought to break your neck!"

Abraham's eyes smiled as he mused, "It's been tried before. No one has succeeded. Just look at me. I'm an old man, and I'm still here. All the neck-breakers are gone."

The tattoo on the inside of his left wrist was visible as he reached for the glass and shoved it back to Martin. The tattoo was Abraham's only souvenir from the Nazi death camps. If it hadn't been for his talent as a master forger, he never would have survived the war. They would have killed him, like all of the others. He had been useful, so he lived. In simple language, he had been too valuable to kill.

Abraham worked now for a variety of clients, forging everything from historical documents to work permits. There was much more work for him than his body would permit. He used the law of selectivity, choosing only the jobs that were the most demanding and personally interesting. He still got a high out of the challenge. He had been on a retainer with Adam for nearly a month, waiting for the call to execute this project. He had been briefed. He understood his part and was primed for the intrigue.

Martin paid for his pint, leaving a healthy tip on the table. Gesturing a thumbs up to the bartender, the two walked out of the cheap pub without exchanging a word. As they walked down the street, Martin hailed a taxi as it rounded the corner. He gave the address of the office he had rented the month before. It was nearly eleven on a Friday night. When they arrived, the building was conveniently deserted.

They proceeded in silence. There was really nothing more to say. Once inside, they laid out the tools for the operation. Martin opened his kit and fitted the harness to the old man. He checked it twice to make sure that it was secure and would not bind Abraham during the ascent. Abraham took off his coat to check the bag of tools that had been tucked securely into a pouch sewn to the lining. Satisfied that all was in order, Abraham slipped the coat back on. Martin then grabbed his kit of tools, and they exited the building by the back door maintaining their silence. Abraham was still clutching the worn paper bag. They walked the short distance to the target building and waited for an absence of traffic.

The two men ducked into the passageway behind the building and Martin searched in the dark for the downspout. It was so dark that his eyes did not readily adjust. The downspout was not easily visible, and this was perfect for his purposes. Shortly, Martin pointed to a chalk mark on the pavement; lining himself up perfectly with the chalked line, Abraham sat down on the pavement and leaned against the building. Abraham pulled out a liter bottle of cheap wine from his well-used paper bag and twisted the screw cap open. He poured a little of the vinegar-like bouquet out onto the pavement next to where he was sitting. The area immediately reeked of cheap rotgut. *Perfect. Just what the doctor ordered.*

The idea was simple. If Abraham was discovered while Martin was above, Abraham would look like a homeless drunk and would probably be ignored. Usually, the bobbies are too busy to mess with a drunk, especially a resting old man. This is what they hoped, anyway. If not, Martin would do what was necessary.

With his eyes now better adjusted to the blackness of the night, Martin continued down the alleyway about three meters further, knowing he would find the downspout. Light-footed, he began to climb the spout with catlike precision. It took him less than twenty seconds to reach the correct floor. Stretching out his left leg, he started to place some weight on the windowsill. A reverberating, grating sound was followed by a loud bang as the corner of the sill broke off. Martin felt himself begin to drop. He was momentarily left hanging by his right hand. His fingers started to slip. Clutching harder, he counted to ten and forced himself to relax. He took a deep breath to muster his strength; in one full swoop, he reached around. His left hand rejoined his right around the pipe. He paused for a brief second to catch his breath and then started to climb again. This time more slowly.

Regaining his position at the proper height, Martin reached out again with his left leg. This time he was careful to place his foot deep into the window's opening. Cautiously and gradually, he shifted his weight. The sill held. Carefully, pulling his right leg to meet his left, he moved onto the sill supporting himself by clinging with his fingertips to a small brick detail just above the window.

Once secure, he moved hand by hand to guide himself as he traversed the three windows necessary. Reaching his destination without further incident, he fussed with the window for a few moments. After several unsuccessful attempts using only his bare hands, he reverted to his tools to unlock the window. Opening the window, he entered the room like a feline and made a thorough inspection to insure that no new alarms had been added.

He reviewed the architect's plan and examined the areas of coverage for the alarm. Satisfied that all was secure, he moved on to phase two. Martin lowered the rope, and Abraham attached it to his harness. Martin effortlessly hauled Abraham up the wall and slipped the old man through the window.

Martin turned on the desk lamp, saying, "You can do your work, here. If you move anything, be sure to put it back where you found it. We want to leave no traces."

"You're bleeding. You had better fix it before you leave a trail through the whole place."

Martin looked at his hand. "Merde. I must have cut it when I slipped."

"Yeah. You scared the shit out of me. That damn piece of concrete bounced and landed right next to me. If you had fallen, you could have come down right on top of me. You would have killed me."

"I guess you're blessed. It must be the good clean living."

Martin, annoyed that his cut was creating extra work, slipped on a pair of rubber gloves. He had planned to use them anyway, and they would keep him from leaking on the floor. He made a mental note to clean up the spots on the window, desk and floor before he left.

Abraham was all business and asked Martin how he intended to get past the motion detectors.

"It's called 'sonar shuffle.' If you move very, very slowly, they can't see you. Timing is the answer."

"Well, don't take too long. I sure don't want to be here when the staff shows up for work on Monday morning. Not only that, I'm an old man and need to take a piss every so often, so you had better get going."

"Use the window. No one will notice. It rains all the time here."

Martin shrugged and moved to the door. He opened it very slowly and only a crack. He reconfirmed his security by examining the area with a specially fabricated periscope. It appeared that no new detectors had been added. The only one that would come into play was located over the door he was opening. It could not see the door. Martin made a complete search again before he was satisfied that it was safe to proceed. Opening the door only wide enough to allow himself a passageway, he wiggled his feet along. He slowly and methodically made his way down the hall.

It was nearly an hour before he reappeared with two file folders and three blank files and forms. "Sorry it took so long. They had locked the damn file cabinet. It took a while to pick the lock. It isn't like in the movies. It sometimes takes quite a few passes to make it work."

"I understand. My work isn't like in the movies either. Let's get going. What do you want me to do?"

Martin handed Abraham the folders. "I need this information copied to this new file folder with the header from this other file."

Abraham pondered for a moment and then said, "So, you want this patient's name transferred to the other patient's history? Is that it?"

"Exactly."

"Got it. Now leave me alone. I need silence, so I can work."

Abraham began his magic. He worked slowly and systematically. He remained focused and determined. A little over an hour later, he presented a new folder filled out in Di's name with Jennifer's notations. "Is that it?" Abraham asked.

"Perfect." Martin took the new folder and placed Jennifer's x-rays within. "I'll be right back." He disappeared down the hall with the new folder in his hand.

About half an hour later, Martin returned. Smiling and nodding his head positively, he closed the door. Looking at Abraham, he said, "Everything is fine. Now forget what you did, old man."

"That's what I do on every job. That's why Adam keeps using me."

Martin nodded. "Let's get the shit out of here."

Martin hooked up the rope to Abraham's harness and checked to be sure that it was secure. Masterfully, he lowered Abraham back to the street level. Feeling the slack in the rope when Abraham touched the ground, Martin released the rope and let it fall to the side of Abraham. Abraham would coil it and sit on it, pretending once again to be an old drunk.

Martin made his usual once-over, going down his checklist to insure everything was in order. He placed the two old files in his kit to be burned later. He cleaned up his blood spots, checking twice that none had been missed. Like a cat, he slipped out the window, closing it behind him. Making his way along the sills of the three windows to the downspout, he descended quickly and silently without notice.

Back on the ground, Martin found Abraham collapsed with his head leaning against the wall. The rope was spread across the ground where Martin had thrown it. *What in the shit is going on?*

Martin called out the old man's name, but there was no response. Abraham was incoherent. He seemed in and out of consciousness. Not understanding what was wrong, Martin tried to pull Abraham up to standing, but Abraham's body was limp. He seemed dazed, like his body couldn't work.

Realizing that something was terribly wrong, it took Martin only a moment to spring into action. He quickly striped Abraham of his harness and emptied the old man's pockets of all the materials he had used for the change of dental records. Martin packed all of these items and the rope into his own kit and set it across the passageway. He then picked up Abraham and carried him to the street. Fortunately, there was no traffic. Martin crossed the street and tenderly propped up Abraham against a building.

Leaving him there, Martin trotted back to the passageway. He broke the wine bottle against the area where Abraham had been seated. Someone would clean up the mess in the morning. In the process any evidence that might remain from the caper would be swept away. Martin then jogged back to the office he had leased and deposited all of the materials that he used for the break-in, along with Abraham's tools.

Only a minute or two passed before Martin returned to Abraham. Shaking him for a response, the old man was still incoherent and seemed worse. His mind racing, his thoughts clear, Martin searched and quickly found a nearby telephone booth. He called for an ambulance. He gave the directions and hung up. Then, he immediately used his cell phone to call Adam. Adam had told him to never use the cell phone to call anyone outside the operation.

No names were passed. No courtesies were exchanged. Only information was provided. "Problem. I think Abraham had a stroke. I've called for an ambulance."

"Merde. Did you complete the job, or do I need to bring in a back-up?"

"Completed without any problems. Everything went perfectly and then… Shit."

"Have them take Abraham to the private clinic. You know the one?"

"Yes."

"Tell whoever is in charge this time of night to call Motti. Forget it. I'll call directly and make the arrangements. Motti should be there by the time you arrive. I want Abraham to have the best. Then get yourself to Paris, at once. I need you in Paris now, yesterday if possible. Whatever it takes. Meet Michael and set up."

"Done." He clicked off the connection.

>-+-<+>-·O-·<+-+-<

It was three in the morning when the phone sounded again.

"He's dead."

"Merde."

"Motti couldn't save him. He was gone before we arrived at the clinic."

"Sign whatever paperwork is necessary to have him cremated and have the ashes delivered to my London flat."

"Adam, I want to be there when you spread the ashes at Dachau."

"Of course. He will finally join his family."

"It always surprised me that the old Jew wanted to be cremated and end up there."

"He always felt that he had cheated fate. When the Nazis killed all of his family and left him alive, he felt singled out for a special mission. He considered the cremation setting things right."

"I know, but it's damned strange anyway."

"When will you be here?"

"By five. Private plane. Michael will collect me at the airport."

"Good. We're on a very tight schedule. We can't afford any mistakes."

"Don't worry. My part will be fine. I'm ready and so is Michael."

"Call if there are any changes."

The lines went dead.

19

Paris, 30 August 1997

The small jet touched down a few minutes ahead of schedule. Martin descended the steps with purpose in his stride and headed across the tarmac to the waiting car. As he approached, the driver was briefly illuminated as he lit a cigarette. Martin opened the passenger door and entered without saying a word. Michael slipped the car in gear; it moved silently into the early morning darkness. A short while later, after driving some distance from the aircraft, Michael turned on the car's headlights. He approached a service entrance, and they passed unnoticed through the airport's exit gate. Finally they spoke.

"Good to see you, Martin. The team's at the garage. They're double checking the cars to make sure everything's ready."

"Any problems?"

"Nothing serious. We had to change the plates on the Fiat. Someone reported the plates as stolen. Not a big deal. We just collected some new ones."

"Belgian again?"

"Of course."

"Are the bikes ready?"

"Yeah, but I thought you'd want to check yours out for yourself.

Other than taking it for a quick spin, we left it alone. Pascal already checked out his."

"Good. How about the team?"

"Blue and White will be in the Fiat. They've been briefed and will perform as instructed. They'll do what's required, nothing more, nothing less. I've used them before. They have two people traveling on their real passports to Bangkok. The people in Bangkok will return within twenty-four hours of the call. Blue and White will have perfect alibis should anyone ever try to trace the car to them."

"Good. You're still going to be driving this car?"

"Yeah. I didn't want to get anyone else involved. The more people involved, the greater the danger something will go wrong."

"What about Pascal?"

"He said he's ready for his part, whatever the hell that is. He's also a complete asshole. Where did you dig him up anyway?"

"He's my godfather. What about the computer setup?"

"Blue and White have spent quite a bit of time on the Virtual Reality trainer. That's quite some video game. It's absolutely brilliant. The kid is still at the flat and has been running different scenarios for Blue and White. He makes me feel like an idiot."

"That kid's a genius. Wake me when we're a few minutes away. I need some rest. I've had a hell of a night."

>-<+>-O-<+>-<

Olbia Airport, 30 August 1997

The white Mercedes arrived at the airport as pre-planned to meet their early afternoon schedule. Dodi and Di were in the rear. Tomas was driving with Trevor in the front passenger seat. Di had already prompted Katherine through their normal coded signals. The final scene was nearly set. The Gulfstream was ready and waiting. They boarded and were soon airborne. Their estimated time of arrival in Paris was a little past three in the afternoon.

Katherine had already placed several anonymous calls to various paparazzi noting the plane's destination and estimated arrival time. The bait had been taken. There would be a crowd awaiting their arrival.

"Dodi, I don't want to have to suffer those bloody paparazzi. I just want us left alone. We only have tonight in Paris."

"We can avoid them. Don't worry about it. I'll call the police and arrange an escort to keep them away."

"You know it won't work. The French police can be very difficult.

They won't do anything. They only agree to help when they can do it their way."

"I'll take care of it. Don't worry. There'll be no problem. No one knows we're coming except for the Hotel. No one from the Ritz would dare tell the paparazzi. There won't be any paparazzi at the airport when we arrive. They might not even know we're in Paris until we arrive at the Hotel."

"I'm sure you're right, but somehow they always manage to find out. I absolutely hate it. Have I ever told you about my friend Michael? He's an expert in geopolitical strategies. He understands how I hate the paparazzi. He told me he has a way we can have some peace from the bloodsuckers."

Laughing, Dodi responded, "What's he going to do, feed them to the lions?"

"No, he'll have them all arrested."

"That would be a genuine miracle. He must have been joking. No one has ever succeeded in pulling that off."

"That's because no one has ever figured out how to do it. It's a very nasty trick but very simple. It doesn't really bother me to play a nasty trick on those bloodsuckers. They deserve it as far as I'm concerned."

"It sounds wonderfully devious, but I can't imagine you ever being nasty."

"Michael has a great plan. It'll buy us some peace, and we can just be ourselves without having to hide."

"What are you talking about? You're so beautiful but you're being very mysterious. You've sparked my curiosity. Tell me about the plan this Michael has concocted. I must know."

"You know how the French are usually slow to react, then they tend to overreact?"

"It's the French temperament, but where's this going? What's his plan?"

"Michael said we should stage an incident. It will look as though the paparazzi placed our lives at risk, just to take our photos. The French police will panic and arrest them all. We can have the last laugh and a little peace this evening."

"This is a bit far out for me. Are you sure this Michael knows what he's talking about? We could never pull anything like that off, especially on short notice. Anyway, it could be very dangerous. I don't want to risk anything that could rob us of even a moment of our time together."

"Michael is in Paris right now. He can arrange it all. I know he can. I've already talked to him and he has the entire plan ready to put in motion. He told me that he has everything he needs ready. You just need to agree. If you say it's okay, I'll call him. We'll be free. He won't try anything that poses a risk to us. The American government even uses him. He really is a genius for this sort of thing."

"I don't want to take the risk today. It's our special day. Something could go wrong. I don't want today spoiled in any way."

Di smiled, reached out and gently touched his cheek. "Let's just see. Maybe I'm worried for nothing, just being a silly female."

"Everything will be okay. We won't have any problems. Trust me, please. I think you're worried over nothing."

She laid her head against his shoulder, and he felt the excitement course through his veins. *She will be mine. What a prize, she's wonderful. No one will ever put us down again. This is the coup of the century.*

Shit, she thought. *I knew this would happen. I feel so badly about leading him on. Shit. I told Adam this would happen, and all he could tell me was to keep my cool. Shit. And now, I even like the guy. He's so sweet. Oh shit, shit, shit.*

>⊷─◦─⊶<

Paris, 30 August 1997

As the aircraft rolled to a halt a little before three-thirty, it was obvious that the paparazzi had been alerted. There were at least two dozen of them hovering. They were impatiently waiting like starving piranhas with cameras dangling everywhere. Di looked out the window. Totally exasperated, she held her head in her hands.

Dodi, reacting to show his control of the situation, telephoned the police and demanded an escort to keep the paparazzi away. The police reminded him that it was not against French law to take photos, while begrudgingly agreeing to provide the escort.

Frustrated, Dodi waited for Henri to load the luggage into the Range Rover. The luggage was to be taken directly to his apartment. Philippe would drive Di and Dodi to the postwar home of the Duke and Duchess of Windsor. Di had asked to see the villa. She had heard so many stories about the grand events that had been staged there over the years.

On the journey to the villa, they were dogged by a paparazzo on a small motorcycle. They played chase but were not able to lose him. He was not overly aggressive, just annoying, like a dull pain that remains constant or a gnat that keeps buzzing around one's head.

When finally secure at the villa, Dodi and Di walked through the mansion and stopped for a time in a quiet room. Sharing an embrace, Di broke their togetherness by bringing up the subject again. "They're going to keep hounding us, just like the one on the scooter. Word is out that we're here, and they'll be everywhere. They'll take this special day away from us. I can feel it."

"Okay. Okay. I give up. Call your friend Michael, and we'll get rid of them."

"Oh, Dodi, you are such an angel. I do love you, you know." She kissed him softly on the cheek, and he held her tightly. A few moments later, she began again. "We must be absolutely secretive about this. If the police realize we've manipulated them, they'll be furious. We'll be under even more pressure. I don't think we should tell Trevor. Let him think it's really happening. The less he knows the better. There isn't any real reason for him to know. If the police question him, he can be completely honest. I don't think he could ever lie anyway. He's just too straight."

Pondering Di's comment, Dodi did not respond immediately. Then, he said, "I agree with you completely. We should keep all of this our little secret. It would be a scandal of epic proportions and a front page story if the press ever caught on."

"Michael told me that we will have to tell the driver. He said it's important to insure that no one is hurt. It makes sense to me."

"Okay, I'll tell Philippe."

"Michael told me that we should use someone other than Philippe. The paparazzi all watch Philippe because he always drives us. It'll be much harder to make the plan work if we use him. Michael thought it would be a good idea to use Henri. He's loyal and well trained for defensive driving."

Again contemplating Di's comments, Dodi took some time before responding. "When I think about it, Michael's probably right. We can use Henri. He's a good man and understands our security needs. I personally like him and trust him completely. He's absolutely loyal and will keep his mouth shut about the plan."

"You tell Henri, and I'll have Michael talk to him to see if they can help us tonight. Oh, I'm so excited. I'll be free at last. Then, we can enjoy our special evening."

"Okay, but you must promise me that if anything looks even the least bit dangerous, we'll stop and forget about everything. I don't want to risk anything happening to you. I couldn't stand it if something happened to you."

"Michael is an expert in these things. He told me not to worry.

Everything will be perfect. I can just feel it. We'll be free, Dodi. Free
from all these bloodsucking leeches."

It was a little after four when they decided to go to the Ritz to wind
down and make their telephone calls in privacy. When they arrived, photographers had already gathered at both the front and back entrances to
the Hotel. Di looked resigned as they took a run for the entrance and
headed directly to the Imperial Suite. Once inside Dodi asked, "Are you
sure you want to go through with Michael's plan? I'll call Henri and tell
him to go ahead, if you really want it."

"Positive. It's our only hope of privacy. Oh Dodi, you don't know
how I've longed to be set free from these leeches."

Dodi went right to work. He called Henri first and told him to expect
a call from a man named Michael. He relayed to Henri that Di had
already spoken to this Michael and that the man had a plan to rid them
of the paparazzi. Dodi instructed Henri to meet with him. Michael would
brief Henri about everything, and then Henri would report back his
assessment of the plan to Dodi. Henri would be their driver for the event
and was to go through with the plan unless he felt that it was too dangerous. If he felt it too dangerous, Henri was to immediately call Dodi.
Next, Dodi called to see if the purchase of Julie Andrews' property was
confirmed. There were some problems, and Dodi became involved in a
long and heated conversation that led to his needing to make several
other calls. He was distracted from Di, as he dealt with his pressing business affairs.

Di took advantage of the unexpected privacy to place her calls. She
made the most important call first. "Hello, this is your old friend. Could
it be worked out for tonight? Dodi is willing to go through with the
plan."

Adam had been expecting Di's call. He responded, "We have time if
we can get to the driver immediately. It will take a while to arrange
everything. Adequate preparation is essential. I don't want to take any
risks."

"Everyone keeps saying that. Henri will do it." She then read Henri's
cell phone number to Adam.

"I have it. We are a go. Remember your instructions exactly. It won't
be long. Are you wearing exactly what you had planned? Jewelry, everything?"

"Exactly. Thank you." As she broke the connection, she became
introspective. *I'm so excited. How am I ever going to place the calls and
not let it show?*

She concentrated, forcing herself to remain in control. It was vital she give no hint. Her excitement was mounting by the minute. She worried that she might say more than she should. She had to be careful not to sound overly bubbly. She placed several calls. It was important to make these last contacts with her friends to express her joy and contentment. She wanted her friends to sense her peace. She felt a little dishonest in that her happiness was not for the reason that everyone thought, but she had no choice. What else could she do? If she told anyone, she would have no escape. She silently mouthed Adam's words. "There is no other way."

Sometime later after completing their calls, Dodi insisted they go to his apartment on Rue Arsène-Houssaye to relax and freshen up for dinner. As they left the Ritz, the paparazzi lingered on their tail, as always. They could go nowhere unescorted by these dogs, so anxious to pick up scraps. But now, it didn't matter. If it were not for the paparazzi, the plan would not be possible. The paparazzi were now a cog in the wheel that was turning.

>─┼─◄▶─○─◄▶─┼─◄

Henri had just finished confirming Di's flight reservations to London for the next day when his cell phone rang. "Hallo."

"Good evening, Monsieur. This is Michael. I believe you are expecting my call."

"Yes."

"I would like to meet with you as soon as possible."

"I'm free at the moment."

"Good. I'm near the Ritz at the Café Costes. Do you know the place?"

"Yes, of course."

"If you can stop in front, I'll come to your car. We can go to my flat. I have sandy hair and will be wearing a navy blue jacket."

"I'll be there in ten minutes."

"Good." The line went dead.

>─┼─◄▶─○─◄▶─┼─◄

"Di, I have a present for you."

"Oh Dodi, what have you done?"

She opened the small, royal blue suede box. Inside she found a diamond ring worthy of a princess. She was stunned for a moment. She knew this was coming, and she had tried her best to stall because she had not wanted to hurt him. She had hoped to delay this moment until after the event. Then, it would not matter. She had given him every excuse in the book. It is strange how quickly a man can become hooked. It had only been a few weeks, and she had been so careful. Her heart went out to him. She felt so very guilty. She had tried so hard not to lead him on, not to give him hope. Now, he was forcing her answer, and she wanted to avoid the subject altogether. It was truly agony for her, because she had started to fall for him in spite of herself. *Damn, why did this have to happen?*

"Di, will you marry me? I know we have talked about it. I know it will be difficult for you because of the Royal family. You have so many reasons for saying no. You have told me all of them so many times, but they don't matter. All that matters is that I know I can make you happy. I just want the chance to prove it to you. I want to marry you as soon as possible. I don't want to beg, but I will if I have to."

"Oh, Dodi, darling. You know how I feel. It's all too sudden. I'm not ready. You know how much I care for you, but I need some time. As the Americans say, I need a little space. I'm so sorry. I don't want to disappoint you. It's just that marriage is such a big decision."

"You can take your time. As much as you want. I love you now, and I always will."

"I love you, too, my darling sweet man. But Dodi, really, you should keep the ring for now."

"No. No. No. I want you to have it, even if you turn me down I want you to keep it."

She looked at the ring for a moment and then placed it on her finger. They kissed, and he caressed her neck. The ringing of Dodi's telephone interrupted the mood.

"I'm leaving right now to meet with Michael," Henri said. "Are you sure you want me to go through with this?"

"Yes, as long as you think the risk is acceptable. I mean acceptable both physically and publicity-wise. I don't want anyone hurt. Most importantly, I don't want to read in a paper that this whole thing was orchestrated by us to get rid of the paparazzi."

"I understand."

He cut the connection and turned to Di.

"Henri and Michael are going to meet to discuss the plan. Are you still sure you want to go through with it?"

"Oh Dodi, it will make me so happy. You know how I hate the paparazzi. I hate the way they interfere with our private lives. I hate the way they're always around, lingering to catch a glimpse of something I do that is unattractive or a little risqué."

"Okay, we'll do it."

"Oh Dodi, thank you. Thank you, darling."

"Tell me yes."

"Dodi, please not now. I'm..."

"No, I didn't mean that. It's the name of the ring. The jeweler called it 'Tell Me Yes.' That's its name, honest."

"Dodi, you're so sweet, but I know what you meant."

"You caught me again."

He put his arms around her waist. Placing his forehead on hers, he said, "I love you more than you will ever know."

20

French country house, 30 August 1997

It was late afternoon when Adam turned to Jennifer. "Everything's a go. The confirmation just came. You're on tonight."

"I'm more than ready. I've waited for this night so long. You will be so proud of my performance. I promise."

"Jennifer, I'd like you to go over your instructions for me, just one more time."

"For Christ's sake Adam, I'm not an idiot. I know exactly what to do. We've been over this a thousand times."

"Humor me."

"Okay, but this is the last time. Listen to me carefully. I mean it. I'll only say it once. I'll get ready here, wearing the costume and accessories that are set out for me. Over that I'm to crawl into my 'bitch in a bag' outfit. Yusuf will drive his little harem to the location, and we'll slip into the toilet area. I'll enter a stall and pull off the bag. Reem will touch up my hair and make-up. Then, I'll sit in the stall taking a world record shit while waiting for your precious Princess to show up. She will brief me on what happened during the day so I won't act like an idiot for the rest of the evening. Then, I'll leave and join Dodi. Then we'll drive off into the sunset. Within a few minutes of leaving the Ritz, we'll be in a minor car accident with some paparazzi. It'll be just like the computer simulation that I've sat through at least fifty times. I'll start to hyperventilate and then faint. They'll rush me to the hospital where I'll be admitted. I'll be placed under observation for a few days and act like I'm having a hard time remembering small things. It won't be hard to pull that off, since I don't know what the hell is going on anyway. The boys and Charles will call, and I am to tell them I'm okay, just a little shaken up. Rosa or some other friends might call, as well. They are not to come to see me. If they insist, I'm to tell you immediately. Then, Yusuf will come to the hospital with his little harem, and we'll do the switch again."

"Perfect. Absolutely perfect. I'm impressed."

"You should be. I'm the best you'll ever have, and don't you ever forget it."

▻┼◅▻─○─◅┼◅

Paris, later the same afternoon

As Henri slowed to a stop, a nattily dressed man in a dark blue blazer approached the car. Henri opened the passenger window, and Michael stooped down and to say, "Good day. I'm Michael. May I join you?"

"But, of course."

As soon as the door was closed, Henri pulled into the traffic amid honking horns. Michael gave him directions and then made small talk, as they drove to the flat that was being used as the project's command center. The rent had been paid through the end of the year. The apartment would not be used again after this evening. As soon as Henri left, a special cleaning crew would remove all the equipment. Then, they would go through the place and completely sanitize it. The crew would be finished before two in the morning. Even if the police questioned Henri immediately after the accident, by the time they arrived at the command center, it would be vacant. As an additional precaution, the cleaning crew was hired through cut outs, and they knew nothing.

When Michael and Henri entered the flat, they found Adam, Martin, Blue and White seated at a table. No greetings were exchanged. The four men just stared with appraising eyes at the newcomers. Breaking the pregnant silence, Michael pointed at the two men seated across the table from Adam and Martin. He said to Henri, "Look at those two men carefully. Remember what they look like. The man on the left is the driver. The other is the paparazzo." Expressionless Blue and White nodded to Henri. Then, without a word, they rose and left the flat.

Henri gave Michael a skeptical glance and raised his eyebrows in an inquisitive gesture. Michael shook his head and waited. As soon as the door was closed, Michael began, "Henri, I wanted you to see these two men so that you could give a description of them to the police. I want you to be able to honestly say to the police that you have never met them before but that you, possibly, have seen them before. You also can tell the police that you think that you could identify them, if you were ever to see them again. If you go through with this, the police will ask you scores of questions. It's important that we protect you by only telling you what you need to know, so you can give honest answers to the questions that you will surely be asked. We don't want to put you in a position where you have to lie to the police. It's always better in these situations to be able to simply tell the truth. Do you understand?"

"Yes, I understand what you're saying, but I don't understand what all of this is about. I must tell you that I have to be satisfied that everything will be safe for my employer, or I'll walk away."

"Agreed. We want the same thing for Princess Di. We will allow no risk to her person."

"Then, convince me."

"First, let's have some coffee. We need to be alert so we can decide together how this will work."

Adam rose to prepare the coffee after taking orders. He knew from the investigation he had conducted that Henri took both flouxetine and tiapride but never both at the same time. Henri often became mildly depressed due to the pressures of his work. Into Henri's coffee, Adam slipped both drugs. The coffee was very strong, and the taste would probably pass.

After the coffee was served, Michael explained the plan to Henri. Martin filled in some of the small details and then took his first sip of coffee. Almost spitting it out he said, "This stuff tastes like cow piss. I'll save you all and make the next batch." The slight chemical taste caused by the medications did not seem to be noticed by Henri. He drank it all without comment and asked for a refill. They were on their way.

Michael took over and said, "Basically, what we intend to do is have a minor accident. The one man you saw earlier will be driving a red Fiat Uno. The other man is, as I already told you, a paparazzo. He will be in the back of the Fiat taking pictures of your car. The driver will bang into the left side of your car, then speed away and disappear. Because the Fiat is so small and light and the Mercedes you will be driving is so heavy, there will be little risk to your car or its occupants. The Fiat's occupants will be at some risk, but these men are professionals and will have no problems. They'll be carrying genuine press credentials from a Belgian paper. Their car will never be found. If you are able to notice the car license number you can even give it to the police. The plates are French. Do you follow so far?"

"Yes, in principle."

"Di and Dodi will be shaken by the accident, and you will rush them to the hospital. There, they will make their escape. You will have to deal with the police and file a complaint about the irresponsible paparazzi."

"That part won't be hard. I hate those bastards. They make my life miserable. I'm always attempting to keep them away from important hotel guests."

Adam felt a sense of peace. Obviously, the drugs were taking hold, and Henri was relaxing. With this combination of drugs, Henri would remain calm in the middle of a nuclear holocaust. Now, all Adam needed to do was convince him to have a couple of drinks, and the stage would be set. This might prove difficult, as Henri was not a drinker, but it was still possible, nonetheless.

Henri remained silent for a few moments as he struggled to assimilate everything Michael had told him. Then, choosing his words carefully, he continued. "I understand the accident. On the surface it seems physically safe enough for my passengers. I agree that the heavy Mercedes being bumped by the lightweight Fiat Uno will be far more dangerous for the Fiat than for my passengers, but I have several questions. First, how will you keep the accident from looking staged? The real paparazzi will probably photograph it. If it comes out that all of this was planned, I'll be out of a job. Second, what if the Fiat is stopped? What will these two men say? Third, what if either the driver or the paparazzo in the Fiat is injured?"

Michael responded quickly. "All good questions. All simple answers. First, we suggest the use of a ploy to distract the paparazzi. Someone from the Ritz can come out and announce that there will be a photo-op in ten minutes. Dodi's normal car and driver can be brought to wait in the area and serve as a decoy. The paparazzi will hover at that entrance to the Hotel. No one will want to miss out. You can leave from the other entrance with your passengers. As soon as you are away, we will arrange for someone to tell the paparazzi that you left with Di and Dodi by the other entrance. The press will madly rush off in pursuit. You'll have a small but adequate head start, so no one will catch up with you until after the event. There will be many witnesses to confirm that the paparazzi left with great speed to catch you. No one will doubt that one of them recklessly caused the accident."

Michael then pointed to Martin. "This man will be riding a BMW motorcycle. He'll be in contact with you at the beginning of your drive on your portable phone and will lead you through the accident. You will merely follow him. He will also be in contact with the Fiat and an additional car that will monitor traffic. He'll insure that the accident is choreographed with no danger to any innocent bystanders. This is very important to us, as well. He'll be behind you as you begin the drive, and as soon as he has a fix on the location of the paparazzi, he'll pass you and be the leader. As the coordinator of the accident, he'll be able to make sure that none of the paparazzi following will see the actual accident. This way nothing will ever look staged."

Without giving Henri a chance to respond, Michael continued. "The second problem has also been considered. Blue and White are being compensated handsomely to keep their mouths shut. There is no doubt that they will. They are professionals. Both carry genuine press credentials from a Belgian newspaper. Their car has French license plates from a wrecked car and cannot be traced. There will be a trailer designed for a racecar parked on a side street near where the accident will be staged. Blue and White will drive to the trailer immediately after the incident and park their car inside the trailer. The two men will then leave for Belgium via private car. A separate person who knows nothing of what is being done will pick up the trailer fifteen minutes later and drive it to Belgium. By the time the police round up all the known paparazzi, there will be no evidence from the event left in France."

"You guys really have your shit together, don't you?"

Appreciating the compliment, Michael went on. "The last problem is that of danger to the Fiat's occupants. The driver is an expert. He's well trained to handle the collision. Remember that he will be bumping into your car. He will control the impact. He will be placing his own life and his partner's life on the line. Neither has any desire to be injured. The driver can handle it. He used to be a stunt driver in Hollywood. He will be cautious and insure, at the most, that there will only be minor injuries. These guys are making damn good money. Believe me, they want to be around to spend it."

"I understand. It sounds as though you have given this all a lot of thought. But there is still the question of preparation, it's not like we can rehearse the accident to work out unknown problems."

"Our work is without flaw. It has to be, as we're working for the Crown. If we make any mistakes, we lose our credibility. Without credibility, we're out of business. We would even have a hard time locating work in the private sector if we screwed up on something as important as this. So, we always take extra precautions. The unforeseen can happen. We know that, and we have a back-up plan. If someone gets hurt, we have a private doctor who will be on standby only a few blocks away. He'll have a Belgian ambulance equipped with state-of-the-art technology to administer aid. If there is a serious problem, the patient will be transported to Belgium for medical care. The plan is solid, but before you make up your mind, I want you to use the simulator we have built. Then, you'll really understand what I'm talking about, and you can make your decision. Please follow me."

The adjoining room was filled with all sorts of technical material and devices. Henri had never before seen so much equipment in any one room. There was hardly any space to stand. A young man of perhaps sixteen or seventeen years of age was sitting in front of several computer screens on an upended wine box. He was tinkering with three different computer keyboards all at the same time. As they entered, the teenage boy looked up. He appeared disgusted by the distraction and then nonplused quickly returned to his tasks.

Henri tripped over a large cable that had been laid across the floor. He caught himself before falling into a huge computer screen that flanked the apparatus that held what looked like a driver's seat. The seat appeared to be out of an 'S Class' Mercedes and was complete with seatbelt, steering wheel, brake and accelerator pedals. There was a tubular framework around the entire contraption, and a maze of hydraulic lines, switches and cables was draped from everywhere.

Michael began, "This device is a little like a flight simulator. It has been designed specifically for this project. Everyone involved has worked with the simulation of his task and practiced the entire encounter many times. We want you to go through the same training so you are confident that the operation can be successful. Then, if satisfied, you can agree to do it."

"You mean you have simulated the accident? I can practice the accident?"

"Correct."

"What do I do?"

"Take a seat, and be sure to fasten your seatbelt."

Henri slipped into the seat and placed his hands on the wheel. Looking at Michael he said, "Okay. I'm ready. What's next?"

"No, you're not ready. Like I already warned you, you need to fasten your seatbelt. The success of this operation cannot be guaranteed unless you and your passengers are wearing your seatbelts. You must remember this."

"I understand all of that, but this is just a video game."

"Believe me. It's like no video game you've ever seen. It's more like an air combat simulator. The movements can be sudden and we even had to attach it to the floor to keep the frame from moving."

Begrudgingly, Henri buckled up. The kid walked over and handed Henri a helmet and gloves. A bundle of cables emerged from the rear of the helmet and connected to the gloves and then wandered across the room before they disappeared into the maze. The kid said, "Please, put these on."

Henri slipped on the gloves and placed the helmet on his head. He went rigid for a moment and then looked like he was trying to catch his balance in the seat. He muttered, "Jesus, Mary and Joseph," as he grasped the steering wheel for balance.

From Henri's perspective, he was seated in an 'S Class' Mercedes waiting outside the rear door of the Ritz Hotel. On command, he touched the accelerator and brake pedals lightly before applying some gas. The whole device shuddered, and Henri muttered "Merde," as he slammed on the brakes to stop. Pulling off the helmet he said, "Merde. I just ran into a parked car. I can't believe it. It was so realistic. I thought it really happened. I heard the crunch of the metal and breaking glass, and I felt the impact."

"The kid does good work," Michael responded. "He built this to our specifications so we could practice this incident without attracting attention."

"It must have cost a fortune. I'm really impressed."

"The cost was not a factor. It was important to do what was necessary to assure there are no mistakes. Everything must be perfect. No one can be at risk. What is money compared to the safety of our charges?"

"Okay, so where do we go from here? What do I do?"

"You need to put on the video helmet again and drive the route. You'll see an arrow appear and flash where you are to turn. A BMW motorcycle will pass you, and you are to follow it. Don't try to go a different direction. The computer is not programmed for any other options, and you'll merely drive into a void. That could prove very disorienting."

Henri took a few moments to adjust the helmet so that it was comfortable before beginning the driving simulation. Michael and Adam watched what Henri was seeing on a separate monitor located in front of the seat that Henri was occupying. Henri looked in both mirrors before pulling out into the traffic flow. He slowed to let a pedestrian run across the street and used his turn signals in accord with the law. On Rue de Rivoli the BMW passed, and Henri followed, exactly as instructed, through the Alma Tunnel. After exiting the tunnel, he came upon a red Fiat Uno. The Fiat swerved and slightly bumped into the side of his car. Henri looked briefly at the driver before speeding away with a barrage of French curses."

Out of nowhere, the kid shouted, "Oh shit," as though he was warning of an upcoming event.

Suddenly, Henri stiffened in the seat and slammed his foot onto the brake pedal. The whole device shuddered, and Henri jerked off the helmet. Henri groaned, "I think I'm going to puke."

"Its cyber-sickness," the kid explained. "It'll go away in a few minutes. Don't worry about it. It's caused by the disorientation that occurs when you go beyond the boundaries of the system. By default, the system resets to the start position."

"That was unreal. It felt like I was really hit by a car. Then, as I sped away, the world turned black for a moment, and I rear-ended a car parked behind the Ritz Hotel."

"Henri," Michael intervened, "let's try it again. This time without testing the limits of the system. Are you a go?"

"Give me a second. Okay? Shit, I need a little space. My heart's racing. Let me take some deep breaths. I need moment to calm down first."

Soon, they returned to the Virtual Reality setup, and Henri made several runs following the route without incident. Satisfied that he was able to maneuver the Mercedes, they added to the scenario. On this run a car pulled in front of him out of the right lane when he was following the BMW in the left lane. Henri, predictably, swerved around the car on the right rather than waiting. Henri was exactly following the profile that they had developed for him. After another ten minutes of scenarios with slight variances, Henri was handling the whole encounter as they had pre-determined. When the events started to happen in real life, he would react similarly and follow the program that they had outlined for him. He would be expecting a red Fiat Uno and the white one would be ignored until it was much too late.

When finished, Henri sat and thought for a moment or two. "This is really impressive. I can handle it with no problem. You're right, Michael. It's a low-risk operation. I'm not worried for my passengers or my employer's reputation. I'll do it. I'll call Dodi and tell him that, for me, everything checks out perfectly. It's a brilliant plan, and I'll get the last laugh on the paparazzi. I'll just step outside to make my call and get his permission."

"That's fine, but be careful of what you say. We don't want anyone to overhear anything. Cell phones are not very secure. Don't say anything specific about the project."

"Oui, I understand."

"After you make your call, we'll review the plan until you're more than one hundred percent satisfied. You already know the route you are to drive. By the time we're finished, it will be second nature to you. Also, we need to verify that your cell phone will work for the project. If it's not adequate, we'll have to make a substitution."

Henri stepped outside the flat, and the other three remained quiet, making no comments to each other. When he returned, Henri said, "Michael, my boss gave me the go-ahead. He wants me to practice until I have it down perfect in every way. I'm to call him when I'm ready. They'll be at the Ritz. He wanted to do it as soon as possible, but I told him that it would be better not to rush. We need time to prepare. I don't want any mistakes. We set a tentative time for midnight. What do you think? If we need more time, we can postpone it a little. But he's anxious to have it done."

"I'm sure we can be ready by midnight. There's very little you still need to do, we have plenty of time. You already have a good grasp of your part, and you seem to handle it well. The other players will have the hard work, and they're already very well prepared."

"You must have been working on this for some time."

"Yes, we've been working on it for quite a while. Let's go to work, and when you're satisfied, we'll uncork an exceptional bottle of wine. We should have a nice toast to the plan."

>-+-◆»--O--◆◆-+-◄

Paris, 30 August 1997

It was nearly eight o'clock when Dodi hung-up from the phone call. "The plan is to do it at midnight. Henri seemed very excited about the whole thing and said that this is really a first-class operation. He said I would be very impressed if I saw what has been organized."

Di threw her arms around his neck and said, "Oh Dodi, thank you, thank you, thank you. This is the most exciting day of my life. You have no idea!"

He was overwhelmed by her affection and held her tightly. Finally, he whispered in her ear, "We'll come back to my apartment when this is finally over, and I'll make tonight a night you will never forget."

"Dodi, I promise you, I will never forget this day. You have been so sweet and made me so very happy."

Glancing at his watch, he said, "We're almost late. We need to leave for our dinner at Chez Benoît. I'll tell Philippe."

Di walked over to the window. "Shit. Dodi, please come. Look at this."

From their window, it was obvious that the media mob had gathered like sharks in a feeding frenzy.

"Di, you know that they'll be gathering at the restaurant, too. Maybe we should just go somewhere else."

"Since Henri is going to drive us from the Ritz at midnight, why don't we just go there? I'm so fond of the dining room."

"Okay. I'll call and have a very private table prepared but not until I've held you tightly one more time and stolen a kiss."

"Only one?"

⊱┈◈┈○┈◈┈⊰

They arrived at the Ritz greeted by a crowd of ravenous photographers and journalists. Making their way through the mayhem, they went directly to the Hotel's grand dining room. As they entered, the whole room became silent. Then whispering sounds began to drift from every direction, as all eyes froze upon them. Di glanced at Dodi, and he put his arm around her shoulders and swept her out of the room.

"This is what I mean. We can't go anywhere. I'll be so happy when this is over."

Trying to comfort her, Dodi said, "I'm so sorry. I know you love the dining room, but let's eat in the Imperial Suite. The staff will make everything perfect for us. I'll see to it. I promise."

⊱┈◈┈○┈◈┈⊰

"Okay Henri. Spill it all back to me. I want to make sure that you're comfortable with everything."

"I've got it. No problem. Philippe will drive the decoy car. He'll wait at the front door of the Ritz. I'll leave by the back door with Dodi, Di and the bodyguard. The bodyguard will be in the dark. Mum's the word. It's important that he knows absolutely nothing of the plan. We're doing this so he'll be surprised, upset and angry when it happens. His reactions need to be perfectly normal."

Michael interjected, "So far, so good. Please continue."

"I'm to drive south on Rue Cambon, then west on Rue de Rivoli, then through the Alma Tunnel. After I depart, someone will tell the paparazzi that we left and they will speed off to try and catch us. As I emerge from the tunnel, no paparazzi will be in sight, because of the tunnel and the sight vectors that lead in and out of the tunnel. Right after I leave the tunnel, I'll be bumped by a red Fiat Uno with a paparazzo taking flash pictures. I am not to panic. I'm to stay cool and professional. All I have to do is follow Martin on his BMW through the whole scenario. I'm to try to match his speed exactly. That way I'll exit the tunnel coordinated exactly with the Fiat. It's very important to match his speed. In principle, I'm to accelerate when I approach the tunnel, to make sure no paparazzi can photograph the accident. After we are bumped, I'm to yell to the bodyguard to get the license number of the car."

"Great. What's next?"

"Di will grasp her chest and complain that her heart feels funny. She might even faint. I'm to take her directly to the Hôpital de la Pitié-Salpêtrière. When I get to the hospital, Dodi and Di will leave immediately by a car that will be waiting there for them. You are taking care of that arrangement. I'm to talk to the police with the bodyguard. I'm to tell the police that Dodi and Di are in hiding out of fear for their lives. They were nearly killed by the crazy paparazzi. The bodyguard and I are to describe the car, driver and the paparazzo as closely as possible."

"Perfect. Are you comfortable with the scenario?"

"Yes. It's just wild enough to work. The police will go absolutely crazy. They'll be frantic to round up anyone from the media who could have contributed in any way. They'll want to avoid an international scandal at all costs."

"Let's check out the phone system. I suggest that you tell the bodyguard that someone is monitoring traffic so that you know how to avoid the paparazzi. That will explain the phone conversation."

Martin put on his helmet. A phone system had been built into it. The system was complex, another electronic engineering feat mastered by Gerard. It allowed Martin to be connected with Henri on one line and, at the same time, have the ability to connect to everyone else on the other. The system was set up so that Henri could only hear what he was told by Martin. Henri would hear none of the information passed onto the other players. All the other players would be able to hear everything. The whole thing was utterly slick. Then, there were override controls to be used if necessary. Adam would monitor the whole conversation in real time, allowing him to be current on the unfolding plan. He would be able to troubleshoot, if necessary. Gerard would be on standby to clean up all of the phone records. He had already hacked into the French phone system for the codes and would erase all records of the phone calls. It would be impossible to trace anything, ever.

"It all seems like a go to me," Michael said. "How about you, Henri?"

"Clear on this end."

"Okay. Let's break out a good bottle of wine. I have two bottles of '61 Châteaux Margaux that are begging to be set free. Let's celebrate a foolproof plan!"

"Michael, please nothing for me. I need to be in top form for tonight, although a bottle of '61 is very tempting."

"Come on Henri. You don't have to do anything. The Belgians are taking all the risk, and Martin will be walking you through it. It's nothing for you. It'll be the greatest coup of your life. Besides that there is still plenty of time."

"Okay. I guess you're right. I have almost no responsibility but only one glass."

Adam returned with the bottle and offered it to Michael. He carefully examined the label and nodded. After the cumbersome ritual of opening and decanting the bottle, they joined in small talk as they sipped their wine and relaxed. Several minutes later, Henri looked at his watch and said, "I had better call and tell Dodi that all is ready."

"Remind him that everyone is to wear seatbelts. We don't want anyone injured by the accident."

Henri didn't bother to leave the room this time. The drugs coupled with the high he was feeling from the simulator made him euphoric. He was relaxed and comfortable. His conversation with Dodi was animated. He expressed his excitement about the creativeness of the caper and affirmed his assurance that all precautions had been taken. Finally, as the conversation ended, Dodi told Henri to remain on alert. Henri would be called when they were ready. Assured that his boss was confident in his judgment, Henri returned to his glass of wine saying, "This vintage is nothing less than exquisite. No man could ever hope to taste a better bottle."

"Let's have another small glass. The night is still young, and you need a little fortifying for your upcoming ordeal with the police."

"That's for sure. They won't be the least bit happy when they find out that they're sitting on a potentially huge scandal. They will probably throw every paparazzo they can put their hands on in jail. I agree. This plan will work."

"Let's drink to it."

Adam and Martin excused themselves telling Michael and Henri that they had work to complete in preparation for the rest of the evening, and they needed to take the kid home. Before leaving, Adam entered the room with the Virtual Reality equipment and drew his finger across his throat. Understanding perfectly, Gerard turned the virus loose. It would make continuous rewrites of the hard disks until the computer was turned off. In less than five minutes, nothing would be salvageable. Not even a top computer expert would have a chance of retrieving anything.

With Gerard's handiwork complete, Adam and Martin passed through the room with their young charge in tow. As he opened the door to leave, Adam looked back at Henri and said, "We have confidence in you. You'll do great. You have mastered the whole script! Sorry to leave you, but this young man needs to be taken home, and we've got one hell of a lot to do."

A few minutes after their departure, Henri asked, "Michael, who is the man who brought the wine? He watched everything carefully but said almost nothing. He seemed much too sophisticated to be just a helper."

"He's an observer from British intelligence. He's making sure there's no possibility of having this turn out wrong. Veto power and all that shit."

"His English sounded almost American, and his French sounded Swiss. I really couldn't place his nationality."

"Blending in is a prerequisite in his line of work. I hate to spoil a wonderful evening, but I guess you should probably leave fairly soon. It would be best for you to go to one of the places that you normally frequent after work. That way nothing will seem unusual if anyone happens to look for you on hotel business. But before you leave, would you like another glass of this most excellent vintage? The night is still young."

21

The French country house, 30 August 1997

It was approximately eight-thirty in the evening when Elizabeth answered the call from Adam. "Yes."

"We're on. It's a one hundred percent go. I just received the final confirmation."

"Timing?"

"Midnight, from the Ritz."

"We'll be there."

"I'll call if there are any changes. Good luck with your baby-sitting."

"Thanks a million and screw you, too."

"Jennifer, that was Adam. We're confirmed for tonight at midnight. Everything is exactly as we rehearsed. We will arrive at the Ritz by eleven."

"Okay. That sounds fine, but there is one more thing I need to get ready."

"What do you mean? You already told me that you're ready."

"Oh, Elizabeth, I am ready. All of my shit is organized and laid out, all that stuff. That's not what I mean. It's just that I've been thinking. Time is one thing that I have had, and it's given me..."

"Just spit it out for heaven's sake. I don't have all night. What is it? What's troubling you?"

"Shit, are you ever bitchy. I'd say it's your period, but you're much too old to be having them. Just give me a minute, and I'll tell you."

Elizabeth shot her an evil glance and said, "I'm listening. Just get on with it."

"Okay. Well, to put it bluntly, I want another raise. I'm doing very specialized work for you. You have even said that I'm brilliant in my role. What I'm doing is worth much more than what you are paying me. I must have an additional ten thousand a month."

"I can't believe you are doing this right now at this time. We have to leave in only a few minutes for your premiere, and you're asking for a raise? Haven't you ever heard about proper timing? Is money all that matters to you? Well, my dear girl, I want you to know, I'm not impressed."

"Elizabeth, really there is no reason to be so snippy."

"Don't test me. It won't be to your advantage in the long run. This is how it is. Listen carefully. I agree to your demand. You may have your ten thousand, but believe me I won't ever forget this. Rest assured, I promise that you will never pull anything like this on me again. You are quickly working yourself out of a job. You've become too bigheaded. You're so over-impressed with your own importance that you have lost sight of reality. You have decided that you are irreplaceable, that we need you. Don't be too sure of yourself, my dear girl. Anyone is replaceable. After tonight, I'll be happy to prove it to you. Tomorrow, I'll start looking for your replacement, and I'll find someone better than you. You have pushed me one time too many."

"Elizabeth, darling, do whatever you want. Go ahead and look for a replacement for me. You have my blessings. Regardless of what you say, I'm not worried in the least. I can do as I please, and you very well know I can. You have no chance of replacing me. I know too much. Soon, I will be one of the most famous women of our time. I will write a book, be on Larry King. Why I might even mention you in my writings, my dear, self-centered bitch."

Elizabeth was silent. She looked at Jennifer stonefaced for a few moments before speaking. Those who truly know Elizabeth would have been terrified; her eyes revealed unspeakable danger. Quietly, almost in a whisper, she responded choosing her words very deliberately. "As I already told you, you have your raise. Don't forget the other things I said either. Now, let's get ready."

"You really mean it? I have my bonus?"

Elizabeth's expression suggested a rage just short of hatred. Realizing she was close to crossing the line of control, Elizabeth forced herself to mask her feelings before responding. "Yes. I'll make a transfer in your account in Geneva on Monday. You have my personal word. Now, please get ready."

Expressionless, Elizabeth turned and exited the room. She went to the kitchen where Yusuf was waiting impatiently. "Are you ready? We will be leaving shortly."

Appearing a little harried, Reem entered the kitchen. Obviously concerned, she asked, "Will we have a photo, or will I need to just work from the original when I see her? I have everything organized and packed."

"Plan to work from the original. I'll try to get a Polaroid to help. But don't count on it."

"The make-up is no problem. I can work it fast. But if the hairstyle is much different, it will take me some time. I know my time line is very limited. If I have an idea, I can do some of the preparation in advance."

"Okay, I'll get on it for you, but there are no guarantees."

><+>-O-<+><

Paris, 30 August 1997

It was about ten in the evening when Adam parked his car on a Paris side street. Turning to Martin, he asked, "Are Blue and White in the dark? Do they have any idea?"

"None whatsoever. They think their job is to kill the Princess. Both think that Michael is the special representative of the Queen and the Queen wants her to be history. They have been told that Michael is arranging the project to save the Crown the embarrassment that would result from the marriage of Di to a foreigner of dubious character. They are aware that the father has had numerous problems with the British establishment and the son has a playboy reputation. They bought the whole package, hook, line and sinker."

"What about Michael? Any suspicions?"

"He thinks he's working for the IRA and that the Queen story is just disinformation for a cover. His pay is coming from an Irish consulting firm. He knows that the IRA unsuccessfully tried to kill both Di and Charles a few years ago. He has no doubts whatsoever that this incident is being staged by the IRA, and I have done nothing to discourage that line of thought."

"Does anyone have the slightest idea about the existence of Jennifer?"

"Not a clue."

"What about Pascal?"

"He's just backup. He'll figure out his part of the operation later, but, right now, he only knows that he is to provide traffic information. Of course, he's prepared for the other possibility, too. But he has no idea of the target's identity, just that she is a blond woman. He will only be activated by the call he places to you. If he gets the go ahead, he will execute the backup plan. He has never seen Blue or White. He thinks that Michael is running the operation. Pascal was told that Michael is a British intelligence agent on special assignment. He accepted it all. You know all about him. It's just another job. He could care less."

"I can't see anything you've forgotten. You've done an excellent job so far. Make the rest perfect. There is no room for error. When this is over, I want you off the continent immediately for at least a year, longer would be better. Where do you want to go? Have you thought about it?"

"Asia. I'll start in Hong Kong and wander around. I haven't been to Thailand for a long time. I'll spend some time there. I'd like to go to Africa too."

"Sounds fine, keep in contact by e-mail. Use the normal procedures. Nothing else is planned for the next year, but things can change quickly in this business. I may need you. Just the same, I want you to keep a low profile, to drop out of existence. If we start another project, I may not use you, especially if it's in Europe, at least, not at first. Enjoy your time off. I need to get myself to the Ritz. We'll see each other when we see each other." Adam slapped Martin on the arm and then extended his right arm around Martin's back and squeezed hard. "Later, old friend."

"You are sure that there is nothing else I need to do? I still have some time."

"We're ready. Just make the rest of the night perfect."

"Ciao."

"Ciao."

><+>-O-<+><

The Ritz Hotel, 30 August 1997

It was just past ten when Dodi picked up the telephone. "I want Henri to drive us tonight. Call him and have him ready. Have him call me here in the suite when he's on the premises."

"Oui, Monsieur."

He replaced the receiver. Looking at Di warmly he said, "From what Henri told me when we spoke, he will be ready around midnight. It won't be long now. Just a couple of hours. Let's just take advantage of our time here alone. We can enjoy our dinner and each other. No one will bother us. We can be completely private."

"Oh Dodi, you are such a sweet, kind man. You have done so much to make everything right for me. I promise you that I will never forget what you have done this day. You are so wonderful!"

"Then, please marry me, tomorrow, tonight, right now."

She placed her finger on his lips, "Oh, my darling, darling, Dodi, please don't do this. Just give me a little time. I promise you an answer tomorrow."

"In two hours it will be tomorrow."

"Dodi, please stop. You're making it too hard for me."

"I don't want anything to be hard for you. I want you to be happy. I just can't help myself. I love you. I want you to be mine forever."

"Just hold me for a while. In a few minutes we can have our dinner."

The telephone rang ahead of schedule. Dodi and Di were just finishing their dessert. The time was perfect. Dodi answered after three rings and spoke only briefly. Placing the receiver back on the hook, he nodded to Di. "Henri is ready. He is confident everything will flow like clockwork. He told me that Michael is an extremely competent planner. He also reminded me to tell you that we are all to wear our seatbelts."

"I hate seatbelts. They are so uncomfortable. They pull across my breasts and wrinkle my frocks. We'll be in the back seat where it's perfectly safe. It will only be a minor scrape."

"He still thinks it's a good idea, and so do I."

"Maybe. Now hold me again."

"Definitely, I'll hold you again, as long as you would like."

"That's not what I meant, you silly goose."

>−+−◇−·O−·◇+−+−◄

Elizabeth and Adam were seated in a quiet corner like two lovers sharing dreams over a cup of coffee. Speaking softly in Jauner-Tüütsch, they covered the last details.

"You have the medication for Jennifer?"

"Yes. I'll give it to her in a few minutes. The medication will be in her blood stream and active by midnight. She should hemorrhage out of control when traumatized."

"Let's hope the trauma is severe enough. Pascal is ready with an injection, if the accident proves insufficient."

"I hate to take the risk. The digitalis might be traceable later." Elizabeth looked a little worried.

"It's just another backup like the switching of the dental records. It will likely never be necessary, but it pays to be prepared."

"Martin seems satisfied that everything will go according to the plan, but I still think..."

Adam interrupted. "Martin's a strange one, but he's one of the most reliable men we have. He's confident everything will go perfectly, and so am I," Adam boasted. Then, more thoughtfully he continued, "I'm still not one to take any chances. You well know my motto about backup plans. They are essential, and this project is no exception. I feel good about this one. Martin verified that Henri has taken the advanced and tactical driving courses for limousines. He maneuvered predictably when confronted with the emergency in the Virtual Reality simulator. Gerard ran several test scenarios, and each time he reacted the same."

"Oh Adam. I almost forgot to tell you. I was e-mailed another crash vector analysis. It was based on the same factors we used the first time, including the use of seatbelts. The only unknown is the exact impact point. Impact could vary from one side of the car to the other, depending upon the car's angle when Henri swerves. The injuries to the passengers could be more severe or less, depending upon the impact point. The G-forces will be strong enough to create the internal hemorrhaging in Jennifer according to the military analysis you have. That's no problem. The new report agreed with the first one we received. Everyone should survive the crash, although the second analysis predicted more serious injuries for Henri and Trevor. The paramedics that show up will concentrate on the front seat passengers because of their injuries. Jennifer should be too far gone before they realize that she is critically injured. With the medication that she will take, the G-forces at 80 kilometers per hour will be sufficient to cause the fatal hemorrhaging. I'm confident of that. Dodi's injuries will be minimal. Everything considered, he will only be heavily bruised and shaken up. He may have some minor hemorrhaging, but without the medication that Jennifer is taking, he'll recover completely."

"Good," Adam affirmed. He continued, "Martin will lead them through the tunnel at 90 kilometers an hour or slightly higher. This will provide an additional margin. I feel certain that Henri and Dodi will keep absolutely quiet about the planning of the accident once this is all over. If they were ever to say anything about the setup, they would be accused of being accessories to murder. Even if either of them ever does talk and the authorities are able to track down anyone, the trail will lead to either the British establishment or the IRA. All our tracks are covered. No one who knows about Jennifer would ever talk, that we know for sure. Most important, Di will be home free."

"Your other idea was a good one too, it will keep eyes looking the other way in any event. Did you get it all accomplished?"

"If you mean the deposits into Henri's account, yes. If Henri is ever investigated, the deposits to his account will lead them on a merry chase. He'll have a hard time explaining them and if they never check, it'll be like Christmas for Henri."

"I still worry about Martin, Yusuf and Reem. I wish they didn't know anything."

"Everyone involved thinks Martin is a minor player, only muscle. All the trails lead back to Michael. Michael doesn't even know Jennifer exists. Martin is leaving for Asia tomorrow as soon as his work is done. He'll remain there for at least the next year. He can get lost there in plain sight with no problem. Yusuf and Reem have never been seen by anyone other than Jennifer and Di. No trails lead to them. No one would ever show an interest in them."

"I still wish that Martin knew nothing about Jennifer. I wish he didn't even know she exists."

"I could see no other solution."

"Agreed. It was a risk we had to take. As the saying goes, better a devil you know. Certainly, there's no love lost between Martin and Jennifer. He'd like to forget he's ever met her, let alone knows her. I'm sure it's okay. I'm starting to understand Martin better. I've spent so much time with him. It's getting easier for me to relate to him. Under the rough façade, he's actually likeable."

"He's a little bit like a pet lion, nice but you have to watch him at feeding times. So you know, Michael will operate under the code name 'Green' and Martin under 'Red.' Gerard will erase all portable telephone records as soon as I give him the word. He has already left town and will be at the country house to finish all necessary business. He ran his shredder program over the Virtual Reality program. Nothing will remain that can be recovered, even if the computer is located before it can be removed from France. The cleaning crew is working this minute and has already disassembled most of the Virtual Reality equipment. It will take until two or three in the morning to remove everything from the flat, have it on its way out of France and sanitize the place. This time line should present no problems. It gives us plenty of leeway. Even if the police learn something at the accident site, there is no way they could be onto the plan or the location of the flat that soon. Oh, I nearly forgot. Did you collect the minidisk player that Jennifer was using? It would be catastrophic to have anyone find it."

"Yes. I left it at the country house. I told her that a recorder we had hidden in the car would record her performance. She didn't seem to care or pay any special attention."

"Anything else we need to cover?"

"No, I don't think so, except that Jennifer has been a real pain in the butt. You can't imagine. She asked for another raise before she would perform again. I gave her my personal word that I would make a transfer in her account tomorrow, and I want to do it. Let's just give it all to charity. I'd better go. I need to make sure she takes her medication early enough before the accident. She's ready to defect. I can sense it. I'm glad that it's nearly over. She's pure trouble looking for a place to roost."

"If she wasn't so self-centered, she might have tried splitting already.

"She's afraid to chance giving up what we can provide."

Well, my dear sister, we're probably lucky she's the way she is. Just think, we've survived so far, and it will be over before we turn around. I'm going to head out to the crash site. I want to be there to activate Pascal, if necessary. See you in Lausanne."

She placed her hand on top of his and squeezed tightly, "I love you."

"I love you too."

>–·‹›·–O–·‹›·–‹

The Ritz Hotel, 30 August 1997

It was a little past eleven-thirty when Di turned to Dodi for more comfort. "Oh Dodi, thank you. Thank you for holding me so close. Could you, somehow, press me even closer to you? I feel so frightened."

"What's wrong. Please tell me. Do you want to cancel the accident? I can do it in a minute. I don't want you to feel frightened. I don't want you to be at any risk. I don't want you to worry about anything."

"No. No. You don't understand. My fright has nothing to do with the accident. Really. I want to go through with it. I know that is something we need to do to insure my freedom."

"Just yours?"

"No. I didn't mean it that way at all. Have you ever heard of the law of unintended consequences?"

"I don't think so."

"A good example is if you were hiking in the mountains in the winter. Imagine yourself climbing a steep and treacherous slope. Finally, after hours of hard work you successfully reach the top. The view is magnificent. Your self-confidence is on a high. You gaze out at the panorama below and feel a sense of awe. You feel absolutely on top of the world and let out a yodel like they do in Switzerland. It's merely an expression of pure joy. The noise of the yodel starts an avalanche, and some skiers down the mountain are buried. The thing you did seemed so innocent and pure, but it had such terrifying results for other people who had no part in your life."

"What does that have to do with anything?"

"It's very simple. I don't worry about any of us in the accident, but what about others? What happens if an outsider who is in no way involved is hurt? It's impossible to think of everything. Sometimes things just go wrong."

"Henri studied the plan. He thinks the risk to everyone is minimal, and there is no risk at all to innocent bystanders. There's no reason there should be any innocent bystanders anyway. Henri told me that he practiced the accident on a fancy video game. He's already gone through it so many times. The next time, the real time, will be nothing. He knows all the variables."

"I want to do it. I need to do it. I just can't help worrying. I would be completely devastated if anyone was hurt."

"It will be okay. Let's look at it as a big adventure. What a wonderful way to begin our lives together. We will never forget it. A new beginning."

"Dodi, I do love you. You always seem to know the right thing to say. I was just being a silly female. Let's get on with it. I really am excited. I mean it. Honest."

"The ring looks so lovely on your hand."

"It will always remind me of your tenderness and kindness, but I would feel better if you would keep it until tomorrow."

"Nonsense. It's yours."

"I'm going to take it off when we go downstairs. Someone will see it, and I don't want to start any rumors until we are ready. Is it okay if I keep it in my bag? It will be safe there."

"Whatever you would like. It's yours. You know that. I need to ask again."

"No, my love. Please, no."

><>-O-<><

"Good evening, Jennifer. Are we having fun yet?"

"A great time, you stupid bitch. Sitting on my arse for an hour in a toilet stall is my idea of a fantastic evening. You people are absolutely daft. My butt cheeks are numb and will probably stick to the seat when I get up. I'm not getting paid enough to do this shit."

"I brought you some wine and a muscle relaxant combined with an anti-bruising agent. It's the same wine that Di is drinking right now."

"Why in hell would I want a muscle relaxant?"

"To keep you from being injured in the accident. We don't want you bruised or to have any problems that will interfere with your acting. Especially, we don't want your face damaged. If your face is damaged, it will hurt your future prospects. It's a risk we can't afford to take, and I'm sure you don't want to run the risk either. This performance will be the most important in your life. It needs to be perfect. When it's finished, you can leave if you want. You'll be able to write your own ticket."

"Okay, I'll go along with all of this shit, but I want more than one glass of wine."

Elizabeth stayed until Jennifer had taken the medication and then excused herself. Reem remained with the girl. A little while later, Elizabeth returned with another glass of wine. It was a very welcome sight to Jennifer, as she had already polished off the first.

⊱─⊷⊷─◯─⊶⊷─⊰

"My Princess, it's nearly midnight. We should go. We don't want to turn into pumpkins."

"Dodi, just hold me a moment longer. Do you mind?"

"What's wrong?"

"Nothing. I'm just fine. Really. Please believe me. Everything is perfect. It's just that I'm trying to find the best way to say good-bye to my old life."

"So, you are going to marry me?"

"Dodi, please don't rush me. I already told you that I need a little more time. Let's just go now. Let's not talk about it. Not right now, anyway."

"If you're sure, I'll call the hotel staff and tell them to alert Henri and Trevor. We'll go down in a few minutes."

"No, please. I'm ready now. Call them and tell them we're coming straight away."

"It would be better to wait. We won't be bothered here. You never know who might see us downstairs."

"No. I would like to get on with it. I've already waited too long. I need to stretch my legs."

"I have a special exercise for that."

Di began to giggle. "Men! You're all alike. Stop teasing me, please. Just make your call, and we'll head down. There is no reason to wait any longer."

22

Paris, 30 August 1997

"Dodi, I need to use the toilet. I'm so sorry I didn't do it upstairs. I'll just be a moment. Promise."

"Let me take you back up to the suite. It'll only take a second."

"No. Really, it's fine. I'll just go here. It's no problem at all."

Elizabeth was standing at the sink washing her hands. She had been there stuck in the pose for what seemed like an eternity. The wait for the appearance of Di had been longer than anticipated. Of all the hazards large and small in her chosen occupation, she had never imagined that having dishwater hands would be one of them. As Di entered Elizabeth nodded to indicate the toilet door, and Di entered. It was very crowded inside. Jennifer was seated with the make-up kit on her lap. Reem, at Jennifer's side, was all business. She took a quick look at Di and began to touch up Jennifer's hair and make-up. Di, speaking softly and concisely, briefed Jennifer on the events of the day, in the event that Dodi mentioned anything and a comment needed to be made. She confirmed that Henri was driving and that Trevor would be the bodyguard. "Other than planning for the accident and normal small talk, the only thing of importance is that he asked me to marry him."

"You told him yes, didn't you?"

"No. I told him I would think about it."

"Shit. His father is as rich as Croesus. Why didn't you say yes? Why wouldn't anybody marry him?"

"I don't need the money."

"No one can have too much money. That's a totally crazy idea. Marry him. You can always leave him later and take half his money. What were you thinking anyway?"

Reem interjected before Di could respond, "Okay, leading lady, you're on."

Jennifer rose, and they all shuffled making just enough room to allow Jennifer to depart the small compartment. Di moved to the toilet as soon as Jennifer left, and Reem began to apply eye make-up to mask her appearance. Jennifer stopped for a moment and smiled sweetly at Elizabeth. Then, as she was exiting the door to meet with Dodi, she looked back over her shoulder at Elizabeth and said, "I'm going to tell him yes."

Elizabeth appeared confused for a second after Jennifer departed. Overlooking the comment, she opened the toilet door and squeezed inside. Reem was finished and was helping Di into the hijab. "Jennifer told me that she was going to tell him yes. What was that all about?"

Di reached for the wall to steady herself for a moment as the blood drained from her face. "She wouldn't, would she?"

Seeing the panic on Di's face, Elizabeth said, "No. No. Don't worry. The girl is a bit of a comedian. It's fine. She was just joking. Don't worry about it."

Reem's face was unreadable, but Elizabeth could tell by her eyes that she wasn't happy either.

When Jennifer exited the toilet area, she made a wrong turn and someone said to her, "Over here Princess. Dodi is this way."

Jennifer, playing her role to the fullest, recovered quickly and responded graciously. "Oh, I'm so sorry. I don't know what I was thinking. I was a little turned around." *Actually, I know exactly what I'm thinking. I'm going to break this story to the press. It's a fabulous story. The Globe will pay a fortune for the exclusive. I'll tell all about the engagement when I'm in the hospital. I'm going to tell them that I was the one who accepted the marriage proposal. Maybe I'll even tell them that I slept with him. I was hired to protect Di from the paparazzi and look what it got me. I'm not going to wear a seatbelt. If I get a minor injury or two, I'll be an even bigger hero. I am on my way to cash in and leave these daft morons behind.*

Dodi and Jennifer were quickly escorted to the car and entered the rear seat. Dodi was seated behind Henri and Jennifer behind Trevor.

Henri turned to remind them to put on their seatbelts, but Jennifer motioned him to stop before he could say anything. Then, ignoring Henri, Jennifer took Dodi's hand. Looking into his eyes and smiling sweetly, she blurted out, "Yes! I'll marry you, you gorgeous man. Let's do it as soon as possible. You are the man of my dreams."

There was a shocked silence in the car until Trevor spoke. "The paparazzi are coming."

Dodi immediately responded, "Get us the hell out of here, Henri. Do it now! Fast! As fast as you can!"

The car swept away from the curb and sped south on Rue Cambon. As they passed Rue Saint Honore, two BMW motorcycles pulled out to follow them. In seconds one of the motorcycles was on their tail, and Henri's cell phone rang. Trevor looked at the driver with a little surprise, and Henri replied, "Someone is watching traffic for us."

Dodi interjected, "It's all right, Trevor. It's someone from the hotel security staff. They are watching the direction the paparazzi take, so we can try to avoid them."

>–+◆–O–◆+–◄

Three Islamic women dressed in hijab left the toilet area. An Arabic man escorted them though the hotel's lobby and out the front entrance to a waiting Mercedes.

The doorman made a passing comment to an assistant as the Mercedes pulled away. "That was a very tall Arabic woman. She was even taller than her husband. Usually, the women are much shorter."

"The car had diplomatic plates," the assistant responded. "I wonder if she was a Princess? It almost seems as though every Arab who stays here is either a Prince or a Princess."

Elizabeth turned to Di, "Is everything okay?"

"I think so, but I feel so unsettled. I don't know whether to laugh or cry. I don't know if I feel relief or concern. For me, today lasted forever. It's all so very difficult and emotionally confusing."

"It will be extremely hard for a while, but each day things will become a little easier. Right now, you might try to get some sleep. You may have to force yourself, but it may be the best thing. We have a long drive ahead of us. We hope to arrive at the clinic before six in the morning."

"I don't think I can sleep. There's so much going on in my head. My mind is racing. My thoughts are spinning. Do you really think that woman might tell Dodi that I would marry him?"

"I'm sure that she was just joking. She thinks she's a real comedian."

"It wasn't very funny. Not for me, anyway. Shit. That would be so unfair. I would never do anything like that!"

"It's really okay. It was just her idea of a joke, she never would do it."

"Oh my God! I can't believe this could happen. No! No! Shit!"

"What's wrong."

Di reached into her bag and pulled out a beautiful ring, "I forgot to give the engagement ring to that woman. What if Dodi asks her to put it on? She doesn't even know that he gave it to me."

"Don't worry about it. Adam will take care of everything."

A police car pulled in behind the speeding Mercedes but lost interest after noticing the diplomatic plates. Soon, they would intersect the AutoRoute and be on their way to Switzerland. With the diplomatic plates, they were exempt and safe from the scrutiny of the police. Yusuf would take every advantage of their immunity, and the trip would be over soon.

>-+-◦-+-<

Michael was driving a midnight blue Citroen XM and was monitoring the conversation with Henri. Martin began the choreography. "Blue, we are just turning on Rue de Rivoli. Confirm that White has powered up the battery pack. Green do you read?"

"Blue, affirmative."

"Green, affirmative."

Blue pulled the white Fiat Uno into traffic and was followed by Green in the Citroen. They both drove in the right lane and paced themselves a little slower than the traffic flow. The hotel Mercedes was a few hundred meters behind them and was also traveling in the right lane. Martin found the gap in traffic he wanted and said, "Henri, everything's clear. I'll pass you in a few moments on a BMW motorcycle. Hang up your phone and try to keep on my tail. We'll talk at the other end of the tunnel. I'll call you back."

On the other line Martin commanded, "Blue and Green into formation. Execute mission as planned."

"Blue, affirmative."

"Green, affirmative."

Martin's big BMW shot past the hotel Mercedes, and Henri joined in the chase. Dodi was in the back seat holding Jennifer's hand, a dreamy look upon his face. He encouraged Henri to speed up so they could keep ahead of the paparazzi. Trevor was watchful, as always, but seemed to suspect nothing. Henri laid into the Mercedes, but the heavy car was unable to keep up with the fast BMW motorcycle and a gap began to open. The Citroen was just entering the tunnel as Martin pulled the BMW even and accelerated past. Henri forced the Mercedes in hot pursuit, but the gap continued to widen as it entered the tunnel. As Martin shot by, the Citroen slowed slightly and watched the oncoming Mercedes. As the Mercedes neared, the Citroen quickly shifted to the left lane and lightly braked. The Fiat remained in the right lane and slowed as well. The heavier Mercedes was still accelerating when the braking Citroen suddenly appeared in the lane directly ahead. Entering the tunnel at nearly 140, the Mercedes took the only available option. Following his training, Henri swerved right to miss the Citroen. The Mercedes made a slight contact with the tunnel wall as Henri fought to bring the heavy car under control. Instead of an escape in the right lane, Henri found himself speeding toward a small white Fiat Uno. Fortunately, there was just enough room for him to swerve to the left and miss hitting the front of the Citroen. Fighting to control the car, Henri swung left to slip in front of the Citroen and miss the Fiat. He lightly clipped the rear corner of the Fiat as he tried to regain control and merge into the left lane. Suddenly, the passenger compartment of the Mercedes was brilliantly illuminated for an instant by a near weapon grade laser fired from the back seat of the Fiat. The light was designed to temporarily blind the target for a few minutes, and it functioned flawlessly. The result was a complete sensory overload. Henri froze in position. From the outside of the car, the light was nearly invisible. Blinded and traveling at a high rate of speed, Henri continued his trajectory and hit a tunnel support column. Michael immediately swerved the Citroen to the right lane and only narrowly missed being hit by the rebounding wreckage of the Mercedes.

There were still pieces of the wreckage spinning on the pavement when Pascal passed the wreck and pulled his BMW motorcycle to the front of the destroyed Mercedes. He made a quick examination of the occupants and called the number he had been given. "Bad wreck in the Alma Tunnel. Be surprised if there are any survivors."

"Say again."

"Two dead for sure. Driver and male rear seat passenger. No question. Front male passenger in very bad shape. Probably won't make it. Female in rear might survive but looks semiconscious. This would be a great advert for why you should wear seatbelts. Only male front seat passenger has one on."

"Get the hell out of there. Your job is over."

"Affirmative."

A few moments later, Adam heard the howl of the BMW as it echoed into the night leaving the tunnel. He waited a few minutes until traffic was beginning to stop and backup to look at the carnage. Pedestrians were starting to gather to examine the spectacle. The expressions were of shock and disbelief. Adam joined the crowd as the paparazzi were juggling for position to shoot photos of the wreck. *Shit! Pascal was right. Dodi and Henri are both gone. Why in the hell didn't they put on their seatbelts? They were told over and over. Damn it all to hell.*

Jennifer was groaning softly. Adam wanted to stay to the end. He wanted to hear everything she might say, but soon the police would arrive. He could not chance being noticed or questioned, so he wandered away.

He returned to his perch above the tunnel entrance and called Yusuf, "It's finished. Don't turn on your radio. There was some collateral damage, and I don't want your passenger to hear about it. Be sure to change out your phone GSM access chip, this one is being deactivated."

"I understand. We'll cross the frontier into Switzerland at the arranged place. We're ahead of schedule. Thanks for the road and traffic report."

Elizabeth immediately realized that Yusuf was covering up something, but she didn't dare say a word. Di was still wound tight and very alert. Sensing Elizabeth's interest, Yusuf told her that the road was clear to Switzerland. Elizabeth tried to put the pieces together mentally. *It must have worked, but something didn't go according to plan. Adam will just have to deal with it. There's nothing I can do.*

"Yusuf, would you mind turning on the radio?"

"I have some great CDs. Could we listen to them instead? The radio static is annoying in this part of France. All that fuzzy talking with background noise blending in and out disturbs my concentration when I'm driving fast. I'd rather not take any risks tonight, if you don't mind."

"Great idea. How about something soothing to help our passenger relax? It would be nice if she could sleep a little. She's been through so much."

"Your wish is my command."

I was right. Something went wrong, and Adam does not want Di to hear about it. What the hell could it be? He didn't abort our trip to Switzerland, so the plan must still be working. I just can't put it all together.

Adam's next call was to Martin. His orders were absolute, as always.

"Finished. Head home." Adam then repeated the sequence to the other operatives. He placed his last call to Gerard. "Clean it up. Erase all calls and cancel the phone service to all of our lines while you're at it. Then go to bed. You're up too late for a kid, and your mother will have my hide."

Within three and a half hours none of his crew, the cars or equipment used in the project would be in France. All residues would be wiped clean. As a precaution, Adam would remain during the cleanup procedures and until the death of Di was released by the media. If all went as programmed, he would not again be contacted by any of his operatives, nor be required to do anything.

After speaking with Gerard, Adam walked the short distance to the Seine River. He thought of the many times through the years that he had stopped to enjoy this gorgeous view of Paris at night. The special glow of the lights in all directions outlining the city was magical to him. Tonight was no different. The same enchantment recurred as he stood and gazed out over the skyline. Yet, somehow something was different. Tonight was not like any of the other nights. He was different. He could not verbalize why, but he felt different. Tonight, he was content with his accomplishments, satisfied with a job well done. He radiated an inner peace and satisfaction. In the past he had always been churning inside, looking beyond himself for accomplishments not yet attained.

After a few moments of introspection, knowing that there was nothing more he could do, he removed the GSM card from his cellular phone. He folded the card to destroy the chip and let it flutter into the water that flowed by like black oil. There was not even a soft splash as it disappeared. He placed a new GSM card in his phone and activated the new phone number.

He looked about a few minutes longer and then returned to the tunnel. There, he became merely one of the many onlookers who were gathering to observe the tragedy. The police had arrived in full force and were seeking out potential witnesses. They were keeping the crowd at bay, so he was unable to move close enough to see clearly. Adam listened to the rumors and waited.

It was taking a long time to extricate the bodyguard and Jennifer from the wreck. Adam wondered if Trevor would survive. He appeared to be in very bad shape. After what seemed like forever, Jennifer was finally removed from the car. By now, she seemed to be deteriorating, although she did not appear to be mortally injured. Jennifer was holding on; they were working frantically on her. He was not at all surprised. She never seemed to do what was expected.

Finally, at a little before two in the morning, the injured were transported by ambulance to Hôpital de la Pitié-Salpêtrière. Bystanders and the press were everywhere, watching and looking and hypothesizing. Different theories of what had happened were being offered as quickly as they could be imagined. The one thing that was certain was that no one knew what had actually happened or wanted to believe it.

Adam drove to the hospital and used a British diplomatic passport to gain entrance to a waiting area close to the emergency room. He tried to look invisible. The police were restricting access, and his diplomatic cover might not hold if push came to shove. He listened to what he could overhear of the conversations among the doctors and nurses as they rushed back and forth. The reports were conflicting. One medic said she was gone; almost immediately, a nurse contradicted his statement and said she was holding on. A few minutes later, Adam heard another nurse whisper, "She's dead." The lack of professionalism was more than Adam could stand. *This is not what I need to hear. Why in the hell can't they seem to agree? After all, it's these very people who are providing the treatment. How can one person say she lives while another says she's dead?*

The uncertainty was more than Adam could stomach. His nerves were on alert. Although seething with anger, he sat and listened quietly in the background, making certain to attract no attention. He knew that the truth would be released. It just would take some time.

It was nearly four in the morning when the news came. They had tried everything but were unable to save her. She had died of massive, internal injuries and hemorrhages.

Adam exited the hospital unnoticed. He went directly to his flat where he showered, shaved and packed a few things. He called Yusuf on the new number and was pleased to learn that Yusuf had already crossed the frontier. Adam affirmed, "I'll meet Elizabeth in Switzerland as planned. Everything is finished here."

Di was sleeping, so not a word was exchanged. Yusuf merely flipped the thumbs up to Elizabeth. She exhaled deeply, feeling as though she had been holding the same breath since the first telephone call.

23

Switzerland, 31 August 1997

The Audi's tires howled as Adam navigated the looping exit from the AutoRoute at the Lausanne turnoff. Downshifting, he began to make his way through the serpentine streets of the city as he maneuvered the route to the clinic. He slowed to pass two stationary radar units, then accelerated to arrive as soon as possible. He had made excellent time from Paris and expected to be at the clinic before eleven. He hoped to arrive before Di was taken to the operating theatre.

Entering the clinic, Adam was shown to Di's room where he found Elizabeth working at her laptop. Elizabeth glanced up and smiled. Adam's expression told it all. Instantly aware of his fatigue, she quickly rose, gave him a hug and guided him to her chair. He collapsed and said, "I thought I might make it before they rolled her into surgery."

"The doctor was anxious to get on with the procedure. He was worried that someone might see her. With the news reports that are snowballing, he couldn't take the chance. The airways are clogged with the story. Nothing else is being covered. Had even one person around here recognized her, there would have been no way to keep it quiet. It would have been a complete catastrophe. She left the room over two hours ago."

"Well, thank God he moved so fast. He did the right thing. Shit. It all fell apart and in a flash... How much longer until she's out?"

"I don't know for sure. He said six or seven hours."

"I'm starved and bone tired. Let's go have lunch. Then, I'll freshen up so we can be here when she awakens. Would you drive? I'm not sure I trust myself right now."

"Let's go to the hotel first. They won't be serving yet, but you can take a quick shower. I'll order from room service, and you'll have time to take a catnap."

"You are so practical. I'd still love you even if you weren't my sister."

She held up her finger to her lips, and he realized his mistake. They had a standing agreement to never talk of such things if there was even the slightest possibility that their conversation could be overheard. He recognized that his fatigue was causing him to make mistakes, and he could afford to make none.

Back in the car, Adam was asleep in the passenger seat before they had turned off the little side street where the clinic is located. Elizabeth was torn as she looked at Adam sleeping with his head against the side window. Should she just drive around for a while so he could continue sleeping? Or would it be better for her to go directly to the hotel? She decided on the hotel, knowing he would get a better nap there. She pulled in front of the hotel and parked. The change in motion startled Adam, and he fought himself to alertness.

As soon as they entered the suite, he stripped off his clothes and asked Elizabeth to awaken him when the food was delivered. He was in bed and asleep before Elizabeth had kicked off her shoes and opened the window to take advantage of the cool breeze that was blowing off the mountains.

She decided she would wait for two hours before ordering. She was a little worried about her brother, realizing that the anxiety of orchestrating this project had taken its toll on him. Rest would do him more good than anything, and he had let down enough to be able to sleep. She was glad he was able to rest, although she had to fight off the burning temptation to awaken him to ask what had really happened. She so wanted to know.

Elizabeth was finding the best and most complete news off the Internet. Information started to flow less than ten minutes after the accident. CNN and the other majors were devoting all of their coverage to the accident, but their reports were often as much as thirty minutes behind what was reported on-line. The networks were relying on the Internet for all their breaking headlines, so the tidbits Elizabeth was gathering from the television were no news to her. The information from the Internet was updated and refined continually, almost every second. There were many conflicting reports, and much of the coverage was only bits and pieces. It was like the fog of a war. No one seemed to really know what had happened. The reader had to sift through mounds of chaff to find a real grain of truth. The only sure thing was that Di, Dodi and the driver were reported dead. *How did it happen? Beyond Jennifer, there should have been no casualties.* The paparazzi were being blamed, and those who were present had been taken into custody. Adam was the only reliable witness, and for the moment he was in no condition to be questioned. *Damn it.*

Elizabeth felt numb and a little helpless as she continued to monitor the news on the Internet and the reports that were being aired by the various news agencies. Checking her e-mail, she was happy to find an update from Michael. The Citroen had been abandoned in an industrial area in Belgium and had already been torched to eliminate all residual evidence. It was a stolen car and would never be traced. Michael was flying back to Northern Ireland within hours. Martin had also e-mailed. He reported that both BMW motorcycles had already been turned over to a freight forwarder and would soon be on their way to Argentina. He was awaiting the pick up of the Fiat Uno; right now it was secure in a private garage just outside of Brussels. It would be transported to South America by ship within the next two days. He confirmed that Blue and White had been paid by Michael and had already disappeared into the Brussels underground. Martin was disassembling the laser and battery pack and would junk the various pieces in several locations. Pascal was flying to Africa today. Elizabeth made a mental list of the things to complete: the Mercedes; Yusuf and Reem; Martin; Gerard and the phone records; and the Fiat. These needed to be resolved today. She could not allow Adam to sleep much longer.

>−I−◄▷−O−◁►−I−◄

Adam was in the shower when Room Service delivered the tray. Elizabeth had awakened him when she placed the order. He entered the well-appointed sitting room wearing a white terrycloth robe with tousled hair. Elizabeth marveled at how amazing it was that he still looked like the young boy she remembered from decades ago. Little had changed except the color of his hair. It had turned so gray. She could not remember it happening. It just happened. Without explanation or preparation, it seemed like he awoke one morning to gray hair. Even the sparse hair on his chest had turned to gray. *We are getting too old. We need a life.* Knowing it was not the time to be philosophical, she allowed Adam to take a few bites. Then, unable to restrain herself any longer, she blurted out, "Okay. What the hell happened?"

"Shit, I don't know. Everything seemed to go off according to plan. But for some reason, Jennifer, Dodi and Henri did not put on their seatbelts. I don't know why. They were all warned and told to wear them. We went over and over the seatbelt requirement. We even made Henri practice in the simulator wearing one. I just can't understand it."

"Did Jennifer say anything?"

"No. She was semiconscious. She mumbled something about marrying Dodi, but I couldn't really understand it. She was fading when I left. I doubt she said anything more. At least, nothing that anyone could have made out."

"With three people dead, do you think we should start some disinformation right away?"

"Maybe. What's in the news?"

"Conflicting reports. Mostly the paparazzi are being blamed."

"If we're lucky, they'll bear all the heat. They are leeches anyway, and no one likes them. The way they act makes them a convenient scapegoat. The Fiat was nearly identical to one used by one of the paparazzi. The blame will probably settle there."

"Let's wait then for a few days."

"With Henri being dead, they will take a blood test for sure. He will probably bear the brunt of the blame, if they give up on the paparazzi."

"He looked fine to me when I saw him earlier at the Ritz. Are you sure that he had some alcohol?"

"He had some wine. I don't know how much as I left. If they start looking past him, we'll begin the disinformation."

"I'd hate to have it hung on him. He was pretty straight."

"If he's dead, it doesn't matter. He no longer has a reputation to defend."

"You're right, of course. It just seems that every time we buy one person's happiness, it's at the cost of too many others. Adam, we're getting too old to do this. I think we are developing a conscience."

"I can't afford one. We'd better get back to the clinic."

"Adam, I'm serious."

"I know, but now is not the time to discuss it. We need to keep the information about the accident from Di as long as possible. She will be furious when she hears about the death of Dodi. The longer we wait, the more stable she will be about it. Maybe we should begin the disinformation now and let it filter back. Then, she might think that the British establishment was behind the accident. We can kill two birds with one stone, so to speak."

"Agreed. But we have another problem. Check this out."

"Gorgeous ring. When did you have time to go shopping?"

"I didn't. That's the problem. Dodi gave it to Di today. Well, actually last night. He proposed marriage. She forgot about it, as she wasn't wearing it. She had tucked it in her purse so that it wouldn't be photographed."

"It's moot now. If anyone else knows about it, they will conclude that someone at the accident scene stole it. We just need to make sure that it doesn't show up at the wrong place. Why don't you have a jeweler, that very private one you know in Geneva, remake it into something different for her? She could keep it then, and it would never attract the wrong attention."

"Good idea. I think I'll keep you around."

⊱┄◈┄○┄◈┄⊰

They were back at the clinic before Di was returned to her room. Elizabeth plugged her laptop into the telephone line in Di's room and logged on to collect her e-mail and updates from the Internet about the accident. Yusuf had turned over the Mercedes to the freight forwarder in Marseilles. Yusuf and Reem were flying to Lebanon the next day. Gerard had not only erased all phone records but even the phone number assignments used by the team. Not only was there no remaining record of the calls, there was no record that the team members' phone numbers had even existed.

Elizabeth sent an e-mail to Gerard asking him to clean up and delete all the e-mail accounts used for the operation. She also instructed him to delete everything from the secure FTP site and fill it with some software files. This was a standard operating procedure used by Adam when winding up all of his projects. Martin and Yusuf would move to the next bank of e-mail accounts to be used for the following project.

While on-line, Elizabeth received an update from Martin. He had turned over the Fiat to the freight forwarder, and it would be out of the country in two days. Martin had booked a flight to Hong Kong and would keep in touch by e-mail. His departure was the next day.

Running down the list she had posted in her mainframe mind, Elizabeth concluded that all of the critical loose ends were either tied up or would be in less than twenty-four hours. She breathed a sigh of relief and looked over at Adam, only to find him soundly asleep in the chair.

As many times as she had seen it happen, she could never relate to how easily her brother could fall asleep. He could close his eyes and be in never-never land almost instantly, no matter the distractions. He had the astute ability to block out all background noise and interference. It was survival for him during periods of high tension. His projects required such a level of commitment that he had trained himself to recharge his resources whenever and wherever the opportunity permitted. It was his remedy for fighting off exhaustion. For him, it worked.

Understanding how worn out Adam really was, Elizabeth continued to work on her computer until she heard the characteristic flutter of gurney wheels coming down the hall. Looking up, Elizabeth noticed Adam was wide-awake. The gurney entered the room with the left rear wheel doing a noisy little dance. Di was drifting in and out of consciousness. She acknowledged Adam and Elizabeth and then instantly drifted back asleep.

Both Adam and Elizabeth would stay until she recovered from the aftereffects of the surgical anesthesia. Then, one of them would stay with her twenty-four hours a day until she was moved to the chalet in Gstaad. It would be long hours over the next few days. It was imperative that they control all access to her until she could be prepared for the bad news. That was the next problem. How would they prepare her? How would they tell her? What explanation would they provide? Adam wished he knew. For the moment, his thoughts were a fog. Everything was overshadowed by the vivid imagine of the accident in his mind's eye. Only one word recurred. *Shit. Shit. Shit.*

>─◄▶─O─◄▶─◄

"Elizabeth, I feel like I was hit by a lorry. I ache all over."

"Darlin', we need to go to work on your vocabulary. It's a truck, not a lorry."

"I wish that you wouldn't call me Darlin'."

"We can't use your old name, and it's not a good idea to use your new name until we are stateside. Darlin' is a term of endearment in the South. You will be called that and 'honey' by sales clerks."

"I'm going to have a lot to get used to."

"Yes, and we need to start now. We would like to travel to Texas in about four months. We have a woman who will come to Gstaad and work with your speech and the use of idioms. She'll help you with mannerisms and gestures, too. She's a very nice lady and has no idea who you are. She lived in Texas for a few years and has worked for Adam before on other assignments. She's very bright and has even worked for the U.S. government assisting in the witness protection program. She's a genius when it comes to preparing a person to fit into a new life style."

"What will she think about me?"

"She won't know who you are. In fact, no one other than the surgeon, his nurse, Adam and I will ever know who you are. It's much better that way. The surgeon and his nurse have worked with Adam several times on other projects. They understand the absolute level of confidence involved. The fewer people who know the secret, the less chance that it might ever escape. This woman will only meet you after the discoloration from the surgery has passed. If she has any curiosity, she knows to keep it very well to herself. She has built a reputation over many years that is unmatched for this line of work. Discretion is the key to her business. By the time you go to Texas, you'll be long past the stage where anyone will likely become suspicious. Someone might think you're a Yankee, but no one will ever imagine your real identity."

"How much time will she spend with me?"

"As long as it takes to prepare you. The speech patterns, voice timbre and mannerisms must become a part of you. She'll help you until they flow naturally. She uses a video extensively and will video you time and time again. You'll be able to watch yourself and adapt what you are doing according to her input. The process will require much energy from you. I have spent some time with her, and she's very thorough. She's a most interesting person. I've found working with her to be extremely pleasant. She grew up in an area of the U.S. where there were many Spanish speaking people. She has acquired a Spanish nickname. I'll let her tell you what it is. Her original birth certificate reads Anita. But I don't think anyone ever calls her Anita.

"Is she Spanish?"

"No. She's an American and claims to be of English extraction, but from her physique and facial features, I'd guess she's an Appenzeller from Switzerland."

"Why do you say that?"

"She's very petite, much smaller than I. Her face is a little rounded. She probably wears a size two, maybe even a children's size. She is very social and vivacious but absolutely no-nonsense when it comes to her work. You'll like her. Everyone does."

"She sounds fascinating. I can hardly wait to meet her. I wanted to ask you about something else. Remember the Old Masters that were purchased for me as part of the financial package?"

"Yes. Of course, I remember."

"I can't get the one that reminds me of Adam out of my mind. I can see the strength of the man this very minute. His image is painted in my mind. It is the General. Do you remember the painting?"

"Yes, very well."

"I asked Adam if I could keep the painting and hang it in one of my new homes. He almost laughed at me, and then he thought about it and said he probably could arrange it, but I haven't heard another word about it. He hasn't forgotten that I want to keep this painting, has he?"

"I don't know. He hasn't mentioned anything about it to me. Knowing Adam, I'd guess he's already made the necessary arrangements. Maybe the painting is already hanging in your home. I'll ask him for you, or you can ask him when he arrives."

"I don't want him to sell the painting. I don't need the money. I have more money than I'll ever be able to use, but I do need the painting. It would be a constant reminder for me of why I was able to do this. It would provide me the courage to face each new day. Without Adam's strength and guidance, I never could have mustered the fortitude to do what I've done. Adam is my General. Can you understand what I am saying? Here, I am talking with you. I don't feel any different than I ever have, but my mind is telling me that I'm no longer who I am. I'm no longer the person I have always been. I'm now someone else. Do you have any idea how strange it feels? Do you have any idea what I mean?"

"Yes, Darlin'. I understand perfectly, more than you can imagine. Someday I'll tell you all about my life. What you are going through at this very moment has already happened to me. I have a new identity. I'm no longer who I was. It's a very difficult and painful story. I'll relate it to you when you are stronger. Now is not the time."

"Oh, Elizabeth, what are you saying? I had no idea. Oh, my goodness. Please tell me what you mean. It would help me to know."

"I'll tell you everything but not today. It's not the right time or place. You'll just have to trust me on this one. Let's talk about something else. Back to the paintings. I know several were purchased. As I remember you have two Van Dycks. One is the Italian General you love. From now on I'll think of that picture as your sixteenth century Adam. The other is a mythological scene, a very lyrical and gorgeous painting. There are three Rubens. Two are the Madonna holding the Christ Child, and the third is a lovely portrait of a young girl. I think there are also two Rembrandts. One depicts the young Christ teaching in the temple, and the other portrays the tale of Joseph and Potiphar's Wife. I'm sure you are familiar with both Biblical stories."

"Could I see the photos of the paintings? I have only seen the photos of my General and the Young Christ in the Temple. The others were acquired since I last talked with Adam about the art purchases. Maybe, I'll decide to keep more than just the General. Rembrandt has always been one of my favorite artists. Maybe I should keep a Rembrandt, too. I'm especially fond of the story of the young Christ teaching. Has Adam sold any of them yet? I hope not."

"I don't think Adam has gotten that far. He wants to wait until you are settled in the U.S. before making any of the sales. The bankers who arranged the purchases have advised Adam about the resale. They are in no hurry."

"I feel like I'm still slurring my words. Do I sound funny?"

"No. You sound just fine. Your lips are a little fuller now, and it will take some getting used to."

"They feel like they are partially asleep. Like after a dentist has done some work."

"Well that's better than pain."

"My breasts are what really ache. My face isn't that bad."

"You had a major reconstruction. I expect that the recovery will take some time. The changes are radical. You'll have some adjusting to do. Not only the discomfort, but you will probably be in shock for a while every time you pass a mirror."

"I guess now there is no going back no matter what."

"Darlin', you hit the nail on the head."

"That was a new one for me. 'Hit the nail on the head.' I'll remember that one. And one other thing..."

"Yes?"

"Thank you from the bottom of my heart."

24

Switzerland, 9 September 1997

"It didn't hurt, did it, when he took out the stitches?"

"No. It sort of stung, but it didn't hurt. Will you ride with me in the ambulance?"

"Of course. Adam will follow in his car."

"I really need you both. You are the only people who know me and who I am."

"Almost correct. The surgeon and his nurse know."

"I guess so. They would never tell, would they?"

"Never. Don't even let the thought cross your mind. The nurse is his wife and their business is based on confidentiality. This work is their specialty. They will not breach the trust that has been placed in them. If they ever told, their reputation would be destroyed. No one would use them."

"I trust you."

The conversation was interrupted by the sound of the ambulance crew coming down the hallway. She was gently helped into a wheelchair and then moved down the hall.

She heard a voice call, "Bye, Darlin'. Y'all have a safe trip, ya hear?"

She turned and to her surprise, it was the surgeon. It sounded so funny to hear him talking with a cross between an American Southern and a French accent. She almost giggled but held back, afraid that she might hurt something. She forced herself to keep a straight face. He smiled noticing her discomfort and said, "It's okay. It won't break, as long as these disguised race car drivers don't drive off a cliff."

She could not hold it back any longer, and a smile crept across her face.

"See that wasn't so bad was it? Make sure that these two take good care of you, and enjoy your recovery."

Adam said good-bye and left to collect his car. He was driving a new Audi. He had taken delivery several weeks before but had immediately taken it to be modified. It was a spotless, aluminum bodied S-8 that had just been returned from the same tuning company that rebuilt his previous car. His S-8 was black with tinted windows. It had been customized with twin turbochargers, resulting in a large number of major engine modifications. All name badges had been removed. Unless an observer knew the car, it was hard to recognize. It had only 3,000 kilometers on the clock and was just now beginning to run free. He had been unable to resist the temptation yesterday and nailed the throttle on the AutoRoute. It was like being shot from a cannon. He was content and loved his toys. He was looking forward to having the chance to play on the way to Gstaad.

As the ambulance pulled from the driveway to begin the journey to Gstaad, Elizabeth noticed a tear in the corner of her patient's eye. "Are you okay?"

"Yes. It might seem silly, but I'm saying good-bye to my first home. I was born here, you know."

"I never thought of it that way, but you're right."

"You two will always be there for me, won't you?"

"Of course. It won't be long, and you'll have new friends. But we'll always be there, if you need us."

"I feel so lonely. Please, never leave me."

Elizabeth reached out and took her hand. Conversation died as the two women each individually dealt with their innermost feelings of what had happened. Both softly shed some tears.

Time was passing without event as the ambulance cruised on the AutoRoute. The driver and his assistant, both of whom had been absolutely silent, suddenly joined in a loud and animated French conversation. Elizabeth asked what had happened, and the driver told her that a black car that must have been traveling at more than 200 kilometers per hour had just passed them. The two men were arguing about the car. The driver thought it was a new model Lexus; the assistant vehemently disagreed, saying it definitely was not Japanese. Elizabeth laughed and with an air of confidence told them that it was an Audi.

"Elizabeth, how did you know that it was an Audi? You didn't see it, did you?"

"Darlin', it was Adam who has yet to grow up. The roads here are his playground."

The two women smiled. Still introspective, they guarded their private thoughts.

>—⊹—◦—⊹—<

Gstaad, 11 October 1997

"Darlin', you look absolutely smashing."

"Look under my eyes. There is still so much discoloration. The skin is darker than it should be. He said it should be gone by now."

"It's looking better every day, and it has been less than six weeks since you had the surgery. Sometimes it just takes a little longer than anticipated. Every person's body heals differently. Don't worry about it. It will clear up."

"When will you let me see the reports of the funeral and everything else? I really would like to know what's happening in the outside world. I can handle it now. I'm ready. I really am."

"I know, and it's time for you to start to put this all behind you. I'll call Adam, and we can go over everything together. Then, we can hook up the TV so you can watch the news."

"That's another word I need to remember. I always want to call it a telly."

"It's amazing that for two languages that are supposed to be the same except for pronunciation, there are so many subtle differences in vocabulary."

"Don't y'all know it."

"Excellent, Darlin'. I'll get Adam."

She was gone but for a moment. When they returned, Adam began, "Good afternoon, Darlin'. Let's sit at the table, and I'll fill you in on everything. You've been wonderful about waiting."

"Thanks. I've tried hard to cooperate. Please, let's talk about the most important things first. Tell me the latest update on my sons."

"They are fine. Although they're still crushed by the loss, they seem to be adjusting as well as can be expected. They are with Charles, and there seems to be new and genuine warmth in him that no one has ever seen before. Everyone is talking about it."

"You know this was probably easier on them than having to deal with allegiances that tugged them first one way and then the other. The best, of course, would have been if Charles and I had been able to make it. But this way, they are free to go on with their public lives, and I will still be able to see them grow up, even though it's from afar. I must be honest. I begrudge the thought of them relating to Camilla. Had I not done this, it would have happened anyway, I was helpless to prevent it. The only difference is, had I done nothing I would have remained a hostage. Now I'm free. There really were no good solutions, once the best one was gone."

"You cannot look back and say 'what if,' now that you have turned the corner. You can do nothing to change what has happened. You have already been dealt a new hand, and it's almost time to play it."

"Dealt a new hand. Is that a Southern expression?"

"It's used everywhere, although it's a little old fashioned."

"Was my funeral a nice, quiet family event?"

Almost laughing Adam responded, "No, not at all. It was what you would call a bit of a theatre. There were miles of people lining the streets to watch the funeral procession. They even had to make the route longer to handle the size of the crowds."

"How sad. Those poor people. I feel awful that they were hurt."

"Actually, they were probably hurt less than they would have been had you lived to an old age. Now, they keep you alive in their hearts. You'll always remain as you were, their Queen of Hearts. They won't be feeling your pain as Charles continues with Camilla. Your legend will live on, and the people who love you will always hold you close."

"Clarify something for me, please. I think about this so often. I'm so curious. How did you ever find a body that could pass for me?"

"Before we get to that I need to tell you some very bad news." Adam prepared himself for the worst. "There is no easy way to break this to you, so I'll just tell you the truth with no sugar coating. The little accident we had planned did not happen at all. Our people weren't even involved. Our team was waiting for the car to emerge from the Alma Tunnel, and it never came out. The car carrying Dodi and your doppelganger crashed in the tunnel. The accident was very severe. It turned out that Henri was taking some drugs and had been drinking. On the way to the location where we were going to stage the incident, he drove much too fast and lost control of the car. The car crashed into a support column in the Alma Tunnel, it was a terrible accident. Henri was not wearing his seatbelt and was killed. Dodi and your doppelganger were also not wearing seatbelts. They both died, as well."

"Oh my God! Oh my God! No! No! I can't believe it. No! Adam, this can't be true. Henri was so responsible. He would never do anything like that. You told me everyone had agreed to wear the seatbelts. Dodi told me Henri was so straight. No! No! No! I don't believe it. It's not possible. I will not allow it. Dodi insisted that we would all wear our seatbelts."

"Here are the newspaper articles. You can see how the story evolved. They talk about the blood test on Henri and everything else. I think you should first read the articles from the Daily Mail. I know you like the paper. We have cut the articles from every issue since the accident, and they are in chronological order. This folder contains the news clippings from the Houston Chronicle. I think it's better for you to read everything before we talk. So much has been reported. After you have the background and when you feel like it, I'll try my very best to answer any questions you have. We can talk as much as you desire. I'm so sorry to have to tell you this horrid news."

They left her alone for a time. Then, Elizabeth came to Di's side when she heard the relentless sobbing. Elizabeth gently wrapped her arms around her and held her for a time. The words interrupted by uncontrollable weeping began to flow, "What a terrible tragedy. Elizabeth, how could such a horrid thing happen? I just don't understand. Adam promised me that no one would be hurt."

Adam reappeared to provide the reply. "We don't know. The incident was supposed to take place on the other side of the tunnel. You know that. The car with your doppelganger never appeared. Our team was all there waiting, but no one saw the accident, because it was in the tunnel. No one really knows what happened."

"It's all so senseless. How could Henri have done such a thing? Dodi is gone. I can't believe it. I will not believe it. I will not accept it. He was such a wonderful man, and that sweet girl who was working for you is gone too. It's all such a useless, terrible loss. I feel awful. I know you promised me that no one would be hurt, but, Adam, this was not in your control, was it? Promise me it wasn't. Oh Adam, please promise me that you had nothing to do with this."

"No. There was nothing we could have done to change the outcome. It was completely out of our control. It really is an appalling tragedy. I wish we could have somehow stopped it. I would have done anything possible, absolutely anything. Please believe me. We had nothing to do with it."

"You know I trust you. I trust both of you with my life. My new one and my old one, as well."

"Now, if it's not too insensitive, I'll answer your question about the body, unless you would prefer not to talk about it."

"No. Please tell me. It's okay. I really want to know."

"We ended up using the body of your doppelganger instead of the body we had set aside. It really worked out better, as it would have taken heavy make-up to make the other body convincing. There was always the risk that someone might have discovered the ruse. This way, we needed to do nothing, only stand back and remain quiet."

"What about her family? What will you ever tell them? Do they know?"

"No. She was an orphan and had no family. There is no one to tell."

"How sad. How terribly, terribly sad."

"Here are the remainder of articles we cut out for you. They are from other sources that we thought might be of interest to you. One of them is even a conspiracy theory that the British establishment was behind the accident. Elton John rewrote 'Candle in the Wind' for you. He sang it at your funeral. You can't turn on the radio without hearing it. We have the CD. You can listen whenever you feel you can handle it. It may be too much for you to take right now. We also have the video of your funeral, if you ever want to see it.

"No. I think that would be a little too ghoulish for me."

"Would you like us to leave you alone for a while?"

"Adam, you are sweet. I think that I would like to be alone with Elizabeth, if that's all right. Do you mind?"

"No, of course not. I don't mind at all. I understand. Your emotions must be raw. You have so much to assimilate. You must be in shock. I'll be here. Just call if you need me for anything."

Di sorted through the other articles and laughed at some of the comments made by her supposed friends. "You would have to be daft to believe some of this rubbish."

"Darlin', we don't use the word daft. You can call them idiots. Rubbish is also not used very often. Garbage is the preferred word."

"Let's leave the language lessons for now, if you don't mind. I am completely serious. I need to ask you a question. Did Adam have anything whatsoever to do with this accident? I know he said that he didn't, but it seems a little too convenient for it to have just happened. If he was involved, I would be devastated, knowing I was the root cause. I would never sleep well again. I need to know the truth. I must know the truth. You must tell me."

"Rest assured that it was just an unfortunate accident. You know that Adam told everyone to wear seatbelts. From the recording you made, even you told Dodi that everyone was to wear seatbelts. The fact that they did not use them is nothing that Adam could ever have changed. Adam could not have had anything to do with the driver's drug or alcohol problems. It was just a senseless tragedy. Yes, it turned out to be convenient for our project, but just think, it could have been you in the car."

"Maybe it would have been better. I am so confused. The news of the other deaths has taken everything from me. I feel deflated. I cannot imagine that Dodi is really gone. I feel badly, of course, about Henri and that sweet girl who worked for you, but Dodi..."

"I can only imagine how you must feel. It was a horrible shock to us as well."

"Elizabeth, please answer me. Is Dodi still alive? Did Adam do his magic for Dodi also? Will I find him one day in America? I can imagine that some day I might meet a man who reminds me of him and when we speak, I will discover that it is Dodi and that he knows me, too. I guess it's silly to ask. If Adam did his magic, he would never tell me anyway. But it does give me something to look forward to. Maybe much of history is just an illusion crafted by men like Adam."

"I really don't know."

"Before this all began, I would not have believed it possible. Now, I know, and it makes me wonder about several people who died or disappeared. Are they really gone or has someone like Adam worked his magic? I guess we will never know if the person who orchestrated it was as good as Adam."

"I know what you mean. But, I have a hard time imagining anyone as good as Adam."

"Are you going to marry him?"

"No. It's not in the stars for us."

"Why not? I can see that you love him, and I'm sure he loves you."

"We are too much alike. To preserve our love and respect for one another, it's better if we remain as we are."

"That seems like a bit of a lame excuse to me."

Elizabeth looked at her and began to giggle. Di then followed in their very private and completely female release of tension and pain.

The afternoon slipped by, and several hours later Elizabeth excused herself, leaving Di with her reflections. Di was going over the newspaper articles again with a dreamy look in her eyes. Elizabeth wandered into the kitchen and sat with Adam who was savoring a cup of excellent coffee. He glanced at her and she nodded. Di had bought the whole bill of goods. Di believed that they had nothing to do with it. He smiled and continued to savor his coffee. Elizabeth prepared a cappuccino for herself, and the two sat together exchanging the silent conversation that only lovers and twins seem to be able to share.

25

Gstaad, 20 October 1997

"Darlin', your tutor will be here today."

"Great. It's not that you and Adam aren't marvelous company, but I crave to learn more and would love to talk to someone else."

"She'll be here in about an hour. You'll like her. She can be a bit theatrical at times, but she is very bright and will help you. Oh, and don't get her talking about dancing unless you have a lot of time."

"Thanks for the advice. By the way, I have a confession to make."

"Oh?"

"I like country music. The music has so much real life in it and became a symbol of sorts for me of what was to come. Of course, it wasn't considered proper for someone in my position to listen to it, and I had to do it surreptitiously. I asked Katherine to buy a George Strait CD for me, and she gave it to me when I was in France."

"Where did you leave it?"

"I knew you would be upset if I left it laying around, so I dropped it over the side of the yacht. It killed me to let go."

"I understand. It's okay. Is there anything else you need to tell me?"

"No, nothing else. But I would like to know what my tutor knows about me?"

"Nothing really. She knows that you're a wealthy heiress who has lived all over the world. She knows you are an American citizen. That you now want to make Texas your home and want to be able to pass as much as possible as an American. A Texan would be even better. I told her that you are easily embarrassed by making mistakes, that what you want is to be able to just blend in."

"Doesn't that seem a little strange?"

"Perhaps, but what isn't a little strange in this day and age? It'll be okay. She actually met the old you at a fund-raiser a few years ago. It will be interesting to see if she develops any suspicions. She would never tell anyone if she did, but we will probably know. She might even ask Adam or mention to him that you remind her of Princess Di. She and Adam have an excellent relationship. She's a very sophisticated art collector. She helped Adam find a number of works for his art collection. She also introduced Adam to the bankers and attorneys who negotiated the purchase of your Old Master paintings, but that was a very long time ago.

"I didn't know Adam is an art collector. That gives us something else to talk about."

"If you will excuse me, I need to get ready and drive into the village to meet her. She hasn't been here before, and if you don't know the town, this place can be hard to find. Oh, she will call you Bobbie. It's an American nickname for Roberta. Americans always shorten given names. I have to fight to be called Elizabeth. Everyone there wants to call me Liz or Beth. She will not be told your new name. That way, if she develops any suspicions, she'll have nothing to tell. We thought Bobbie would be a good name and easy to remember for you."

"I have had two important women named Elizabeth in my life. You are my angel. The other was from much farther South."

>─┼─◆─○─◆─┼─◄

Gstaad, 24 December 1997

"Darlin', do you think you're ready?"

"I feel pretty good about it. Nervous yes, but I want to start. My several weeks with the tutor gave me so much insight. I'm sure I'll make a lot of mistakes, but you'll be there with me. We can make it work. We will do it. It's been over three months now, and my emotions are finally fairly stable. I haven't had a good cry for a couple of weeks. With Christmas tomorrow, I've been worried I would be a wreck. I'm surprising myself. I really am okay."

"Adam felt it would be better to travel on Christmas Day, so that you wouldn't have to think about it. You will miss the TV broadcasts and the seasonal loneliness. The timing is right, too, for entry into the U.S. There will be large crowds returning from the Mexican beaches, and it will be easy to get lost in the masses. The more people, the less any one individual will stand out. It's called hiding in plain sight."

"Actually, the best part will be that I'll be in Houston for the New Year's sales. Neiman Marcus, here I come."

"Now that's the attitude."

"I really miss my boys. I try not to think about them, but I miss them so much. I crave to hold them. Shit, here I go..."

Elizabeth held her as she began to sob. Adam entered and was at a loss. He handled the situation in a typical male fashion. He beat a hasty retreat, pretending he hadn't noticed. Elizabeth began to cry with her, and the two clung to one another ruining their make-up. It was Di who ended up consoling Elizabeth, who had a difficult time getting hold of herself.

"Elizabeth, why are you crying? I'm really okay. Please don't worry. It's just that with Christmas and everything, I was overwhelmed for a moment. I am strong though, and I can handle it. I know I can."

"I'm so sorry. Please forgive me. I was reminded about a terrible loss that I had in my life many years ago, and it just bubbled to the top."

"Do you want to talk about it? I have broad shoulders, and I'm a good listener."

"No. I'd rather not. Not now, anyway. It's a little too painful to discuss, even after all these years. It always overwhelms me around the holidays. Each year I think I have won the battle, but it overcomes me just the same. Someday I'll tell you everything."

"Does it have to do with your change of identity?"

"Yes."

"Can I have a few minutes to say good-bye to this place? It's the only home I can claim to have known, discounting the clinic where I was born."

"Of course. Would you like me to leave you alone?"

"No. It's okay. I just need to say good-bye in general. Not only to this place but also to my old life. I'll always cherish the memories of this place. The little chip in the newel post at the bottom of the banister. It caresses my hand every time I turn to go up the steps. It's a little like an old friend. It was so sweet of Adam to bring that little painting for me that was in my room."

"Did you bring everything?"

"Everything I own is in my bag. I feel a little like a refugee."

"Now you sound as theatrical as your tutor. You have two homes filled with possessions in Texas. No refugee ever had it so easy."

"You're right, but sometimes it's comforting to feel a little sorry for yourself."

"I wouldn't know."

"Bullshit." Di turned on Elizabeth only to see her begin to giggle, and Di realized that she had been had.

"Great use of the expletive. Sounded just like a Texan."

The two women held hands as they left the chalet for the car. Adam opened the car doors for them and locked the house while the two settled in the back seat of his Audi.

At the airport terminal in Zürich, Adam dropped his car keys, the parking lot ticket and the parking slot location in an envelope. Then, he posted it to a garage owner who would collect the car, prepare it for storage and take it to his home in Zug, where it would rest until his return to Switzerland. He had fallen in love with his new Audi, and both the women found it amusing that he could find such joy in an automobile, of all things.

>─┼─◈─○─◈─┼─◄

Acapulco, 3 January 1998

The golf club flashed through the air and barely caught the top of the ball. The ball shot off, skimming across the ground at a sharp angle to the direction intended. "Bloody hell."

"Darlin', you can't say that. Say shit, damn, crap or even rats, but never bloody hell."

"I hate this game."

"You loved it on the last hole when you made par."

"That was different."

"You need to relax. You're too tense when you swing."

"Do you think I'll ever get the knack of it?"

"Sure. It just takes time. It'll be a great way for you to meet people. Golf's a very social game, and most well established Americans play. If you go to the Ladies' Day activities, you'll make friends. You just need to remember not to say 'bloody hell' when you top the ball."

"Okay. I've got it. Shit. Shit. Shit."

"Let's try it the South Texas way. Make it two syllables, 'she-it.'"

"She-it."

"Perfect. Now you sound like a Texas golfer."

Elizabeth and Di began to giggle as they walked to their balls for the next stroke. Di addressed her ball and was about to swing when Elizabeth said, "Stop. Take ten deep breaths. Relax, or you'll do the same thing again."

Di forced herself to relax, and Elizabeth could see the tension fade from her body. She began her back swing, and it was like poetry in motion all the way through the swing. The ball sailed straight toward the pin, bounced twice and rolled onto the green stopping next to the cup. "She-it, I like this game!"

"Perfect. I think you have it."

"I have a long way to go before I'll be able to play like you."

"Nonsense. You're a natural and your height is a wonderful advantage. Remember Alaina, the girl you played with in Switzerland?"

"Yes, she was so nice. But what I really remember is that she could hit the ball so far and straight. It was a little discouraging to play with her."

"You just need some practice, and I guarantee you will do even better. There are so many nice courses around Houston and Dallas. You'll have such fun learning the different courses. There are also lovely resorts in the Texas Hill Country. We can take a few days there if you like. In fact, San Antonio is a favorite area for me. I love the golf there, and the city is fabulous. Adam and I have a place near there in the hill country. It's one of our favorite escapes when we want to get away from it all."

"You and Adam will spend some time with me, won't you?"

"You know we will. One of us will always be in town with you for the first year or even longer if you still need us. Usually, both of us will be there. It's a part of the package. Who knows what will happen. You may get sick of us and want us to leave."

"Elizabeth, please listen to me. I want you to stay with me because you want to, not because staying is a part of the package. I need your friendship, not your professionalism. Please don't get me wrong, I appreciate all you've done and keep doing for me. There are days I wish all of this was only a dream and I would awaken to my old life. There are days when I'm glad it worked out. But regardless of these feelings, what happened is in the past. There's nothing that can be done to change the outcome. What's done is done. I don't think I'll ever need your services again, but I desperately need your genuine friendship."

"You have that. You know you do. We have a bond that's forged in adversity, and it will always be there."

"I hope so."

"Cheer up. We fly home tomorrow. Your tan looks great! You look great! You look five years younger."

"I'm still a little surprised when I pass a mirror. He really did me a favor by taking out those little, ugly wrinkles next to my eyes. I had no clue of what to expect, and it's still quite strange. At times, I have to remind myself that I'm not seeing a phantom. That what I see in the mirror is me. I must admit, I have come to like it."

"Great. Now let's see if you can sink that putt."

"Bravo."

>─┼─◆〉─○─〈◆─┼─◄

Texas, 4 January 1998

The plane made a slight shudder and began its descent into Houston Intercontinental Airport. The seatbelt light came on at the same time the pilot made the announcement that they had begun their approach and would be on the ground in about fifteen minutes. Di reached out and put her hand on Adam's arm and gave it a slight squeeze.

He lifted her hand passing it over his cheek and kissed it tenderly. "It's okay. We're nearly there."

She leaned over and whispered, "I'm just a little frightened. I don't think I can pass if the man at the passport control starts asking me questions."

"Just look at me with adoring eyes. He'll think we're lovers and wave you right through with me."

"I already look at you with adoring eyes, you stupid man."

"Great! Keep it up, and they'll think we're newlyweds having our first fight."

"You know what I meant. You are absolutely impossible."

There was another slight shudder when the plane began its final approach, and then it landed so smoothly that it was difficult to tell when the wheels first touched.

"Great pilot. That was the best landing I've felt in years."

"Adam, any pilot who gets me down in one piece is a great pilot."

"Touché."

Elizabeth was sitting a few rows behind, next to a fat bald man who was doing his best to impress her with his worldliness and charm. He was failing miserably, although he was gallant enough to bring her carry-on down from the overhead bins. She offered a polite "thank you" and started the slow airline shuffle down the aisle toward the exit ramp.

Di and Adam were dressed in tourist garb. She was wearing one of those Mexican dresses that are sold everywhere, and he was wearing an Acapulco Princess tee shirt. They looked just like a thousand other tourists returning from a thousand different destinations of the paradise in the sun. Elizabeth fell in line behind them as they entered the maze that was designed to keep the international passengers from having a chance to pass contraband to an accomplice on the other side of the custom's control area.

Di took Adam's arm, and the two approached the customs and immigration agent who was checking passports. Adam handed the two passports to the agent who looked at them superficially and asked where they had been.

"Just a little vacation in Mexico. It was fun, but it's great to be home," Adam commented.

Unimpressed by Adam's chattiness, the immigration agent stamped the custom's declaration, and they walked on towards the baggage claim carousel. They waited there for a few minutes before Elizabeth joined them. She said nothing but could not hold back a small smirk from ghosting across her lips.

"Okay. What did you do? I can tell you are up to something." Adam asked.

"Not a thing. Would I do something improper? You know me."

"Fess up, Elizabeth. What did you do?"

"That charming, obese man who was trying so hard to impress me was telling me that he was very important and that everyone always pays a lot of attention to him. When I went through the passport control, he was two people behind me. I told the agent that the fat man kept saying to me that he hoped no one checked his bag."

Di looked at her and said, "That was nasty. I can't believe you did that. I hope you never get mad at me."

"Believe me, that was nothing. I can be really nasty if I want to, but I've decided to put that part of me aside. I'm throwing away my nastiness. Never again."

"I don't believe it." Adam interjected.

"Oh look, Adam. There's my bag."

They loaded a cart and made their way toward the 'nothing to declare' exit. They handed their customs' declarations to the agent at the exit and were waved through doors.

They had done it. They had arrived, safely and without notice. Di
was close to bursting. She was keeping it together but barely. She first
flung an arm around Elizabeth, and then motioned to Adam to join the
embrace. Positioned in the middle of the busy corridor somewhat block-
ing the normal flow of traffic, the trio hugged one another for some time.
Pulling back and looking directly into Adam's eyes, Di could no longer
ward off the tears as she said. "Adam, please take me home."